To the Romantic Novelists' Association
– without whom I would not be a published author
– Happy 60th Anniversary!

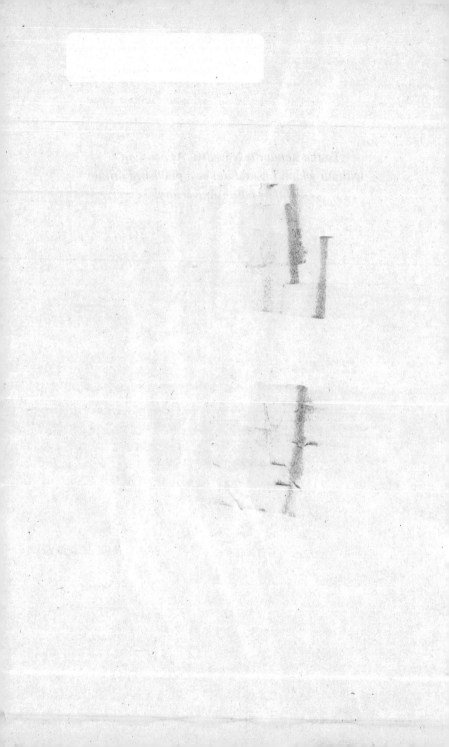

Christina Courtenay is an award-winning author of historical romance and time slip (dual time) stories. She started writing so that she could be a stay-at-home mum to her two daughters, but didn't get published until daughter number one left home aged twenty-one, so that didn't quite go to plan! Since then, however, she's made up for it by having eleven novels published and winning the RNA's Romantic Novel of the Year Award for Best Historical Romantic Novel twice with *Highland Storms* (2012) and *The Gilded Fan* (2014).

Christina is half Swedish and grew up in that country. She has also lived in Japan and Switzerland, but is now based in Herefordshire, close to the Welsh border. She's a keen amateur genealogist and loves history and archaeology (the armchair variety).

To find out more, visit **christinacourtenay.com**, find her on Facebook /**Christinacourtenayauthor** or follow her on Twitter **@PiaCCourtenay**.

By Christina Courtenay

The
Runes
of
Destiny

CHRISTINA COURTENAY

REVIEW

First published in 2020
by HEADLINE REVIEW
An imprint of HEADLINE PUBLISHING GROUP

1

Cataloguing in Publication Data is available from the British Library

ISBN 978 1 4722 6824 2

Typeset in Minion Pro by Avon DataSet Ltd, Arden Court,
Alcester, Warwickshire

Printed and bound in Great Britain by Clays Ltd, Elcograf S.p.A.

Headline's policy is to use papers that are natural, renewable and recyclable
products and made from wood grown in well-managed
forests and other controlled sources. The logging and manufacturing processes
are expected to conform to the environmental regulations
of the country of origin.

HEADLINE PUBLISHING GROUP
An Hachette UK Company
Carmelite House
50 Victoria Embankment
London EC4Y 0DZ

www.headline.co.uk
www.hachette.co.uk

Chapter One

Kneeling in a muddy trench in the middle of an archaeological dig might be considered a dirty and boring job by some, but it was just what Linnea Berger needed right now. The rhythmic scraping of a trowel on soil was soothing, mind-numbing, creating an inner peace she had been craving for weeks. And who cared about a bit of mud?

'Finding anything, Linnea?'

She looked up into the kindly face of Uncle Lars. He wasn't her uncle really but the grandfather of her best friend Sara, as well as her dad's boss. Lars and his family had been a huge part of her life for as long as Linnea could remember, hence the honorary title.

'Nothing much.' Although to be honest, she hadn't really been paying attention. *Oops!* She glanced quickly at the heap of soil behind her, hoping she hadn't missed anything vital. It was a good thing her dad wasn't here or he'd have told her off for sure.

'Well, what's that then?' Lars pointed at a cream-coloured patch that was just emerging from the soil in front of her. He hunkered down and smiled, the grooves around his eyes deepening. 'Keep trowelling. I think this could be good.'

'Oh, right.' Linnea refrained from making a face. She'd learned by now that the finds an archaeologist considered 'good' usually proved to be something extremely mundane and boring, like a glass bead or a rusted piece of metal that resembled nothing more than a pitted lump. But then she didn't have their expertise in the minutiae of Viking life, which was what they were exposing in this field. Lars's enthusiasm was infectious, though, and she always enjoyed watching him at work.

Lars and Haakon, Linnea's father, oversaw archaeological digs every summer. Since the age of six, Linnea had been dragged along, even though she'd never been all that keen. It was just an inevitable part of her summer holidays, and as Lars usually brought Sara, who was the same age as Linnea, at least they'd had fun when the hard work stopped each day. The two girls had hit it off right from the start and had been best friends ever since. Although Linnea normally lived in the UK these days, while Sara had stayed in Sweden, their bond remained strong.

The archaeology bug had never bitten Linnea, or at least not in the practical sense. Instead she'd become fascinated by runes and the Viking language – Old Norse – to the extent that she was now a PhD student in that subject at the University of York. It required a certain amount of knowledge about the culture, of course, and a love of all things Viking, which she'd acquired through her parents. But she'd always preferred to read about the period rather than dig up the evidence first-hand.

That all changed with the accident . . .

She continued to scrape and Lars joined in, pulling his own trowel out of a back pocket. What began to protrude from the dark earth was ivory in colour and slightly domed. Linnea swallowed hard and hesitated. It couldn't be . . . could it? Tense now, she levered off a large piece of soil and was suddenly face to face with a gaping eye socket, its dark, mournful stare directed straight at her. She jumped and emitted a small shriek.

Lars didn't seem to notice. 'Well, hello! What have we here?

I do believe it's the first grave of the site. Excellent! Just what I was hoping for.'

Linnea wasn't listening. Confronted with the reality of death and the remains of an actual body, she'd tuned out. The only word that registered was 'grave', which sent her mind into a spin. It was far too close to home. Her surroundings disappeared and instead she was in the back of a car again, travelling at way over the speed limit, and then everything imploded. *The screech of tyres braking too late, the vicious crunch of metal being compressed, the tinkling of shattering glass and the screams of people who knew they were on an unstoppable path to destruction, taking their last breath ...*

How did you forget? Was it even possible to make your brain delete something like that, once experienced? Linnea closed her eyes and tried to stem the rising tide of panic that assailed her every time she relived those moments, but it didn't work. *Breathe, Linnea, breathe. In slowly, hold it, then push the air out through half-closed lips.* The therapist's instructions were clear, but she couldn't do it. It was impossible. A cold sweat broke out between her shoulder blades. Her hands started shaking, her heart fluttered against her ribs in a frantic dance and somehow her lungs weren't big enough for the air to get through ...

'Hey, Linnea, are you OK?'

She blinked and returned to reality – a field in the wilds of the Swedish countryside. Sunshine on her face, a soft breeze caressing her hair and cheeks, and Uncle Lars peering at her with concern written all over his face. At last she managed to suck in the much-needed breath, but her heart was still going ballistic. Was she OK? No, not really. The fact that she'd escaped almost unscathed while Sara's parents hadn't made her feel worse, not better. Survivor's guilt, even though she'd only been a passenger, the accident not her fault. She tried to focus on Lars, putting up a hand to push against her ribcage as if she could calm her heart from the outside. *At least Sara is going to be OK, focus on that. Breathe!*

'Um, yes. Yes, I'm fine, thanks. Just . . . you know, remembering. He . . . it . . .' She nodded in the direction of the trench, but couldn't bring herself to look a second time at that baleful eye.

'Oh sweetheart, I'm so sorry! I should have realised. Come on, let's get you away from here. You've gone as white as . . .' Lars glanced at the skull in the ground, then quickly looked away. 'I mean, we don't want you fainting now, do we?'

'I'm OK,' she repeated, but didn't resist when he pulled her out of the trench and tucked her arm into the crook of his elbow, steering her towards the food tent.

Linnea was grateful. She didn't think her legs would have carried her away from the horrible sight of the skeleton – she shuddered at the mere thought of the word – without Lars supporting her. His kindness made her want to cry, but she'd run out of tears ages ago. The well was dry.

'Let's get you some coffee and a chocolate bar. You've had a shock. Entirely my fault. I get too carried away. Poor girl . . .' He patted her arm and found her a seat at a camping table while he went in search of coffee.

If only she could be stronger, like him. It was his son and daughter-in-law who had died in that car, after all, and his granddaughter seriously injured. But he seemed to be coping with the grief by burying himself in his work. The only outward sign was the profusion of new wrinkles on his brow, and the occasional sombre, contemplative expression.

For Linnea, however, it wasn't that easy. It had become impossible for her to concentrate on translating obscure old texts or memorising the syntax and grammar of Old Norse and related languages. Her brain seemed unable to function the way she wanted it to, preferring to dwell on the terrible waste of two lives cut short far too early, and giving her no peace. And her anxiety attacks had grown worse – every time she stepped out into the York traffic and heard car brakes screeching or horns blaring, her breathing became laboured and her heart rate went into overdrive.

It was unbearable and she'd just had to get away for a while. Joining this dig was a godsend. Or at least it had been until a moment ago . . .

Lars returned with a mug, a bowl of sugar lumps and a chocolate bar. 'Here you go. Put lots of sugar in that coffee; best thing for shock, or so I've been told.' He made a face. 'I really am sorry, my dear. I'm a thoughtless old man. When I'm working, I don't let real life intrude. I mean, of course I'm just as sad as you are, but I simply don't allow myself to think about it during the day. And digging up skeletons is part of my job, always has been.'

'Don't worry about it. Not your fault.' And it wasn't. He didn't mean to be insensitive. Linnea just had to toughen up, stop associating everything with what had happened. She'd been doing better this week, forgetting about it for several hours at a time, but that creepy, empty eye socket had brought it all back in techni-colour detail.

She still had no idea how she'd escaped the accident with only minor injuries, but she knew one thing – if Sara's dad hadn't been driving too fast as usual, he and his wife might have been alive now. Linnea was still angry with him for being such a speed freak. For never listening. Hadn't Sara and her mum told him over and over again it would end in tears? Although they'd never imagined it would be something this awful . . .

'Earth to Linnea?'

'Huh? Oh, sorry, I was miles away.' Linnea blinked away the images, willing them to stay buried in her subconscious. She had to let it go. *Had to*. Especially now that Sara was finally getting better and might be out of hospital soon. She would need Linnea's support if she was to recover fully. 'What were you saying?'

'I said how about I let you loose with a metal detector instead? Then you don't have to do more than indicate to the others where to dig and you won't get any nasty surprises.'

'Sure.' Linnea had to admit that sounded better.

'Come on then, finish that coffee and I'll show you what to do.'

She swallowed the last of the hot drink and shoved the remaining chocolate in her mouth as she followed Lars out of the tent and over to a stash of implements. He picked up a metal detector and showed her how to use it. 'If you get a strong signal, put down one of these markers for now.' He handed her a bag of plastic pegs.

'OK. Where do you want me to start? Or am I part of a team?'

'No, it's just you today. Try over in the next field, behind that hedge. The geophys guys haven't been in there yet, so it's virgin territory.'

'Right.' She hesitated, then reached up to give him a quick hug. 'Thanks for having me here, Uncle Lars, you're the best.'

His cheeks turned a bit ruddy. 'It was the least I could do in the circumstances. It was my son who nearly . . . Anyway, glad I could help, if only in a small way.'

But Linnea knew he would have helped out whatever the reason. He was that kind of man. When he'd heard that her dad's summer project had been delayed, he hadn't hesitated in offering her a place on his own dig with immediate effect, allowing her to get away from everything when she needed it the most. And it was working. Just not when faced with . . . skulls. She suppressed a shudder.

As she set off towards the field, she knew she was very lucky to have Lars in her life.

*

Starting on the other side of the hedge, Linnea began to methodically scan the ground with the detector. Every now and then it gave off a beep, signalling something of interest. Without thinking too much about it, she marked the spots and carried on. As she walked, she tried to steer her mind in a happier direction – the beautiful birdsong coming from all around her, the soft caress of the wind on her face, the wonderful scents of burgeoning leaves and flowers. It was peaceful, she couldn't deny that, and her therapist was right – it was time to start enjoying life again.

'She means that you need a man,' had been Sara's comment when Linnea told her about this advice. Happily settled in a relationship herself, Sara seemed to think that having a boyfriend was the answer to everything, but Linnea wasn't so sure.

'No, I think she was trying to tell me that moping won't bring your mum and dad back. That me being miserable isn't helping anyone, least of all myself. Besides, there aren't exactly a whole bunch of guys queuing up to date me.'

That wasn't quite true. She'd had offers – fellow PhD students and guys hitting on her in pubs or clubs – but she wasn't interested. There was only one man she wanted: her tutor, Daniel. He was ten years older than her, and she'd had a crush on him since the first time they'd met. With their shared interest in Old Norse, history and academia, he'd seemed perfect for her. It didn't hurt that he was tall, dark and handsome – such a cliché – although Sara didn't agree.

'He's too intense. The archetypal nerd,' was her verdict the one and only time she'd met him.

'Is not! I'd rather have him than some rugby-playing type, all muscles and no brain.' Linnea hotly defended her crush. And she wasn't the only one who had noticed Daniel – he always seemed to have a gaggle of starry-eyed female students around him. 'But it's all academic anyway, as he never seems to notice me except as someone who can take on some of his research workload and do his filing.' Not that she minded helping him. It was a great excuse to talk to him.

Her mobile pinged and she stopped halfway along the field to fish it out of her pocket. Speak of the devil . . .

Hi Linnea, haven't you had enough of the archaeology malarkey? We're all missing you at the department, especially me ☺ *D x*

It was the weirdest thing, but when she'd told Daniel she was taking time off to go to Sweden, it was as if he'd suddenly realised that he was about to lose her and couldn't bear it. Ever since she arrived, he'd been texting her, and the tone was growing warmer. Today's message actually made her blush. There was a smiley face and that *x* – a kiss? Linnea stared at the screen, her heart hammering in her chest for a different reason now.

How should she reply?

'Oh, sod it, what does it matter?' she muttered, typing quickly. She was probably imagining the increase in interest anyway.

Not quite yet, although I'm missing you all too. But the peace of the countryside is soothing and I'm starting to enjoy it here. I'll be back soon enough – I'm sure you can find someone else to do your filing for you ☺ *L x*

She added a winking face to show that she was joking, although there was an element of truth in there, a niggle of doubt. Why was he suddenly so keen? Did he just need her as an unpaid assistant, or did he actually miss her? But if he only wanted a skivvy, there was no need for the kiss at the end of the message, was there? And he had plenty of other students – both male and female – who could help him out with stuff.

The reply came almost immediately.

No one as good as you! Don't stay there too long – I mean it! D xx

Linnea couldn't think of anything to say to that, so she just carried on with the metal detecting, while daydreaming of Daniel's darkly handsome face. It wasn't just his looks she admired, though. He was brilliant in his field and a respected professor, one of the youngest at the university. They'd had some spirited discussions about Norse dialects, and just having someone to talk to about obscure matters like that was amazing. They were on the same wavelength, two peas in a pod. Had he finally realised that?

By the time she had reached the third corner of the field, she was feeling much more optimistic, and had started weighing up her options for the future when the detector suddenly went berserk, jolting her back to the present. The beeping seemed to be going almost off the scale. She stared at the machine and passed it over the same spot several times.

'Whoa! What have you found?'

She knew she ought to just place a plastic marker here and move on, but her curiosity was well and truly piqued now. Something about the machine's insistence stirred up feelings of excitement, and without thinking, she bent down to use the end of the marker to scrape at the soil, removing it layer by layer. In between, she passed the detector over it, and each time it almost screeched at her. 'OK, OK, take it easy,' she muttered. At a depth of perhaps a foot, she spotted something with a dull shine. 'Aha! Got you.'

Gone were all thoughts of the correct excavating procedure that her dad had drilled into her at length over the years. She forgot about context, layers and recording the surroundings of every find so it could be properly dated. The glimmering object called to her, and she shovelled the soil away as fast as she could. It was only when she held a magnificent silver brooch in her hands that she registered what she'd done.

'Oh, *shit*!' Lars was going to kill her.

She took a deep breath. Well, the damage was done now so she might as well have a look at her find first before taking it to Lars. Brushing the soil off with the edge of her T-shirt, she followed the design with one finger, taking in the exquisite swirls and decorations. Although the brooch was tarnished, she could see animal heads picked out in gold filigree with a narrow gap between their gaping jaws. When she turned it over, she found a runic inscription scratched into the surface. 'Oh, you're definitely Viking then. Wow!' This was amazing; Lars would be so pleased. Well, apart from the whole context thing, but hopefully he'd forgive her for that . . .

Once she'd cleaned the soil off, the writing was as clear as the day it had been done and, being an expert on various runic alphabets, Linnea had no trouble reading it.

'*Með blóð skaltu ferðast,*' she whispered. '"With sacrifice you shall travel"?' Or . . . no, it said *blóð* not *blót*, so 'blood' rather than 'sacrifice'. What did that mean? She frowned as she followed the long pin with one finger down to the very tip and absent-mindedly tested its sharpness. 'Ouch!' Damn it, she should have been more careful. Blood welled out of her tender skin and she wrapped part of her T-shirt around it. Good thing it was black, or the stains would never come out.

'*Með blóð skaltu ferðast,*' she said again, puzzling over the meaning of the phrase. 'Travel where?' But in the next instant, a wave of dizziness hit her with the force of a small tsunami and made her reel. She cried out, holding on to the brooch as if it could anchor her in an upright position, but the whole world began to tilt on its axis and she felt as if she was spinning out of control. Nausea slammed into her gut and she gulped for breath, leaning forward to steady herself against the newly dug soil.

'What the . . . ? *Aaarrgghhh!*'

A loud racket reverberated inside her head and ears, as if a huge crowd of people were all hissing and shouting at her in unison, and the spinning intensified. She moaned out loud, terrified of what was happening but unable to make sense of it. It couldn't be the sight of blood – she'd never been scared of that – and the May sunshine wasn't strong enough to cause heatstroke, surely? But she felt so ill . . .

Just when she thought she was going to be violently sick, the dizziness stopped and everything went black.

Chapter Two

It wasn't every day you found yourself sitting on the ground surrounded by a horde of Vikings. Well, perhaps not quite a horde, but certainly more than half a dozen.

Linnea had absolutely no idea how she'd got here, but staring up at the group of men looking down at her, she felt very small and vulnerable. She assumed they must be re-enactors; they were certainly taking their roles seriously, their expressions uniformly fierce and menacing. When one of them took a step towards her, she scuttled backwards instinctively and held up a hand to ward him off.

'Whoa, take it easy there! I don't want to be part of your little war games. Go play with someone else.'

She had to admit they looked authentic. Wearing well-made period costumes that were realistically dirty in places, they were bristling with gleaming weapons – knives, long-handled axes, bow and arrows, and in one case even a sword. And was that a . . . a dead deer hanging from a branch carried by two of them? *Yuck*. They must be pretending to be a hunting party. The one who'd come closer – a blond guy with eyes like a frozen blue lagoon – started shouting something at her in what sounded like a weird dialect of Icelandic. She wasn't listening, though, as she suddenly remembered what she'd been doing before she fainted.

'Yesssss!'

She was still holding the most amazing penannular brooch of pure silver, decorated with intricate animalistic motifs. Heavy and big, its circumference was at least three inches, and it had a very long, sharp pin for use when fastening a cloak with it. So sharp, in fact, that she remembered pricking her finger on it when she'd tested the tip. There was a droplet of blood coagulating on her skin to confirm it.

'Awesome!' she murmured. It was the kind of find most archaeologists could only dream of, and yet she was just a helper who'd been playing around with one of the metal detectors. How lucky was she?

A laugh bubbled up in her throat, but the blond guy was still shouting, and as Linnea peered up at him, her laughter faded away. She was fluent in both Old Norse and Icelandic, having studied them as part of her degree, and she couldn't help but register the word for 'thief' once he'd said it about three times. She was surprised he knew that much. Most re-enactors only learned things like greetings or common commands for attack for the purposes of their fake battles. And no one was quite sure how these were supposed to be pronounced. It was all educated guesswork. That probably explained the accent. Either way, she still felt dizzy and vaguely nauseous, and definitely not in the mood to be harangued. She hadn't stolen anything. Couldn't he see that she was right next to the dig site?

'Oh, be quiet,' she muttered. 'You're just jealous.' When he didn't stop talking, she added, '*Þegi þú!*' – 'shut up' in Old Norse – in a louder voice. She'd bet anything he didn't think she knew how to speak that language.

It worked – he stopped mid sentence, so he obviously understood those words as well. Unusual.

In fact, there was a collective intake of breath and the entire group went silent, staring first at Linnea, then at shouty guy. What, they'd all understood? How could that be? She blinked at them in surprise, but the man's pale blue eyes narrowed, and with a hiss of fury he snatched the brooch out of her hands and barked an order in the same language. 'Bring her!'

'Hey, give that back! It's *my* find!' Linnea lurched to her feet, even though an attack of the spin monsters threatened to overwhelm her. But before she'd taken even one step, her arms were gripped by strong hands and she was almost lifted off the ground.

'What the . . . ? Let go of me, you bastards!' Kicking and screaming, she attempted to free herself, but it was useless. These were muscle-bound pretend warriors, probably on a daily dose of steroids, and their grip on her felt like iron clamps.

The guy on her right muttered, '*Þegi þú?*' and chuckled. Linnea gathered that he thought it was hilarious that she'd said that to their leader. But she didn't see anything funny in her situation. Where were they taking her anyway?

She looked around to see which tent they might be heading for. Were they going to report her to the dig's director? They'd catch cold at that since Uncle Lars would never believe the claim that she'd been stealing. He'd vouch for her. Besides, he was the one who'd told her to have a go with the metal detector in the first place.

But she soon noticed that she had an entirely different problem to contend with – the tents were all gone. Every last one of them.

What the heck?

The dig was due to continue all through the summer, so what had happened? The team of archaeologists had also disappeared, and there wasn't a single trench in sight. Linnea began to panic. How long had she blacked out for? Had she somehow moved away from the site during that time? No wonder Blondie and his mates thought she was absconding with treasure trove.

'Hold on. *Wait!* I can explain . . .' she protested, and pulled at the vice she was being held in. 'Come on! You can't seriously believe I'd run away with a socking great Viking brooch? What would I do with it? Look, if you take me back to the dig, I'll sort this out with the director. He's my uncle, well sort of, and—'

But the leader turned abruptly and marched up to her, standing almost nose to nose. 'Be quiet,' he said in Norse, the words clipped and angry, 'or you might not live to see the end of this day.'

Linnea's mouth fell open and she had to make a conscious effort to close it again. She ought to have been scared, but she was too angry. 'Are you threatening me?' The nerve of the guy. They weren't living in the Middle Ages.

But as he went back to the front of the group without answering, she caught sight of their destination in the distance and nearly choked on a gasp. They were heading towards a clutch of buildings, the largest of which was a massive Viking-style longhouse.

And Linnea knew for a fact there were no such buildings anywhere near the dig site. So where the hell was she?

There were some days when you wished you hadn't got out of bed and others when you couldn't get up fast enough. Having slept on a disgusting flea-infested straw mattress in a dark wooden hut, Linnea was definitely in the second category today, even though neither option was very appealing. And it wasn't as if she was able to go anywhere.

She was locked in.

She didn't know if there really were bed bugs, but her imagination supplied them and she was itching all over. The mattress had been hard and uncomfortable, rustling every time she moved, and she wouldn't be at all surprised if it contained all sorts of vermin. It didn't help that she'd only had a scratchy woollen blanket for cover, but beggars couldn't be choosers and the nights were still cold this time of year. She kept it wrapped around her now but couldn't suppress a shiver, partly from revulsion, but also because she was freezing.

And scared. Very scared.

Ever since her arrival in the pretend Viking settlement the previous day, she'd been stuck in here. At first there had been some light seeping in through holes up near the roof, but when night fell, no one came to give her illumination of any kind and she'd been left in complete darkness. She'd tried to get out while she could still see, even going so far as to climb up to the rafters using old shelves as footholds, but those holes – air vents perhaps? – were too small to squeeze through and the door remained locked and solid. All she had to show for her efforts were a couple of splinters and a grazed knee.

So far she had only been given one meal and some water. The food was some sort of porridge – at least she thought that's what it was supposed to be – but it was more like eating wallpaper paste with bits in, and there was no sweetener or even a berry or two to add taste. These people obviously believed in re-creating an authentic experience, but Linnea would have infinitely preferred a piece of bread.

She suppressed a sob of despair and fury and went to test the door for the umpteenth time. Still locked. She kicked at the offending mattress to give vent to her feelings. Despite the gloomy interior of the hut, she saw a dust cloud rise up and envelop her. It made her cough, which in turn made her even more cross.

'They can't do this! Bastards!' It had to be illegal, keeping a person prisoner.

Had it really been necessary to lock her up like this? She'd assumed it was only until the police arrived and she was reported for the alleged theft, but the hours had passed and nothing happened. If only they'd give her a chance to explain that she hadn't been stealing the brooch at all, but no one came to talk to her.

Instead they seemed to have kidnapped her. Why? And who were these people? Some crazy sect living a 'green' life out in the countryside? She'd heard of the Amish in America following an older lifestyle without modern trappings, and speaking an ancient dialect of German, but never anything like that in Sweden. She couldn't make it out.

'Bunch of loonies,' she muttered, yawning and pacing back and forth out of sheer frustration. She hadn't actually slept much at all as she'd been on edge, not knowing what they were going to do with her. And just as she'd been about to nod off, some dogs had started howling in the distance. It had sounded just like a pack of wolves, eerie and sending shivers down her spine, but as wolves had been extinct for at least a hundred years it couldn't have been. Huskies, maybe? Who knew?

The worst thing was not knowing how she came to be here. Not here as in the pretend Viking settlement – they had clearly walked – but the place where she'd woken up yesterday. How had she ended up so far away from Uncle Lars's dig? She'd only been in the next field; she remembered scrabbling in the soil to free the silver brooch from its hiding place. Of course, she shouldn't have touched it until one of the archaeologists had recorded its exact location, but she'd been carried away by the excitement. And then she'd pricked her finger on the pin.

The next thing she recalled was a sensation of tumbling head over heels into nothingness, and then waking up in a different place, surrounded by Vikings. She shook her head. No, *pretend* Vikings. But what did they want with her, and why hadn't they just taken the brooch while she was unconscious? It made no sense.

Too anxious to sit still, she continued to pace the hard earth floor of the hut and became aware that her finger was throbbing. When she peered at it, the tip was swollen. 'You'd have thought I would have learned a thing or two from reading *Sleeping Beauty*,' she muttered, 'like *not* pricking yourself on spiky objects. What a moron . . .' But how was she supposed to know it was so lethal? The damned thing had been lying buried for at least a thousand years; it should have been blunt.

What if she had blood poisoning because the wound had become dirty and infected? It would explain the blackout, but in that case she ought to be dead by now. She pulled up her sleeve and checked her arm. She'd read somewhere that if you had septicaemia, you'd get what looked like black lines running up your arm or leg, or wherever you were hurt, towards the heart. Or was it red spots? Either way, her arm was as pale as usual, nothing alarming to see. No, she was being silly – you didn't get an infection with blood poisoning that quickly.

Her stomach growled loudly, and as if on cue, the door was thrown open. Hopefully that meant more food, but caution had her backing towards the far wall. She didn't trust her captors in the slightest.

Instead of bringing a meal, however, the blond man who'd seemed to be the leader yesterday walked in and grabbed her upper arm. 'Come with me. Jarl Thure wants to see you. Do you understand me?'

Linnea blinked. He was still speaking that strange version of Icelandic, the words recognisably Norse. His grammar and syntax were definitely much older than the modern language. Exactly like Old Norse, in fact. Was he a Scandinavian language scholar too, with re-enactment as his hobby? Or was this sect, or whatever

18

they were, trying to revive the old language, as well as re-creating the living conditions? Those were the only explanations she could come up with.

OK, fine. If he wanted to pretend, she'd play along for now, just to show him he couldn't fool her. 'Yes, I understand,' she replied in her best Norse accent. Apparently it wasn't good enough, as it made him frown. Well, she wasn't used to speaking the language, only studying ancient texts.

'Where are you from? Your speech is strange,' he commented, but he didn't seem to require an answer as he tugged her out of the hut and started striding towards the longhouse.

Linnea had to half run to keep up with him. She clutched at the blanket to keep it anchored around her shoulders as the chilly morning air hit her. At about five foot nine, she wasn't short, but he had to be over six foot, and his powerful legs made short work of the hill leading up to the double doors of the impressive hall. For a moment she forgot about her predicament and just stared in awe at the enormous building. It must be at least thirty metres long and maybe five or six metres wide, with timber walls and a pitched roof covered in wooden tiles. Was it 'shingles' her dad had called them when he'd described a longhouse to her once? Possibly.

Smoke puffed out of a hole up at the top of the nearest gable end, the lazy swirls being caught by the breeze and dissipating slowly. Both gables were decorated with carved finials, as was a smaller roof over the doorway, which was near one end of the longer side of the house. It stuck out slightly like a built-in porch. Who had created this, and so near to the dig site? Why hadn't Uncle Lars mentioned it? Surely he would have wanted to be part of such a reconstruction project – he was crazy about anything to do with Vikings. Or were these people religious zealots who didn't welcome normal Swedes?

'Inside.' The blond man pushed her in front of him and through the doors, where Linnea was hit by what felt like a wall of woodsmoke. She coughed and rubbed at eyes that watered instantly. They entered a passageway first. To the right was some sort of storage area – she glimpsed barrels, sacks and other containers on the floor and on shelves and tables – but they turned left into what appeared to be the main room of the building. A large, cavernous hall, it seemed almost divided into three parts as there were two rows of sturdy posts all the way along holding up the roof timbers. The internal walls were made of vertical planks, but the floor was stamped earth, just as in the hut where she'd spent the night.

There was a huge stone-built raised hearth at one end of the middle section, with a cauldron to one side, suspended from a roof beam by an iron chain and hook. Next to this, on the floor, stood a newly filled log basket. Smoke rose towards the ceiling, and Linnea could see now that there was a hole at both ends of the building up by the roof to let it out. But a lot of it hung around inside first like some evil miasma and seemed to permeate everything in the room.

There were women and children in here, not just pretend warriors. That made her feel better until she caught one of the ladies glaring at her. Was everyone around here completely into their role play? What about a bit of sisterly solidarity? They were all busy in one way or another – cooking, sewing or looking after babies – and it was such an ordinary scene it made Linnea pause. None of it seemed forced or as if they were re-creating the past. It felt as if it *was* the past.

Wow, they're good!

Most of them sat on benches – or rather low platforms – that had been built along the walls. These were quite wide and covered in furs and pillows, making them ideal both as seating and presumably for sleeping on. A couple of the kids were also using them as some sort of race track until a woman's hand shot out and stopped them by grabbing the back of their loose tunics. 'Enough!' she hissed, but the little boys just wriggled out of her grasp and ran outside to continue the game, shrieking with laughter. Various cooking vessels and pottery storage jars, baskets and casks were lined up against one wall, while a tired-looking girl kneeled on the floor grinding flour on a stone quern. It looked like extremely hard work – the quern stone was massive.

Before she had time to look about further, Linnea was forcibly propelled towards a man sitting in a carved wooden chair that had been placed on top of the platform at one end of the long room. It made him seem like a king on a dais, though this was no castle. Behind him were colourful wall hangings depicting human figures and animals, but Linnea didn't get a chance to study them. The man had an expression of acute dissatisfaction on his face that must be permanent, since it had etched deep lines either side of his mouth and around his eyes. Although why he was so disgruntled was a mystery, since he was clearly in charge.

'There you are! You took your time,' he grumbled.

His clothing had to have been a lot more expensive than anyone else's, as his overtunic had bright red silk panels along the top and was trimmed with fine braid interwoven with gold and silver thread. He also had a cloak edged with fur thrown over one shoulder. Mink or even ermine, perhaps? Something soft anyway. On his fingers he wore a multitude of rings – both gold and silver – and he also had numerous arm rings that shimmered in the light from the fire. His weapons were finer than the ones Linnea had seen on her captors, including a sword with an intricately decorated hilt and an axe inlaid with a silver pattern, both leaning against the chair. He wore a belt with a shiny buckle; the strap end, which hung down, was tipped with an equally shiny decorative metal fitting in the shape of some sort of animal head. But what made her really mad was the fact that his cloak was fastened on his right shoulder with *her* brooch. *The utter bastard!*

'I was busy, but here is the woman I found, brother.' The blond man had come to a halt in front of Thure – if this was indeed the so-called jarl or chieftain he'd been talking about. 'I'm thinking of taking her to Miklagarðr to sell. With that hair she should fetch a better price there than in Birka.'

'Who says she belongs to you, Hrafn? She was found on my property with my pin in her possession. I believe that gives me the right to punish her. And then maybe I'd like to keep her . . .' Thure smiled, but it wasn't a nice smile. His eyes glittered strangely as he contemplated Linnea, letting his gaze linger on her body rather than her face. She had to suppress a shiver. There was something so primitive and savage in that stare, she wanted to physically recoil. She forced herself to stand still.

'No, she was found outside your boundaries by me. I have claimed her.' Blond man – or Hrafn, as he seemed to be called – stood his ground. 'If there is any compensation to be paid, I will do it. You have your brooch back, but by all means raise it at the next *þing* if you wish.'

Linnea knew that the *þing* was a primitive court of justice in Viking times, and was astonished that these people would even go as far as to re-create one here.

Thure didn't appear to like this suggestion one little bit, though other men standing and sitting in a semicircle around him had nodded in agreement with Hrafn.

'Very well,' he bit out. 'You owe me half her value. Don't try to cheat me. I'll be there to see how much you get for her.'

Linnea was starting to wonder if this was some surreal nightmare. First of all, these people were taking their play-acting way too far. Were they making it up as they went along or had they practised beforehand? But for what purpose? There was no audience here. And second, how come they all knew how to speak this variant of Old Norse? Because there was no denying it *was* Old Norse – the more she listened, the more certain she was of that – and they were more fluent in it than she was despite her many years of study. The words just flowed out of them, as if they'd been used to this language from birth. How could that be? No one was these days. *No one!*

But never mind that now – she finally had her chance to explain and she had to grab it with both hands and get out of here. 'Excuse me.' She cleared her throat. 'I would like to protest most strongly. I didn't steal anything. I found the brooch in the ground using a . . .' She couldn't think how on earth you'd say 'metal detector' in a language that had been around a thousand years before such machines were invented. 'Well, a . . . thing, and I wasn't going to keep it. Why would I?'

This question was greeted with hoots of laughter. Even the grumpy Thure's mouth lifted on one side. 'Why indeed?' A guffaw escaped him, but then he turned back into a sourpuss again. 'Where are you from? What do you here?'

'I'm from England, Norðimbraland to be exact,' Linnea grudgingly told him, since she was currently living in what the Vikings knew as the kingdom of Northumbria. 'Although I was born here in Svíaríki,' she added for clarification. Not that it was any of his business. 'And my father is from, er . . . Hordaland originally.' She used the Norse word for the part of Norway where her dad had been born, as it hadn't actually been a unified country back in Viking times. These people were clearly sticklers for history. She wanted to show them she could be too.

Thure peered at her. 'Why are you so far from home?'

'I was visiting my . . . um, uncle.'

'Hmm. Well, where is he now?'

23

'Nearby.' At least she hoped he was, but she couldn't be sure of anything any more. In fact, she was so exasperated, she wanted to scream. Scared and anxious, she had a really bad feeling about all this, but knew instinctively that it would be better not to show any fear. *Concentrate on the anger.* This sect, or whatever they were, weren't normal, but perhaps they could be reasoned with. 'I felt sick and fainted, then when I woke up, this . . .' she couldn't think of the Norse word for 'brute' and just pointed at Hrafn, 'this man was shouting at me. Now please, let me go. I'll find my own way back, thank you very much. Enough of these games. I'd rather not spend any more nights in your stinking hut. A fine way to treat your guests.'

Hrafn looked at her strangely, then shook his head and turned back to Thure as if she hadn't spoken at all. 'I'll give you a quarter of her value, not a single weight of silver more. You can be present at the sale if you don't trust me. The ships are almost ready. We sail the day after tomorrow.' He gave a curt nod and moved his grip down to Linnea's wrist, tugging her along behind him as he left the longhouse.

They were outside before she'd had time to protest, but now she'd had enough.

'*Hey!* Doesn't anyone around here listen? I'm not your property. I'm a free woman and I am leaving now. You can't keep me here against my will. Do you hear me?' Her voice had risen an octave and she was struggling to free herself from his grip.

He stopped abruptly and she walked into him, inadvertently breathing in a big lungful of his scent. It wasn't unpleasant – no BO, no excessive aftershave, just a slight hint of wool and a lot of woodsmoke, which was somehow more bearable outdoors.

'I should think every man, woman and child around here heard you, *bikkja*. Now unless you'd like me to put you in chains, like a thrall going to market, I suggest you keep quiet and do as I

24

say. You're not going anywhere other than to Miklagarðr with me.'

Miklagarðr? He had to be joking. That was what the Vikings had called Istanbul. He'd said something about the ships being ready soon. These people weren't seriously thinking of re-creating a journey from Sweden all the way to Turkey in a longboat, were they? That would be insane.

'But my uncle—'

'Will soon be found too if he is anywhere in this area. Now come along to the bath house. You are exceedingly dirty and I would have you bathe and change.'

Chapter Three

Hrafn was seething. What manner of women did they raise in England? He'd met some outspoken and argumentative ones in his time, but this one was unsurpassed.

'What is your name?' He realised she was struggling to keep up with his long strides and slowed down slightly.

'Linnea. Linnea Berger.'

'Lin-*ee*-ah?' Hrafn had never heard that one before.

'Yes, you know, like the little pink flowers that grow in the forest? You must have seen them. They look like tiny bells. Named after the famous . . . er, man, Carl von Linné.'

'Who?' He shook his head. He knew the flowers she meant but had never heard them called that. 'And Berger what?' He stopped again and looked her up and down. She was quite a delectable sight, he had to admit, despite being filthy and dishevelled. She had let the blanket drop slightly and he glimpsed lush curves hugged by the strange tunic she was wearing. She also had on what appeared to be a pair of men's trousers. Perhaps she had been pretending to be a boy? Although for what purpose, he could not discern.

'Huh?' She frowned at him.

'Linnea *what* from Berger?' He emphasised the last part. 'I'm

Hrafn Eskils*son* of Eskilsnes, so the son of Eskil. Whose daughter are you?'

'Oh.' Her frown deepened. 'Well, Linnea Haakonsdóttir then. And I'm not from a place called Berger; that is part of my name.'

'So why did you not say so? Why only Berger?' He regarded her with suspicion. There was something not quite right with her but he couldn't put his finger on it.

'It's . . . um, how my family is normally referred to in England.'

Hrafn raised his eyebrows at her. He'd never been to England, but he knew people who had and was sure he'd have heard about such a strange custom. He shook his head. She wasn't telling the truth, but right now he didn't have time to make her.

'What age are you?'

'Twenty-two years. Why, how old are you?'

'Me? I have seen four-and-twenty winters.' He had no idea why he'd even answered her. The question was impertinent, coming from her. He studied her anew. She looked much younger than twenty-two winters. Why had she said years? No one counted their age like that. Either way, she fairly shone with vitality and youth. Well, he could always lie to a prospective buyer. Who would believe a thrall?

'There are clean clothes and soap over there. Hurry up. I have other things to attend to.'

Hrafn had closed the door of the bathing hut – at least that's what Linnea assumed this was, since there was nothing in here except a huge wooden tub filled with water, a smouldering hearth, and some benches along the walls – and was leaning on it with his arms crossed. She tried not to notice the muscles bulging under his lightly tanned skin, but it was hard to avoid as they were noticeable even through the material of his tunic. He looked dangerous, his features forbidding and impatient. He was obviously very strong and determined, and she was alone with him in a small hut.

Shit! She was in serious trouble here.

Her breathing became erratic and every muscle in her body tensed, ready for fight or flight. Neither was really an option, though, with him blocking the only exit. She'd never make it past him, and if she tried, he would probably be even more pissed off. Did he seriously want her to take a bath with him standing there? No way, even though the water looked extremely tempting, considering the bed bugs she'd been worrying about earlier.

'Why do I have to have a bath right now?' she asked, stalling for time while trying to find a way out of this situation. It did seem crazy – surely there were other priorities, such as discussing why she was being held captive at all. And whether he was going to contact Lars this morning to ask for a ransom or whatever other demands he had.

'I want you to be presentable when we leave, and you can't put on clean garments in that state.' He threw a disdainful look at her clothes, which admittedly were covered in dried mud and dust. As for her hair, she didn't have a mirror, but she seemed to have lost her clip, so the tangled mess was tumbling around her shoulders and down her back. She guessed it was more of a rat's nest than a hairdo really. Plus she'd been lying on the ground so there was probably dirt in it as well.

She focused on his words rather than her appearance. Maybe there was still a chance to reason with him? 'But I don't want to go anywhere with you! Just take me back to my uncle, then there's no need for any of this.' She swept out a hand to indicate the tub.

Hrafn rolled his eyes. 'Are all English women this obtuse? I found you, I captured you, I claimed you – you are my thrall now. That means you go where I say and do whatever I ask or there will be unpleasant consequences. Understand?'

Thrall? And unpleasant consequences? Linnea didn't like the sound of that. What had Vikings done to errant slaves? Did they whip them or beat them, like the slave owners of the American South? During her extensive reading of Norse sagas and folklore, she'd never paid much attention to this aspect, but she'd heard of thralls being killed and buried with a dead master, so clearly their lives weren't worth much. This was the twenty-first century, though, and Hrafn couldn't get away with keeping her for long or mistreating her. She wasn't his slave; slavery had been abolished a long time ago. No, Lars must be going frantic by now, and he'd have the entire police force out looking for her. Surely they'd find her soon.

In the meantime, perhaps it wouldn't hurt to be clean. She still had that crawling feeling all over, as though tiny insect feet might be walking on her skin. Yuck.

'Fine. You can leave now.' She nodded dismissal and tried to act composed. 'I am perfectly capable of washing myself. If you don't trust me, ask some of the women to stand guard.'

One corner of his mouth quirked upwards. 'I wasn't about to help you, if that is what you think. But I need to keep an eye on my property or someone else might try to . . . er, assist you.'

Linnea sent him a death glare, forgetting her fear entirely as fury coursed through her. 'For the last time, I'm not a . . . a possession! What is wrong with you all? This is the year 2017 – you can't just grab people and say you own them! Hold me for ransom if you must, but I am no one's thrall.'

'The year what?'

'Two thousand and seventeen.' She said it slowly, as if speaking to a moron. 'The era where everyone is free and no one has the right to hold anyone against their will.' She didn't mention the more backward countries of the world, where virtual slavery was probably still in existence.

Hrafn shook his head. 'We don't count years that way. You must be one of those who follow the carpenter's son. Josis, was it? But everyone knows that there are both free men and thralls. That is just how life is, so you had best become used to it quickly.'

'Jesus,' Linnea corrected automatically. How could he not know Jesus's name? Or was he still play-acting? He kept using the Viking word for slave – *þræll* – and for some reason it sent a shiver down her back. He seemed so adamant that this was normal, but who was he trying to fool?

She crossed her arms over her chest. 'I am *not* bathing with you in here. Go stand outside if you're worried about others.'

Hrafn took a couple of steps forward until he had her backed up against the tub. He was fast and agile, there in a flash before she had time to react. She tried to lean back, but that would just have made her fall in. 'Do *not* give me orders, do you hear, and don't contradict me! You are to do as I say or else. Now undress, wash and change or I'll have someone do it for you. Several of Thure's men expressed an interest. Is that what you want?'

Linnea drew in a sharp breath and muttered, '*Bastard!*' in English, but he didn't react to the insult so she tried Swedish instead. '*Jävla idiot!*' Still no reaction, apart from a raised eyebrow. *What the hell?* But his gaze didn't waver and it was pure ice, showing that he meant every word. She could also feel his chest pushing against hers; at such close quarters he was overwhelmingly large and masculine. Exactly the type of guy she'd told Sara she didn't want, and the complete opposite of Daniel, who she was sure would never behave like this. Daniel would have . . . well, she didn't know exactly what he'd have done, but he wasn't here. This brute was, and he most definitely wasn't a gentleman.

As if to confirm this, a flash of desire lit up his eyes for an instant, and he lifted a handful of her hair as though admiring the rich golden colour, but then he stepped back and dropped it. 'Make sure you wash that too. And don't use a lot of soap or it will bleach too much. I think the men of Grikkland will prefer your natural colour.'

Staring at him, she swallowed hard. This could not be happening. But the sharp edge of the wooden tub digging into the back of her legs felt very real. Steam wafted up from the water and floated in lazy wisps towards the ceiling, where moisture formed, only to drip down again occasionally. It wasn't a dream. She was in a Viking-style bathing hut and this man was about to watch her take a bath.

A spark of defiance lit up within her. *Fine, let him!* She wasn't shy about her body and usually went topless on the beach. Plus she'd been skinny-dipping on numerous occasions with friends. Bodies were just that – bodies – and if you'd seen one, you'd seen them all. Sort of. But if he tried anything, he'd be sorry – she'd shove a handful of soap in his eyes, if not the entire thing. She turned her back on him and began to undress, pulling her grubby T-shirt over her head.

'What in the name of Odin's ravens is that?'

She'd been about to unhook her bra, but now she turned and faced him with a frown. 'My bra?' she asked in English, but he looked blank so she surmised he really didn't speak that language. Unusual, as most Swedes did, but still . . . How on earth did you say bra in Norse? 'My . . . breast-holder?' she tried, then almost giggled. It sounded so stupid.

Hrafn's eyes had lost their chilly blue edge and were verging on deep indigo as he stared at her chest. Linnea's mouth tightened. 'Have you seen enough?' she snarled. 'It's not even a very nice one.' It was black with lacy panels, but not special in any way, and she'd had it for ages. Thankfully it wasn't see-through either.

'Give it to me.' He held out his hand and she flashed him an

31

irritated glare. He wanted to hold her bra while she washed? What a pervert.

'Whatever,' she muttered in English, then turned around and undid the fastening before taking it off and throwing it over her shoulder for him to catch. She didn't check to see whether he did or not. Instead she untied the drawstring on her sweat pants, stepped out of those and her knickers, and climbed into the tub, still with her back towards him. The water wasn't boiling hot, but it wasn't too cold either, thank goodness.

There was a rustling noise behind her, and when she glanced back at Hrafn, he was holding her bra in one hand and her knickers in the other. Definitely a pervert. *Just great!* Was he going to rape her next? Soap probably wouldn't be enough to stop him, if so. This day was going from bad to worse. Her stomach was full of butterflies dancing a violent tango and nausea rose in her throat. How on earth had she ended up in this situation? It was insane.

And where were the bloody police when you needed them? Couldn't they hurry up?

While he focused on her clothes, she scrubbed herself with the slightly abrasive soap, which didn't smell particularly nice, and managed to wash her hair with it too. After dunking her head in the water several times, she looked around for a towel and saw a piece of linen nearby. 'Would you mind handing me that, please?' And although she hadn't expected Hrafn to do it, he came over and gave it to her.

She held it in front of herself as she stood up, then wrapped it around her body and climbed out of the tub. 'Is there a comb I could use?' She sat down on one of the benches, scooting as far away as possible, very wary of him. Wearing only a thin towel, she was definitely at a disadvantage and extremely vulnerable. He had only to rip it off and . . . But he wasn't even looking at her. He was gazing into space, his eyebrows lowered in concentration.

'Huh? Oh, borrow mine.' He fished a comb out of a leather pouch that was hanging off his belt and held it out to her. It was beautifully crafted out of some sort of animal bone, the tines close together, and with a pattern cut into the top part. Just like a real Viking one. And it had the patina of much use, so Hrafn must be fussy about grooming. She glanced at him briefly; yes, his hair was immaculate – shoulder-length and shiny, framing a handsome, if somewhat harsh, face. His hair was that surfer-dude type of dirty blond that was strangely appealing, and he had darker blond stubble and eyebrows to match.

But damn it all, she didn't want to find any part of him handsome. He was a kidnapper. A modern-day slave trader. And most likely a complete nutcase.

Linnea sighed and began to try and unravel the knots in her hair. It was long, almost down to her waist, and thick, but mercifully straight. She had no idea how curly-haired people would have coped with such a primitive comb – it must have been a nightmare for them to use. It took her ages, but she managed to tame her own tresses at last. When she looked up, Hrafn was back to frowning at her underwear, pulling at the elastic in her knickers as if he'd never seen anything like it before.

'Most perverts –' she used the English word because she didn't know how to say that in Norse either – 'just smell them and be done,' she commented, wrinkling her nose.

'Most what?' His gaze fixed on hers. 'Smell them?' Now his eyebrows came down into a ferocious scowl. 'What do you take me for? An *argr*?'

Linnea knew that was a terrible insult for a Viking, implying a man was sexually deviant, and realised it would have been much more prudent to keep her mouth shut. Too late. She'd have to brazen it out now. 'I don't know you, do I?' she said with a shrug.

33

'But you seem to be studying my clothing with great interest, and I thought—'

'You thought I was going to take you right here, after smelling your clothing?' He finished the sentence for her and she felt her cheeks heat up. 'No, you'll be more valuable as an untouched maiden. You *are* untouched, I take it?' he added, as if the possibility that she wasn't had only just occurred to him.

'I am not discussing that with you.' Linnea raised her chin, but in two strides he was standing before her again and she jumped to her feet. There was no way she wanted him looming over her in that threatening way. 'What?' The word came out as a squeak, betraying her fear.

'Do you have a husband? Or have you ever had one?' His gaze was intense, as if those pale blue orbs were trying to drill their way into her thoughts.

'No.'

'A betrothed? A master?'

'No! Well, apart from you . . . or so you say.' Linnea stared back, trying not to blink. Normally she wouldn't stand her ground like this. Confrontation wasn't her thing, but there was something about this man that made her want to act defiant. What right did he have to be asking such personal questions?

'I mean someone you have lain with?'

'No! I have not had any such master.' And that was the truth. That didn't mean she was necessarily a virgin, but she wasn't telling Hrafn that. It was none of his business.

He held her gaze a fraction longer, then stepped to the side, allowing her to go over to the pile of clothes he'd indicated earlier. Lifting them one by one, she could see they were made in the Viking fashion – a long linen chemise with sleeves, old and patched, but mercifully clean, and an overdress of coarse wool in a boring brown colour that was the same shape, only with three-quarter-length sleeves and a shorter skirt. It might reach about halfway down her calves. A piece of braided wool, presumably to use as a belt, and a matching shawl with a crude pin to fasten it completed the ensemble.

'You can wear your own shoes for now, although they are a bit strange.' Hrafn considered her footwear, a pair of Roman-style sandals she'd put on yesterday morning as the weather had seemed fine enough for summer shoes. They were simply made, with just a thin sole and leather straps that criss-crossed her feet and ankles, but they were comfortable.

She hadn't really registered what he was wearing, but now saw that his shoes also seemed to be made out of soft leather and tied with a cord, although admittedly they were a different style, and definitely not sandals. His clothing was the same as Thure's, but of plainer materials – a linen shirt, a thigh-length woollen tunic with a belt, and narrow trousers. Unlike the cord given to her, his belt was of finely tooled leather, again like the one Thure had been wearing but less ornate, although the bit that hung down had a decorated end made of silver. From the belt hung an assortment of items – a large knife, which for some weird reason was strapped horizontally across his abdomen, a small whetstone – or hone stone as some people called it – with a hole at one end so it could be suspended from a thong, two leather pouches, one large and one small, and a strange-looking key. He wasn't wearing his sword today, as presumably he didn't need it at home, and nor was his battleaxe in evidence. Linnea shivered at the thought of those weapons, but she had a feeling he was just as dangerous without them.

'Can I have my underclothes back, please? *If* you have finished with them, that is?' She held out her hand for the bra and knickers, but he shook his head.

'No. None of the women wear such things. I shall burn them.'

'What? But—'

He held up a hand. 'Hurry now, or I'll drag you out of here naked.'

Clamping her teeth together in frustration, she turned her back on him again and started to dress, keeping the towel on until it was covered by the chemise. '*Infuriating sod! Just you wait until the police get their hands on you . . .*' She continued to mutter to herself in English while she wriggled her way into the dress, tied the belt and put her sandals back on. As the dress seemed to be made of wool, she'd expected it to feel itchy, but the linen of the undergown protected her skin from the scratchy material, and in fact it just felt nice and warm. It helped that the sleeves and hemline of the chemise were longer too. The shawl she just picked up to carry for now. It was very odd not to be wearing underwear, but sort of liberating at the same time. In winter it had to be fairly draughty, though, so she was glad it was early summer at the moment.

Hrafn was holding the rest of her normal clothes and fiddled with the drawstring that tied her sweat pants. 'You have strange garments where you come from.' A coin fell out of the pocket and he picked it up. It was a silver ten pence piece, which Linnea had forgotten about, and he studied it. 'El-eesa-bett? I don't know of any countries with a queen of that name. She is a queen, I take it? She'd have to be in order to have her likeness on a coin.' He took a knife from his belt and poked at the coin, his lip curling. 'And your silver is worthless.'

'I guess you haven't travelled much then, but at least you can read,' Linnea snapped. 'Elizabeth the Second is the ruler of England, Bretland and Skotland.'

Hrafn's eyebrows rose and he gave her a disbelieving look. 'She can't be. From what I hear, there are several kingdoms in England alone. And yes, I can read Roman writing, as well as ours. I learned on my last voyage – I *have* travelled, you see. Now, enough of this. Let's go.'

'But—'

'Out!' He dragged her with him, and Linnea decided she'd have to argue some more with him later. How could he not have heard of Queen Elizabeth? And what did he mean, several kingdoms? Unless it was all just part of the play-acting. In Viking times Britain had been divided, of course, and maybe he was sticking to the known facts of this game.

A game she was really beginning to hate.

Chapter Four

'You can make yourself useful while we wait to set off on our journey.' Hrafn took Linnea over to a small house where a group of women sat sorting and carding wool, spinning it and winding it into balls of yarn, while two others worked at weaving cloth on an upright loom that was leaning against the wall. He addressed the oldest one. 'Estrid? Can you look after my thrall, please? She's not to leave your sight, understood?'

'Yes, Hrafn, as you wish.'

Estrid was his aunt on his mother's side and she was getting on in years, but he trusted her to keep an eye on his captive. Unlike most of the other people here, she was loyal to him and his two younger brothers, rather than their older half-brother Thure, who ruled these domains. Although, naturally, she was careful never to show Thure any disrespect. Hrafn's mother had died giving birth to his youngest brother, Geir, and, being childless herself, Estrid had brought them up as though they were her own. For that privilege she'd had to put up with Hrafn's father Eskil's unwanted attentions, but the one and only time Hrafn had asked her about it, she'd said it was a price she'd gladly paid.

He owed her for that.

'I couldn't leave the three of you to be brought up just by *him*,' she'd added, as if that explained everything. And perhaps it did, as his father had been a difficult man.

Unfortunately, she'd had no power over Thure's upbringing, which was why he was cast firmly in his father's mould – greedy, power-hungry and vicious. All things Estrid had taught her nephews not to be.

He nodded his thanks to her now and left, ignoring the glare he received from Linnea. Honestly, what was wrong with her? Did she not have any sense of self-preservation? She ought to try and be nice to him, ingratiate herself so he'd treat her well, but it was as if she hadn't understood that at all. He'd never personally owned a thrall before – he didn't normally deal in them as trade goods – but he was sure they didn't usually behave like this. Thure's certainly didn't. He shook his head and beckoned his two brothers, Rurik and Geir, who were loitering nearby. They followed him into the forest without a word.

Rurik had only recently returned from a lengthy stay in Birka, where he'd been learning the art of silversmithing and making jewellery. At twenty-one winters, he was three years younger than Hrafn, but roughly the same size, and people often commented on the likeness between them, although Rurik's hair was more of a golden blond and slightly wavy. The two of them were alike in many other ways too – pragmatic, capable and determined – though Rurik was more easy-going, not taking life as seriously as Hrafn did. Perhaps because he'd never had the responsibility of being the eldest.

Geir was only eighteen, but was already showing signs of overtaking his older brothers in both size and height. He'd always been a serious boy who enjoyed being outdoors and working with his hands. Skilled in carpentry, he could make almost anything out of wood and knew exactly which type of tree was best suited to a particular item. He was also keen on hunting, although he preferred to go off into the forest on his own. Hrafn worried when Geir disappeared for days on end, but his fears had proved to be unfounded and the youngster usually came back with a great collection of pelts. He'd even killed two bears and now proudly wore a bear's claw hanging off a leather thong round his neck. Perhaps some of the animal's strength would be transferred to him. He was certainly still growing and had filled out a lot lately.

Hrafn stopped in a clearing some distance from the settlement, where they couldn't be overheard, and turned to his brothers.

'This stays between the three of us,' he began, although he knew he could trust them with his life. He'd had Linnea's strange clothing clutched under his arm, but now he unfolded it and laid each garment out on the ground in front of them. 'Have a look at these.'

His brothers kneeled down and picked up the clothes, one by one. 'What in Thor's name is this?' Rurik held up the thing Linnea had called a breast-holder. The mere word made Hrafn hot all over and he remembered how the scrap of material had hugged her assets, drawing attention to them in a way that had had him hardening in an instant. He tried to explain this to his brothers, and although they hooted with laughter at first, he saw them swallow when their imaginations supplied the image he was conveying.

'*Skítr!*' Rurik threw it at Geir, who held it up to the light, looking through the material, which was like a spider's web in black. 'And that?' He pointed at the even smaller scrap Linnea had been wearing on her nether regions.

'That I cannot fathom out. Just look at this.' Hrafn demonstrated how the top part had something inserted into it that made it possible to stretch the garment, and yet it became tight again as soon as you let go. The small black tunic she'd worn was similar in that it bounced back into shape after being stretched. It was uncanny.

'Huh?' Geir tried it too, several times, then shook his head. 'Is this some kind of *trolldómr*? Is she a *völva* who can do magic?'

'I don't think so, but we will have to keep an eye on her. There is something not quite right about her.'

He showed them the coin as well and asked them if they'd heard of an English queen of that name. Neither had.

'She keeps saying that everyone is free where she comes from, but surely people have thralls everywhere? I do not understand.'

'Let us all observe her and we will see. That shouldn't be a hardship – she's not exactly a troll.' Geir chuckled, his usually serious gaze twinkling for once.

'No, you should get a good sum for her at the market in Miklagarðr.' Rurik nodded. 'She is very comely indeed, and that hair, well—'

'Thank you, I know.' Hrafn cut him off. The last thing he needed was for his brothers to be lusting after his thrall. It was bad enough that he'd wanted her himself, if only for a moment. Last time he'd been on a trading journey he had learned that the men of Miklagarðr valued untouched females, and he was determined to keep Linnea that way. Something that might prove quite a problem.

He agreed now that there was nothing they could do other than watch Linnea's every move. 'Before we go, help me make a fire, please. I'm going to burn all this. I don't want anyone else to see.'

For himself, he had no need to see Linnea dressed in her breast-holder ever again, since the image was firmly etched into his brain. As was the sight of her standing naked in the tub with that glorious hair tumbling down, even if it was only the back view. He just wished he could stop thinking about it.

*

'Here, girl, make yourself useful.' The older woman called Estrid handed Linnea a drop spindle – really just a smooth stick with a round weight at one end – and a pile of carded wool, then pointed at a stool that was currently unoccupied. 'Sit, sit.'

'Er . . . I don't know how to spin wool.' Linnea stared at the items in her hands, then at some of the other women, who were busy using their own spindles. They seemed incredibly deft, woollen thread appearing as if by magic in long strands, and were obviously into old-fashioned handicrafts in a big way. Everyone in the hut fell silent and stopped what they were doing to goggle at her. She had the feeling she'd just grown at least three heads.

Estrid tutted. 'I took you for a high-born woman. What *can* you do then? Weave? Make decorative bands?'

High-born? What did she mean by that? Linnea must have looked blank, because the woman added in an exasperated voice, 'Can you do carding at least?'

'Er, no, but I can learn.' It didn't look that difficult. Two other women had been carding as she came in, just brushing the wool with some sort of combs that had handles and long, slightly bent tines. Then inspiration struck. 'Or I could make something out of the wool? What do you need – socks, warm garments for children, mittens?'

She was ace at knitting; it was her go-to method of relaxation. And hadn't she read somewhere that Viking women knitted? So she wouldn't be ruining their re-enactment games by doing something that wasn't authentic. The only problem was, she couldn't remember the word for knitting in Norse, but Estrid seemed to cotton on.

'Ah, you mean *nálbinding*. Very well, help yourself to materials. We always need socks and hats.'

Linnea couldn't see any knitting needles, only some sort of

42

crude sewing needle made of bone. 'I need long, um, needles. Like sticks.' She decided to play along with the re-enactment for now, and held out her hands to show the required size. 'About this big? It's how we do it where I come from.'

Estrid's patience was clearly running out, as her mouth tightened into a thin line of disapproval. 'I have no idea what you are talking about. Come, sit by me and I'll show you how to do *nålbinding*. It's easy. Even a child can learn.'

That put me in my place! But Linnea did as she'd been told and watched as Estrid gave her a crash course in the strange technique. It seemed incredibly fiddly and took her a while to understand, but she did sort of get the hang of it eventually. It was actually like a mixture of crochet and knitting, using a large bone needle to make the stitches. She found it clumsy and slow, but decided it wouldn't be politic to mention that.

They were in a sunken building where the lower parts of the walls had been dug into the ground about half a metre then covered with planks. The rest was built out of wattle and daub, and whitewashed on the inside. Benches lined the walls, apart from on one side where two big upright looms were standing, although only one was being used at present. Its warp was weighed down with loom weights that looked to be made of clay. Linnea had seen similar ones at Uncle Lars's dig, though most of those were broken. It was a very primitive way of weaving, but effective nonetheless. Daylight spilled in through the door, and a little bit more illumination came from an opening high up near the roof. She guessed that would also double as a chimney if the weather was cold. The place was cosy, and in any other circumstances she might have enjoyed spending an afternoon here practising handicrafts.

But right now she was an outsider and on tenterhooks the whole time, her ears straining to hear what was going on outside.

Would the police arrive soon? And what would happen when they did? Would they search the place for her? If she really had been kidnapped, Hrafn might try to hide her away somewhere. She'd have to make her presence known in that case. But how?

As it happened, she needn't have bothered thinking about it, for no one came.

By evening, she had one slightly lopsided sock to show for her day's work. 'Hmm, yes,' Estrid grunted when she inspected it. Linnea had a suspicion she was being kind, even though she looked as though that word wasn't in her vocabulary.

No one else had spoken to her during her time in the hut, but Linnea had listened to their conversations and marvelled yet again at their language skills. They were all speaking Norse as if they'd been born to it; much better than she herself did, even though she'd spent years studying it. At one point, she tried asking for more wool in Swedish to see if it was possible to jolt them out of their role-playing. 'A different colour would be nice,' she added.

'What did you say?'

She received only puzzled glances until she repeated her request in Norse. It was as if they truly didn't understand modern Swedish, but how could that be? Even if they were some sort of odd sect, surely the Swedish government wouldn't let them get away with not going to school?

Even their topics of conversation were old-fashioned – children's illnesses, their hopes for a good harvest this year, gossip about various couples, the master's latest concubine – *concubine, what the hell?* – and, most strangely of all, how some of their husbands were going off on a trading journey to places they called Garðaríki and Grikkland.

'And possibly even Serkland,' one woman added in awed tones.

Linnea mentally translated Garðaríki as Russia – or what

would become that country long after Viking times – Grikkland as Byzantium or the Eastern Roman Empire, although nowadays it was Greece, and Serkland as 'the land of the Saracens', or the Middle East. She was thoroughly confused as to why they should refer to them this way, but it was obviously part of the whole theme.

She tried to ignore the strange thought that popped into her mind – that she had actually ended up in Viking times for real.

That just wasn't possible.

Hrafn didn't see Linnea again until the evening meal and assumed Estrid had kept her busy. He tried to occupy himself with other things, as he didn't want to spend too much time thinking about her. Time and time again, however, he'd had to force himself to concentrate on what he was doing, blinking away those images of the young woman in her strange clothing, and in the bath with nothing on at all.

'The trolls take her!' he muttered, but in that exact moment she walked into the hall with Estrid, and his breath caught in his throat. *Skítr*, but she was beautiful now she was clean. Darkness was falling outside, and in here there were only oil lamps and the hearth, but both cast a golden sheen over Linnea's hair, which hung in a loose plait over one shoulder. She must have braided it to keep it out of the way, but wayward strands escaped and surrounded her face, drawing attention to her delicate bone structure, pert nose and full mouth. There was a healthy glow about her and she exuded vitality in a way none of the other women present did. Perhaps she really was a *völva*? How else could she look so good after the long, hard winter? He exhaled slowly in order to calm his heartbeat, which had increased fourfold.

'Ah, Hrafn. Do you wish your thrall to serve you this evening?' Estrid had come to a halt in front of him and he tried to focus on her, but he didn't miss Linnea's outraged squeak. She opened her mouth to say something, but he held up a hand to forestall her. He didn't want any scenes here. The last thing he needed was to draw attention to her. Or rather, more attention, since there were already quite a few men ogling her.

'No, thank you. I am quite capable of serving myself. But she had better sit next to me so I can keep an eye on her.' He held out a hand to Linnea. 'Come.'

At first he thought she would refuse, but she must have been hungry, and after a slight hesitation, she followed him over to a bench behind one of the trestle tables that had been erected all around the hall. He noticed she ignored his outstretched hand, but he hadn't expected anything else. They scooted on to the end of a bench, Linnea last. Hrafn leaned forward and grabbed a couple of wooden platters, waiting for the serving women – all thralls belonging to Thure – to reach them with the dishes on offer. Without asking, he put food on both his own and Linnea's plates – an ember-baked turnip each, some boiled fish and a dollop of pea stew from which emanated a faint scent of wild garlic. 'Eat,' he said, his voice coming out more gruffly than he intended.

Linnea looked at the food. 'What do I eat with?'

'Huh? Oh, we'll have to share my knife.' He put his eating knife between them, then called for one of the serving women to bring an extra wooden spoon.

Linnea watched as he picked up his turnip, trying not to burn his fingers, then asked, 'Isn't there any bread?'

Hrafn stared at her. She was much too outspoken and demanding for a thrall, but he supposed he'd have to make allowances, as she wasn't used to her situation yet. 'No. There's not much grain left this time of year, so we make do without.' She ought to know that, unless she came from the sort of rich estate where the jarl could afford to buy grain all year round. 'And the harvest wasn't very good last year.'

She frowned but seemed to accept his reply and started eating. Clearly she was starving, as she devoured the turnip quickly, and he remembered with a pang of guilt that she hadn't been fed since yesterday. Her strange garments had made him forget all about giving her something this morning, and Estrid would have assumed she had already eaten.

'Forgive me,' he muttered. 'I forgot to give you *dagverðr* this morning.'

She stopped with a piece of turnip halfway to her mouth and something flashed in the depths of her dark blue eyes. Then she quirked an eyebrow at him. 'You didn't do it on purpose then? To starve me into submission?'

He felt his mouth stretch into a smile. 'No, although I probably should have. You are the least submissive thrall I've ever had the misfortune to come across.'

She huffed. 'Maybe because I'm *not* a thrall,' she muttered.

'You are now,' he stated firmly. And that was the end of the discussion as far as he was concerned. Not for Linnea, though.

'Listen, I don't know what is happening here, but if it's a ransom you want, I'm sure my uncle can arrange it. Can't you at least contact him and ask? He'll have the . . .' She hesitated as if she didn't know the right word to use, then said something in a foreign language. '. . . the police out looking for me by now, and when they find me, you'll be sorry. Please think about it!'

It was an impassioned speech and clearly heartfelt, but Hrafn didn't understand her. If by *police* she meant her uncle's men, then he'd warn Thure to be on his guard. Her uncle could not possibly be anyone of influence around here or Hrafn would have heard of him. He knew just about every person of note in these parts. She had to be bluffing, but if it made her more compliant, he had nothing to lose by playing along. Besides, a ransom might be better than dealing with her on a daily basis.

'Very well, I will think on it.'

He returned his attention to his food, although he kept an eye on Linnea at the same time. He saw her carefully picking the bones out of the fish, making a face when she still managed to put one in her mouth. The pea stew was tasted with caution, but she must have liked it, as it disappeared in a few bites, as had the turnip.

'How did you fare this afternoon?' he asked, more to make conversation than because he was genuinely interested in women's work.

Linnea sighed. 'Estrid thinks I'm useless because I can't do any of the things the other women were doing.'

'What, nothing?' He stopped eating to stare at her again. What manner of home had she come from where they hadn't taught her any useful skills?

She shook her head. 'No. She taught me *nálbinding*, but I would normally do it in a different way – knitting.'

'Nitting?' He'd never heard that word, although it sounded a bit like *níðingr*, which was something completely different.

'Yes, it's more or less the same thing, but much faster, and I'm good at it. But Estrid didn't have the right implements so I had to do it her way.'

'What do you need?' He found himself genuinely interested now. As a small boy, he remembered watching his mother doing *nálbinding*, and although she was quick, it was a fairly laborious way of making socks and hats. If Linnea could do it faster, that would be a good skill for her to pass on to others. Besides, they'd need warm clothes for the journey.

'Oh, five polished metal or bone sticks, about this thick and so long.' She showed him by pinching her fingers together for the width and holding her hands out to demonstrate the length. 'But I don't suppose there is any way of obtaining them here.' Another deep sigh.

Hrafn didn't comment, but he knew someone who could definitely make sticks like that for her – Rurik. He was very tempted to ask his brother; he'd like to see this new technique in use. Yes, perhaps he'd have a word with Rurik later.

With her plate clean, Linnea reached for the cup of ale that had been left for her by another thrall. She took a sip and choked, staring into the cup in disgust. 'What *is* that?' she spluttered in between coughing fits.

'It's just ale.' Hrafn was puzzled. 'Is that not what you normally drink?'

'Not tasting like that.' She shivered visibly, like a dog shaking itself. 'That is so bitter.'

'Would you prefer some whey?'

'Whey? No, thank you. Can you even drink that?'

'Of course.' Hrafn shrugged. 'Well, if you don't like the ale, go without. There's always water in the beck outside.'

He couldn't understand it. Was she used to drinking nothing but mead? That was only for the very rich or extremely special occasions. He decided to ignore her. She'd become used to ale or die of thirst.

'Let us listen to the *skáld*. He's going to tell us the story of Loki and the Lady Sif's golden hair,' he said. Glancing at Linnea's shiny plait, the tale seemed apt, and for a brief moment it occurred to him that Linnea could be the goddess in disguise, come to plague him for some reason. But she seemed much too human to be a deity, and he immediately discarded that thought as ridiculous.

'If that's what passes for entertainment here, I don't suppose I have a choice,' Linnea huffed.

But once the *skáld* began his tale, she became as enraptured as everyone else. The man really was very good, and although Hrafn had heard this particular story many times before, he admired the way it was delivered. He sipped at his ale and noticed that Linnea made a face each time she tasted hers. That made him frown. What was wrong with it? It tasted good to him. He could only assume she had been spoiled all her life – as witness her soft, uncallused hands.

Well, no one was going to spoil her here.

Chapter Five

'This is where I'm sleeping?' Linnea couldn't believe her ears. This, this . . . oaf expected her to sleep with him? And in a hall full of other people too? What were they – the night's second lot of entertainment? 'No way!' she said in English.

'What was that?' Hrafn had led her outside to a disgusting privy she'd already had to use a few times today – with bits of moss the only available toilet paper; what was wrong with these people? – then back inside and over to one of the bench beds built into the wall of the longhouse. Now he was holding out a woollen blanket and glaring at her as if she was really trying his patience.

She took the blanket and sniffed it automatically. It didn't smell bad and was of much finer quality than the horrid one she'd slept under last night. But at least she'd had that – and the bed – to herself.

'I'm not sleeping with you.' She tried to imbue her voice with as much force as possible without shouting. Other people had already gone to bed and probably wouldn't appreciate a slanging match between her and Hrafn disturbing their sleep.

He rolled his eyes. 'Not *with* me, next to me,' he clarified, then swept a hand out to indicate a few of Thure's men, who were watching their exchange with interest. He lowered his voice.

'You're not safe otherwise. If I put you with the thrall women in their hut outside, you'll have a steady stream of visitors all night, I can assure you. Is that what you want?'

'I . . . No!' Linnea swallowed hard. She'd already noticed some of the men here sending her lascivious glances – well, most of them, actually – and one or two had managed to brush against her as she passed them. A shiver went through her. Sleeping next to Hrafn was definitely preferable, but how could she be sure he meant what he said?

It was true that he hadn't hit on her a single time and seemed supremely uninterested in her charms, such as they were, but who was to say what would happen in the dark of night?

'Can't I sleep next to Estrid?' she tried, grasping at straws.

Hrafn snorted. 'She wouldn't want to share her bed with a thrall.'

'Well, why would you?'

'Because you're mine and I'm trying to keep you from being molested. I told you, you'll fetch a much larger sum in Miklagarðr if you're untouched.'

'And what if I'm not?' Linnea hissed.

Hrafn narrowed his eyes at her. 'Then you and I will both be in trouble. Now lie down and go to sleep, woman.'

In the end, Thure made the decision easier for her. While she'd been talking to Hrafn, he'd come up behind her, and the first she knew of his presence was when a large hand groped her backside. She jumped and twisted around, scuttling out of the way. 'Hey!'

Thure smiled. 'Just making sure you'll be worth the large profit Hrafn and I are hoping for.' He glanced at his half-brother. 'Nice arse on her. What say we sample the goods to be absolutely certain?' His hand reached for Linnea's left breast, but before he could make contact, Hrafn whisked her out of the way, pulling her behind him.

'No. We are none of us touching her, understand? I told you the Grikkjar pay more for maidens.'

Thure's eyes narrowed and he made a face like a child about to have a tantrum. 'This is my hall and I'll have you know that here I do as I wish, when I wish it.'

Hrafn stood his ground. 'Not with *my* property you don't. I've not sworn fealty to you and I never will. Besides, you have countless other women; there's no need for you to have this one.' He nodded towards a doorway at one end of the hall. 'Look, Bodil is waiting for you. She'll see to your every need, no doubt.'

Angry sparks glimmered in Thure's bloodshot eyes, but then his mood changed abruptly and he smiled condescendingly, shaking his head. 'You are nothing without me, little brother, and one day you'll learn that, but very well, I'll humour you for now. Just remember, you wouldn't be going on this trading journey if it wasn't for me.'

As he sauntered off, Hrafn muttered, 'Yes I would, one way or another.'

Linnea wasn't sure what was going on between the two men, but figured she didn't need to know. And she'd rather take her chances with Hrafn than with that bastard Thure.

She crawled on to the bench, trying not to notice how dusty the planks were or how manky the furs that covered them. These seemed to be a random collection – sheep, wolf, deer, cow and even a badger – but all looked worn and dirty. Probably a haven for bed bugs, and she was about to add to their feast. *Ugh!*

'What is the matter?' Hrafn had been watching her.

'Nothing.' Linnea didn't think there was any point complaining. She scooted over, lying right up against the wall, and he stretched out beside her like a human shield. If she was honest, she did feel safe, if a bit on edge. He was so big, and made of solid muscle; if he decided to have his wicked way with her, there wouldn't be a thing she could do about it. But he'd seemed very determined that she should stay a virgin, an outdated notion if ever there was one. Well, if it helped to keep her from being raped, she wasn't going to complain.

She wouldn't admit it to anyone other than Sara, but she was still 'untouched', as he'd put it. A late developer, she'd attended an all-girls' school in England and been a total swot. By the time she'd caught up with her classmates physically, they'd left her far behind when it came to boys and partying. Linnea had never had the chance to catch up.

At uni, she'd been determined to at least lose her virginity, but somehow the right guy never came along. Drunk nerds weren't very appealing, and she had a suspicion the more attractive guys would laugh at her for her inexperience. Burying herself in her studies was so much easier than having to tell someone that it was her first time and please could they be gentle with her. No, that would have been beyond embarrassing. And after that, she hadn't wanted anyone other than Daniel, who until recently had shown no interest in her as a woman.

Had he been told she was missing? Had her parents? Lars must have alerted everyone by now and they'd be out scouring the countryside for her, probably thinking the worst. *Oh, God!* Her poor parents. They'd be going out of their minds with worry, as would Lars. And he'd be blaming himself, even though it wasn't his fault. But why hadn't they come looking for her here yet? She couldn't have gone far after she blacked out, and if the police had tracker dogs, they should have been able to follow her scent easily.

It was very strange, but all she could do for now was wait and hope to be rescued.

She sighed and pulled the woollen blanket firmly around her. Hrafn's bed might be hard, but it was a good deal better than the stinking hut. She closed her eyes and was asleep in seconds.

*

'Have you contacted my uncle yet?'

Another day had gone by with surprising speed and Hrafn had been very busy with preparations for the trading journey. Thure, as usual, left everything up to everyone else, and wouldn't bestir himself until it was time to actually set off. The lazy son of a *bikkja* . . . Hrafn pushed down the resentment that always rose within him at the thought that Thure had inherited everything from their father when he was the least worthy of Eskil's four sons. But such was life, and he was determined to make his own way in the world, and be free of this place and any connection to it as soon as possible. Trading was his route out of here and away from Thure.

Now he found Linnea blocking his way, her hands on her hips and with eyes shooting angry sparks at him. She'd spent the day with Estrid and the other women and he hadn't given her much thought.

'What?' He glared at her, having forgotten the conversation about her uncle entirely.

'You promised to find out if he would ransom me. Remember?'

'Oh, that. Well, I couldn't find him. No one has heard of a man called Lars Mattsson around here. He must have gone back to England.'

He was about to walk away, but she grabbed his arm. 'He's not *from* England, he is a . . . a Svíar, like you.'

He looked at her hand, then up at her with raised eyebrows. She seemed to realise what she was doing, blushed to the roots of her hair and hastily removed it. That was better; at last she was learning her place.

'I see.' He shrugged. 'He's still not to be found anywhere, so I'm afraid I have no choice but to take you with me. We leave in the morning.'

'Where are we going? And don't say Miklagarðr.' She held up a hand. 'We couldn't possibly be going all that way in such a small boat.' They both glanced down towards the edge of the nearby lake, where Hrafn and Thure's ships were tethered to a jetty.

'Small? I'll have you know it takes a dozen people and quite a large cargo. And it's a ship, not a boat.' Hrafn glared at her. What did she expect – a vessel fit for a queen? 'Any bigger than that and we won't be able to carry it between rivers.'

'Carry it? You can't be serious!'

'Linnea, I don't have time to stand here arguing with you, and I've told you before, it is not your place to question my orders. As I said, we leave in the morning, so you will see for yourself. Now kindly go back to whatever duties Estrid has set you. I have matters to attend to.'

Her mouth set in a mulish line, which oddly enough made him want to kiss her. He bit back a curse. He shouldn't be thinking about her mouth at all, let alone in that way. It would only drive him mad. How on earth was he going to survive a long journey in her company?

'Fine. Estrid said to give you these.' She held out a pair of socks that were the oddest things he'd ever seen – one large and slightly lopsided, the other so small he doubted it would fit more than his toes – and added, 'I made them.'

He detected a touch of defiance in her voice, as if she knew how awful they were but was daring him to comment on it. 'Er . . . thank you.' He took them from her and tried his best not to laugh, even though he could feel his mouth twitching. He could see now what she had meant about only just having learned how to do this. It would be most unkind of him to ridicule her work, but by all the trolls, these were priceless. He manfully swallowed a chuckle. 'I'll, um . . . add them to the rest of my clothing.'

'You're welcome.'

*

Linnea stomped off, having seen the smile he'd tried to hide at the sight of her handiwork. Although he would have been fully justified in laughing at those horrible socks, she still felt hard done by. She'd done her best. Besides, she was cross with Hrafn for lying about her uncle, and even more angry with herself for actually thinking he was going to try and find Lars. The annoying man was clearly enjoying this charade about taking her to be sold somewhere. Was it some perverted mind game, or did he just enjoy keeping her on tenterhooks?

It was so frustrating.

But Estrid and the others were all playing along too, and Linnea was becoming increasingly uneasy as the day passed and no one slipped up. No mention of modern things whatsoever, not a hint of contemporary language even from the children, and no gadgets of any kind. Estrid even went as far as to give Linnea a sack with a few items to take with her on this pretend journey.

'Hrafn's orders,' she explained. 'I've put in an extra serk and overtunic, a warm cloak in case you have to overwinter somewhere, two pairs of men's trousers – linen and wool – a comb and a small eating knife and spoon. Some soap, although Hrafn will have brought some, needles and thread, and balls of yarn for you to make more socks and whatever else you need. Oh, and five metal sticks, which Rurik brought just now. Apparently Hrafn asked him to make them for you, although the gods only know what for and why he's humouring a thrall.' Her mouth twisted in disapproval, but Linnea hardly noticed. She opened the bundle, located a long, thin container made of birch bark, which contained the sticks, and pulled them out to inspect them.

'Oh, wonderful!' she breathed. It was strange how Hrafn could be such a brute one minute, then order these to be made for her the next. She was amazed he'd even remembered their conversation. Made of bronze, by the look of it, they weren't perfect, but they would certainly do as knitting needles. She was tempted to make a start immediately, but knew it would be better to leave it for another day. 'Thank you.'

'Don't thank me, it was Rurik's doing.' Estrid's frown didn't let up. 'I'll tell Hrafn he will need to buy you some better shoes soon, even though you are a thrall. I expect he'll want a good price for you, which means he has to look after you well.' She sniffed, as if thralls didn't deserve nice shoes or extra clothing. Linnea couldn't understand how anyone could even pretend to believe that owning and selling slaves was OK – it was despicable.

And yet if she really was going somewhere, having some form of luggage was a bonus, since her own things were still back at the dig site. 'Thank you again,' she said grudgingly. What else could she say? *Stop pretending that this is for real! I'm on to you!* But whenever she tried to talk to anyone here about modern things, they went blank and treated her as if she was mad.

The only good news was that they were leaving this place tomorrow. Surely they'd have to pass by normal civilisation? Then Linnea should be able to attract someone's attention to the fact that she was being held captive by these loons against her will.

She went to bed that night feeling optimistic.

Their journey began early in the morning, with Linnea sitting at the back – or stern – of Hrafn's ship. Apparently he owned a quarter of it, as it was shared with his two younger brothers and Thure. She gathered this type of ship was very expensive and Hrafn hadn't had enough money to buy or have one built for just him. Thure had a ship all his own, though, and had placed himself at the front, again acting as if he was a king. His grumpy expression hadn't changed much.

'Hurry up!' Linnea heard him shouting at everyone. The men rowing both boats were his, apart from the two who Linnea now knew were Hrafn's brothers, and most were strong, lean males in their twenties. Six in each boat, although only four rowed at any one time, they worked well together, as if they were used to rowing as a team.

Linnea wasn't the only female. There was a blonde girl sitting next to Thure, fawning over him in what Linnea considered a sickening way. She was the mistress Hrafn had pointed out, and she'd heard Estrid and the other women gossip about her too – Bodil? Yes, that was her name. Thure mostly ignored the poor thing, but she didn't seem daunted. No doubt she was used to his moods.

The two ships travelled side by side as much as possible, and several times Linnea noticed Thure's eyes resting on her instead of Bodil. It was as if he was still evaluating her for possible use, despite Hrafn's refusal. She couldn't mistake the man's intent when his gaze started at her face, then moved deliberately down her body as far as he could see and back up again. She shivered. He did nothing to hide his lustful expression, and when she glared back at him, he smiled. It made her skin crawl, and she was all the more determined to escape as soon as possible.

In the ship's prow sat a Saami girl with shining blue-black hair and pretty features. She didn't speak much, but had greeted Linnea before boarding. 'I'm Eija,' she said, and added, 'I've heard we are picking up a couple more women along the way.'

Linnea just nodded. This whole thing was getting more and more bizarre, but she was totally focused on trying to spot the nearest modern town, or even a summer cottage or farm. Anywhere there would be normal, decent people who could potentially help her. And hopefully a phone.

But there was nothing.

The boat glided along, low in the water, smoothly propelled by the oars. Hrafn was sitting right in front of her, facing her, and unlike his half-brother, he was rowing with the others, while his brother Geir was steering. It would seem there was no room for freeloaders here, not even if you were the captain, as Hrafn clearly was. It was a warm day in late May, and most of the men wore only linen shirts that showed the outline of their muscles as they rowed. Linnea tried not to stare at Hrafn's arms and upper body, which were definitely impressive. Either he worked out a lot or the physical labour around the farm kept him fit. Rowing probably helped too.

He was concentrating on the rhythm, but from time to time he peered at her. 'What are you looking for?' he finally asked, demonstrating that she had failed to glance around her surreptitiously.

'Um, houses. I didn't know your place was so far from everywhere else.' Linnea tried not to show her confusion. The ship was built so that both prow and stern looked the same, presumably to make it easier to row or sail it in either direction, and both ends were slightly raised. That gave her a good vantage point from which to observe the passing landscape, but so far she'd not seen any signs of civilisation. The dig site had been only a couple of kilometres from a small town, and she was sure it had been surrounded by at least a few houses and farms. But it was as if she'd ended up in the middle of nowhere, with forests as far as the eye could see. How could that be? Had Hrafn and his goons carried her some distance before she woke up?

'There's one.' Hrafn nodded. 'My friend Haukr owns that settlement. He and his wife have just had their first child, a son.'

Linnea's gaze fastened on the passing shore, and yes, there were some houses at last, but they looked exactly the same as

Thure's – all built in the Viking style, and with not a single car or other modern trapping anywhere to be seen. The name Haukr rang a bell for some reason, but she couldn't put her finger on it right now.

'Jesus!' she breathed. What the hell was going on? Was everyone around here nuts?

As they continued the journey, she became increasingly anxious, her stomach muscles clenching and her thoughts whirring. They passed several more places of habitation – each and every one of them Viking, or at the very least old-fashioned. Linnea was grabbing the side of the boat so hard her knuckles were turning white.

'Relax,' Hrafn said. 'You are safe in this ship; it won't capsize. And even if it did, I can swim, so I'd save you.'

'And me,' Geir added. The youth was so close, he couldn't fail to have heard their conversation, and he sent Linnea a smile that she gathered was meant to be reassuring.

She frowned at them both. 'I'm not worried about that, and I can swim too. But . . .' She bit her lip. How could she tell them what she really feared? That she was going mad. Or that she'd ended up in some sort of alternative universe. Or—

'There it is!' someone called out. 'Birka.'

Linnea turned to look and gasped out loud. As they rounded a peninsula and headed into a large bay on their right, she saw a town spread out before her. But it wasn't a modern one. It looked exactly like the large-scale model of Viking-age Birka that she had seen not three weeks ago when Uncle Lars had taken her on a trip there. Then, the bay had been empty and on the shore there were only a few modern houses with a restaurant and a museum telling the story of this place. But now . . .

She stifled a cry of distress and stared at the shore as they approached.

Now there were three or four semicircles of houses fanning out from the bay and climbing up the gentle slope, surrounded by earthworks with a palisade on top and wooden watchtowers at regular intervals. To the right of the town, up on a hill with far-reaching views, lay some sort of fort, presumably to add extra security, and Linnea glimpsed men up there manning the walls. Some of the houses in the town were also built of wood, others made with wattle and daub, but they all had their gable ends facing the lake. Roofs varied – a few were steep, with fancy carving on the top of the gable finials, while others were plain and thatched. Most had smoke coming out of them in gentle wisps through holes either end. In between ran narrow streets, and as they came closer, Linnea could see that each had a walkway of planks down the middle, presumably because they became too muddy to walk on otherwise. These walkways led all the way down to the shore and connected with a number of jetties.

There were boats and ships of every size moored or anchored in the harbour. And people everywhere. People who were all dressed in Viking clothing and going about their daily business – fishing, trading, building, laughing, arguing . . . Not just a group of re-enactors, but hundreds of them. Even a thousand maybe. And the jetties were impressive – some possibly as long as thirty or forty metres, and wide enough for there to be market stalls set up on them where traders and customers mingled.

But . . . no electricity. No modern boats. No tourists. Not a camera or mobile in sight.

Dear God, this couldn't be true! *No, no, no!* It just wasn't possible.

Linnea's vision blurred. She blinked to clear away the tears that threatened to spill out of her eyes, but she couldn't stop a sob from escaping. There was no way this town could have been built in the last few weeks, and it was equally as certain that she was looking at Birka, because she remembered the place clearly. There was only one conclusion she could reach.

She really *had* ended up in Viking-age Sweden. How on earth could this be?

Chapter Six

'Watch out for the underwater palisade!' Hrafn shouted over to Thure, having sent a man to the front of his own ship so that he could locate the large sharpened poles and guide them past. They were there to deter invaders, but if you knew about them, they could be avoided. As he began to row again slowly, Hrafn heard an anguished sob from Linnea's direction and turned to look at her. 'What ails you, woman?'

He frowned at her in concern. She was blinking furiously and another sob escaped her. As they neared the jetty, she sat immobile, staring at the houses as if she was looking at a *draugr* – someone returned from the dead. Her face was completely drained of colour, and he noticed that her hands were shaking, despite hanging on to the side of the boat for dear life. What in Odin's name was wrong with her now?

'Huh?' She turned dull eyes towards him.

'Do you feel sick from being on board the ship? If you are going to faint, put your head down between your knees.'

As the boat came to rest against the jetty and one of the men jumped off with a thick rope to tie them to it, Hrafn bent forward and pushed Linnea's head down. She didn't resist, just gave another strangled sob and let her head hang between her knees.

Her long hair, which she wore loose today, fell like a curtain, shimmering in the sunlight. Hrafn had the urge to bury his fingers in the thick mass to feel its softness. He muttered an oath. This was not the time to be thinking of such things.

'Rurik, can you direct the men for now, please? I'll bring the thrall when she's feeling better.'

Rurik nodded and began to give orders. A couple of the men would stay on the ship to guard the trade goods already on board, while everyone else went ashore to their lodgings. Hrafn had agreed with a merchant friend, Leifr, that his crew could sleep at his house for the night. That way they had the afternoon to gather the rest of their cargo, and then they could be off first thing in the morning. Thure and his men were bedding down elsewhere, probably with another merchant, although Hrafn didn't care which one. He didn't like any of Thure's friends.

'Can you stand now?' He put out a hand and lifted Linnea's face, which had the effect of framing it in tousled golden tresses, making her look beautiful but tragic. Her eyes were wide, filled with tears, and so dark blue they were almost violet; her gaze distant as though she was in shock. He could feel her trembling still. 'Come, let us go and sit by the shore. You'll feel better then.'

She didn't reply but allowed him to guide her on to the jetty and dry land. He led her along the water's edge until they found a quiet place where they could sit on a couple of large boulders. Linnea needed only a gentle nudge before sinking down on one of them. Her expression was still dazed, and her face continued to be devoid of colour.

Hrafn was worried. If she was sickening for something, he couldn't take her with them, but what should he do with her? No one here would want to look after a woman who was ill in case she had something infectious, especially not a thrall. He reached out and turned her face towards him so that she had to focus on

65

him, and he saw her blink a few times. One large tear rolled slowly down her cheek, and somehow that one droplet affected him more than a whole waterfall would have done.

'What is the matter? Did something bad happen to you here in Birka in the past?' It had to be more than seasickness the way she was acting.

Linnea shook her head. 'No, I . . . You wouldn't understand.' Her voice was nothing but a husky whisper, as if she didn't have the strength to speak properly.

'Let me decide that,' Hrafn ordered. He had to get to the bottom of this.

A flash of her old spirit returned as Linnea sent him a challenging look. 'Very well, but you won't believe me. It's almost impossible to explain, but . . . I don't belong here. I'm from the future.'

Of all the things Hrafn might have expected her to say, that definitely wasn't one of them. 'What?' He leaned back, regarding her with raised eyebrows. She might as well have told him she was the goddess Freya – he couldn't have been more flummoxed. In fact, he might have been more inclined to believe that.

'I know it sounds strange, but I think I have travelled through time. Remember I told you I lived in the year 2017? Well, this . . .' she swept a hand out to indicate the whole of Birka, 'this town ceased to exist sometime around the year 980. That means I have come from a time more than a thousand years into the future.'

Hrafn just stared at her. By all the gods, she was completely insane. How had he not seen that before? True, he'd heard her asking some weird questions and speaking a language that sounded oddly like his own although not one he understood, but still . . . This was beyond anything. He shook his head. 'You are deluded.'

And yet she seemed so sincere. So sure. So . . . normal.

She gave a strangled laugh. 'I can see that's how it must appear to you, but I swear, I was here only a few weeks ago and all those houses over there were gone. The streets and the people too. All that was left was a tranquil bay and mounds of grass.' She snorted. 'Do you know what's really amusing? I thought *you* and all your people were the ones who were deluded. That you were just playing at being Vikingar . . . er, I mean Svíar from this time – you don't call yourselves Vikings, do you? I couldn't understand why you wouldn't admit that it was just pretence.' She closed her eyes and another tear escaped, making its way down her flawless skin. 'But you're for real.'

Hrafn was stunned. 'Prove it,' he said finally. He had heard that the gods sometimes played tricks on humans, particularly Loki, the god of mischief, but he would need to be thoroughly convinced to believe something this outrageous.

Linnea spread her hands in a helpless gesture. 'How can I? I didn't bring anything other than my clothes and that coin, which you said was worthless. I don't know what you did with any of it, but either way, they don't really prove anything. I wasn't even wearing something with a zipper.'

'A what?'

'A way of fastening garments. I can't explain. I . . . Oh, dear God, what am I going to do? I need to get back. I have to find a way . . .'

'No!' Hrafn surprised himself with the vehemence in his voice. 'You're not going anywhere other than with me. If you're not ill – other than possibly in your head – you are coming with us tomorrow. I don't believe a word of what you're saying. This is some ruse to make me release you so that you can try to find your uncle – well, it won't work. Now come, we need to go to Leifr's house.'

Linnea opened her mouth as if she intended to protest, but then closed it again. It was as though an awning came down over her face, the light in her eyes dimming until they lost their sparkle completely. 'Fine,' she whispered. 'What's the use? I have no idea how I got here in the first place, so I can't go back anyway. You might as well sell me to the highest bidder or . . . or kill me.'

Her mouth trembled, but she stood up.

Hrafn didn't reply; just took her arm and marched her off towards the town's narrow streets. He'd wasted enough time on this contrary woman.

Linnea walked along in Hrafn's wake, dazed and completely frozen on the inside. She was in Birka, probably sometime in the ninth century. *The bloody ninth century! Jesus* . . . It seemed impossible, but unless she was having a really long dream – or nightmare more like – this was all real. There were details here she couldn't possibly have imagined – things that the large-scale model of the town she'd seen at the museum didn't show. Wear and tear on the walkways, slaves toiling to carry heavy burdens down towards the jetties, children, dogs, chickens and other animals scurrying about the place . . . And noise, everywhere a cacophony of sounds.

It was all too much.

She started taking in her surroundings. Wooden houses side by side with the wattle-and-daub ones, with small alleyways in between. Crude picket fences, craftsmen working in their front yards or just inside open doorways, women with toddlers hanging on to their skirts, haranguing older children. At one point, the street opened up into a small square with four or five old trees, their branches covered in new leaves. In between, offerings to the gods could be glimpsed in the form of rotting carcasses, slowly swinging to and fro. Linnea turned away, even though the animals had clearly been dead a long time. She swallowed down another sob and put her hand up to cover her mouth. The smell of this place . . . it stank of rubbish, faeces and humanity en masse. She wrinkled her nose and tried to take shallow breaths. Were there diseases lurking here? The fetid air certainly couldn't be wholesome.

But maybe that would be the best thing for her – to catch something horrible and die quickly. Because what was the alternative? To be taken on a trading journey in a tiny ship all the way to Istanbul and sold in a slave market? She felt hysterical laughter bubbling up in her throat but managed to keep it from escaping. No, her brain couldn't possibly be making this up.

'In here. And don't even *try* to tell that idiotic story to anyone else or you'll be very sorry,' Hrafn hissed, and pulled her though a gate in a low fence and towards an open door.

Linnea wanted to laugh again. What good would that do? No one would believe her anyway – they'd all react the way he had – and even if they did, they couldn't help her. How had she travelled through time? She had no idea. It shouldn't even be possible, and yet it had undoubtedly happened. If only she knew how . . .

She stopped dead in the doorway, lost in thought, but Hrafn seemed to have run out of patience and tugged on her wrist. 'Move, woman!' he whispered.

She followed him into the merchant's house while still trying to accept that the concept of time travel wasn't just a far-fetched theory – it was very real indeed.

Hrafn left Linnea and the Saami girl, Eija, in the care of Leifr's wife and daughters. They knew not to let new thralls out of their sight, even though there was nowhere for them to run. Birka was situated on a small island in the middle of a lake, and escaping would be pointless, but there were still those who made the attempt.

Leifr was a jeweller who specialised in polishing amber and other beads, using them to make necklaces that tempted the local ladies. Amber was a fairly soft material that could be carved with a knife and have holes drilled through it without too much effort, although mostly a lathe was used to polish and shape the raw pieces. It was also perfect for selling abroad, the more intricate creations especially. Hrafn had made a deal with Leifr that he would sell as many as the man could make. They were to share the profits equally, since Hrafn had been to the land of the Balts to fetch the raw amber for Leifr to work with, thus cutting out the middlemen, and was also the one making the perilous journey. It seemed fair, and they trusted each other.

It was with Leifr that Hrafn's brother Rurik had spent a few years learning the trade of silversmithing and bead polishing. He had his own collection of amber jewellery to sell now, which pleased Hrafn because he wanted his younger brothers to be able to escape from under Thure's control just as he himself was doing. Geir wasn't interested in the finer things, but had amassed a collection of beautiful furs – wolf, lynx, marten, fox and even those two bears. Hopefully they would give him the riches he needed.

'I want land of my own,' he'd told Hrafn. 'I could do so much better than Thure. He hardly ever involves himself in the day-to-day running of his domains, just leaves it to others.' He had sniffed. 'That's plain stupid, but then we know he's a lazy *aumingi*.' There was no arguing with that, but Hrafn knew Geir would need a lot of silver in order to buy lands for himself. Probably more than those pelts would raise.

Hrafn had been on several previous trading expeditions, and the profits he made he'd invested in buying his share of the ship and even more furs to take with them now, as well as walrus tusks – which most people called 'fish teeth' – iron ore and sacks of eiderdown. He'd learned last time that these, and the amber, were the items most sought after in Grikkland. All in all, he was pleased with the cargo they'd be bringing.

Of course, the most profitable commodity of all was thralls, but Hrafn still felt they were a lot of bother. He was bringing four females altogether, but they were going to be a real nuisance. Especially Linnea . . . He sighed inwardly. It was an incredibly long and arduous journey. Did he really want to bring an insane woman with him?

As if he'd read Hrafn's mind, Leifr clapped him on the shoulder and commented, 'That was a comely thrall girl you brought, the golden-haired one. Where did you find her?'

'Comely, but not quite right in the head,' Hrafn muttered.

'Really? That's a shame, but makes no difference, unless she's violent.'

'No, I don't think so.' Hrafn hadn't noticed any violent tendencies in Linnea. And as Leifr said, what did it matter if her mind wasn't all there when she was so beautiful to look at? The men of Grikkland wouldn't find out about her lack of sanity until Hrafn was long gone, along with the massive amount of silver he would receive for her.

'I found her when I was out hunting,' he told his friend. 'She was just lying there, next to the forest track. I have no idea where she'd come from or how she ended up there, but no one has tried to claim her.' He shrugged and decided not to mention that Linnea had been in possession of Thure's brooch at the time.

That was another conundrum, actually, because hadn't Hrafn noticed his half-brother wearing the brooch that same morning before going hunting? And yet no one at the settlement had seen Linnea before he brought her back there. So how could she possibly have stolen it?

*

71

Linnea spent most of the night awake, her mind a jumble of thoughts. Denial, fear, confusion and disbelief warred with one another. She just couldn't make sense of her situation. Time travel shouldn't be possible unless someone had invented a time machine, like in some of the sci-fi stories she'd read. Science was, after all, making leaps and bounds every day in the twenty-first century, and hadn't Einstein said time travel was possible in theory? Yes, she remembered reading something about wormholes. Or maybe black holes? But she hadn't heard about any such inventions, and she'd not been anywhere near a gadget other than the bog-standard metal detector, and she very much doubted that had anything to do with it.

Magic? Could what she had gone through be some sort of supernatural phenomenon? Was there a wormhole in that field? But she'd never believed in such things for an instant. That kind of stuff only occurred in fairy tales.

Still, she couldn't doubt that she was lying in a house in Birka, probably in the eighth or ninth century. It was inconceivable that her mind should have made up the snoring humans surrounding her, the hard straw mattress underneath her, the scratchy woollen blanket that covered her, or the house itself. Rough walls and an earth floor, a few bits of furniture – a table, benches and some stools – plus lots of utensils, some of which she had no idea what they were for. If she didn't know that, she couldn't have imagined them either, could she?

If she allowed herself to accept the fact that she really had been transported back to Viking times, the next challenge was how she was going to return to her own era. That would only be possible if she could figure out how she got here in the first place and then, somehow, reverse the process. She really needed to go back to that field to see if there was anything strange about it – did it contain a time portal of some sort, perhaps? – but she had no idea how to find it. And judging by Hrafn's reaction, he wasn't going to take her either.

Which meant she was back to square one, and as morning approached, no nearer to finding a solution. It would seem she was well and truly stuck here – a slave in ninth-century Birka.

Bloody hell!

A memory suddenly surfaced of an evening in York, about a month ago. She'd been in a pub with Daniel and some of his students when one of them, a Norwegian girl by the name of Karin, had dropped into the seat beside her, saying, 'Hey, do you want me to cast the runes for you? It might help.'

'What?' Linnea had been staring into space, lost in dark thoughts, while people chatted and laughed all around her. She shouldn't have come to the pub. It had been a mistake; she wasn't ready for socialising or enjoying life. It seemed wrong somehow, after the accident. She'd focused on Karin and frowned. 'You want to tell my fortune here? Seriously?'

'Why not? No one is paying attention to us.' Karin smiled. 'Sometimes it helps to know where you're going when you feel lost.'

'Hmm, maybe.' She did feel lost right now, very much so. And what harm could it do? It was just a bit of fun. Not a word that had been in her vocabulary lately. 'OK, fine, go for it.'

Karin had already pulled out a leather pouch. She shook it, then closed her eyes and extracted what looked like three bits of old bone with writing on them. 'Ready to find out your destiny?'

'I thought this was done with stones,' Linnea commented.

'Sometimes, but these are antique rune staves I inherited from my Icelandic grandmother. Very powerful they are. Magical. Now, let me see . . . Oh, this is Thurisaz and it's reversed.' She hesitated. 'That means danger and defencelessness. I . . . Sorry! Maybe this wasn't such a good idea after all.'

But Linnea's interest was piqued now. 'You mean even more danger than I've already been in? Go on, what else do they say?'

'Um, well, this is Hagalaz.' Karin tried to smile brightly. 'It's telling you there will be some disruption to your plans, but that gives you a chance to rethink things. Basically, you're just being tested and then everything will work out fine.'

That last bit didn't sound very convincing, and Linnea sent the girl a sceptical look. 'Really? Sounds perfect. Not!'

Karin ignored the sarcasm and held up the third rune. 'Look, this is very positive – Degaz, the rune for transformation and awakening. See? You will come through the dark times and be given hope. So all will end well.' She quickly collected up the rune staves and put them back in the pouch. 'There, didn't I tell you? Just focus on the fact that you will have joy in your life again soon.'

Linnea nodded. That wasn't the message she'd taken from the runes, and Karin seemed on edge, as if she was uncomfortable with the predictions and had left out something vital. But what did it matter? It was only a joke. 'I'll . . . er, keep that in mind. Thanks for trying to cheer me up.'

'Any time.'

Lying in the darkness of Leifr's house now, Linnea felt a shiver travel the length of her spine. It hadn't been a joke – Karin's runes really had shown her destiny. From the girl's reaction, she must have sensed the seriousness of the prediction and that the runes were right. Linnea was in danger and defenceless. And oh Lord, was she ever being tested.

She could only hope that the final rune was telling the truth as well and she'd come through this dark time. But how?

Chapter Seven

'She's awfully quiet this morning. What's the matter with her?' Rurik whispered, and nudged Hrafn's shoulder. They were standing on the jetty watching the last of the provisions being loaded on to the ship, as well as the four thrall girls, including Linnea. Smoked meat, dried fish, two sacks of dried peas and a barrel of pickled kale, as well as ale. It wouldn't last the whole journey, but they'd be purchasing other things along the way.

'I don't know. She made up some ridiculous story yesterday, no doubt to try and make me set her free, but I didn't believe a word of it. Now she's probably sulking.' Hrafn sighed.

He'd taken out her strange coin again when he woke before everyone else, and studied it in the morning light. It wasn't made of proper silver, he was sure of that, but it certainly looked like that material. He'd never seen any metal that imitated real silver so well. The writing was Roman – as he'd told Linnea, he had learned to read that during his last voyage when spending time with a foreign merchant he'd got on well with. He could decipher the name she had mentioned – *ELIZABETH II* – and the rest read *DEI GRA REG FID DEF*. He assumed those were words in the Roman tongue, perhaps a curse or magic formula, but there were four markings he didn't understand at all – *2016*. They weren't letters as far as he could see, except for one that looked like an elongated version of the Roman O.

The depiction of the queen was incredibly detailed and lifelike, and Hrafn marvelled at her strange hairstyle and headdress. She was clearly an elderly lady, but looked dignified and firm. He supposed she would have to be very strong if she was ruling a kingdom on her own. On the other side of the coin was an animal that he had been told was a lion. He'd seen depictions of them during his travels, and although he wasn't sure if they existed somewhere or were imaginary creatures, this too was an amazingly meticulous image. The beast had the same sort of headdress – or hat? – as the queen, and looked powerful and proud. Around the edge of the coin were the words *TEN PENCE*, presumably more Roman, and another two of those letters he couldn't read. Possibly they were an *I* and an *O*, strangely shaped.

He'd hidden the coin away again in an inside pocket, deciding he'd make a hole in it and hang it round his neck when he had a moment. It could be a powerful amulet, who knew? And perhaps he would ask Linnea about the letters he didn't understand, even if he couldn't be sure that she'd tell him the truth. The coin might be part of some elaborate ruse on her part, although that seemed a bit too organised for someone who was mad. It was more likely she was a *völva*, but one who'd inhaled too much henbane smoke. He'd heard this could have a strange effect.

'Are we ready to go, or are we waiting around all day?' Thure slapped Hrafn on the back so that he almost pitched head first into the water, jolting him out of his thoughts. Thankfully Rurik grabbed him at the last minute.

'Whoa, brother!' Rurik sent Thure a death glare, but the man was oblivious.

Hrafn scowled at Thure. 'Everything is ready, I believe.' He didn't add that they'd been waiting for him to wake up. He had been told that a lot of ale had been consumed the night before at the place where Thure had lodged, and he could well believe it. His half-brother was squinting at the sun, and there was a greyish tinge to his skin as if he wasn't feeling too good. Hrafn silently thanked the gods that he didn't have to share a boat with the man at least.

'I see you found some thralls for me to sell.' Thure glanced at a group of three women who stood huddled together waiting to board his ship. Through narrowed eyes he studied them critically. 'Not the best-looking wenches I've ever seen, but I suppose they'll do. Good thing you're taking the Saami girl, though. I'll not have her.'

Considering he'd spent weeks trying to find the prettiest thralls with blonde or red hair and comely figures – not an easy task when other traders had the same objective – Hrafn was very tempted to punch Thure, but he knew it wouldn't do any good. They had to travel together for a long time, and falling out before they'd even left wasn't going to help. The man hadn't shown any interest in seeing the women before now so he only had himself to blame. 'They're Mercians. I bought what was available,' was all he said in the end. He didn't know why Thure would object to Eija – although she wasn't blonde, she was undoubtedly beautiful in an other-worldly sort of way.

Some men went on raids during the summer months and brought back thralls they'd captured, but that wasn't Hrafn's way. He never just helped himself to anything that didn't belong to him – he traded honestly for profit. That meant he'd had to travel to a couple of different market places during the spring in order to find exactly the type of women he was looking for. There were towns where an assortment of thralls were sold, and he'd brought his purchases back to Birka, leaving the women in Leifr's care while he went back to Eskilsnes to finalise preparations for the journey.

Thure made a face. 'Why aren't they in irons, though? They are thralls, going to market. We can't have them running off at every opportunity.'

'I don't consider irons or chains necessary,' Hrafn said in clipped tones. 'The women are surrounded by strong men – how are they going to run away? And where to? Besides, I selected them for their beauty; do you really want to mar that by scarring them with chafing irons all the way to Grikkland?'

'I suppose not, but if we lose any of them, it will be up to you to replace them.' Thure turned towards his ship. 'Well, let's be off then. You'd best lead the way since you've made this journey before,' he added grudgingly.

'Ouch, that cost him dear to say,' Rurik murmured under his breath, and chuckled.

'Yes. We had better hope he actually listens to me, or this venture could be even more arduous than it normally is.'

The two ships set off, full to the gunwales with people and cargo, most of which was stored in the middle and covered with animal hides to protect it from the elements. Hrafn took turns to row with the rest of his men. He hated being idle and enjoyed the sensation of finally being under way after months of planning. They headed towards the open sea, passing forested shores and numerous small islands. At first the islands were wooded, but the further out they went, the more they consisted mostly of bare rocky outcrops. Hrafn stuck to the right-hand side of the lake, as he knew they wanted to go south down the coast. Once clear of the lake and into the sea, they pulled in the oars, storing them along the inside of the ship, and hoisted the square sail. The wind would do most of the hard work from now on.

'Secure the oars,' Hrafn ordered, then took the steering oar and settled himself at the back of the ship, just behind where Linnea sat. She seemed to be in a complete daze, staring at the scenery but in a way that made Hrafn suspect she wasn't seeing anything at all. Her body was still, and it wasn't until they reached the sea that she started to move. He saw her frown when the waves began to roll the ship, and then she turned pale, as did a lot of other people on board.

'If anyone feels sick, hang over the side, please!' he shouted, well aware of what ailed them. He'd discovered last time that he was one of the lucky few who didn't suffer from seasickness except in extreme conditions, but he knew it afflicted most people, at least to begin with. And the last thing he wanted was a ship full of vomit.

At first the ship cut smoothly through the water, but as the wind picked up and the waves increased, it wasn't long before some of the crew members were casting up their morning meal. His four thrall girls – Linnea, two women from Frisia, and Eija, the Saami girl – soon followed suit. After a particularly violent bout of sickness, Linnea glared at Hrafn as if it was all his fault.

'Why aren't you ill?'

He suppressed a smile at the accusing note in her voice. 'Not everyone is affected by the sea, and the waves aren't that bad today.' He shrugged. 'I'm lucky, I suppose.'

'I'd say,' she muttered, and leaned over the side once more.

Rurik was an interesting shade of green, but managed to hold on to the contents of his stomach. Geir, on the other hand, seemed fine. 'Can you make sure everyone drinks some water,' Hrafn called out to him. 'If not, they will grow weak. And it doesn't matter if they throw it up again; some will remain in their bodies eventually.'

They'd brought casks of rain water and Geir went round with a small bucket and a scoop, forcing everyone to take at least a few sips.

Towards afternoon, they reached the beginning of a wide

channel between the mainland on the right and a long island on the left. Hrafn immediately turned sharp left, rounding the northernmost tip of the island and sailing partway down its eastern coastline. As darkness fell, they made landfall and set up camp on a sandy shore. Hrafn and Geir lifted the thrall girls on to dry land, and he felt Linnea shiver.

'I am never going on a ship ever again,' she hissed. 'You can just leave me here to die tomorrow.'

He laughed. 'I'm afraid that is not possible. And believe me, you will start to feel better soon. Most people get used to it.'

She shook her head as if she didn't believe him, her eyes dark pools of despair, and he sent up a prayer to the gods that she wasn't one of the unlucky ones who never adapted to the sea at all.

Linnea couldn't remember a time when she'd felt so sick, not even after a student union party where someone had spiked the punch with way too much vodka and everyone had the hangovers from hell afterwards. Her body seemed mauled and battered, and she barely managed to take a few sips of a broth cooked by Hrafn's brother, although she had to admit it settled her stomach.

Most of the men recovered faster than her and were soon sitting round a campfire drinking ale.

'Urgh, how can they?' she muttered to Eija.

The Saami girl just shrugged. 'They're men. It's what they do.'

As the evening wore on, the men began to cast longing glances at the thrall women, who sat in a separate group, whispering together. It wasn't difficult to guess what they wanted, but Hrafn must have noticed too, because he stood up and said in a loud voice, 'No one touches the women, understood? We can't be arriving in Miklagarðr with pregnant ones. Who'd want to buy those?'

'But they'd get two thralls for the price of one,' one of the men dared to joke, but the look Hrafn sent him had him raising his hands in a peace gesture.

'Whatever you say. I'm sure we can find willing ones along the way.'

'Exactly.' Hrafn's tone didn't invite further comment, and although there was some muttering among the men, they obviously saw the sense in what he'd said.

'Maybe I'll let you share Bodil when I tire of her.' Thure guffawed and seemed to relish the look of horror on his mistress's face. 'I just need to break her in properly first.'

Linnea was disgusted at his comments and felt very sorry for Bodil, but hopefully Thure was only joking in an evil way. He probably enjoyed seeing the poor girl quaking. What a bastard. He was still sending Linnea lascivious glances from time to time, though, so perhaps he was already tired of Bodil.

For the most part Linnea was lost in her own thoughts and stayed close to Hrafn, half hidden by his broad shoulders. She didn't interact with anyone other than Eija, but eventually nature called and she slipped away to the nearest clump of bushes. Just as she'd finished, an arm came round her neck from behind and she heard Thure hiss, 'Keep your mouth shut if you know what's good for you. This won't take long.'

'What? *No!* Didn't you hear what Hrafn said?'

He chuckled. 'My little brother is not in charge. I am.'

A clump of icy fear pooled in Linnea's stomach, and for a moment she couldn't move her limbs out of sheer terror. 'No, you can't! I belong to Hrafn. He'll kill you if he—'

'*Þegi þú, bikkja!*' He put his hand over her mouth and fumbled with something, then started tugging her skirts up.

Linnea tried to focus. She'd taken a self-defence course a few years back but she was having trouble remembering what to do. It was one thing learning it in theory; quite another when faced with the reality of an attack. It was as though her entire body was paralysed, every muscle unable to function, especially her brain. *No, I can't let this happen!* The thought of what he intended galvanised her into action, and she started to struggle in earnest. He probably saw her as a meek slave who wouldn't dare fight back once he showed her who was master. Well, she'd show *him*.

Taking a deep breath, she forced herself to concentrate, and some of the lessons came back to her. She made her body go suddenly limp, like a dead weight, which had the effect of making Thure lose his grip a little. That gave her the opportunity to stomp down on his foot with her heel as hard as she could, then kick backwards into his shin. As she was only wearing her Roman sandals, this wasn't as effective as it would have been with boots or heels, but he swore and it was enough for him to let go.

She surged forward, intent on escaping, but Thure snarled and managed to grab her arm, spinning her around. 'Not so fast. We're not done yet.'

'Oh yes we are,' Linnea muttered. He had moved his hands to her waist and was about to pull her close, but she remembered another manoeuvre that would hopefully have a more lasting effect. Swiftly she brought her own hands up and placed them on either side of his face, something he hadn't expected. His eyes opened wide. *Excellent!* She didn't hesitate, but dug both thumbs into his eye sockets, pushing as hard as she could. Thure cried out and let go of her waist, bringing his hands up to pull hers away from his face.

She hung on for a short while longer, then gave one last vicious push and let go, swinging her arms up and around to get out of his grip. It worked, and when he immediately put his hands over his eyes, groaning in pain, she ran, not stopping until she threw herself down on to the ground next to Hrafn, panting and shivering.

'Linnea? What in the name of . . . ? What's happened?' He stared at her, taking in her dishevelled appearance and no doubt wild-eyed look.

Her legs were shaking so much with delayed reaction, she was glad she was sitting down. Taking deep breaths, she pulled them up and wound her arms round her knees, leaning her forehead on them. 'N-nothing,' she muttered. 'Just . . . Someone obviously wasn't listening to you p-properly.' Her teeth were chattering now and she couldn't seem to stop them.

'Who?' Hrafn's voice was low and deadly, boding ill for whoever had dared to molest what he clearly considered his possession.

'D-don't know,' she lied. 'It was dark.' Much as she hated Thure right now, she was sure it was better not to sow discord between the half-brothers. Nothing had happened after all, and next time she'd ask Hrafn to go with her to stand guard. Why the older man had thought he could get away with this, she had no idea. But then he was probably used to having whatever he wanted with no thought for the consequences. Well, he wasn't having *her*.

'Were you harmed in any way?' Hrafn's question was loaded, and she knew what he meant.

She shook her head. 'No, I . . . broke f-free and ran.'

'Good.' He didn't press her further, but when Thure stomped past everyone soon afterwards, snarling for Bodil to come with him to bed, Linnea saw Hrafn give his half-brother a long, considering look. He waited until Thure had gone, then told Linnea they'd best bed down for the night as well. 'We have a long day ahead of us tomorrow,' he added.

She could only nod, and when he lay down with his back touching hers, she felt the fear ebbing out of her and exhaustion taking over. She was safe, for now anyway.

*

Hrafn didn't go to sleep straight away, but lay staring into the darkness. He hadn't missed the look of fury Thure had sent Linnea's way as he stormed past the fire. So the *aumingi* had tried to take Linnea against her will, had he, and that despite knowing she was Hrafn's property, and that all the thrall girls were to be left alone? It made his blood boil, but he knew from experience it was never a good idea to confront Thure head on. There was a certain satisfaction in thrashing the man in a fair fight, but somehow he always got his own back in more devious ways. Hrafn was done with him, and as soon as this journey was over, he hoped never to see his half-brother again. Good riddance.

Thure would have to make do with Bodil – why else had he brought the girl? But he always coveted what he couldn't have, the greedy *argr*, and Hrafn had to admit that Linnea was a cut above the rest of the women, a prize worth having. She wasn't there to be enjoyed by anyone during the journey, however, even himself. Therefore he'd have to be extra vigilant from now on. He must keep her untouched.

Hrafn couldn't be sure that Linnea was a virgin, of course, but she didn't make eyes at any of the men and he'd not seen her seek them out or interact with anyone intentionally. She hadn't even tried to use her body to entice him into treating her kindly. Instead, she just appeared to expect him to. Again, this pointed to a very privileged – not to say spoiled – upbringing. But where on earth had she come from? If she really was from England, what had she been doing alone in his country?

It was a conundrum he wouldn't solve any time soon.

Linnea slept like a log, exhausted from the shock of so nearly being raped, not to mention hanging over the side of the boat for most of the previous day. But she felt far from rested; rather, she was on edge the whole time and still panicked whenever she thought about the fact that she was in the ninth century – *the ninth century!* – on a journey with Vikings who were going to sell her. She tried not to allow herself to dwell on it. What was the point? There seemed absolutely nothing she could do about it, and the further they travelled away from the field where it had happened, the slimmer were her chances of going back. It would seem she had no choice but to accept her fate, at least until she could figure out how she had ended up here in the first place.

Was there such a thing as destiny? She'd heard the women talking about the Norns, three goddesses weaving the strands of fate. Well, if they could kindly weave her back to the twenty-first century, she'd be eternally grateful. Not that she believed in the Norse gods, but it was the only thing she could hope for now.

She tried to concentrate on the here and now. The prospect of another day on board was not in the least appealing either. There was no way of avoiding it, though, and reluctantly she sat down in the stern next to the other women. Luckily the sea was calmer today, and as long as she kept her gaze firmly on the horizon, the urge to be sick stayed in the background.

'You look almost human,' Hrafn commented as he took his place at the steering oar. Linnea had gathered it wasn't called a rudder because those hadn't been invented yet. Instead it was more like an extra oar or paddle on the right-hand side of the ship, with a handle of sorts.

She shot him a look of acute dislike. 'No thanks to you,' she muttered, not in the mood to be teased, although perhaps he was trying to make her forget what had happened the night before.

'I really shouldn't allow you to speak to your master in that way,' he said, but one side of his mouth turned up in a lopsided smile, so she gathered he wasn't too bothered.

The annoying thing was that he was right. If she really was in the Viking age – and she didn't doubt it now – he had complete power over her and she ought to treat him with deference. It was a sobering thought. She supposed she should count herself lucky *he* hadn't raped her or mistreated her in any way so far, apart from that night spent in the stinking hut. He more or less ignored her, apart from making sure she was always supervised by someone.

Now why did that irritate her? It wasn't as though she wanted him to be attracted to her.

She sighed and concentrated on the horizon. Although she didn't want to admit it, she was actually enjoying the ride today. The ship was gliding through the waves quite quickly, and she felt exhilarated as it gathered speed. She'd had no idea a Viking ship could be so fast. Sunshine warmed her cheeks and the breeze teased her with its salty tang. It was almost like being on a holiday outing . . .

Except she was a slave, on her way to be sold. That put a dampener on things.

'Do you know where we are?' she asked, some perverse part of her wanting to goad Hrafn a little. 'Because it all looks the same to me.'

His smile turned into a full-blown grin, which gave him the look of a devil-may-care pirate. 'Of course. I've sailed this way many times and I remember every detail.'

Linnea barely heard his reply. She was staring at his face, absorbing the effect of that grin. He was properly handsome when he wasn't cross, with his dark blond hair, deep-set clear blue eyes, straight nose and determined jaw. A jaw that had been clean-shaven yesterday when they left Birka, and now sported a day's growth of golden-brown stubble. And when he smiled, his eyes flashed, throwing sapphire sparks at her like the sea. She was mesmerised against her will.

'What?'

His question pulled her out of her trance and she shook her head. 'Nothing.' What was she doing admiring the guy? Was she insane? He was going to sell her, for Christ's sake.

She turned away from him and tried talking to the other women instead, but the two Frisians – Ada and Gebbe – had started to feel ill again as soon as they set foot on board the ship and didn't have the energy to speak much, and Eija mostly sat and hummed to herself. It was as though that kept her in her own little world, protecting her mind from what was happening to her. Linnea could see where she was coming from. Their prospects were very bleak indeed, if they even survived this journey. And God only knew how many men these poor women had had to submit to before they were bought by Hrafn. From what she'd read, thralls were those captured during raids in foreign lands. Didn't such raids usually include pillage and rape? It made Linnea furious just to think about it. *Bloody barbarians!* Was Hrafn even sure they weren't already pregnant?

That wasn't her problem. Anyway, he'd been so adamant about no one touching them, he must have made sure somehow.

They headed straight out to sea, towards the east, and as they sighted land again, Hrafn said, 'We are sailing towards an island called Gotland.'

Linnea gathered from this that they had spent the night on Öland, one of two large islands situated to the east of Sweden in the Baltic Sea. Gotland was further out but not too far. A couple of hours perhaps? As Hrafn seemed in conversational mode, she dared to question him further. 'And then what?'

'We will stop there to buy barley or other grain, if there is any available, to add to our supplies, and then carry on straight across the sea to the land of the Balts. They are a day or so east of Gotland if we are lucky with the winds.'

The land of the Balts had to mean one or other of the Baltic states – Latvia, Estonia or Lithuania. Linnea's geographical knowledge of that part of the world was a little hazy, but she had a vague idea that Latvia was the country that stuck out the most and would therefore be closest. 'Why are we going to Lat— I mean, the land of the Balts? Shouldn't you be aiming further north if you want to go to, er, Grikkland? There's a big bay, isn't there? And then the mouth of a river.'

Hrafn stared at her. 'How do you know that? Have you been there?'

'No. I, um . . . heard about it from someone.' How did you explain to a Viking that you'd done geography at school and could tell him what the entire world looked like? Or that you'd just read a book, which Uncle Lars had recommended, about Vikings travelling to Byzantium? He wouldn't believe that any more than he had her time-travel claims.

He hesitated, as if he wanted to question her further, but then thought better of it. 'I want to pick up more amber first,' he said eventually. 'It is much sought after everywhere, and one can find it on the beaches, where it's free. What better than trade goods you don't have to barter for in the first place? Although it's possible to acquire larger pieces from the Balts as well, which we will do.'

Linnea had to admit his logic was faultless. 'Are you sure you can pick it up just like that?' She couldn't believe it would be that easy.

He smiled again. 'I'll show you.'

Chapter Eight

They arrived at a place called Paviken before midday. It was in a secluded bay that created a perfect natural harbour, and was reached via a narrow entrance strait. There were jetties built along the sides where ships could be moored, just as there had been at Birka. Hrafn left his brothers to tie up while he went ashore to confer with Thure, who, as usual, was happy for someone else to do the work.

'I'll stay here and make sure our ships are safe while you go in search of grain to buy. Get the best price you possibly can – we don't want to pay a fortune to greedy merchants.'

Hrafn just nodded. To be honest, it was a relief to be doing the haggling on his own, as Thure had a habit of rubbing people up the wrong way. While they talked, he debated whether to mention again that Linnea was out of bounds, but judging by the unusual redness of Thure's eyes – and what were those strange marks on his eyelids? – she must have managed to inflict some damage. Hopefully that would deter the man from further such attacks, and in any case, Hrafn wouldn't let her out of his sight from now on.

He couldn't resist a quick comment, though. 'What happened to your eyes? Been staring into the wind?'

Thure sent him an icy glare, his mouth tightening. 'No. I walked into a tree branch in the dark last night, if you must know.'

A likely story, but Hrafn refrained from snorting. 'Right, well, I'd best hurry then.' He was about to set off when he remembered something and turned back to his own ship. 'Linnea, come with me,' he ordered.

She looked up from where she'd been sitting with the others, blinking in surprise. 'Me? Why?'

He almost smiled. Her expression indicated extreme wariness, as if she suspected that being singled out in this way boded ill. Some perverse streak made him prolong her uncertainty. 'I'll tell you along the way. Geir, you'll stay with the ship, yes?'

'Of course, but please don't come back without grain. I don't think I can stomach weeks of nothing but dried fish.'

Hrafn gave his little brother a friendly shove. 'We do have other provisions on board already, you know.'

Lifting Linnea over the ship's side, he set her down on the jetty, trying not to notice how her beautiful hair brushed his hand in a soft caress as the long plait swung over her shoulder. Instead he grabbed her wrist and began to tow her towards the town. She was still looking apprehensive, and after yesterday that was entirely understandable, so he gave in to the urge to soothe her fears. 'I'm going to buy you some shoes. Estrid said you couldn't go all the way to Grikkland in those.' He pointed at her strange footwear. 'And the craftsmanship will be better here, I'd wager.'

'Oh, I see.' Her brow cleared, and she started to take in her surroundings. 'Where are we? Visby?'

'No, this is Paviken, further south. Have you been to Visby, then?'

'Once, when I was little. My parents took me and my siblings there.' Her mouth tightened as if the memory made her sad, but she took a deep breath and continued. 'It was a pretty place.'

Pretty was not exactly how Hrafn would describe the trading town of Visby, but he made no comment. Instead he blurted out, 'You're tall for a woman.'

Linnea laughed, which made him stop and look at her. 'Sorry,' she said, still smiling, 'but that was a bit unexpected. I suppose I am, at least compared to the other women you've brought.'

'Compared to most women,' he amended. The top of her head reached at least as far as his nose, if not slightly further, which made her the perfect height for him . . . He stopped that thought right there. Linnea wasn't for him. She was a thrall, to be sold for as much silver as possible. He shouldn't be noticing anything about her, other than her potential value. It was time to end the conversation.

'Come. It's this way.'

Linnea was surprised that his friendliness evaporated so suddenly, but he seemed to be a mercurial man and she couldn't make him out. She definitely hadn't expected to be bought new shoes, but an hour later she was the owner of a pair of Viking-style leather ankle boots. Soft, supple pieces of leather had been sewn together to form a dainty shape, fastened with a toggle around the ankles, and with flat soles and slightly pointy toes. The shoes smelled new, that wonderful scent of freshly crafted leather, and Linnea couldn't help but be pleased with this gift, even if it was for practical purposes. He'd also bought her a very plain leather belt with a small pouch attached to it.

'To keep essential things in,' he said.

'Thank you,' she murmured as she trailed behind him on the way to the second grain merchant. The first had proved unwilling to haggle much, and Hrafn refused to waste time on the man, or so he'd said.

'You're welcome.' His raised eyebrows told her he hadn't

expected thanks, which made her glad she'd said something.

Hrafn haggled to his heart's content with the second merchant, then brought out a set of folding scales from his pouch in order to measure out the required amounts of silver. Linnea watched fascinated as he took the scales out of a case that appeared to have been specially made to hold the slightly bowed beam and little rounded bowls with chains, and fitted them together. Impressed by his deft use of the weights that went with the scales, she had to smile when the merchant stepped inside his booth for a moment and Hrafn whispered, 'I prefer to use my own, then he can't cheat me.'

'Aren't the weights all supposed to be the same?' To Linnea, who'd grown up in a world where everything could be measured to the gram or millimetre, it seemed strange that weights might not be standardised.

'Yes, there are set measures, but you will always find those who try to cheat by a small margin. I won't have it and usually compare with my own.'

She could understand him being cautious if that was the case.

While he concluded his business, she took in the scene around her. Stalls and workshops were selling all manner of goods, including handicrafts and food. It was a far cry from a modern market, without any of the colourful exotic fruits Linnea was used to. Instead there were mainly boring things like turnips, swedes, beets and grain, as well as meat and dairy products. She heaved an inward sigh, her mouth watering at the thought of a juicy mango, plump tomatoes or even a chocolate brownie or two. Would she ever eat any of those things again?

The traders were all shouting to advertise their wares and attract customers, and the resulting racket was deafening. The surrounding area was none too clean – a combination of dirt, dust and animal excrement – but the fresh breeze from the sea blew away most of the noxious odours. Linnea wandered over to a nearby stall with a table full of jewellery, gazing at some of the pieces with longing. There were basic bead necklaces, which she didn't rate much, but alongside them were more sophisticated items, such as the double brooches used to fasten the apron-like overdresses worn by some of the women. They looked like bronze or silver tortoises and shone in the sunlight. She also spotted gleaming silver bracelets, rings and even the odd torque. The craftsmanship was excellent, but to her surprise, Hrafn steered her away with the words, 'My brother can do better than that.'

'Oh? Which one?'

'Rurik. He's a silversmith and maker of fine jewellery. And he's very good, even if I might be accused of being biased.'

'My friend Sara makes jewellery too.' The words were out before she had time to think them through, and something inside her twisted at the thought that she might never see Sara again. When Hrafn turned a questioning gaze on her, she immediately regretted having mentioned it.

'Your friend is a smith? Where does he live?'

'Not *he*; she. And yes, she is, but only for small items. I mean, obviously she's not strong enough to make, er . . . swords and things.'

'I should think not. I'm surprised she's allowed to do any smithing at all.' He steered her back in the direction of the ship.

Linnea sighed. 'I know you don't believe me, but in the future – during the time I come from – women do all sorts of things that you consider manly pursuits only.'

He shot her an irritated glance, but then seemed to humour her. 'Like what?'

'Well, for instance, in my time a woman can be the leader of a trading expedition such as the one you're undertaking. She can run her own workshop, be a shoemaker or jeweller or whatever profession she wants, even a warrior. There are no restrictions on what women can do. And we are given the chance to learn, to acquire knowledge. Have you heard of the Christian monks who write down histories of people, for example?'

Hrafn gave a curt nod of acknowledgement. 'I have heard of them. They are like our skalds, but they can't retain the knowledge in their heads so they write it down instead on bits of calfskin.'

'Yes, well, where I come from, everyone is made to remember all kinds of knowledge – how to write, how to count and add up, history and various other matters. Everyone can read, women as well as men, starting from a young age.'

'It sounds unnecessary, all this learning.' The look Hrafn gave her was sceptical. 'Who is left to farm the land and look after livestock? Cook and store food?'

Linnea smiled. 'There are those who do that too, after they have learned enough. Once we reach a certain age, we choose a profession.'

'And what is yours? I thought you a high-born lady who did nothing at all, other than embroidery or some such, judging by the softness of your hands.' His tone was scornful, and Linnea gathered he didn't have much time for such women.

She shook her head. 'It's difficult to explain, but my profession is to learn as much as I can about your language and pass that knowledge on to others.'

'What?' Hrafn's eyebrows almost hit his hairline as he stared at her. 'Why can't they just come here to learn?'

'Because your language does not exist in the future. Or at least, not in the form you know it. We call it Old Norse. By the year 2017 it has turned into five or six different languages, most of which you probably wouldn't understand. The way people speak changes constantly, and after hundreds of years, a language is very different to how it was originally.'

'You have a very fertile imagination, I'll say that for you. But I still don't believe you.'

Linnea shrugged. 'I didn't think you would, but it's the truth. If you like, I can teach you things in order to try and convince you.' She might as well, seeing as how she was stuck here with him.

'No thank you. Although . . .' He pulled something out of his pocket and held it out on the palm of his hand. Her ten pence coin. 'What do those letters mean?' He pointed at the number 2016.

'Those are numbers – two, nothing, one and six. Together they make two thousand and sixteen, the year this coin was made.'

'How?'

'I will teach you, but we need some sand or something to write on.'

Hrafn seemed torn, as if on the one hand he didn't want to believe this either, but on the other he was eager to learn. Curiosity won the day. 'Very well, you can show me, but not right now. We will wait for a quiet moment. Now hurry, I need to bring men to fetch the grain I've just bought.'

Hrafn's mind was spinning. This woman was definitely some sort of *völva*, as his brothers had said, else why would she have so much knowledge? He didn't believe her tales of what women could do where she came from. That had to be lies; he was sure he'd have heard of such strange goings-on otherwise. And she couldn't possibly have travelled through time, except perhaps during shamanistic rituals. He knew that wise women and seeresses often performed ceremonies called *seiðr*, where they might free their souls from their bodies and go elsewhere. Was that what she meant?

But she described everything so matter-of-factly, as if she'd really lived in the future. It was a ludicrous idea.

'I need three men to help me carry grain,' he shouted as they returned to the ship. 'Let's go!'

The grain had been put into oiled sacks to protect it from the weather and the sea, and together he and the men carried enough supplies for several weeks back to the ships. Thure grumbled about the price, but Hrafn cut him short.

'If you think you could do better, please feel free to go and try.'

Thure muttered something, but let it go. 'Well, I'm going ashore to find some ale and a good meal. I take it we're not continuing until tomorrow?'

'Wrong. We need to sail to the other side of the island, ready to set off across the sea at first light. By all means have a meal, but please hurry. I wish to leave as soon as possible.'

More grousing from Thure, but when Hrafn reminded him that the longer it took them to reach Miklagarðr, the more silver they had to spend on feeding the thralls they were going to sell, his half-brother gave way. 'Fine, I'll be back shortly.'

He took Bodil, who was trying to cajole him into buying her something from the jewellery stalls. Hrafn felt sorry for her when Thure vented his frustration by smacking her across the back of the head. 'Cease your whining, woman. I've bought you enough to fill an entire coffer already.'

'Ow! You never—' But one look at Thure's expression made Bodil stop. She wasn't very bright, but she was clever enough to know when to shut up.

Hrafn cast a glance at Linnea, who was now chatting to the other thrall women. There was no doubt she was a lot more intelligent than the likes of Bodil, but she also seemed to be an extraordinary liar. He didn't want to contemplate the weird things she had tried to tell him, because she couldn't possibly be right.

By keeping busy, he managed to suppress all thoughts of Linnea's strange claims.

They set off later than Hrafn wanted, judging by the grim set of his mouth, and Linnea thanked her lucky stars she wasn't the one he was cross with. She had by now been told that Thure was only a half-brother to the other three, and anyone could see they didn't get on. Not that it was surprising – Thure seemed impossibly up himself, and was forever complaining about something or other. If he hadn't been the jarl, she was sure Hrafn would have heaved the man overboard at the first opportunity and told him to swim for it.

'To the oars, men! We'll have to row for a while; the wind is in the wrong direction.'

Linnea was grateful Hrafn wasn't making her and the other women row as well, although maybe he would another day. She knew how to, but only a small rowing boat, nothing this size. It looked like hard work, especially with contrary winds to battle, but no one complained and they worked as one, falling into the rhythm easily.

Eventually the wind became more favourable and the sail was hoisted again. It was huge for such a small ship, or so it seemed to Linnea, and apparently made of woollen cloth that had been treated with something greasy to make it waterproof. She leaned to one side so as not to be smacked in the face by the bottom of it as the wind whipped it around, but the men soon had the corners tied down.

They followed the coastline north, then east, past islands and beaches. Linnea knew this was definitely Gotland, because she spotted the curious rock formations called *raukar*, which were a distinct feature of that island and the neighbouring smaller one of Fårö. Linnea had never seen the strange limestone stacks before, except in photos, and marvelled at them now. They were quite beautiful.

They finally made landfall once more just as it was getting properly dark.

'Pull the ships up, as high as you can!' Hrafn's voice rang out, commanding everyone's attention, even though Linnea had a suspicion it ought to be Thure giving the orders. He, however, seemed to have fallen asleep. Too much ale with his meal earlier?

They had entered a huge bay with a perfect sandy beach several kilometres long. Linnea guessed this must be the famous Sudersand beach, where tourists came to spend lazy summer days in her time. It was supposedly a perfect holiday paradise when the weather was favourable. Right now it was deserted, and a cold breeze blew in off the Baltic. Linnea shivered as she was lifted out of the ship and put down on the sand by Rurik.

'Thank you,' she murmured.

'Welcome.' He smiled at her and she was struck by his resemblance to Hrafn. He had the same devil-may-care grin, but although he too was good-looking, his smile didn't disturb her the way Hrafn's did.

She walked away, suppressing that thought, but the words 'Stockholm syndrome' flashed into her mind. 'No!' she muttered to herself. She was not going to allow herself to become attracted to her captor. Absolutely not. He was to all intents and purposes a savage. A barbarian with no concept of human rights. She shouldn't even like him, not one little bit.

'Linnea, help the other women cook some traveller's porridge.' Hrafn pushed a small iron cooking pot into her arms and pointed further up the beach, where someone was making fires out of driftwood. 'You'll need this too.' He held out a large wooden spoon and a simple tripod with a small chain and hook at the top.

'Right.' She didn't seem to have any option, and it made sense for them all to take turns cooking. Geir had done it the night before, after all, so it would seem it wasn't just a job for women. Hopefully the others would be able to tell her how to make the porridge, as she was fairly sure it was very different to the dish she would refer to by that name.

She watched as Hrafn made another fire with wood his brother had collected. Instead of matches, he brought out a fire steel and a piece of flint. The fire steel looked a bit like a metal handle, and he held it in one hand while striking it with the flint. A shower of sparks rained down on to some dry grass that he'd arranged on top of the wood, and soon there were glowing embers that he blew into flames. It looked so easy, but Linnea guessed it probably took a lot of practice to get it right.

Eija seemed a bit surprised that Linnea had never cooked before, but showed her what to do. 'Cut some smoked pork into tiny pieces first, and some onions, then boil them in water for a while,' she instructed. 'This makes a tasty stock. When the onions are soft, add the barley and cook until that too is soft, then it's ready.'

She demonstrated with her own cooking pot, which seemed to be made out of some kind of stone. Linnea remembered Uncle Lars showing her a vessel like that, although the one he'd found had been in pieces.

'Vikings used soapstone a lot,' he'd told her. 'It's easy to carve, and pots made out of that material could be put right at the edge of the hearth – they can take the heat. As you can see, though, they break very easily, so you have to be careful not to drop them. Easily done, as they're so heavy! The good thing about them was that they could be fixed with something like iron staples, and then they could still be used.'

Eija's pot wasn't broken and it looked a lot shinier than the sherds Lars had dug up. She measured out meat, onion, barley grains and water, and Linnea copied her. It seemed easy enough, but she wouldn't call it porridge if it had meat in it – more like risotto. Not that anyone here would understand that word, of course . . . The fires were going nicely by now, and Linnea set her tripod over one of them and hung the little cauldron on the hook. Once the meat and onions were done, she added the barley grains and let them simmer until they'd gone mushy.

'Don't forget to stir or it will get stuck,' Eija reminded her. Linnea did her best but longed for a Teflon saucepan. How did these people live without one? The washing-up must be a real pain. She almost groaned out loud – no doubt that would be her job too later on.

'Are we adding any flavouring?' The ingredients didn't seem massively exciting.

'I don't think we have any.' Eija shrugged. 'Not even salt. We're using some seawater to give it a little bit of taste, although this particular sea seems to be rather brackish so it won't help much.'

The resulting gloop did not look very appetising, although to be fair, neither did risotto if you thought about it. But Linnea was so hungry she dug in anyway and found it surprisingly tasty. Best of all, it filled her belly in a most satisfactory manner. She had a feeling, though, that she was going to become really sick of porridge, with or without added ingredients.

'Come, we're sleeping on board the ship.' Hrafn appeared while Linnea was trying to scrub the pot down by the water's edge, using sand and some sort of hard reed stems recommended by Eija to get rid of the stubborn bits of porridge that had stuck to the insides despite her stirring. 'Are you ready?'

'Er, give me a moment. Will you . . . will you stay close by, please?'

He nodded as she handed him the pot and tripod and went to squat behind some bushes. For a fleeting moment, she considered not going back, but what was the point of staying here alone in Viking times? She might as well stick with the devil she knew.

'Why are we sleeping in the ship?' she asked, as she trailed behind Hrafn along the sand.

'To keep our goods safe.'

She looked around at the deserted landscape. 'But there's no one here!' Not for miles, as far as she could see.

'We were seen leaving Paviken with fully loaded ships. There might have been people who noticed, and thought they'd like to make an easy profit by following us and surprising us in the dead of night.'

'Oh.' She hadn't thought of that. 'That's not . . . very nice.'

Hrafn laughed out loud as he dropped the cauldron and tripod into the ship, then put his hands around her waist to lift her on board. 'Why would you expect anyone to be nice?'

Linnea had no answer to that. In his time, it was obviously every man for himself. There were no rules of behaviour, no restrictions if you were unscrupulous. In silence, she wrapped herself in her blanket and bedded down back to back with Hrafn on the hard planking at the bottom of the ship, next to all the valuable goods. Some of the men were already asleep nearby, by the sounds of their snoring.

'Geir is taking the first watch, then he'll wake me when he starts to become tired,' Hrafn explained.

'Should . . . should I take a turn?' Linnea didn't know what was expected, but her question brought forth another chuckle.

'No, I don't think that will be necessary. This is men's work, in any age, I'm sure.'

'Suit yourself,' Linnea huffed, but was secretly glad she'd get to sleep the whole night through.

Chapter Nine

As it turned out, she didn't. Sometime in the early hours, she woke herself with a strangled scream and sat up abruptly. Her heart was pounding fit to burst through her ribcage, and she was shaking uncontrollably. Panic knifed through her, its sharp blades tearing into her mercilessly.

The nightmare had returned.

Travelling along a foggy road covered in treacherous black ice, the Swedish forest passing by in a dark blur. Sara's mother urging her husband to slow down a little, and him grumbling about morons who didn't put their fog lights on, but still keeping his foot down. Linnea and Sara exchanging a look of resignation – they both knew Jonas never paid any attention to speed limits. He was an impatient man, forever in a hurry. A thicker patch of fog made him step on the brake just a fraction, but it was too late because they were going round a steep bend and the unforgiving ice gave the tyres no traction. And there was a car coming from the opposite direction, also unable to steer properly . . .

In her dreams, it all happened in slow motion, but in reality it had only been a matter of seconds. Headlights meeting, the impact of the two cars as they collided, the noise of the crash and the strangled screams . . . Then she woke up, still screaming.

'What ails you, woman?' The gruff voice and a hand on her shoulder brought her back to reality. Hrafn.

She was in his time and there were no cars here. But she was still in danger, albeit of a different kind. He probably wouldn't appreciate being woken from his slumber. 'Nothing,' she muttered. 'Nightmare. Sorry.'

'Sounded like you were being skewered alive.'

'Something like that.' She swallowed hard, trying to blink away the images of the accident and instead focus on his face in the semi-darkness. His hand still rested on her. Perhaps he was half asleep and had forgotten to remove it, but she didn't mind. It was comforting. Safe. She almost snorted. How could he make her feel safe when he was her captor, taking her on a journey to sell her? But somehow he did. She sighed. 'I was in an accident, just after ... er, midwinter. Two ... wagons colliding. My friend's parents were killed and she was badly injured.'

'And you?' Hrafn sounded fairly awake now.

'Only a few scratches.'

'Then it was not your time to die.'

'I know, but my mind can't stop reliving those moments. It was frightening.' She shook her head. The therapist had said it would take time, but it had been months now and she couldn't forget. 'And I can't help but feel guilty somehow. For still being alive when they're not, you know?'

She saw him raise his eyebrows at her. 'That makes no sense. It was not for you to decide who lived and died; that was in the hands of the gods. Or the Norns. Were you driving the wagon?'

'No, but—'

'Then there was nothing you could have done. No blame is attached to you.'

It sounded so simple when he put it like that, and she knew he was right. She just had to somehow make her brain accept it as fact. She sighed. 'Thank you.'

'What for?'

'For . . . I don't know, not just telling me to go back to sleep, I suppose. For listening.'

He shrugged and gave her shoulder a brief squeeze, then let go. 'Sleep now, woman, I have guard duty to do.'

It took her a long time to fall asleep again, though. As she watched him grab his weapons and leave, her thoughts returned to the accident yet again, and the other person who had survived it – her best friend Sara. She'd be coming out of hospital soon, although she would still need a lot of physiotherapy to help her recover fully from her injuries. It was a miracle that she was still alive; for a while it had been touch and go. Linnea had planned to be there when she was discharged, but obviously that wasn't going to happen now. What would Sara think when she heard that her friend was missing? Would it set her back?

'Oh, I hope not,' Linnea whispered into the night. If she tried really hard and pictured Sara in her mind, perhaps her thoughts could reach her. She snorted out loud. That was a silly notion, but then so was time travel. Who was to say it was impossible?

She concentrated fiercely. 'I'm OK, Sara. Don't give up on me, please. Continue to get well, and be strong.' Hopefully one day they'd see each other again.

They were leaving at daybreak and Hrafn found it difficult to wake Linnea. She was curled into a ball, like a butterfly cocoon, her golden hair spilling out over the coarse blanket. He had a brief vision of a gorgeous creature emerging from its chrysalis as she sat up and the material slid off her, but the image was ruined by her sullen expression.

'It can't be morning yet,' she protested. 'Look, it's still dark.'

Hrafn just shook his head. 'You'd best accustom yourself to waking early. A thrall has many chores of a morning.'

In return, he received a dark glare. 'Well, how come you look so bright-eyed and alert? You must have been awake for at least a couple of hours during the night.'

He had, and she'd been the one to wake him initially with her nightmare. But he shouldn't have encouraged her to talk about it – what master would do such a thing with a thrall? – so the incident was best forgotten. 'I slept well the rest of the time. Now go ashore for a moment if you need to, then we're off. I'll keep watch.' He took his place by the steering oar and watched her as she went to do what was necessary. On the way back, she stopped at the water's edge to wash her hands and face. It looked as though she also tried to scrub her teeth with sand before spitting out the brine.

'What in the name of all the gods were you doing?' he asked when she returned to the ship and clambered aboard. 'Why were you drinking seawater? You hate ale that much?'

She glared at him again. 'I was cleaning my teeth as best I could. How are they supposed to last a lifetime if they're dirty? Not that sand works anywhere near as well as toothpaste.'

'What's that?' Hrafn was thoroughly confused. Sure, he rinsed his mouth with water every morning, but put sand in there? No.

'Something like lye, but for teeth.'

'Lye?' He made a face. 'That would be disgusting.' Although he had to admit she had perfect white teeth, so perhaps there was something in what she said.

'Never mind, you wouldn't understand.'

She settled herself next to Eija and the two Frisian women. Hrafn saw her shiver and draw the blanket around herself once more. He swallowed a sigh – what a cosseted woman she must have been all her life. So fragile, and unable to cope with the

105

weather or rising early. How would she survive being some man's toy? Because he was fairly sure that would be her fate. No female thrall owner would buy a woman that beautiful. Her looks guaranteed a male purchaser, no doubt about it, and Hrafn knew exactly what that man would want to do with her.

Because he wanted it too.

Taking her himself would be pure self-indulgence, however. The world was full of women, and if he needed one, he could just find one next time they stopped at a settlement. There were always those who'd do anything for payment. In a way, it was a shame he couldn't take one of his thralls. Ada and Gebbe were both comely – he'd purchased them for that reason after all – as was Eija. But they were to be his means of leaving Thure for good, and nothing could be allowed to stand in the way of that. Giving in to base urges would be plain stupidity. He masked his irritation with himself by issuing a string of orders, and soon they were on their way again.

Around midday, he had Geir distribute dried meat and ale to everyone on board. Most of them accepted, including Linnea, although a few were still suffering from the effects of the sea. Linnea was pale, but without the green tinge she'd had the first day. He noticed that she asked for rainwater instead of ale, though, and he wondered about that again. Never had he met anyone so particular with the food and drink they took. It was ridiculous; if she didn't like what she was given, she should go without.

Towards late afternoon, the wind picked up, and consequently the waves grew higher. There were groans from quite a few quarters, and crew members began to hang over the sides of the ship again.

'Keep watching the horizon,' Hrafn told Linnea, and it worked for a while. In the end, though, she succumbed as well, and lost what little sustenance she'd taken. He couldn't blame her; the ship was rolling quite considerably, the timbers groaning and the big square sail flapping wildly. His hair whirled around his head, becoming wet from the salty spray, and with a curse he found a piece of leather to tie it out of the way. Some strands soon worked themselves loose, though, and irritation built inside him. He had to stare quite hard at the horizon himself and tried to ignore the discomfort building inside him. When he finally sighted land, he heaved an inward sigh of relief – he didn't think he could have hung on to his midday meal for much longer.

'Land!' he shouted, hoping to encourage those who were looking greyer than seals. 'We'll camp here tonight and sail up the coast tomorrow. Look sharp, I need help pulling the ship up on to the sand.'

Thure's ship had managed to stay more or less alongside them during the day, thanks to its able helmsman. Hrafn was grateful for that, as it was better travelling in numbers in case of attack. There were always those who preferred not to have strangers on their territory, and he knew from previous trips that traders weren't always safe.

Not many people wanted an evening meal, but most forced down at least a few sips of broth and some ale. The night passed like the previous one, with a couple of men on guard at all times. Hrafn wasn't taking any chances.

'Linnea, come for a walk with us.'

'What? Where?' She looked up at Hrafn, and had to shield her eyes with one hand against the glare of the morning sun. The high winds of the previous day had given way to a softer breeze, and she was grateful. It should make sailing easier. She was surprised he wasn't off at the crack of dawn again, like yesterday.

'You'll see.'

Linnea, Hrafn and his two brothers set off along the water's edge.

'It's the perfect day for it, just after a storm,' Rurik commented with a contented smile. 'Let's get started.'

'What exactly are we doing?' Linnea was confused, and watched as Rurik and Geir bent to poke at a clump of seaweed that was being sloshed around by the waves.

'I promised to show you where to find amber, remember?' Hrafn put a hand on her elbow and steered her towards a tangled line of seaweed slightly higher up the beach. 'It often washes up after bad weather, and because it's a light material, it gets caught in this.' He bent to riffle through the briny mess. 'See? Here's a little piece.'

He straightened up, holding something out to her on his palm. Linnea smiled. 'Oh! Is that really amber?' But there was no doubt about it. Shiny and treacle brown, this was the real thing. And you could just pick it up? How amazing was that?

She strode over to the next seaweed clump and began to sort through it. 'There's nothing here.' Disappointed, she stared over at Hrafn, who was picking something up.

He shot her a quick glance. 'There isn't always. Try the next one.'

She did, and to her delight she found a respectable piece of what was recognisably amber. Not the see-through kind – she supposed you had to polish it for that – but a lump with a slightly dull surface. Still, definitely the right thing. 'All right!' she hissed in English, punching the air. The other three regarded her with raised eyebrows, but she ignored them and carried on to the next clump. 'Hey, this is fun!' She laughed out loud. Perhaps there were some perks to being trapped in the past after all. She'd have to remember this and do it again if she ever managed to return to her own time.

As they searched, the men placed their finds in pouches hanging off their belts. Linnea did the same, and was very grateful now that Hrafn had bought her that belt. By the time her back started to protest against the constant bending, she had quite a nice little pile of brown and yellow amber, and was feeling content.

As Hrafn caught up with her, she frowned as she remembered that she was his slave. 'I suppose I have to give all these to you now.' She knew her tone was insolent, and she could probably be punished for talking to her master like that, but she couldn't help it. Hunting for amber had been such fun; it completely spoiled the day having to hand over her booty.

To her surprise, he smiled and shook his head. 'No, keep it. Who knows, you might even be able to buy your freedom with it one day.'

Linnea shivered. 'Is that possible?'

'Of course. Everyone has a price, although I'm not sure how it works in Miklagarðr. You will have to find out.'

She looked at her amber haul inside the pouch. 'Is this enough to pay *you* to let me go?'

'Er . . . let me have a look.' He poked around the little pile, then shook his head. 'I don't think so.'

'I see.' She bit her teeth together hard to stop herself shouting at him that he shouldn't get her hopes up only to dash them again. 'What will I have to do to earn the rest?'

His expression darkened. 'Nothing. I don't want any sort of payment from you – I'm selling you to someone else.' He gave her a quick once-over, as if he had briefly contemplated payment in kind, but then looked away. So he didn't even want to sleep with her. Was she too lowly for him? Not that she shouldn't be grateful for that, but still, it was galling to be so summarily rejected.

'Why?'

'I'm a trader with no permanent home. I have no need for thralls.'

That kind of made sense, but Linnea was still annoyed and frustrated. *Infuriating man!* She turned away, and even though she was tired and hungry now, she continued her search for amber. Having something to barter with might come in useful, even if it didn't work with him.

'Let's take a break and eat something.' Hrafn pointed at the sand and Linnea sank down on it without much enthusiasm. Since their talk about the possibility of her buying her freedom, she'd not said a word to him and he was sure she was sulking. But really, what had she expected? And he'd been telling the truth. He was planning on spending the next few years on constant trading expeditions and didn't have a permanent home other than Thure's hall, which wasn't a home in any sense of the word. Thralls were for those who needed help with farming and domestic chores, neither of which applied to him. One day perhaps he'd settle in Birka or one of the other larger trading places, but for now he was always on the move.

'Here, have some ale.' He handed Linnea a small leather skin and saw her take a few cautious sips, her nose unconsciously wrinkled. 'You still don't like it?'

'No. Sorry. Is there any water around here?' She glanced behind them at the sand dunes and, further inland, some scrubby bushes.

'I doubt it. You'll have to wait until we're back on the ship. We still have rainwater.'

He'd brought pieces of smoked meat and she chewed on those without complaint, staring out over the constantly moving sea, watching the gulls swooping and shrieking nearby. 'It's beautiful here, but a bit bleak,' she commented. 'Does anyone live here?'

'Well, yes, the Balts. There is a settlement along here somewhere. I sent two of the men to look for it, as the people there might have larger pieces of amber to sell. There's a quarry not far away and the quality is excellent. These –' he indicated the pouch containing his finds from the beach – 'are just extra.'

'Will you have them polished, or do you sell them in their natural state?'

'A bit of both. As I said, Rurik is good at polishing amber and he'll do as much as he can each night. He's brought his equipment.'

They sat in silence for a while, then Linnea turned to him, her eyes lit up as if she'd just thought of something. 'I was going to show you those numbers. We are surrounded by sand, so is this a good time?'

'I suppose.' Hrafn didn't want to admit that he was eager to learn, but he'd always been interested in new knowledge.

'Great! I need a stick.' She stood up and found one nearby, then smoothed out a large square of sand next to them, writing down ten symbols. 'These are the numbers from one to nine, and then this other one is called zero – that means nothing.'

'Is this Roman? I thought they counted with their letters.' He'd heard about that but not learned how.

'They did, and no, these are Arabic. Er . . . from Serkland, I believe. I can teach you the Roman ones later. I know how to do those as well.'

Was there no end to her knowledge? He frowned but paid attention as she made him copy the numbers with the stick and learn them. After a while, she erased the whole lot and wrote down random ones to test him, then made him write as she called them out. Hrafn caught on quickly and was glad his mind had always been good at retaining knowledge. Someone had once told him he'd make a good *skáld*, but entertaining people wasn't for him. He preferred to be a listener.

When she was satisfied that he seemed to know all the numbers, Linnea smiled and said, 'Excellent! Now I'm going to show you how to continue after nine.'

She carried on until he got the hang of it, and it seemed very simple. 'Interesting,' he commented when she stopped after showing him how to write ten thousand, a number he'd never even contemplated using. 'And all this you learned in your homeland?'

'Yes. In the future.' When he was about to protest, she held up a hand. 'I know, I know, but I can carry on teaching you more things until maybe one day you'll believe me. Next time we're on a beach I will show you how to add these numbers together, like if you've bought three things that cost . . . I don't know, five pieces of silver each, how much is that altogether?'

'Fifteen.' It was the sum of the fingers of one hand three times, he knew that.

'Yes, but there is a way of getting to that answer by writing it down.'

'I don't see the point of that. Most of my trade is done by bartering, or if I pay with silver, it is weighed, not counted.'

'Well, in the not-too-distant future you'll find that everyone starts to use coins as payment. When your country has its first king, he'll issue his own coins with his name on them. Then you'll need to know how to add.'

Hrafn snorted. 'And you are sure of this? It seems most unnecessary.'

But Linnea didn't give in. 'If you live long enough, you'll see that I am right. They already use coins in England, and the land of the Franks, I think. And the Romans did it hundreds of years ago. No reason why your people shouldn't do the same eventually.'

'If you say so. We'd better go back to the ship now.'

He called out to his brothers, who had stayed at the other end of the beach, and together they set off. Hrafn's head was whirling with newly acquired knowledge, and it was exhilarating. Much as he hated to admit it, Linnea made an extremely interesting travelling companion.

They spent one more night on the Baltic coast while they waited for Hrafn's men to return. When they did, they had what seemed to Linnea to be a huge quantity of amber – large pieces that could potentially be made into stunning jewellery. One lump in particular was passed around, as there was an insect trapped inside it; even Thure was impressed by that, although as he hadn't acquired any himself, he was soon back to his usual sullen self.

'Should fetch a good price,' he commented. 'But my furs will be worth much more.'

Linnea secretly doubted that. The people of Istanbul could probably get hold of all kinds of pelts from whatever natives lived in Viking-age Russia, but she didn't say anything. Hrafn would have to prove his half-brother wrong, and she was sure that he would. He was clearly more intelligent, and she'd been impressed with how quickly he'd caught on during their lesson the previous day. He might not be a university professor like Daniel – strange how she hadn't thought about *him* for days now! – but he seemed eager to acquire knowledge for the pure joy of learning something new.

That evening, Rurik sat slightly apart from everyone else and started work on some of the pieces. He had set up a basic lathe, but with a stone attached for polishing the amber. Linnea longed to go over and watch him, but he appeared to prefer solitude, and everyone else left him alone so she had to content herself with watching from afar. On Hrafn's urging, she'd given Rurik everything she'd found that morning.

'He'll keep it safe for you, and if he has time, he'll polish it. That way it will be more valuable,' he'd said. 'He'll take a few pieces as payment, but it's a good bargain for you.' It made sense to Linnea, and she saw no reason not to trust them. What did she have to lose anyway? She was still hoping to be back in her own century long before they reached Istanbul.

To her surprise, Rurik came over to her the following morning, just before they boarded the ships. 'I thought you might like something to remind you of your first time searching for amber. Here. It's one of the ones you found.' He handed her a leather cord threaded through a hole in a smooth amber nugget.

Linnea blinked back sudden tears at his kindness. 'Thank you! I . . . That is wonderful!'

He smiled but shook his head. 'It is nothing. May it give you good fortune.'

Hrafn, who'd been standing nearby, frowned at this exchange and muttered something to his brother, but received only a playful shove in return. That made his brows come down even lower, but Rurik didn't seem bothered. Linnea pretended she hadn't noticed anything and tied the cord round her neck, absurdly pleased with this trinket. Rurik was right, it probably wasn't worth much, but it was the fact that someone had taken the time to think about her that made a warm glow spread inside her. She might be stuck in a godforsaken age, but there were still kind people here.

They sailed north. Linnea was becoming used to judging their direction by the sun's position, and in any case, she knew they had to go north first and then into the Gulf of Finland if they were to sail along Russian rivers towards Turkey. The journey was monotonous, but at least she didn't get seasick again, and they stayed close to land, which meant there was always scenery to look at. Ada and Gebbe became a little more talkative, as they were feeling better too, but when Linnea questioned them about their past, they shook their heads.

'We prefer not to dwell on what was. It only makes facing the future that much harder,' Gebbe said.

'I suppose that is true.' Naturally Linnea couldn't mention that her own past lay far into the future, and therefore her circumstances were different. But perhaps the Frisian girls were right. Should she try to make the best of the here and now, and resign herself to her fate?

No, she couldn't do that. She had to figure out a way of returning to her own century.

Glancing over at the other ship, she saw Thure's brooch flash in the sunlight, and sudden inspiration struck. *Whoa, the brooch!* Could that be the key? Was it magical somehow? She almost snorted, because that sounded insane, but was it any worse than believing in wormholes and time portals?

Her mind went back to the day she'd found it. She'd been so excited and amazed, but then it had all turned into this nightmare. One minute she'd been digging up the brooch, studying it and reading out the runic inscription. The next she'd pricked herself with the pin and that was when it happened – she'd started to feel sick and fainted. When she woke up, she was in Viking times. She didn't believe in magic – and definitely not because of touching or holding an ancient object – but then she hadn't believed in time travel either, and look where she was. Yes, it had to have been the brooch; it was the most likely explanation.

The main question was: how did it work? And could the process be reversed?

The runic sentence had to have something to do with it. She'd heard of runes used in magic rituals and curses, as well as for fortune-telling. Perhaps these particular ones had a hidden function. She had said the words out loud – that seemed important –

and they'd mentioned blood and travel, two things that had happened. That must be it: sacrifice some of your blood and recite the sentence holding the brooch. The only way of proving whether she was right was to get hold of the brooch again, but how? It seemed firmly welded to Thure's shoulder, and he'd never let her anywhere near it. He couldn't wear it all the time, though. There had to be days when he didn't need a cloak and put it away among his belongings. It was the beginning of summer now, and the weather would grow warmer; then he was bound to take it off.

Linnea vowed to watch and wait. At least she had some hope now. It was worth a try, and until she had proved that it didn't work, she wouldn't give up.

Chapter Ten

On the second day, they entered the mouth of a river and the men had to row again. 'Linnea, can you take the steering oar? Then all six of us can row at the same time.'

Hrafn's question – or more likely command – jolted her out of a daze. 'What, me?'

'Yes, it's not difficult. Didn't you say women of your . . . country could do anything? Here, I'll show you.'

There was some snickering among the men, and a few good-natured jibes, but the principle was simple. Push the handle of the steering oar forward and the ship turned left; backwards and it went right. Linnea got the hang of it fairly easily, but she still felt a bit nervous. What if she steered them into one or other of the riverbanks? But Hrafn kept an eye out, and told her to correct their course whenever he deemed they were straying too far to one side.

From her studies, which had included the history of the Vikings, and that book she'd read recently, she guessed they were on the Neva river, where modern-day St Petersburg would eventually be situated. It was a waterway with many twists and turns, not making it easy for the rowers or her, but at least there weren't any rapids. They spent one night on its banks, with guards posted to keep an eye out for possible unfriendly locals, then continued for another day. Eventually the river opened up into an enormous lake, which had to be Lake Ladoga – it was so vast it couldn't be anything else.

'Keep to the right-hand coastline,' Hrafn shouted to the men in Thure's ship, who had come up alongside them after they'd entered the lake. 'We will reach another river, and partway down that is the settlement of Aldeigjuborg, where we'll stop for a few days.'

Aldeigjuborg? Linnea hadn't heard that name before, but if it was downriver from this lake, she assumed he meant a place that in her time was called Staraya Ladoga. If she remembered correctly, it had been one of the earliest Viking trading settlements in Russia, and it lay on the Volkhov river. She hoped it wasn't too far away.

Another hour of rowing south on the wide, but beautiful, meandering river brought them to Aldeigjuborg, situated on a bend on the left-hand bank. Hrafn was relieved to reach the trading town just before it became properly dark. He hadn't wanted to spend a night by Lake Ladoga. The locals were for the most part peaceful in this area, but one could never be sure. Aldeigjuborg was safe and had wooden fortifications – with some recent additions in stone – and a small earthwork fortress near the harbour. As he'd learned from his previous visits, most of the inhabitants lived inside the town walls, while their cemeteries and sacred groves lay outside. Just before reaching the jetties, they passed a row of impressive burial mounds that were so huge they were visible from quite a distance. Hrafn had been told they contained some of Aldeigjuborg's former chieftains and most important merchants.

The population was not as large as that of Birka, but the

place always seemed to be teeming with people of different ethnicities – Svíar like himself, Balts, Slavs and Finns, as well as the occasional merchant from faraway places like Grikkland and Serkland. They all appeared to live in harmony, and mixed happily with each other. It was an exciting place, and he had contacts here – a friend, even – who would give them a warm, dry place to sleep.

As before, guards were left with the two ships. 'Don't let *anyone* come aboard, no matter what,' Hrafn instructed.

He and Thure made their way through the streets with everyone else following. The buildings were made of timber and came mainly in two fairly uniform sizes – small dwellings with space for only a few people, and larger ones that could house a dozen or more. Hrafn knew that most of them contained workshops of one kind or another, but at this late hour everyone had finished for the day, and the noise and bustle had ceased. Instead the smell of cooking hung in the air, enticing and in some cases exotic with the scent of foreign spices. His stomach growled in response. He hoped his friend Olaf would have a meal to offer them.

Linnea stayed close to his side like a restless *vættr*, or wraith, scanning their surroundings with big eyes. He had to resist the urge to take her hand while leading her along the narrow streets. Their fingers occasionally brushed one another's, until he hooked his hand firmly in his belt. She was a thrall and ought to keep her distance. He shouldn't encourage familiarity, but in all honesty, he couldn't blame her for craving his protection. Despite her obvious anxiety, he could see her taking note of everything, and glancing in through the occasional open doorway with curiosity.

'What sort of things are made here?' she asked, as if she couldn't contain her thirst for knowledge any longer.

'All sorts – glass beads, bronze items like belt buckles

and suchlike, pottery, things made of bone and antlers, wooden objects –' he pointed into a house where a lathe stood deserted for the moment, visible through the open door – 'made on one of those or carved, and leather items. I could have bought you shoes here, but I trusted the man at Paviken more.'

'I see.' She flashed him a tiny smile, as if she was grateful for the information, and something inside him heated up for an instant.

He coughed. 'Er, we are on our way to a friend of mine, Olaf, who deals in amber like us. I met him on my first journey here, some years ago. He will let us sleep in his hall.'

'How kind,' she murmured.

'I would do the same for him,' Hrafn told her, although of course he couldn't at the moment since he didn't have his own dwelling yet. In principle, though, he would be happy to offer Olaf hospitality at any time.

'If I remember correctly, the ruler of this place is called Oleg. Sounds similar to your friend's name. Perhaps it's the Slavic way of saying it.'

Hrafn stared at her. 'Who told you that?' He didn't think any of the other men they were travelling with knew this. He was the only one who'd been here before. Oleg was indeed the ruler of Aldeigjuborg and had been for the past six or seven years.

Linnea sighed. 'I learned about it recently. It stuck in my memory, I suppose.'

He shook his head. It was uncanny the way she seemed to know so much, but he still didn't believe her tale of being from the future. There could be people in England who had heard about Oleg, and she might have learned from them. That explanation would make much more sense. Or even more likely, she could have divined this knowledge in her role as *völva*. Wasn't that what a seeress did? He'd have to be on his guard; women like that could be dangerous, especially to men. He carried on walking without answering her, and she stayed silent for the rest of the way too.

One of Thure's men had a relative with whom he and some of his men would be staying, and as Hrafn had been here before, he led them there first, and left them to be greeted by their host. He hoped Thure wouldn't make a nuisance of himself, but it wasn't his problem for now.

A few streets further on, they came to Olaf's house, one of the larger type, and Hrafn was pleased to be greeted with a huge smile. 'Hrafn, my friend, it's good to see you!' Olaf pulled him into a bear hug, and since he was a large man with more than his fair share of flesh around the middle, Hrafn really did have the impression that he was being crushed by such a beast.

He laughed. 'It's great to see you too. I hope you don't mind, but I bring you house guests for a few nights. I'll give you recompense, of course.'

Olaf waved the offer away. 'No, no, you know you're always welcome. Mila!' he shouted. 'We have guests!'

His tiny Slavic wife came bustling over with a smile and smacked her husband on the arm. 'No need to shout, I'm not deaf. And I have eyes in my head. Welcome to our home, all of you. Please take a seat and I will bring you ale.'

'Thank you, Mila.' Hrafn gave her a brief hug too, careful not to seem too familiar. She was dark and pretty, and he could see why Olaf had chosen her, but he knew that she was also a hard worker and helped her husband in every way.

They settled down on benches along the walls, facing the fire that blazed in the middle of the room. Hrafn introduced his brother Rurik to Olaf – Geir had chosen to stay with the ship for now – and watched with pleasure as the two men began to discuss amber, a subject where they obviously had a lot in common.

Linnea and the other thrall women had been shown to the bench furthest away from the fire, but when he glanced her way she didn't seem fazed. She was still taking everything in, as if storing the images in her memory, and even drank some of her ale without grimacing. Hrafn hid a smile. Perhaps she was getting used to the beverage – it would be as well for her if she was.

Linnea had just had an epiphany. Staring at everything around her, she'd suddenly realised how privileged she was to be experiencing all this first hand. Why hadn't that occurred to her until now? If she ever managed to return to her own century – and that was still a big if, unfortunately – she ought to try and remember as much about life in Viking times as she could, in order to tell Uncle Lars and all the other archaeologists who strove to understand what it had really been like. The tiny details of everyday life that they could only speculate about, and would never know for sure, unless she could describe them.

Not that they'd believe her, of course – why would they? She could hardly take it in herself, and she was here, right in the middle of a real-life Viking trading post. *In Russia, for heaven's sake!* Sitting in a small hall – maybe ten metres by fifteen, with a raised central hearth and wide benches along the sides – where the smoke from the fire stung her eyes and settled in her hair and clothes. Drinking bitter home-brewed ale. Breathing in the slightly damp, musty smell of the wood all around her. Watching actual Vikings interacting with each other. Perhaps she ought to view it as a miracle? It was certainly magic of some kind, because there was no other way of explaining her presence here. Not that she could think of anyway.

Her eyes kept returning again and again to one Viking in particular. She swallowed a sigh. Why couldn't she stop looking at him?

Hrafn stood out, there was no disputing that fact. He wasn't the loudest or the biggest, but he was extraordinarily attractive – or was that just Stockholm syndrome talking again? Had to be, because she didn't like the muscle-man type. She wanted someone like Daniel – intelligent, sensitive and courteous. Didn't she? Then why was she finding it difficult to even remember what Daniel looked like? She clenched her fists in her lap. It was impossible not to notice Hrafn, though, and with the light from the fire playing across his sculpted cheekbones and proud nose, gilding his dark-blond hair and emphasising his physique, how could she not stare?

'The wife seems nice.' Eija broke into her thoughts with her quiet comment. 'I've never seen one of the Svíar married to a foreigner before. We are usually just thralls.'

'Perhaps there weren't any other women available out here in the wilderness,' Linnea speculated. Although it certainly looked as though Olaf was happy with his choice of wife. Several times, as she passed him with mugs or plates of food, he grabbed her for a kiss or swatted her backside. Those weren't the actions of a man who had been forced to wed by necessity.

'I'd like to stay here.' Eija stared wistfully into the fire. 'If I can't go home, I mean. Perhaps some man would take me to wife without looking at me as if I'm a troll.'

Linnea felt her eyebrows rise. 'A troll? What are you talking about? Eija, you're beautiful! No one could think you ugly.'

'Oh believe me, they do. I don't have your pretty hair or eyes, do I?'

'No, but yours are every bit as nice, just a different colour. Where we are going, almost all the women have black hair, so you won't stand out for that reason. Only the shape of your eyes will be unusual, but I'm sure some man will love them.' She crossed her fingers behind her back, hoping that she was right.

Eija blinked. 'How do you know about the women of Miklagarðr?'

'Oh, I've been told by someone who went there. It's true, you'll see when we arrive.' *If we ever get there.* It was by no means certain, and she sincerely hoped she'd be long gone before then herself. Back to civilisation. Somehow that seemed like an unkind thought now because these people *were* civilised. They lived in accordance with certain codes of conduct, and the fact that these were different from her own didn't make them uncivilised. Still, in many respects they were barbaric, and there was no getting away from that fact. She and Eija were living proof of it.

The Saami girl smiled and put a hand on Linnea's arm, squeezing it. 'Thank you for trying to make me feel better. You are very kind.'

Linnea smiled back. 'Not at all. I'm just telling you the truth.' And she was. She only wished she could take Eija with her if and when she left this era.

'You shouldn't stare at her. You'll give her ideas.' Olaf elbowed Hrafn and chuckled. 'Or are you thinking of keeping her for yourself? I can see why.'

'What? Who?' But Hrafn knew exactly who his friend was referring to. Linnea. His eyes had strayed in her direction much too often if even Olaf had noticed. *Skítr!*

'Your golden thrall. She's a treasure and no mistake. Will make you a tidy profit, I should think.'

'Oh, her. Yes, I hope so, although I'm a bit worried about her mind. She's very unpredictable and, er . . . prone to lying.'

Olaf leaned forward and considered her. 'Seems docile enough to me. And what does it matter if she lies? Won't be your problem once she's sold.'

'True. I'm worried she won't cope well with the journey,

though. I have to tell you, it seems she's been treated like a queen all her life and has no practical knowledge whatsoever. She's as fragile as a butterfly's wing.' Hrafn shook his head. 'How is she going to survive all the way to Miklagarðr?'

'Ah, she'll adapt. Everyone does, or so I hear. Never made the journey myself and have no wish to, but by all accounts, parts of it are enjoyable.'

Hrafn thought of everything he'd heard and memorised about the route to Grikkland. 'Enjoyable' was not a word that had ever been mentioned. But he decided not to share any more of his worries, except one. 'Well, I keep her close at all times and she'll be sleeping in my bed.' He held up his hands. 'Without me touching her, I swear – I do want a good price for her.' He lowered his voice. 'The truth is, I can't entirely trust the other men. Apart from my brothers, they're all in Thure's pay, and as you said, Linnea does draw the eye, if you know what I mean.'

'I understand. Very sensible of you. I'd do the same.' Olaf laughed. 'Although how you sleep next to her and don't . . . Well, you must really want that profit.'

'I do.' Hrafn knew his reply was curt to the point of rudeness, but he was fed up with discussing Linnea. He debated the issue with himself every night; he didn't need Olaf's input. At the end of the day, it always came back to one thing: his intense need to escape from Thure and never be beholden to his half-brother ever again. For that he had to acquire wealth; as much as possible in as short a time as was feasible. Selling Linnea would help him achieve this goal, and if it meant he had to keep his hands off her, so be it. That was the price he had to pay for his freedom.

It was time to change the subject. 'Tell me about your son – looks like he's thriving.'

Mila had just given birth to a baby boy last time Hrafn was in Aldeigjuborg, and now the little one was toddling around on as yet unsteady legs. While Mila was busy with her guests, her mother kept an eye on the child.

'Jaroslav – yes, he's a sturdy little thing, isn't he?' Olaf's voice was imbued with pride.

'Indeed he is.' Hrafn thought it showed how much the man loved his wife that he'd given his son a Slavic name. But although he was secretly amused by the strange-sounding combination of 'Jaroslav Olafsson', it was a sign of how the people of this town were becoming integrated, no ethnic background better than another. That seemed to him a good thing. They all had a common goal – to make their town prosper. As long as they worked together to achieve that, it didn't matter where they came from. Perhaps he ought to settle here himself one day.

Olaf leaned over to whisper, 'He'll be getting a sibling before the midwinter *blót*, but that's a secret for now.'

'Excellent – congratulations!' Hrafn slapped his friend on the back. 'Perhaps I will see him or her on the way back. In the meantime, I brought something for Jaroslav.' He pulled a carved figure of a dog out of his pouch. He'd done it himself during the past winter and was pleased with how it had turned out. Although he could have just bought a toy, he wanted the gift to be more personal.

'Why thank you, that's very thoughtful of you!' Olaf's eyes lit up and he called for Mila to bring the little boy. 'Look what Hrafn has for you, Jaro!'

Mila sent Hrafn a smile and thanked him on her son's behalf. Jaroslav burbled something unintelligible and gave him a big grin, showing off six or seven tiny teeth, the size of barley grains. He seemed very happy with his new possession and waddled back to his grandmother to show her. Hrafn was pleased. He'd brought other gifts for his host and hostess, but they could wait until morning.

Chapter Eleven

'You girls might as well do some washing for your masters while you're here. Collect any dirty laundry in your shawls.'

Mila was a whirlwind of activity early the next day, not allowing Linnea or any of the other thralls to lie abed for long. Hrafn had told her he was off to do business with Olaf all day, and that the women were to stay with Mila and do as she bid them. She hadn't reckoned on washing clothes, but it made sense, and to tell the truth, it would be wonderful to put on something clean. Although she'd given up trying to sniff herself after a few days, she was still enough of a twenty-first-century woman to want to feel fresh. *Oh, for a hot shower, some proper soap and shampoo, and deodorant!*

So far, she had tried to wash in the sea and rivers they'd passed, using a wash cloth she'd found in her pack, but it wasn't a very satisfactory way of keeping clean. She'd changed her under-gown – or serk as it was called here – but she only had one extra and knew she'd have to make do with that. The men all dunked their heads in water and washed their hands with soap every morning, she'd noticed, but of course the rowing made them sweaty. When asked, every one of them produced several linen shirts and other items of clothing, and the women had quite a pile by the time they set off on the short walk to the river.

'I've brought soap,' Mila told them. 'We can all bathe as well, once some of your clothes are dry.'

It sounded heavenly, although Linnea wasn't sure what the water temperature would be like. She'd brave anything, though – short of ice – in order to feel clean and sweet-smelling again.

The river seemed very wide and flowed sluggishly in the morning sunlight. In a few places it was still and mirror-like, reflecting the surrounding trees and low-lying landscape. There was a small sliver of pebbly beach, with grasses, bushes and birch trees behind it. Linnea recognised some of the wild flowers as similar to those that grew in Sweden – cow parsley and buttercups among them. In some places, water lilies could be seen along the edge of the river, surrounded by reeds, and despite the noise coming from the town, it was a serene and beautiful place.

But they weren't here to take in the scenery, and Linnea realised she was yet again at a disadvantage. Drawing Eija slightly to one side, she whispered, 'Can you show me what to do, please? I've, um . . . never washed clothes before.' Well, she had, obviously, but only in a washing machine.

Eija's eyes grew round, as if she'd never heard of such a thing, but she must have felt some residual gratitude from the night before, because she just nodded and said, 'Come, kneel next to me.'

In a low voice, she gave instructions, and as it wasn't exactly rocket science, Linnea soon got the hang of it. Doing laundry in a river with a very basic type of soap was hard work, however, and she was extremely glad when they were down to the last garments.

'Let's bathe before doing those,' Mila instructed. She reminded Linnea of Napoleon – small, dark and dictatorial – a thought that made her smile to herself until she remembered that there was absolutely no one here she could share that joke with. She was an alien in a foreign land – or time, rather. A sobering thought.

'Won't anyone see us?' she asked Mila as the women began to strip off.

'No, we have this stretch of the river to ourselves.' Olaf's wife smiled and pointed to the trees behind her. 'And I've left two of my women on guard over there, just in case some man decides he wants a peek.'

Linnea smiled back. 'Good thinking.'

The water was very cold, but not unbearably so. She had learned from experience that it was best to just throw yourself in and not try to do it gradually. It was like ripping a plaster off in one go. Her body quickly became used to the chill, and she revelled in the feel of the coarse soap as she used it to wash herself from head to toe.

'God only knows what this is doing to my hair,' she muttered in English. Lye soap – which was what she believed it to be – couldn't possibly have any of the properties her luxurious shampoo and conditioner at home did. She wasn't looking forward to a session with the little bone comb to try and untangle it, but at least it smelled reasonably good and wasn't greasy. She longed for a toothbrush as well, but had to make do with rinsing her mouth with water and rubbing her teeth with the edge of the serk she was about to wash.

They emerged from the river and dried themselves off on their old undergarments before putting on the clean ones and laundering the final dirty items. Linnea couldn't help but feel they'd done a good job, and there was a certain sense of pride in having accomplished something.

She hoped Hrafn and the other men would be grateful, but doubted it. After all, it was expected of her now.

'So can you take all of this to sell for me? Do you have the space?'

Just like with Leifr, Hrafn had an agreement that he would take

Olaf's pieces of jewellery and amber to Miklagarðr as well as his own. In return for selling them, Olaf would give him part of the profit, which seemed a fair deal. They would both still make more than enough.

'Yes, I'm sure we can squeeze in one more box. Linnea could sit on it, in fact, as she and the other women don't have chests for their belongings.'

Hrafn could have bitten his tongue, and swore inwardly, but if Olaf noticed that he had mentioned Linnea again, he didn't comment, just nodded and smiled. 'Excellent. Thank you, my friend. I trust you to do your best when it comes to haggling over prices. Shall I give you an indication of how much I'd like for each one if possible?'

'Yes, do.'

They spent some time going through the various items Olaf had produced. Like Rurik and Leifr, he was a smith, although his style was different. Where Rurik created delicate silverwork in traditional ornate styles with animals and swirls, Olaf's pieces were more influenced by the Slavic designs favoured by his wife and her people. They featured circles, triangles and straight lines rather than any naturalistic motifs, an interesting fusion of his own heritage and theirs. Although Hrafn secretly thought them clumsier, as the patterns were often square and sharp rather than flowing the way Rurik's were, he would never dream of saying that to his friend. Either type would probably sell well in Grikkland, and indeed their merchants often sent traders this far north to obtain both kinds.

In fact, the entire town was focused on producing trade goods of one sort or another, a lot of it aimed at the southern markets. There were workshops in almost every house, as he'd told Linnea. As well as the various handicrafts, there were locals who dealt in timber, honey, furs and thralls – most of the latter caught during raids further east. There was a never-ending demand for human labour, and although Hrafn preferred not to deal with them himself under normal circumstances – this longer journey was the exception – he was aware of the huge profits to be made.

As well as the local produce, items came here to be traded from as far away as Frisia, Frankia and the Roman Sea to the south, more commonly called the Grikklandshaf by his people. Especially sought after were the Frankish swords, which were true master-pieces of workmanship. Hrafn had one himself, bought with the profits from his first ever trading voyage. It was double-edged and pattern-welded to make it extra strong and durable. It wouldn't break under even the most vicious of enemy blows, he was sure, and he took good care of it, storing it in a leather-covered wooden scabbard with a lining of wool. The oiliness of the wool stopped the blade from getting rusty. He absolutely loved it, even though the handle wasn't terribly ostentatious the way some could be. Thure's was one such, inherited from their father, and Hrafn was secretly pleased he hadn't had to take it over but could choose for himself. It suited Thure, though, the overblown decorations exactly to his taste.

Coming from the other direction were things he hoped to obtain himself in Miklagarðr – silver, red beads made out of something called carnelian, rock crystal, silk, glass and exotic spices. All these could be found here in Aldeigjuborg, but at a vastly inflated price, which was why he wanted to go and fetch them himself. It would make a huge difference to his profit, but there were countless dangers attached to the journey, and he had prayed to the gods to keep them safe.

'When will you leave?' Olaf brought him back to the present, having wrapped the box of jewellery in oiled cloth, even though there was little risk of water damage to such items.

'We'll set off two days hence.' Hrafn snorted. 'My half-brother wants to rest before continuing. As though he's done any hard work so far . . .'

Olaf grinned. 'Maybe with a bit of luck the Pechenegs will get him. Make sure he's at the front to lead his men in case of attack.'

Hrafn chuckled. 'Good idea, although knowing him he'll let everyone else do the dirty work. Mind you, he does like a good fight, so who knows?' He sighed, growing serious once more. 'I try to focus on the fact that if this venture succeeds, I'll never need to see him again. I will be my own man, not dependent on him for anything.' He'd confided in Olaf how matters stood between Thure and his half-brothers, so the man understood him perfectly.

'Sounds like a good plan. Now, did you want to go and haggle with my friend Beorn for some furs? He told me he'd just received lynx and marten of excellent quality.'

'Why not? We can pile them on top of what we already have, I'm sure. Or . . .'

'. . . Linnea can sit on them.' They both burst out laughing and Olaf added, 'The poor girl will topple out of the ship at this rate. You'd best let someone else have these.'

Still laughing, they headed for Beorn's house.

'Do you have anything to occupy yourselves with, or shall I put you to work helping with the cooking?' Mila asked when they returned to the house. She had her hands on her hips in true tyrant mode, but Linnea knew it wasn't ill meant. It was just that in Viking times – or any time before the twentieth century really – no one could ever afford to be idle as there were always tasks to be done.

'I'm happy to help with cooking.' Ada shrugged.

'And me,' Gebbe said. The two of them were ushered towards one end of the hall.

'I have some, er . . . *nålbinding* to get on with,' Linnea said.

She'd been itching to try her new knitting needles and this seemed an opportune moment. They were in a warm, dry house and not out on the salty sea or a misty river. Her yarn shouldn't become too wet or tangled here, and for some reason she had a burning desire to show Hrafn that she really could make socks – better than the pair she'd given him before anyway.

'Me too.' Eija pulled a half-finished hat and some yarn out of her pack, and settled down next to Linnea. 'I'd rather stay with you, if you don't mind,' she whispered. 'That woman is tiny but scary.'

'I don't mind at all. It will be nice to have company.'

Taking a ball of yarn, Linnea began to cast on. The new needles felt a bit strange to begin with, but they were the right length and circumference, and once she'd adjusted to them they worked very well. At first, she was concentrating on her task, and it wasn't until a while later that she noticed she was the focus of everyone's attention. By this time she'd done five rows, using four needles to make up the top of the sock and knitting with the fifth, and the women were all staring at her handiwork. The ribbed part was emerging, and although the wool was crude and probably very itchy to wear, Linnea wasn't having any trouble working with it.

Mila's mother walked over to stand right in front of her, peering down. She was wrinkled and grey-haired, as well as bent and birdlike, but Linnea had seen her lifting her hefty little grandson without any trouble and knew that looks could be deceptive. There was something very determined in the old lady's dark eyes that spoke of an inner strength as well as the physical one. 'That seems a very fast way of doing it,' she commented, and the others nodded. 'You'll have to show me how some time.'

Linnea debated with herself – should she teach these women a skill that wouldn't be invented for several centuries, or keep it to herself? In the sci-fi stories she'd read, there were always bad consequences when the protagonist tried to change history in any way. But then what harm could it do? Women would develop this technique eventually, and it might as well be now. 'I'd be happy to, when you're not busy,' she replied in the end, and Mila's mother seemed satisfied with that.

Towards evening, the men returned, but unfortunately they brought Thure with them. As he entered the hall, his eyes roamed around and settled on Linnea for an instant. She saw something flash in their depths and knew that he hadn't forgiven her for not giving in meekly to his demands. Nor for hurting his eyes – they'd been a bit odd-looking for a few days after that incident. He wasn't going to intimidate her, though, she was determined about that. Hrafn would protect her from now on, and there wasn't a thing Thure could do about it. She glared at him before continuing with her knitting.

'Mila, this is my brother Thure. Olaf has kindly invited him to eat with us this evening.'

Linnea watched Hrafn make the introductions. Although he seemed outwardly calm and polite, she already knew him well enough to detect an undertone of irritation. From that she guessed Thure had more or less invited himself, perhaps in order to get to know Hrafn's friend. But as his gaze returned to her again, she couldn't help feeling he had an ulterior motive.

'Eija, can you stay with me at all times this evening, please?' she whispered to the Saami girl. 'I don't trust the jarl. He seems to have set his sights on me and . . . um, I thwarted him once before. He hasn't forgotten or forgiven, by the looks of it.'

'Of course.' Eija's eyes narrowed. 'I don't like him either. The way he looks at us makes my skin feel as though it has maggots on it.'

Linnea chuckled. 'Exactly.'

'We'll stick together, don't you worry.'

Linnea thanked her and was relieved to have at least one ally in this strange environment.

'I thought you said you didn't trade in thralls,' Olaf commented during the evening meal. 'What made you change your mind?'

Hrafn took a draught of ale before replying. 'I listened to what other merchants had to tell me and realised that if I wanted to make a really good profit on this journey, the thralls were necessary. I still don't like bringing them, though. They're going to be a right nuisance while travelling along the rivers.'

'What, you don't think they can help carry your ship?' Olaf guffawed, his eyes dancing with amusement.

Hrafn dug his elbow into his friend's side. 'You know they can't. Women might be strong, but they're not that strong. And I didn't select them for their muscles.' He sighed. 'I've thought about it and decided they'll have to be the ones to ferry the logs from one end to the other as we drag the ship along the ground. We'll have to make sure the logs aren't heavier than two women can manage between them.'

'If necessary, I'll make mine help with the boat,' Thure put in, spitting out a chicken bone inelegantly. 'Women may want you to think they're weak, but they are a lot tougher than they let on.'

Olaf smiled. 'Perhaps, although I'm inclined to agree with Hrafn – there are certain things that are beyond them. I suppose you'll just have to try it and see.'

'We don't want them to arrive in Miklagarðr all scrawny and muscular from overwork,' Hrafn put in. 'They need to seem appealing and womanly to the prospective buyers. You know, soft and enticing. Otherwise how will we obtain a good price?'

Thure grunted. 'You may be right about that, but we can fatten them up on the last leg of the journey.'

Hrafn gave up. There was no point arguing with Thure. He

would do whatever he wanted, no matter what anyone else said. Hopefully Hrafn would prove his point by selling his thralls for much more silver than his half-brother.

'How do you like living here?' Thure asked Olaf. 'It's quite far from your homeland.'

'Oh, I'm very happy here. Aldeigjuborg is a lively place with people always coming and going. There's never any chance of becoming bored, and I get plenty of trade from both directions.' Olaf patted his stomach. 'As you see, I'm doing well for myself. Much better than I could ever have done at home.' He nodded towards his wife, who was sitting with little Jaroslav now. 'And I have Mila and my boy. Couldn't have asked for better. What about you? Do you have a wife and family waiting for you?'

'Me?' Thure looked as though he'd never even considered the possibility, although Hrafn knew for a fact that Estrid had been on at him to form a suitable alliance with some powerful neighbour's daughter. 'No, time enough for that when I go back.' He winked lasciviously. 'So many women to sample before tying myself to just one, you know?'

'Right.' Olaf's smile was lukewarm. He was obviously a man wholeheartedly converted to living with one woman only. Hrafn envied him in a way, but at the same time he was relieved not to be responsible for others just yet.

He glanced towards Linnea and the other three thralls he'd brought. Well, he was responsible for them at the moment, but it was temporary, and soon he'd be free again. He ignored the sudden longing for a home to go back to, and perhaps a toddler or two running towards him with open arms, the way little Jaro was doing to his father. He would have that soon enough, he told himself. He had to be patient.

Chapter Twelve

Another day of chores and knitting followed, and Linnea was surprised at how content she felt here. Now that she was over the first shock of finding herself in the Viking age, it was almost like taking part in an adventure. Everything was new and exciting, and there was much to see and learn. She spent most of her time listening to the other women, and watching how they performed various tasks. Everything they did was time-consuming, but no one complained.

She thought about all the modern conveniences she'd left behind – hoover, washing machine, dishwasher, cooker, heating . . . And the food. She'd kill for a piece of chocolate, or a burger and some fries, but at the same time the sugar craving had more or less gone. Here she hadn't eaten a single sweet thing, because there just weren't any. When asked, Eija had explained that she had tasted honey once or twice, but that it was rare, as bees' nests had to be located in the forest and each one contained only so much. No one seemed to have hit on the idea of keeping bees in hives as yet. Weird, but presumably they didn't find it necessary to even think about it.

'What do you add to your morning porridge if you want to make it special?' Linnea asked.

'Berries when they're available, and sometimes butter.' Eija shrugged as if she'd never considered it.

Butter? That seemed odd to Linnea, but she'd be happy to try it at some point because just barley and water was very boring, if filling.

She'd just started on sock number two when one of Mila's thralls came over to them and said, 'Your master's man is outside asking for you. Says you're to come with him so he can show you something.'

'Me? Oh, very well.' Linnea bundled up her knitting and put it away.

'Do you want me to come with you?' Eija was frowning, clearly remembering their chat of the night before.

'Yes, please.' Hrafn might just want to buy her something else that needed to be tried on, like the shoes from Gotland, but it was best not to take any chances. With Eija by her side, she'd definitely feel safer.

Outside the door, one of Thure's men waited to escort her. It was a man she'd often seen helping out on Hrafn's boat. Vidar, she thought his name was. He threw Eija an irritated glance, but didn't comment on her presence or order her to stay behind, as presumably he would have done if he'd had any nefarious purpose in mind. 'This way,' was all he said, and headed off down the street without waiting to see if they followed.

Linnea wondered what Hrafn could possibly need to show her. Perhaps he wanted her to have a prettier gown to wear when she was sold. The boring homespun brown she had on was far from attractive, it had to be said.

Vidar led the way towards the edge of the town, and down to the riverside. There were storage huts here, presumably owned by various merchants, and people coming and going along the jetties and riverbank. He stopped outside one of the huts and nodded. 'He's in there. Hurry, he doesn't like to be kept waiting.'

Something about the way he wouldn't meet her eyes made her cautious, and instead of walking briskly inside, she stopped by the doorway and looked in. Eija was right next to her. It was dark and gloomy, but she could make out the shape of a man standing in one corner. Before she had time to say anything, however, she was given an almighty shove from behind and flew into the hut, landing on all fours on the dirt floor. 'Ow! What the . . . ?'

She heard Eija protest, as if she'd been yanked away, and Vidar's gruff voice telling her, 'Not you, girl. You're not needed here.'

The door slammed shut and the man inside strode over to it, pushing down a bar to lock it. 'Good day, Linnea,' he said, and turned around.

Thure.

She scrambled to her feet and turned to face him, bunching her fists at her sides in impotent rage. *The lying, ruthless bastard!* And Vidar too. If she ever got her hands on him, he'd be very sorry. But first she had to deal with Thure.

'You don't take no for an answer, do you?' she spat. 'Why can't you understand that I am not yours for the taking? I belong to Hrafn, and he's made it very clear that I am not to be touched. What do you think he'll say when he finds out about this?'

Thure had remained silent, and now that her eyes had accustomed themselves to the gloom, she could make out his smirk. 'My little brother knows I do what I like and there's nothing he can do about it. Now, you and I have unfinished business.'

'The hell we have,' Linnea hissed in English.

She looked around to see if there was anything in here she could defend herself with, but it seemed to be a storage space for furs. Hah! So he thought he'd attack her somewhere comfortable, did he? Sex on soft pelts, what could be better? Well, she'd rather die than sleep with this self-righteous toad.

'Come here.' Thure stepped towards her and grabbed her arms just above the wrists. 'And no tricks this time. I'd like to keep my eyes intact, if you don't mind.'

'But I *do* mind,' she muttered. 'I should have gouged them out last time, when I had the chance.'

He laughed. 'Such spirit, I like it! I will enjoy bedding you all the more if you fight me every step of the way. Not like Bodil – that girl is so boring. Always "yes, Thure, whatever you say, Thure".' He did a poor imitation of a woman's high-pitched voice.

'You should be grateful she'll have you,' Linnea snarled. 'Everyone else finds you repulsive.'

'Time for you to shut up, I think. There are better uses for your mouth, and before we leave here, I'm going to make sure I sample them all.'

His grip on her arms tightened and he twisted so that her skin burned. Linnea drew in a hissing breath but managed not to scream. She wouldn't give him the satisfaction. She tried kicking him in the groin, but he'd obviously expected that because he blocked her with his leg, quick as a flash. 'I don't think so,' he muttered, and forced her backwards.

She felt a pile of furs touching the back of her knees and knew that she would soon have Thure on top of her, and then it would be too late for her to do anything. He was so much bigger and stronger. She had to act now or she was lost. Gathering all the strength she could muster, she pretended to go limp just like the last time, as if all the fight had gone out of her. But when Thure started to lean in as though he was going to kiss her, she pulled her head back and brought her forehead down on to his nose as hard as she possibly could. As headbutts went, it was a superb one, and to her satisfaction she heard a crunching noise. *I hope his nose is broken. Vile bastard!* He howled and let go of her arms to bring his hands up to his nose. Linnea didn't hesitate, but broke free and ran for the door.

She'd managed to lift the bar up and open the door before he was upon her again, trying to drag her backwards with both arms around her waist. She screamed at the top of her voice and grabbed hold of the door frame, hanging on for dear life while using her heels to kick backwards at his shins.

'Help! Someone help me, please!'

'*Þegi þú!* No one . . . is going to . . . come to your . . . rescue,' Thure panted from behind her, although he was clearly struggling, which gave Linnea some hope.

'Help! I'm—' But Thure somehow clamped one hand over her mouth, cutting off the rest of her scream.

'Get inside,' he hissed, heaving her away from the doorframe with one last effort.

Linnea bit his hand, but although he swore, it didn't stop him from slamming the door shut and flinging her to the floor. All the air went out of her as she landed badly on one wrist. Intense pain shot up her arm and she was afraid she'd broken something. How was she supposed to fight him now?

A sob escaped her, but she scrambled backwards and managed to get to her feet. There had to be something here she could use as a weapon, surely. Weren't furs cut with knives? Groping behind her with one hand, she searched desperately for something, anything, with which to hurt him. But the softness didn't yield so much as a needle, and despondency gripped her. Thure was going to win and there was nothing she could do about it. *Bloody hell!*

He slapped her hard, making her ears ring, and she blinked to clear her vision as he threw her down on the nearest pile of pelts, landing on top of her so hard she couldn't breathe. With one hand he tried to force her head forward so he could put his mouth on hers, but she twisted violently and tried to headbutt him again.

There was blood running freely out of his nose, and some of it smeared her cheek, but she didn't care as long as she didn't have to feel his lips on hers.

The other hand was tugging at her skirts. Linnea heard the material rip as she struggled to get him off her. She could feel herself weakening, and when he twisted the wrist she'd damaged earlier, she cried out in pain. The knowledge that she wouldn't be able to hold out for much longer hit home, but there was only one thing she could do – make this as difficult for him as possible – so she continued to fight him every step of the way.

'Look at me, *bikkja*! I want you to remember this moment, because I certainly will.' He grinned and grabbed her face again to attempt to force her to look into his eyes, but in the next instant, the door to the hut flew open and crashed into the wall.

'Get . . . *off* . . . her!'

Thure's head snapped to the side as someone hit him hard and shoved him on to the floor. Relieved to be rid of his dead weight, Linnea drew in a couple of much-needed breaths, then blinked and tried to sit up. Without thinking, she leaned on her bad wrist and cried out again.

'Linnea? Are you hurt? Can you stand?' Hrafn placed an arm under her shoulders and pulled her into a sitting position. 'By all the gods, your face! What . . . ?'

'It's not my blood,' she whispered. 'It's his.'

'Huh?' Hrafn turned to stare at Thure, who was kneeling on the floor now, glaring at the two of them. Blood streamed down over his mouth and chin, clearly visible in the light from the open door, and stained his tunic.

'She broke my nose,' he snarled, putting up a hand to cup the bloody mess. 'She'll pay for that!'

Hrafn's expression hardened. 'I'm glad, or I would have done it myself.' He got up and took his half-brother's hand to pull him to his feet, but as soon as Thure was standing, he grabbed the front of his tunic with both hands and slammed him into the nearest wall. Linnea could see that Hrafn was taller and more powerfully built, and his stance was quintessentially menacing. Putting his face close to Thure's, he said in a low, icy-cold voice, 'If you *ever* touch her again, I'll kill you. Do you understand? She is mine and mine alone. You may be the big jarl at home, but there are things that are out of reach even for you. I allowed you to come along on this trip because you supplied some of the men and paid for your own ship, but I can easily find others to travel with. So think hard, *half*-brother – if you want to continue on this journey, you will swear an oath never to lay hands on this woman again. Yes? If not, you're on your own and I will go without you.'

Thure's mouth twitched, going from mulish to sulky to resigned. Finally he nodded. 'I swear by all the gods never to lay hands on this woman again.' Then he turned to spit on the floor in Linnea's direction, snarling, 'May the trolls take you!' before heading for the door. He flung over his shoulder, 'We leave in the morning,' as if he had to have the last word and show that he still possessed some authority.

Hrafn didn't reply. Instead he stood watching his half-brother leave, then went to help Linnea. 'Can you stand, or shall I carry you back to Olaf's? I'm so sorry this has happened. I honestly didn't think he'd try anything here in the middle of a town or I would have left someone to guard you.'

'I c-can walk by myself. Just give me a moment.'

He put his arms around her, and she allowed herself to lean into his broad chest, breathing in the familiar scent of him as he hugged her tight. Listening to his steady heartbeat calmed her, and she had the sensation of having come into a safe harbour. Which was ridiculous really, considering the fact that this man's plans for her weren't all that much better than those of his half-brother. What on earth was wrong with her? With a sigh, she forced herself to take a step back.

'We'd better go. Y-you knew he was going to d-do something?' She accepted his help in the form of a supporting arm around her waist and leaned into him, trying not to allow herself to think about what had so nearly happened just now.

'Of course. I'm not blind. You hurt him that night on the beach, didn't you?'

She nodded. 'Poked his eyes.'

He gave her a lopsided smile. 'Good, but he doesn't take rejection well, so I was sure he'd try again. Only I was convinced he would wait until we were out in the forests, and I would have been on my guard. It was madness to attack you here. Anyone could have seen.'

'No. He had Vidar fetch me and shove me into that hut, then he barred the door. No one was paying attention. And Eija, who was with me, couldn't do anything. I think Vidar took her away. Even when I managed to open the door briefly to shout for help, everyone turned a blind eye. They must have thought I was Thure's thrall. And by then, Eija was gone. Oh, what if she's been hurt too?'

'Don't think about that now. I'll deal with it. Vidar, eh? Then he's not going any further on this journey, I'll see to that.'

Linnea put a hand on his arm and looked up at him. 'I don't think it was his fault. He was only doing as he was told. Thure probably threatened him.'

'Hmm, we'll see.' Hrafn didn't seem convinced and she let it go. It was up to him, after all.

When they arrived back at Olaf's house, she was relieved to find Eija there, seemingly unhurt. Her friend came rushing over. 'Linnea! What happened? Are you—'

'She'll be fine. Keep your voice down, please.' Hrafn called

Mila over and told her quietly what had happened, while Eija stood nearby, listening wide-eyed. 'Please don't speak of this to anyone else. Can you help Linnea get cleaned up and find her a new gown? She'll need to rest for a bit. Say that she fell and hurt herself. It's partly true anyway.' He took hold of Linnea's wrist, which was red and swelling up. 'I'll find someone who can take a look at this for you. For now, pretend you have a headache.'

'Thank you. And . . . thank you for . . . for rescuing me. How did you know?'

His mouth tightened. 'I guessed when I arrived back here unexpectedly early and found you both gone. I'd left orders you weren't to leave the house. It shouldn't have been necessary to rescue you at all. It's fortunate this town isn't very big and I met someone who remembered seeing your hair. Now, please, let Mila take care of you.'

'My mother is skilled with herbs and ailments. I'll ask her to look at that wrist.' Mila held out an arm for Linnea to lean on. 'Come, you had better lie down before you collapse.'

Hrafn nodded. 'Thank you. I'll be back later.'

Hrafn couldn't remember when he'd last been this furious. It was as though a black cloud had enveloped him the moment he'd seen Thure lying on top of Linnea while she struggled in vain. The *niðingr* had definitely crossed a line today, and it was time his high-and-mightiness realised that there were limits to what could be tolerated. At least he'd sworn an oath not to touch Linnea again, but the way his devious mind worked, that was no guarantee he wouldn't hurt her through other means. Hrafn had to be even more vigilant if he was to bring her safely to Miklagarðr. He ignored the little voice inside his head that told him Linnea might face something even more unpleasant there. That was not the point.

He went in search of Vidar, whose face turned ashen at the sight of him. 'Hrafn! I . . . Is all well?' He was sitting on the jetty next to Thure's ship; presumably it was his turn for guard duty.

Hrafn pulled him to his feet by grabbing the front of his tunic. 'You know it isn't,' he hissed. 'What possessed you to allow Thure to hurt my thrall? Didn't you hear me say that none of the women were to be touched on this journey?'

'I . . . I . . . yes, but the jarl is different, isn't he? I mean . . . he is in charge.' Vidar's eyes were frantically looking for a way out, but Hrafn wasn't having it.

'He may be in charge at home, but he has no say over my possessions, and he's not in charge of this journey. I think your travels end here – you'll have to find your own way home. I care not how. Now get out of my sight.'

'No, please, forgive me! I . . . I have wanted to do this for so long. Please let me come! I'll swear fealty to you and you alone. I'll do anything you ask, just don't make me go back empty-handed. I couldn't. What will everyone say? My wife . . .'

He seemed genuinely contrite, and more than a little desperate to continue on the journey. Hrafn calmed down and tried to think rationally. Could he trust the man? Looking into Vidar's eyes, he believed he could. He hadn't hurt Eija, after all, but brought her back safely to Olaf's house. Thure had no doubt manipulated him somehow – he was good at that – and made him believe he was within his rights to take Linnea. She was correct, it wasn't Vidar's fault.

'Very well. Swear fealty to me, and if Thure ever asks you to do any such thing again, or you overhear him asking anyone else to harm her, you are to come to me immediately and tell me, is that clear? I'll not travel with anyone who is untrustworthy. We face a lot of dangers and need to be able to rely on each other fully.'

Vidar nodded. 'I swear. You have my oath. I'll speak to you first in future.'

'You do that or you will regret it immensely, you have *my* oath on that.'

Hrafn gave the man one last death glare, then turned on his heel and marched off in search of his brothers. He had to warn them to be even more on their guard from now on, as he was sure they hadn't heard the last of this. Thure was as devious as Loki, the god of mischief. Hrafn only wished he could fetter his half-brother for eternity, the way the other gods had done with Loki, with venom forever dripping into his face. It would have been a fitting punishment.

For now, all he could do was be alert to every eventuality.

Chapter Thirteen

'There, child, that should make the swelling go down in a day or two.' Mila's mother, whose name was apparently Bela, tied the linen bandage in place and patted Linnea's arm. 'You're lucky it's only sprained, not broken. That would have taken weeks to heal, months even.' She tutted. 'Men! Always causing trouble . . .'

Linnea almost smiled at that; it sounded so much like something a twenty-first-century woman would say. It would seem that nothing changed through the ages. 'Thank you, I appreciate your kindness and your, er . . . skill.'

The old woman had first ascertained that nothing was broken, then put together some smelly concoction that she plastered around Linnea's wrist before tying on the bandage. It was anyone's guess whether the foul stuff would have any effect with regard to healing, but Linnea figured it couldn't hurt, and it felt good. She had heard about wise women of the past who had great knowledge of healing herbs and the like. There was no harm in giving it a go, since she couldn't exactly rush off to A&E.

More was the pity.

'Now drink this down. It's just willow bark infusion. Should help soothe your aches and pains.' Bela held out a cup and Linnea obediently swallowed the contents. It had an earthy smell and flavour, with a slightly bitter undertone, but it wasn't unpleasant.

'Thank you.' She'd heard of willow bark being used as a pain-killer, since it contained more or less the same substance as modern aspirin, and it occurred to her that it would be useful to have some to hand on their journey. 'I don't suppose you have any more of this? I'm thinking we might need it during our travels.'

Bela nodded. 'That would be wise. I can give you a small pouch, but it might be best if I teach you how to find it yourself.'

'Find it? In the forest, you mean?'

'Well, usually near the river or water of some kind, but yes.'

The old lady went on to describe how Linnea should seek out the fresh thin twigs at the end of a willow bush's branches. 'They have to be alive, mind,' she cautioned. 'No dead wood or it won't work.' She was to collect a handful and then strip the bark off it carefully, while trying not to include the innermost part of the twigs. 'That makes the infusion more bitter,' Bela explained. 'Scrape all the bark off, and don't worry if you can't manage with the tips of the branches. You can just put those in whole, it doesn't matter. Chop it all up into tiny pieces and leave them to dry for a few days. You can then store it in a pouch or other container, as long as it's kept fairly cool.'

Linnea nodded, taking it all in. 'And how do I make the . . . er, infusion?' She'd almost said tea, as that was what it looked like, but of course the old woman wouldn't know what that was.

'Add one or two spoons of the dried bark to a cup of water and put in a pot. Simmer gently for a while but make sure it doesn't boil, then leave it to stand before drinking.'

'Thank you so much, I'll remember.' Linnea was genuinely grateful. It was actually terrifying to be stuck in an age where there were no chemists or doctors, and no medicines as she knew them available. Now she would at least have aspirin, a small comfort.

Bela brought her a pouch. 'Here, take this to begin with, then you can make more yourself.'

'What would you like as payment? I have some amber . . .' Though she had no idea what would be a fair price when bartering.

'No need. Consider this a gift. I enjoy passing on my knowledge to those who will listen.'

Linnea thanked her again and then lay down on the bench she'd shared with Hrafn the night before, pulling her blanket around herself as best she could with one arm.

'Here, let me help you with that.' Eija came over and perched next to her. 'Are you truly unhurt? When Vidar forced me to come back here, I was so afraid for you.'

'Thank you, I'm fine. Although things could have been very different.' She told her fellow thrall what had happened, speaking in hushed tones so that no one else would hear. 'But please, don't mention it to anyone. We just have to be very careful from now on.'

Eija nodded. 'I'll stay with you whenever the master can't, I promise. Now you had better rest.'

Linnea's eyelids were drooping, so she didn't argue, just thanked her friend once more before exhaustion claimed her.

'How is your wrist?' Hrafn had shared his story with both younger brothers and with Olaf, and was now back at the latter's house in time for the evening meal. He'd found Linnea sitting on the bench staring into the fire, her face unusually pale and her expression sombre.

'Huh? Oh, it's you.' She jumped as if her thoughts had been far away. A thousand years into the future? Hrafn snorted inwardly and dismissed that thought. It simply wasn't possible.

He sat down next to her and she moved over to make room for him. 'Your wrist?' he asked again, picking it up gently to inspect the bandaging. Mila's mother appeared to know what she was doing, as it was neat and tidy.

Linnea pulled her arm towards her and cradled it protectively against her stomach. 'It's throbbing but at least it's not broken. Bela said it should be better in a few days.' She managed a wan smile. 'I'm afraid you'll have to find someone else to do the steering.'

He grinned back, glad that she was able to joke, if only a little. 'That I will. And I'm glad it's just a sprain.' He added in a whisper, 'Else I would have had to break one of Thure's bones in return.'

Her chin came up and a spark shot through her eyes. He'd noticed before that their deep blue colour changed depending on her mood. When she was angry or defiant, they turned almost violet. Shaded by long dark lashes, they were beautiful anyway, but the extra sparkle definitely added to their appeal. Not that he should be noticing, but still . . .

'I thought I already did,' she said. 'How's his nose? I hope it will be really ugly from now on.'

Hrafn stifled a laugh. 'It already was – he takes after his mother, who I gather was well dowered but sadly lacking in beauty, though don't tell anyone I said so.' He nudged her with his elbow and marvelled that he could share such a feeling of companionship with a thrall. Perhaps it was wrong of him, but right now he was enjoying their banter.

Geir, whose turn it was to come and sleep at Olaf's house rather than guard the ship, ambled over and sat down on the other side of Linnea. 'What's this I hear? You've been brawling?' He chuckled. 'You should leave that sort of thing to us men.'

'Believe me, I'd be happy to. But perhaps it was good training. I've been hearing about the perils of the next part of our journey.'

Hrafn, who was a bit put out at having his conversation with her interrupted, frowned. 'Who from?'

'Oh, the women were talking as we did the laundry. They said there are wild tribes along the rivers who might attack us.'

'It's true,' Hrafn admitted, 'but we will be prepared at all times, and won't let anyone hurt us or steal our goods. No need for you to worry.' He made his voice sound confident, although secretly he knew there was a strong possibility they wouldn't make it. It was a risk he was prepared to take. Cowards never prospered and he was not afraid to die fighting – it was the best way, after all, and might even gain him admittance to Valhalla. Not that he really cared either way.

Before now he hadn't given a thought as to how such an ambush could affect his thralls, however, and glancing at Linnea, a stab of anxiety shot through him. Even though he was going to sell her, that would be to a prosperous man most probably, not a wild tribesman who would treat her harshly. He'd have to make sure she wasn't captured by such a one.

Or any of the other women either, he amended silently. He should be thinking of all of them, not just her.

'Here, Linnea, have some ale. Have I told you about the time Hrafn beat up Thure when we were younger?' Unusually, Geir's eyes were dancing with merriment as he prepared to tell his tale. Hrafn was sure his brother was merely trying to entertain Linnea in order to stop her brooding about the happenings of the day, but he resented being the subject under discussion.

'Don't listen to him,' he muttered. 'He exaggerates.'

'No, I want to hear. Tell me, please?' She turned her pretty eyes on Geir instead of Hrafn, and he felt suddenly bereft.

He shook his head and grabbed the mug of ale a serving girl offered him, taking a large swig. This would not do. He was developing feelings for a thrall, and he couldn't afford to do any such thing. He needed the riches she would bring, not her.

Never her.

Then why did he have such a strong urge to keep her by his side for always?

The urge grew even stronger that night. A light sleeper, Hrafn was woken by whimpering and someone pushing hard on his chest as if trying to get away from him – Linnea.

He grabbed her good wrist with one hand and shook her shoulder gently. 'Linnea!' he hissed, all too aware of the many people sleeping around them. 'Stop it! Wake up.'

He heard her suck in a huge breath and felt her shudder. 'Hrafn?' she whispered. 'What in . . . ? Oh, did I wake you again? I'm so sorry.' She tried to pull her hand away, but he held on in case she wasn't fully awake yet. He didn't want her falling off the bench; she was on the outside tonight in order to avoid her injured wrist coming into contact with the wall.

'Another nightmare?' They would appear to be a regular occurrence, and he surmised that the incident with the wagon had been truly terrifying if she was reliving it so often.

'Y-yes. But not just the . . . er, wagons this time. I usually wake up when they crash together, but . . .' She swallowed hard. 'This time Thure got out of the other one and was coming for me and I was stuck. I couldn't get away . . .' Her whisper grew so faint, Hrafn barely heard that final sentence, but he could guess the rest.

He swore under his breath. *The Jötuns take Thure!* Without thinking, he wrapped his arms around her as he'd done just after the attack. It was only to help calm her down, nothing more. She was shaking and he rubbed her back in a soothing motion. 'I won't let him hurt you again, you can be sure of that. You must try to put it out of your mind.'

She nodded against his shoulder. 'I know. It's just . . . we have no control over dreams, do we?'

'True.' He hesitated, then blurted out, 'I sometimes dream of the night my mother died. I was summoned to say farewell. As I'm the eldest, she told me to look after my brothers, and I wake up just before I have time to promise . . .' He shook his head. Why was he telling her this? Baring his soul to a stranger, and a thrall at that? It was madness. And yet it felt right.

'How old were you?' Linnea pulled away slightly and seemed to be peering at him through the darkness. There was only a faint glow from the hearth, and he was glad because that meant his expression was hidden.

'Six winters. She had just given birth to Geir. I did give her my oath, only I'm not sure she heard me because she may have passed into the afterlife already.' He shrugged. 'I've done my best to keep my promise, so I've no idea why that particular night haunts me. As you say, our minds have a will of their own sometimes.'

Linnea placed her palm on his chest. 'Thank you for telling me and for . . . bearing with me and my nightmares.'

He had the urge to grab her hand and hold it against his heart, but resisted. He'd been soft enough already this night and it was time to stop that. 'It was nothing. The least I could do when my half-brother was responsible. Now please, try to sleep. We leave at first light.'

As he lay down with his back against hers, he frowned into the darkness. It was all too easy to let things slip when talking to her. He'd have to be more guarded in future. Nothing good could come of being familiar with her, of that he was sure.

After such a disturbed night, Linnea didn't feel ready to tackle the next part of the journey, and knew she'd be reluctant to leave Olaf and Mila's comfortable home. She was even more unenthusiastic when she became aware of a grinding pain in her lower abdomen that could only mean one thing – the monthly curse.

'Nooo!' she groaned quietly. What on earth was she to do about that here? She hadn't the faintest idea how Viking women dealt with such things. There was only one way to find out – ask Eija.

She thanked God for her friend, who took charge as soon as Linnea had stammered out a convoluted explanation about not having any of her things with her. 'Don't you worry, it is not my time at the moment so you can borrow mine. Put on some linen trousers and come with me.'

Eija rummaged in her pack and then led Linnea outside to the privy, where she handed her a bundle of pads. These appeared to have been made by *nålbinding* and were thick, multi-layered rectangles of wool. 'You'll have to rinse them out each night, of course, or you can put some moss on top if you want, but I'm sure you know that already.'

She didn't, but kept quiet about that. And moss? No thank you. Bad enough having to use it for other things; she shuddered at the thought of all the creepy-crawlies it might contain. 'Thank you, Eija, you are too kind. I'll try to make some of these for myself for next time. Perhaps you could show me how?' That didn't sound right, as presumably she ought to know how already, so she backtracked. 'I mean, yours look much better made than the ones I owned.' Throwing her arms around the girl, she gave her a spontaneous hug, which made Eija blush.

'Oh, it was nothing. I'm happy to help.' She clearly had no idea just how much of a lifesaver she was.

Soon afterwards, it was time to set off.

'We look forward to seeing you on the way back,' she heard Olaf say to Hrafn as they said their farewells. 'Be careful, my friend.'

A stab of something akin to jealousy shot through Linnea – or was it wistfulness? No one expected to see her here again, no matter how kind they'd been to her. Instead, they'd be welcoming back a rich man laden with silver, silk and other exotic items. Her life, and those of the other thralls, in exchange for all that. It was taken for granted that this was normal, and not a single person present felt sorry for her or even wondered what her feelings on the matter were. *Bastards!*

And yet she knew it wasn't cruelty. It was simply the way things were here. Why should they question something so intrinsically part of everyday life? She was the outsider, the strange one to whom this seemed barbaric. Eija and the other girls might bemoan their fate, but they didn't blame Hrafn and his people for human trafficking. Their own countrymen did the same. It was just bad luck when you were the one captured and sold.

'I shall miss this place,' she whispered to Eija as she sat in the stern of the ship, staring at the settlement of Aldeigjuborg, which was fast disappearing into the morning mist.

'And I.' Eija's cheeks turned pink and Linnea peered at her with interest.

'Any particular reason?'

'No. Well, maybe. No, probably not.' The colour spread all the way down her neck.

'Tell me. We have all day with nothing to do, so you might as well.' Linnea smiled encouragingly. 'I can keep a secret.' Boy, could she ever.

Eija took a deep breath and bent her head. 'Very well. Did you happen to notice Master Olaf's apprentice, Einarr?'

'Shy young man with reddish-blond hair?' Linnea guessed. She'd seen him scurrying around, and he'd been with his master to wave them off.

'Yes, him.' Eija's colour deepened further. 'He . . . he spoke to me, several times. Seemed very nice and . . . he didn't appear put off by my looks.'

Linnea smacked her friend lightly on the arm. 'I told you! There's nothing wrong with your looks. I can quite see why he was taken with you.'

'Oh, I wouldn't go that far, but . . . well, it has given me something to dream about.'

The mood plummeted like a stone thrown into a well, and Linnea had to swallow a curse. Of course there was no point Eija mooning after Olaf's apprentice – she'd never see him again. 'I'm sorry,' she whispered, taking Eija's hand to give it a squeeze. 'At least that's proved to you that men find you attractive, right? There are bound to be lots of others.'

Eija managed a smile. 'Yes. Don't worry. I'm not stupid enough to have thought that anything could come of it, but I will be better able to cope with whatever I have to endure now, because in my mind I can go back to this place. To Einarr. Do you see?'

'Mm-hmm.' Linnea did see, but at the same time she wanted to cry. For herself, for Eija, and for all the thousands of humans who had ever been in this situation – helpless chattels with no say in their own future. If only there was some way she could take Eija back to the future with her, but she wasn't even sure she'd ever make it herself.

Her thoughts were interrupted by Hrafn. 'Eija, your turn to take the steering oar. Linnea can sit next to you and tell you what to do. The men who aren't rowing need to rest or we will never get anywhere.'

For the rest of the day, the two of them sat silently side by side while Eija steered. It was a companionable silence, even if they were both lost in sad thoughts, and Linnea took comfort from the fact that she wasn't alone. Whatever happened, she had Eija and the other women until they reached Istanbul. She hoped to have stolen that infernal brooch long before then, at which point she'd have to leave her new-found friends, but she didn't want to think about that now. It might not even happen.

'Here, you might as well make yourselves useful while we row.'

They had stopped at midday for a rest and a quick meal on the right-hand bank of the river, and Hrafn had fashioned makeshift fishing rods out of strong sticks, thick thread and some metal hooks he'd brought for the purpose. He held them out to Linnea and the other women, including those from Thure's ship. He'd briefly considered asking Thure himself to do some fishing, but didn't want to even speak to him at the moment. He was still too angry.

'I don't want to fish.' Bodil wrinkled her nose. 'They are so slimy when you land them.'

'Then perhaps you don't want to eat either?' Hrafn's questioning gaze made her cheeks turn bright red. She huffed, but didn't make any further protests.

'You will have to take turns,' he told them. 'I've only made four, but any fish you can catch will be a welcome change to our normal diet. We'll just need to dig for worms to use as bait. Gebbe, can you find containers of some sort to put them in?'

The Frisian girl nodded and went over to the ship, coming back with two small pails.

Rurik had fetched a spade and helped them turn over the soil. To Hrafn's surprise, Linnea didn't seem at all fazed and happily picked up the fattest of the wriggling worms. Some women disliked them, he knew, and he'd been sure a high-born lady such as her would consider this beneath her. 'Have you fished before?' he asked, as they walked back in the direction of the ship.

She nodded, her eyes twinkling. 'Oh, yes. Uncle Lars taught

me and my siblings how to *meta* – well, that's what he called it. I know how to put the worms on the hook too, although I'm not good at killing the fish if I catch one.'

Hrafn smiled. 'I'm sure someone else can do that. I only hope they are biting today. I should have brought nets, but I forgot. Perhaps we can make some.'

He took his seat in his usual place, at the back on the bench in front of Linnea. No one had questioned his decision to sit there, although Rurik and Geir had ribbed him a couple of times.

'You just want an eyeful of pretty women to spur you on to row harder,' they'd joked, but he had let it go. Hopefully they wouldn't realise that he was only watching one in particular, and although he knew he shouldn't, still he remained in the same position each time they boarded.

'Ugh! I don't want to touch those.' Gebbe made a face as they watched Linnea baiting a hook.

'Here, you two can have this one.' She handed over the finished rod and started on the next one. 'Eija and I will share this. I can hold it with one hand, but if we catch anything big, I'll need help. My wrist won't be much use against a massive fish.'

'I doubt you'll be that lucky,' Hrafn muttered. He had heard tall tales of monstrous catfish in this river, the size of a small boat if the fishermen were to be trusted, but he'd believe it when he saw it, and in any case, they probably wouldn't bother with something as tiny as a worm on a hook.

By fishing almost continuously throughout the afternoon, the women managed quite a respectable catch of mostly salmon and pike-perch, but also some smaller perch and a local species of fish Hrafn didn't know the name of. He threw back any that were too small, and the ones he didn't recognise – you never knew if they were edible or whether they contained too many bones – and kept the rest. Pike-perch had a huge amount of bones, but were so tasty most people were prepared to put up with that. Perch were better, but usually quite small, and you needed large quantities of them. Salmon were clearly the best – fat, with large bones that were easy to pick out, and the pink flesh slightly oily and rich.

'Good work,' he praised them as they made landfall at dusk on a small, mercifully uninhabited, island in the middle of the river. 'If you can do as well each day, our evening meals will be considerably tastier and we won't need to waste time on hunting.'

'We might get bored with fish,' Linnea commented, then shrugged. 'But I suppose it makes a nice change from porridge.'

Hrafn laughed. 'How did your family put up with you?' he wondered out loud.

'What do you mean?' She blinked, clearly puzzled.

'You have more likes and dislikes when it comes to food than anyone I have ever met. A king would be easier to please, I swear. Most people just eat what is put in front of them.'

'Oh, that.' She sighed. 'Well, if you'd grown up eating the kind of food I was given, you'd be the same.'

'You'll have to describe it to me sometime.' He held out a sharp knife. 'Since you're so good at fishing, are you able to gut them too? Or shall I ask Eija?' He was sure the Saami girl would be adept at such a task.

'No, I'll do it. My wrist doesn't ache as much now.'

'Oh, I'd forgotten . . .'

Linnea held up her hand and wiggled the fingers. 'No, it's fine. I can move these and that's all I need. Besides, I'm right-handed and I'll only need to hold the fish with my left.'

'Very well, but if it starts to hurt, tell me.'

He handed over the knife, and wondered briefly why he wasn't worried about the possibility of her using it on him. She'd been so angry when he had first captured her, but now she was calmer, more accepting of her situation. Was she only biding her time?

He glanced at her and saw her briefly watching Thure, who of course made no attempt at helping with the fish his thralls had caught. Perhaps Hrafn needed to keep an eye on Linnea too in case she took revenge. There was something lurking in her gaze as it rested on Thure, but it was gone as quickly as it had come.

Yes, she would bear watching as well. She was up to something.

Chapter Fourteen

They made good progress at first, despite having to row upstream. The Volkhov river was sluggish and didn't put up too much resistance, and the men were well used to the hard work by now. Linnea marvelled that they could keep it up for hours on end, fuelled only by the occasional drink and piece of dried meat, but no one complained. At least not on board their ship.

Thure's was another matter. After two days where his men took turns with the steering oar, leaving only one rower to substitute with, Hrafn finally lost his patience.

'Thure, for the love of Odin, surely you can do the steering? It's not exactly hard work. Even my women can manage it. We're constantly having to wait for your crew to catch up with us, and at this rate we won't reach Miklagarðr before next winter.'

'I'm the jarl,' Thure hissed. 'The one providing the victuals and pay.'

'We're mostly eating fish caught by the thralls, and you won't have anything to pay anyone with if we don't reach our goal. Or do you not know how to steer? I can have Eija teach you.' Hrafn's eyes were shooting angry sparks. Linnea could see clearly that he wasn't backing down and secretly cheered him on.

Thure glared back for a while, his mouth a study in mulishness, but eventually he shrugged. 'Very well. If you're in such a tearing hurry, I can hold on to the steering oar for a bit. I'm bored anyway.'

'Good,' was Hrafn's only reply before he turned his back on his half-brother and stalked off.

Linnea hurried to lower her eyes. She didn't want Thure to notice her, especially not with *Schadenfreude* in her expression. Best thing would be if he forgot she even existed, but during the past few days she'd still felt his malevolent gaze on her from time to time. Although she tried to ignore him, it made her shiver. She couldn't forget those terrifying minutes in the storage shed when she'd thought all was lost.

Come to think of it, though, in some convoluted way he'd done her a favour, because the terror of that near-rape had almost completely erased her memories of the car accident that had preyed on her mind for months before she ended up here. Apart from that night at Olaf's house, whenever she had the usual nightmare now, her mind skimmed swiftly through the collision and it was the threat of Thure coming towards her that had her in a panic instead. It was as though the accident was fading into the past, and only the present held any fears.

Would her memories of the twenty-first century disappear altogether if she stayed here long enough? She didn't want that; had to hold on to them if she was to find a way to return. To that end, she spent a part of each day thinking about her family, Lars, Sara and everyone she'd left behind. If nothing else, it helped to pass the time. As it was June now, Sara should definitely be out of hospital. It was a shame Linnea wasn't there to celebrate this milestone with her as she'd planned, but she was stuck here, at least for now.

Her thoughts also kept coming back to Thure's brooch. She was convinced it was the key to returning to her own century, and that somehow she must steal it for real. But he still made her very uneasy. She definitely didn't want to be alone with the man again; he was creepy as hell. And sneaking a look at his belongings would be near impossible, surrounded as she was by other people all the time.

Quite apart from the fact that he slept in some sort of tent away from everyone else each night, he also had Bodil clinging to him, limpet-like, most of the time. Linnea wanted to scream at the girl to let go because she was convinced Thure felt no obligation towards her. Most probably he'd use her until they reached Istanbul and then sell her. With her white-blonde hair she'd be just as valuable as Linnea herself – or perhaps slightly less because she was 'used goods'. Worth a lot nonetheless. This didn't seem to have occurred to Bodil at all, who acted as though she was somehow better than the other girls. Linnea didn't have the heart to disillusion her.

She hadn't had a chance to speak much to the three other women who belonged to Thure. She'd been told they were Mercians – so in effect English, as she guessed that meant they were from the Midlands – and their names were Ælfgifu, Emma and Mildred, but they stuck together and didn't say much. They allowed Bodil to boss them around, and Linnea assumed they must be used to such treatment. She couldn't imagine what they must have gone through – being captured somewhere, perhaps watching their families killed or taken away from them, their houses burned . . . then brought to Sweden and sold. Horrible.

She shuddered as she thought about what her own fate might be, but at least she knew her family was safe. Somewhere a thousand years into the future . . .

Her thoughts were interrupted by Rurik. 'How about we sing to pass the time? Might help with the rowing too, eh, Hrafn?' He raised his eyebrows at his brother.

'I suppose.' Hrafn didn't look thrilled, but perhaps saw the sense in keeping boredom at bay. Rurik hadn't waited for his approval in any case but was already in full flow.

To Linnea's surprise, Hrafn soon joined in, and some sort of ballad with a rousing chorus rang out among the trees lining the riverbanks. Rurik, who seemed to have the best voice – strong and melodic – occasionally did the verses on his own, but everyone helped with the chorus. The words were simple and the fourth time round, Linnea decided to give it a go. It felt strange to be singing about some long-lost hero's deeds, but she liked it all the same.

She exchanged looks with Hrafn, who seemed to be enjoying himself now, and they sang the final chorus in harmony. It wasn't until they'd finished that she noticed everyone else had gone quiet, but then Rurik laughed and clapped Hrafn on the shoulder.

'You two should sing by yourselves. You are well matched.'

Hrafn scowled. 'Don't be a *fífl*, brother. You're the one with the best voice and well you know it.'

'True,' Rurik said with a grin to show that he was being immodest on purpose. 'But your deeper one goes better with Linnea's. We'll have to teach her some more.'

Linnea could feel her cheeks burning. 'Maybe later,' she murmured. 'Sing something else, please, Rurik.'

He must have caught the pleading look in her eyes because after hesitating for just a moment, he started on another song. Linnea turned away to concentrate on her fishing rod. Singing with Hrafn probably wasn't a good idea, no matter how well matched their voices were.

It was a good thing their ships were so broad and flat, as the river was very shallow in places. Linnea remembered from her reading that Vikings had been able to travel the waterways of Russia for just that reason – most of their boats had a really shallow draught and therefore didn't get stuck. It also made them ideal for landing on beaches, as they were easy to pull up on to sand or shingle.

After about a week – she lost count of the exact number of days – they came to another large settlement. 'Oh, is this Novgorod?' she blurted without thinking, looking around her at the activity on both the shore and a large island in the river. 'Or, no . . . Gorodisce, was it?'

Hrafn looked up and regarded her with his head to one side. 'We call it Holmgarðr, but I believe to the natives it's Ryurikovo Gorodisce. How did you know? Did Mila tell you?'

'No, I . . . learned about it long ago.' Linnea turned away, but she couldn't quite hide the flash of sadness that shot through her. Would she ever read a book again? And was there any way all her learning could help her here?

Hrafn's expression told her he wasn't sure whether to believe her, and she supposed she could easily have heard the name of this place from someone in Aldeigjuborg, but he let it go. Instead he pointed to the island. 'That is where many of the merchants dwell, while the *konung* – or *knyaz*, as they say here – has his hall up there.' He nodded towards the right-hand bank of the river, where a large hall sat on top of a hill.

'Oh, yes. Isn't his name Rurik, or was it Oleg?'

'Rurik, the same as my brother,' Hrafn replied, throwing her a suspicious glance. 'Oleg was the name of the leader at Aldeigjuborg, remember?'

'I know, but there seem to be a lot of people called that in this country, and Rurik will be succeeded by someone called Oleg too.' Linnea was sure of that, but at Hrafn's narrowed gaze she didn't insist or repeat how she knew it.

He shook his head as if he despaired. 'Maybe you are a *völva* after all. Can you perform *seiðr*?'

'A wise woman, me?' Linnea laughed. 'Hah, probably the opposite. But at least now I know roughly which year this is.' She nodded to herself, satisfied. 'Rurik established this place in approximately 862 and then Oleg is supposed to have ruled between about 880 and 910, so I'd guess this could be around 870 perhaps?' She didn't know why it mattered to her, but knowing roughly which era she had ended up in seemed important. 'They'll call it Novgorod eventually.'

Hrafn's eyebrows rose. 'I don't know what you are talking about. Rurik has only been ruling for a handful of years, so I'd keep quiet about his possible demise if I were you. Even if you are able to see into the future, no one wants to know when they're going to die, least of all a king.'

'I told you, I'm not a *völva*!' Linnea protested. 'I'm definitely neither wise nor a seer. But I'm not stupid either. Of course I won't say any such thing.' She shot him a look of irritation. Honestly, what did he take her for?

Eija had been humming to herself as usual and didn't seem to register their conversation, while Ada and Gebbe sat at the front of the ship today. Linnea hoped no one else had heard her either. She didn't want them to think her mad or some kind of witch, the way Hrafn obviously did.

'Are we stopping here long?' she dared to ask. By now she'd realised it wasn't her place to question his decisions in any way. If she did, she would only draw attention to herself, but at the same time she was curious.

'No, one night only. We have all the trade goods we need already.'

As they neared one of the jetties built on the island, he stood up and addressed the two ships' crews. 'We will remain here overnight while Thure and I go in search of extra grain and other foodstuffs, but I would prefer it if you all stay on or near the ships,

167

please. I don't entirely trust the people here, and we don't want to be robbed. All you women, stay close to the men.'

'*Yes, sir,*' Linnea muttered in English.

Eija nudged her. 'What does that mean?'

'Oh, I was just replying in my own language, the way you would to the commander of a group of warriors. He's so over-bearing, isn't he?' Linnea said, but she knew he was only doing his job, which was to keep them and their cargo safe. After what had happened with Thure, she should be grateful.

Eija giggled. 'He's a man used to leading. I doubt he even thinks about the fact that he's always issuing orders.'

'You're probably right.'

And if she was completely truthful, Linnea liked the way he took charge. He was very sure of himself and his abilities, a man comfortable in his own skin. There was something very attractive about that. A little voice in her head uttered the traitorous opinion that someone like Daniel would have been next to useless here. His leadership skills were sadly lacking and, if she was honest, she'd always found his inability to hold his students' attention somewhat disappointing. Although personally she'd enjoyed his lectures because she wanted to learn, he'd never been able to control the rowdier element who weren't as eager to absorb his pearls of wisdom. Here he wouldn't have survived a week, never mind years. She felt very guilty for thinking that, but if you had to be stuck in a hostile environment with anyone, who better than Hrafn?

Although she'd rather not be here at all.

She could see what he meant about this place though – as soon as they'd moored the ships, they attracted the attention of the people of Gorodisce. A couple of shifty-looking individuals in particular eyed them speculatively, and Linnea was suddenly very happy to stay on board.

'Why are they looking at us like that?' she whispered to Eija. 'Those men over there, see? There's something . . . I don't know, hungry about them.'

She felt Eija shiver next to her. 'Yes, you're right. Perhaps they take us for easily deceived travellers. I do hope the master knows what he's doing.'

'Me too.' Linnea couldn't wait to leave this place.

Holmgarðr was a large island, and Hrafn had heard tell that it would take several days to walk around its perimeter. The areas not covered by houses, lanes and walkways were forested for the most part, and the rest was thick bush and undergrowth. It wasn't a place he'd ever want to live in, as it seemed a bit dirty and cramped, but thankfully they would be moving on quickly.

'Shouldn't we go and visit the *konung*?' Thure asked as they met on the jetty before going off in search of the nearest grain merchant. Hrafn hadn't wanted to bring his half-brother at all, but he didn't have much choice unless he wanted to pay for all the food himself.

'No, I doubt he wants to be bothered with every trader who passes by on the way south,' he said dismissively. Overlords interested him not at all, and he preferred to keep out of their way in case they decided to interfere in his business.

'But I'm a jarl,' Thure persisted. 'I'm not just anybody.'

Swallowing a sigh, Hrafn regarded the man he'd had to put up with for as long as he could remember. He had lost count of the number of times Thure had pointed out his higher status, as if being born first somehow made him the better man. Ever since Hrafn had realised his half-brother enjoyed the power it supposedly gave him, he'd ignored it. The end of this journey, and the day when he was rid of Thure once and for all, could not come soon enough.

'Listen to me. If we go and ask to see Rurik of Gorodisce, he might agree, but I am fairly certain he will expect you to bring him something by way of a gift. Now do you wish to part with any of your trade goods just for the privilege of sharing a meal with a *konung*? Because if not, I would suggest we hurry up and do what we came here for, and then leave as quickly as possible.'

He held Thure's gaze while the meaning of his words sank in, then watched in satisfaction as his half-brother's cheeks turned ruddy and his mouth twisted. 'Very well, I will take your word for it, although I doubt the man would be that avaricious.'

There was no doubt in Hrafn's mind at all, but he refrained from saying so since he'd won this minor skirmish. 'Good, then let's buy some grain. We have a very long way to go before we can purchase any more.'

'My good men, welcome to Gorodisce! May I be of assistance?' A dark-haired man with keen sparkling eyes approached them. He was dressed in fine clothing, his trouser legs wide and puffy, showing that he could afford the amount of cloth necessary, and his tunic covered in panels of silk and edged with fur and braids. 'I can take you to the best merchants and make sure you aren't cheated.' His words were accompanied by a broad smile showing very white teeth.

'Thank you, it is very kind but I'm sure we'll manage.' Hrafn put a hand on Thure's arm and tried to steer his half-brother away. There was something about the foreigner that made him wary, despite the apparent friendliness. No one helped you out of the goodness of their heart. Not when it came to business. No doubt he would expect something in return.

'Oh don't be so grumpy, Hrafn. We could do with some assistance to speed things up.' Thure pulled his arm out of Hrafn's grip and ignored the warning look the latter shot him. 'What is your name? I'm Thure, and this is my first visit to your island.'

Hrafn almost groaned out loud. How stupid could you be? Thure had as good as given the man permission to fleece him. But there was no stopping him now and he'd already set off with the man – Casmir by name – as his guide. Hrafn strode after them, determined not to be fooled.

'How fortunate that it is not *my* first time here,' he said loudly. 'I hope we are heading for the same merchant I used when last I visited.'

He'd make sure they did.

Linnea stayed on board the ship and watched the teeming quay-side, where goods of all types were being bartered and exchanged. The people scurrying about were a curious mixture: tall, fair-haired Scandinavians for whom the name Rus had first been coined – although no one seemed sure where the word came from, with suggestions ranging from 'men who row' to their hair colour, or just a derivation of the Finnish word for Sweden, Ruotsi – smaller dark-haired Slavs and lots of other ethnic groups in between. She guessed some were Finns and Balts, while others were perhaps from further south – Bulgars or Khazars. Although if she wasn't mistaken, most of those tribes had been hostile to their northern neighbours.

The Slavs were easy to pick out because their clothing was different and their women wore earrings and headdresses with big rings hanging over their temples, as well as lots of pendants made of various metals. The Balts sported ornaments with geometric designs that Linnea had seen previously, although their clothing was more similar to that of the Vikings. Many people here appeared to have adopted a mixture of styles, though, which made it difficult to tell them apart. According to the books she had studied, Oleg of Novgorod had eventually united them into one state called the Kievan Rus, although that was obviously still a few years into the future. It was definitely noticeable that the inhabitants of Holmgarðr were assimilating and becoming one nation, irrespective of their origins. A melting pot, kind of like the United States of America in her time. Fascinating.

There was something about the hustle and bustle, however, that made her breathe a secret sigh of relief when Hrafn and Thure returned, followed by some thralls carrying barrels – containing ale perhaps? – and more sacks of grain. Presumably barley yet again, but she was becoming used to it now, and porridge was definitely preferable to going hungry. With them was a gaudily clad man with a wolfish smile, who seemed very happy when Thure invited him on board his ship to share a skin of wine.

'I've been saving it for a special occasion,' he declared loudly, 'and now seems a good time. Come, Casmir, have a seat. This is my lovely Bodil.'

Lovely now, was it? Linnea suppressed a snort, and when she happened to exchange glances with Hrafn, his mouth quirked and she could see that he was thinking the same thing. It wouldn't surprise her if Thure lent the poor girl to his new friend. She was only lovely when he wanted her to do something for him.

Soon there was quite a party atmosphere on Thure's ship, with several of his men joining in and a few of Casmir's cronies coming aboard too. Linnea heard Hrafn whisper to his brothers to go over there and keep an eye on their goods, which was probably an excellent idea. Eventually the foreigners took their leave, apparently without anything having gone missing.

'Good riddance,' Hrafn muttered as he sat down next to where Linnea was already lying on the hard planks.

'Aren't you going to sleep?' she asked.

'No. I don't trust Casmir not to return with several henchmen. He's seen exactly what we have now – well, everything on Thure's ship anyway – and I'd rather leave here with all our trade goods intact.'

Hrafn spent the night on the jetty with the other guards posted there. It would seem he wasn't taking any chances. It made Linnea jittery and she slept fitfully, plagued by dreams in which a demonic-looking Thure featured. She was pleased when they set off again at dawn, as soon as it was light enough to see, and before most of the town's inhabitants had begun to stir.

'We'll be crossing a lake today,' Hrafn told those sitting near him. 'Ilmen, I think the people here call it. It's fairly big, but we should reach the other side before nightfall. We can follow the coastline on the left for a while first and find somewhere to stop for a meal. Later, when we come to a large bay or inlet, it's time to head straight across.'

'Have you journeyed this way before?' asked a man sitting opposite. Linnea was glad, since she wanted to know the answer to that as well.

He shook his head. 'No, I've never been further than Holmgarðr, but I've spoken at length with men who have – and who lived to tell the tale – and I memorised their instructions word for word.'

The other man, who went by the name of Odd, laughed. 'You're like a *skáld*, committing things to memory. Will you be telling us tales next?'

Hrafn's mouth quirked. 'No, I leave that to others better suited for the task. I don't deal in tales, but in reality.'

His words were joking, but Linnea sensed that there was a serious message underlying them. This was no pleasure jaunt. It was going to be dangerous in the extreme, and there was no guarantee any of them would live beyond the next few months, including her.

Chapter Fifteen

They spotted the large inlet about an hour after breaking their fast, and Hrafn told Eija to change course. 'We need to go directly south from now on. Keep the sun on your left until midday, then on your right,' he instructed, although he would be sure to check for himself from time to time.

They were heading for the mouth of a smaller river on the opposite side of the lake. It was the beginning of the true adventure, as far as he was concerned, since it was new territory for him. From now on, they had to be alert at all times as danger could lurk behind every tree trunk they passed. The founder of Holmgarðr might have started to unite the peoples of this area, but there were always lawless men who cared nothing for such things and disobeyed every ruler. Hrafn was sure they would come across more than a few, but he was determined to be prepared.

'No more singing,' he ordered. 'From now on, we don't want to draw attention to ourselves in any way.'

'Spoilsport,' Rurik muttered, but Hrafn knew his brother understood.

Rurik had changed places with Odd, and he and Hrafn worked well together, equally as strong and taking even strokes of the oars. 'Will we go *down* any rivers, rather than just up?' his brother asked. 'We seem to have done nothing but row for weeks now.'

'Yes, but from what I've heard, you may come to wish we weren't.' Hrafn remembered the warnings he'd been given. 'Once we reach the final river, which is incredibly long, apparently, there will be rapids and other dangers to avoid. I'd rather be rowing upstream than fighting to keep the ship from being smashed on rocks.'

'Hmm, I suppose. And at least we won't get bored.' Rurik grinned and lowered his voice, glancing towards the ship behind them. 'Well, apart from some people.'

Hrafn snorted. 'Thure is busy steering, can't you tell? It's such hard work, isn't it, Eija? Especially with a sore head.'

The Saami girl, who'd been in her own little world as usual, looked at him with dark eyes. 'I'm sorry, what?'

'Nothing.' Hrafn knew he shouldn't joke with her, but when he glanced at Linnea he saw her hiding a smile. At least she'd understood the humour, and she was clearly listening to their conversation.

Rurik must have noticed as well, because he nodded towards her wrist. 'Is it healed yet? I see you've removed the bandages.'

'Yes, I'm going to take over from Eija in a while.' Linnea flexed her hand and stretched her fingers. There was still some bruising, but it was fading to yellow and pale purple. 'It feels fine now. In fact, I might as well do something while I wait my turn.' She bent to rummage in her pack and brought out what at first appeared to be her *nálbinding*. On closer inspection, however, Hrafn could see that she had four of the metal sticks he'd given her all threaded with wool, and as she began to work with a fifth one, she alternated between them, seemingly going round in an endless circle.

'What are you making?' he asked, almost against his will. He really shouldn't be so friendly with her. It was making life more difficult, blurring the lines that ought to exist between them.

'Socks.' She smiled impishly, her eyes dancing in the sunlight. 'Hopefully better than the ones I gave you before.'

He grinned back and couldn't resist teasing her. 'That wouldn't be hard. I couldn't wear those unless I had the toes cut off one foot.'

Rurik regarded them with interest. 'What's this? Are Linnea's skills at sock-making no good?'

'I'll show you some time.' Hrafn chuckled.

'I make excellent socks, thank you very much, but only when I can do it my way. Like this.' Linnea indicated her strange set-up. 'Estrid tried to teach me your way, but as I'd never done it before, it's no wonder I made one sock larger than the other. You would have done too.'

'Well, I for one have no idea how you have the patience for any of it,' Rurik declared. 'I look forward to seeing the result, and if you have the time, I wouldn't mind a pair of new socks.' He gave her his best smile, making Hrafn long to smack him over the back of the head. Rurik was usually a favourite with women, able to charm even the most serious ones, but strangely enough Linnea didn't look as though his flirtatious glance was affecting her in the slightest. There was no fluttering of eyelashes or rosy cheeks, which was the normal response to Rurik's advances. Intriguing.

Instead she nodded and said calmly, 'I'll see what I can do.'

As they continued on their way, Hrafn glanced at Linnea's work now and then, and couldn't help but admire the strange technique. He'd never seen socks quite like it before. As one emerged, he could see that she'd managed to make it so that the top part stretched when she tugged at it. Perhaps this was how her own strange clothing had been made, only with smaller stitches. But those hadn't been of wool, nor linen either. He wanted to ask her about them, but knew that would only invite further strange tales of travelling through time.

What if she really had, though? How would he feel if he'd ended up a thousand years before – or after – his own time? Exceedingly lost, he imagined. If Linnea was telling the truth, he couldn't but admire her spirit. Since that first week, she hadn't complained much at all, and was even able to joke with him and Rurik. That showed courage, something he admired greatly.

And if she *was* from the future, he ought to try and make use of her knowledge.

'Linnea, you promised to explain about the Roman way of counting. Can you teach me and Rurik, please?'

She looked up. 'What, now? But I don't have any sand.'

'Try writing on the ship's planks with water,' Hrafn suggested. 'Or do you need a lot of space?'

'No, that could work. Very well, I'll try.'

'What's this? More counting?' Rurik, who together with Geir had been taught the Serkland way by Hrafn one evening, perked up. Rowing was boring, and anything that took their minds off the monotony was good.

Linnea put away the sock and found a mug to fill with lake water. Then she began to draw with one finger on the planks in front of their feet. 'This won't be perfect because I'll have to do it upside down in order for it to be the right way up for you, but here . . . This is a Roman number one.' She made a straight line up and down, like the beginning of many of the runes Hrafn knew how to use. 'Sometimes they add tiny lines at the top and bottom, like this, but that's mostly for decoration and isn't strictly necessary.'

She continued with more signs that she claimed meant five, ten, fifty, a hundred and a thousand, then showed them how to put them together in order to form the other numbers.

'That's ingenious!' Rurik stared at the number 199, for which Linnea had used five symbols.

'It seemed easier the Serkland way,' Hrafn muttered. 'Here you have to add or take away numbers in your head first.'

'True, but it still makes sense.' Rurik beamed at Linnea. 'Thank you for showing us. Who knows, we might have use of this when we reach Miklagarðr.'

'Yes, thank you.' Hrafn hadn't meant to sound ungrateful, but he did prefer the first system she'd taught him.

'You're welcome.' Linnea threw what was left of the water overboard. 'I doubt you'll need it in Miklagarðr, though. They don't speak or write like the Romans any longer. I think their main language is Greek . . . er, what you call the *grikkskr tungu*. But perhaps they still use these for counting.'

'How do you know that?' Rurik stared at her with raised eyebrows, while Hrafn just digested the information. However she'd come by her knowledge, he was beginning to believe that she spoke the truth at least. She would have no reason to lie about things like this because they'd find out for themselves eventually. If there was *trolldomr* involved, there was nothing he could do about it.

'Oh, I . . . um, heard it somewhere. Eija, do you want me to take over now?'

'Huh? Oh, yes please.' Eija looked at the sun, which was past its zenith. 'Shall I fetch everyone something to chew on?' she suggested diffidently.

'Good idea.' Hrafn's stomach growled as if in assent. It was going to be a long time until their evening meal.

By dusk, they had sighted the opposite shore of the lake, and also the mouth of a fairly narrow river. Linnea couldn't remember its name, but assumed it would allow them to continue in a southerly direction. Not today, though, as the rowers had had enough and they needed to set up camp for the night.

'Look, the river seems to fork in two and there's an island in between. Let's stay there,' Hrafn suggested. 'Hopefully no one lives here.'

That proved to be the case, and although it was a bit marshy, they found wood for campfires and began to cook the fish caught that day, as well as some turnips Hrafn and Thure had bought. These roasted slowly in the embers at the edge of the fire.

'We'd better sleep in the ships. There are midges and mosquitoes here as it's so damp,' Geir commented. 'I hate those little beasts, but they love me.'

'Good point.'

It was a bit squashed, but they managed to all squeeze in, lying like sardines at the bottom of the ship. As usual, several men took turns doing guard duty and Linnea was grateful she didn't have to. She wondered if Hrafn didn't ask her or the other women simply because they were female, or was it the fact that they were thralls and therefore perhaps not trustworthy? It was probably best not to ask. Either way, she wouldn't have any idea what to do if they were attacked.

She found it difficult to get comfortable on the hard planks. Although she'd become used to sleeping on the ground, rolled into her blanket and with her pack as a pillow, this wooden surface was even less yielding. When she wriggled for the umpteenth time, Hrafn grunted and elbowed her lightly.

'What's wrong? You're like a worm on a hook,' he murmured.

'Sorry. I suppose I'm not as tired as you since I didn't spend all day rowing, and these planks are so rigid,' she whispered back. There were snores coming from all around them, and she didn't want to wake everyone else.

As always, he was lying with his back towards her, but now he turned over. Linnea sensed him studying her in the darkness, and although the moon was absent, she could make out the general shape of him. 'Here, use me as a pillow,' he said softly, and reached out to pull her against him. He put an arm around her and cradled her head on his shoulder. Instinctively, she placed one hand on his chest and felt his steady heartbeat under her palm.

'Are you sure?' It was definitely more comfortable, but it seemed like this might be a bad idea for other reasons. 'I mean . . .'

'For the love of all the gods, woman, I've told you I won't molest you. Now go to sleep or we'll never get under way tomorrow.'

'OK,' she whispered in English. He was just trying to be nice, after all, not coming on to her, and she had to admit she felt safe and cosy lying like this, even though it was wrong on so many levels.

'What's that?'

'Oh, it means "fine" or "very well" in my language.'

'Well, good. Sleep now, *unnasta*.'

Linnea drew in a sharp breath. Had he just called her 'dearest', or did she imagine it? But he probably only meant it the way London cab drivers called you 'love' without being in the slightest bit acquainted with you. She was reading more into it than had been intended, and that was ridiculous. Hrafn might be kind right now, but he was still a hard-hearted trader who cared nothing for her. She would do well to remember that.

And yet as she closed her eyes, she couldn't help wondering what it would be like to lie like this with him if he was more than her owner . . .

Despite being completely exhausted, Hrafn found it impossible to go to sleep himself once he'd gathered Linnea into his embrace. What a *fífl* he was, to be sure, imagining he could hold her in his arms and feel restful. Of course having an armful of soft woman would give any man ideas of what he'd like to do with her. It was entirely normal, but he'd promised her – and himself – he wouldn't touch her, and he was determined to stick to that.

It was a relief when Geir came to fetch him to take his turn at guard duty.

'This river is much narrower, and we'll need someone on lookout duty in the prow of the ship,' he ordered the following morning. 'The last thing we need is to collide with underwater obstructions. If it starts to look shallow, we'll have to cast out lead lines to make sure. I don't want any holes in the hull. Ada, Gebbe, can you take turns, please?' The Frisian girls had seemed bored and listless the previous day, and he didn't want them to fall into a decline.

'Yes, will do.' Their expressions brightened, which was good.

'I can help too, as it's not my turn to row.' Geir, who'd been at the back of the ship, headed for the prow. Rather than make his way across the benches, however, he jumped up on to the nearest oar and began to use them as stepping stones, lithe as a cat.

'For the love of Thor, brother, get down!' Although he'd often played this game himself, Hrafn had visions of Geir falling into the water and being smacked on the head by a heavy oar. They couldn't afford any accidents.

Geir just laughed and continued. 'I need some exercise.' As if to prove his point, he went backwards and forwards one more time, ducking out of the way of Hrafn, who tried to grab him.

Thankfully, the men whose oars he'd skipped across were grinning and holding them steady, and it only took him a matter of moments to reach the front of the ship a second time. Hrafn swore under his breath, but knew there was no point arguing with Geir. And secretly he was proud of his brother's fearlessness.

Soon they were under way again, rowing steadily, with Thure's boat following as usual. Since leaving Holmgarðr, Thure had been unusually silent, but he continued to steer his ship and Hrafn was relieved that he had at least embraced that task. It gave him something to do other than complain. Despite this, while rowing alongside them on a wider stretch of the river mid morning, he apparently couldn't stop himself from griping at least a little bit.

'Are you sure we're going the right way?' he shouted across to Hrafn, nodding at the sun, which wasn't on their left as it ought to be. 'Seems to me we're heading west, and you said Miklagarðr is due south.'

Biting his teeth together to stop himself saying something he'd regret, Hrafn replied, 'Yes. The rivers won't always go in a straight line. That is not nature's way, is it? I am told this will eventually take us in a southerly direction. We have to be patient.' Not a word Thure was familiar with, as he well knew.

'As long as you're sure . . .' Thure left the sentence hanging, as if to cast doubt on Hrafn's authority yet again, but thankfully none of the other men paid him any attention.

As the day wore on, Hrafn could tell they were indeed going south and was therefore not unduly concerned. No one had said this would be easy, else every man would be undertaking the same journey.

Late that afternoon, Linnea leaned forward and touched his knee. 'I think there's someone following us,' she whispered.

'Huh?' Hrafn had been lost in the rhythm of rowing, but her words jolted him into full alert. 'What do you mean?' He stared at Thure's ship, which was some twenty arm-lengths behind them.

'Not Thure. Another ship. Well, a smaller boat, I think. I've glimpsed it a couple of times now, but whoever it is they're being careful to stay back. It's only when we go round a bend and you can see through some of the trees that they're visible.'

A sensation of foreboding slithered down Hrafn's spine. He nodded at Linnea. 'Thank you for letting me know. We can be on our guard now.'

He started whispering to Rurik, who in turn conveyed the

message to the next man, and so on. Linnea leaned close to Eija, presumably telling her as well, but as per his orders, everyone carried on rowing as if there was nothing to alarm them.

'We'll need to tell Thure and his crew,' Rurik muttered.

'Yes, but it must wait until we stop for the night. I doubt those following us will make a move before then. They're probably hoping to surprise us after dark, if indeed their intent is nefarious.'

They found another uninhabited island covered in forest, and Hrafn ordered everyone to set up camp by the shore while he went to speak to Thure. Soon every man and woman among them knew what was happening, and one by one the men fetched their weapons from the ships and hid them under their clothing. Hrafn's plan was for them all to eat, then pretend to go to sleep as usual, but no one was to close their eyes until he said so. The thrall women were given a sharp knife each, just in case there was more than one boatload of attackers coming, and Hrafn was sure they'd defend themselves if they had to. Who wouldn't? It might be a 'kill or be killed' situation.

He kept an eye out during the meal, but there was still some summer evening light and nothing happened. Two men were posted as guards; they'd been told to pretend not to be very vigilant, and perhaps stand and whisper together.

Everything was ready. He only hoped Linnea hadn't been mistaken, because then he would look like a fool and Thure would never let him live it down.

Chapter Sixteen

Linnea lay on the ground next to Eija, her senses on full alert. Every tiny sound seemed magnified in the still night air, and it was a strain to listen against the constant background murmur of the river. What if she'd been wrong, and the boat following them was entirely harmless? They couldn't be the only traders travelling this route. Hrafn would be so angry with her if it was a false alarm, but on the other hand, surely it was better to be overly cautious?

A mosquito buzzed around her face and she tried to swat it away stealthily. Damned insects never gave up. *Oh, for some mozzie repellent!* But the tiny creatures were probably the least of her problems right now. She discerned a slight scraping further along the island's shore, like wood on sand, and opened her eyes wider. Was she imagining things? But no, this was followed by a soft splash or two, as though feet had been carefully placed in the water, then the occasional snap of a twig among the trees. If she hadn't been listening out for it, she doubted anything so quiet would have been noticeable, but as it was, she heard it and hoped the others did too.

For a moment longer, everything remained still and quiet, but then a cacophony of noise exploded around her. Hrafn's cry of '*Núuuuu!*' echoed along the shoreline as dark shapes hurtled out of the undergrowth. He and his men sprang to their feet, and fierce fighting began as a couple of torches were lit and stuck into the ground. Steel clanged on steel, sparks lighting up the darkness. Sickening thuds and shrill screams bore testament to a weapon well aimed or a direct hit. Scuffles, grunts, groans and muffled curses seemed to surround them.

Linnea huddled close to Eija, Ada and Gebbe. 'Let's stay together,' she hissed.

'Yes, safer that way,' Ada muttered.

The four of them stood facing one way each, back to back, but luckily their attackers were kept at bay by the men. Linnea could see the Mercian women doing the same, while Bodil shrieked and tried to stay behind Thure. On the one hand it appeared to take for ever, but at the same time she was aware that only a few minutes had passed when further torches flared into life, lighting up the scene before them. She drew in a sharp breath at the sight of the devastation that surrounded them.

'Jesus!' she muttered.

'Sweet Freya!' Gebbe let out a muffled sob.

'It's over,' Ada whispered, rubbing her friend's shoulder. 'We were never in danger. The master saw to that.' Her voice was quivering a little, showing Linnea that she too was shaken despite her bravado.

'Anyone hurt?' Hrafn's voice rang out. 'Account for yourselves!'

A few of the men were still grappling with attackers, although it looked to Linnea as though most of the strangers had been killed. One by one they called out their names and that they were unhurt, or at least not badly wounded. There were quite a few bruises and some nasty cuts, but none had died.

'Thure? Where are you?' Hrafn glanced around the camp looking for his half-brother, who hadn't spoken.

'Here.' Thure stepped forward into the light, clearing his

throat. 'I'm here.' He was unusually subdued and wore an expression of shock. At first Linnea wondered if he was just a coward who had never fought before, but then she saw what he was staring at.

The dead face of Casmir, his new friend from Holmgarðr.

Hrafn glanced at the man too, but didn't comment. He had to be a veritable saint not to utter the obvious 'I told you so', but perhaps he figured that Thure had learned his lesson and didn't need it rubbed in. 'Take the ones who are still alive back to their ship and tie them up,' he ordered. 'Someone will find them soon, I have no doubt, as there are always ships going up and down this river. As for the rest, we will pile them up further along the shore. Their comrades can bury them when they are free, if they so wish. Hopefully they'll tell anyone else wanting to ambush us that we're not that easily overpowered.'

'Anyone skilled in how to treat wounds?' Geir called out, walking over to his brother Rurik, whose arm was covered in blood.

Linnea exchanged a look with Eija. 'We can try,' she said. 'But we'll need something to bind it up with.'

'I'll fetch a linen sheet we brought for that purpose.' Geir headed for the ship.

'And the cauldron and soap,' Linnea shouted. 'We need boiling water.'

He frowned over his shoulder but didn't argue.

Soon she and some of the other women were busy washing and bandaging cuts, while Hrafn and the remaining men dealt with the attackers, dead or otherwise. Linnea tried not to look too closely at maimed bodies and staring eyes, and was glad the darkness hid most of the gory details. It brought the memories of the car crash to the fore again – she'd never forget the sight of Sara covered in blood, unconscious and so pale she'd thought she was dead too – not to mention that skull she'd found with Uncle Lars. She shuddered. No one else seemed to want to be in charge of healing. She got stuck in and that helped her to push all other thoughts to the back of her mind. It was a relief when the others listened as she told them to use boiled water and soap. Everyone except Bodil, that was.

'Why can't they just go and wash in the river? I don't want blood all over my tunic. So unnecessary,' she complained.

Linnea refrained from rolling her eyes. Bodil still seemed to think she was somehow better than the other women just because she was Thure's favourite. 'If you don't want to help, I'm sure we can manage without you,' she replied, a bit more waspishly than she'd intended. 'It was the old lady in Aldeigjuborg who taught me to treat wounds this way,' she added, in order to avoid awkward questions. She figured it was better for everyone to think a wise woman had given her advice, since she couldn't explain about germs and infections.

'Very well, but you can do the washing. I'll tear the linen into strips.' Bodil looked down her nose at Linnea, who decided it wasn't worth arguing over.

Only one man needed stitches and thankfully Eija volunteered to do that. Linnea wasn't squeamish, but the thought of using a crude Viking needle on someone's skin was more than she could handle. 'Just make sure you boil the needle and thread first,' she whispered to her friend.

'If you say so.' It was fortunate that Eija had developed a healthy respect for Bela during their stay at Olaf's house, and she didn't protest.

'Come, let's go and sit together in the boat,' Linnea suggested when everyone had been patched up. She and the other women huddled in the stern, wrapping their blankets around themselves and trying to calm their breathing.

'Well done, Linnea,' Eija whispered.

'What do you mean? Everyone helped.'

'I don't mean about the wounds. It was thanks to you that we weren't all killed this night. You noticed the boat following us.'

'Oh, that. It was pure luck that I happened to be staring that way.'

That was the truth, but from now on she'd be on the lookout on purpose. All the time.

By tacit consent, no one spoke about the ambush, or at least not within Thure's hearing. Hrafn hoped that the bodies they'd left behind – and the few attackers still alive – would leave a clear signal to anyone else who might be following that they were not to be trifled with. He'd had a word with Linnea, and she was now taking turns with Eija to keep watch, as were Mildred and Emma in Thure's boat. They wouldn't be taken by surprise next time either. If there was a next time.

'Did you manage to get any of them to talk?' Rurik asked as they collected up the enemy's weapons to take with them. They would make a great addition to what they'd brought themselves; you could never have too many.

'Only one spoke our language, and he merely said that this was the way Casmir and men like him operated.' Hrafn shrugged. 'After Thure's behaviour, they thought we'd be easy to overwhelm. Can't blame them for that.'

'True. Well, they've done us a favour, I suppose, as now we'll be on our guard even more.'

After a few days, the river became so shallow that they could not continue. 'The lead lines are telling us it's dangerous here,' Ada called out. 'Look.'

Hrafn sighed inwardly. Transporting the ships across country

188

was not something he'd been looking forward to. It was awkward in the extreme, but unfortunately necessary.

'Right, everyone with an axe, set to!' he ordered. 'We need perfectly straight tree trunks, about a handspan in width and two arm-lengths long.'

'Are you building a large bonfire?' Thure muttered with a smirk.

'No, they're to roll the ships' keels over, of course.' Hrafn hoped his clipped tone indicated that he did not appreciate stupid jokes at a time like this. 'The rest of you, keep watch in case of another attack. The locals must know that we have to stop here, and therefore we're vulnerable.'

Thankfully no ambush materialised, and the short tree trunks were soon produced, with any twigs hacked off to make them smooth and easy to roll over the ground. Hrafn considered the available manpower and scratched his week-old beard. 'We'll need six men to move each ship. Two women to keep a lookout ahead and behind us, and the rest of you – yes, that includes you, Bodil; this isn't a pleasure jaunt – I want you to pick up the logs at the back of the ships as soon as we've passed over them and bring them to the front.'

'Odin's ravens, but this is going to take for ever!' Thure threw up his hands, but when Hrafn directed a death glare in his direction, he subsided. 'Very well, I'll go in front and keep watch with the women. Bodil, stop whining and do as you're told.' His mistress had been whispering to him, clearly unhappy at having to do some actual work for a change. She sniffed and stomped off to join the other women.

Hrafn noticed that his own thralls and the Mercian women didn't complain, but merely took up their positions and set to work as soon as the men had manoeuvred the ships out of the river and on to dry land. It was a laborious process, but they made good progress, and by the end of the day they'd reached the next stretch of navigable river. With a huge sense of relief, they made camp for the night, and Hrafn congratulated everyone on a job well done.

'I'm pleased to see how well you all work together,' he praised them. 'Unfortunately this was only the first of many such days, but I promise you the rewards at the end of the journey will be worth it.'

At least he sincerely hoped that was the case.

The others didn't look convinced, and a narrow-eyed glance from Linnea reminded him that there would be no rewards for the thralls, but most of them were too tired to argue. They lay slumped on the ground, barely managing to eat their evening meal. He could feel his own muscles protesting after the long day's work, and couldn't help but wonder if he'd been mad to think they could succeed in this venture.

'We must,' he muttered to himself. Succeed or die trying, those were the only options. Going home a failure was not to be contemplated. And they would all become used to the hard work; that was the nature of the human body.

One day, they might even thank him for bringing them. Well, some of them . . .

Linnea was starting to wonder if they would ever get to a proper wide river again. Transporting the ships across land was very tedious. Every time they thought they'd be able to row for a long stretch, the river suddenly narrowed again unexpectedly, which meant shallow waters. It was also full of twists and turns so that you never knew when these smaller parts were going to appear. She sincerely hoped Hrafn knew what he was doing, as they seemed to be in the middle of nowhere.

The first few days of portage – she knew it was called that in her time, although no one used that word here obviously – had felt endless, and she'd been physically exhausted each night, but now she was growing stronger. She'd never been keen on exercising, preferring a good book on the sofa to going to a gym, and knew she'd been carrying a few extra kilos, especially round her middle. Miraculously, these were disappearing, and that wasn't entirely due to the healthy – but boring – fare, although that probably helped too. There were no crisps, biscuits or chocolate bars to reach for whenever she needed a boost, only the ever-present bits of chewy smoked meat or dried fish. Strangely enough, she had almost stopped craving sweet things entirely. She only had the odd moment of 'if only . . .'

Several weeks passed, although Linnea lost count of the days so she couldn't be sure how many. They tried to head in a southerly direction at all times, making use of whatever small waterways or lakes they could find when the main river dwindled and disappeared. Sometimes these would allow them to travel easily for a day or two; sometimes they only made slow progress with portage. Finally, after an extra-long stretch of carrying the ships through forest, they encountered a river that appeared to be navigable for a long way. Everyone heaved a sigh of relief.

'Oh, I do hope this is the Dniepr,' Linnea muttered to herself. If it wasn't, and they'd gone the wrong way, she was afraid they would never get out of this godforsaken country and reach Istanbul. Not that she particularly wanted to get there, but at least then she wouldn't have to carry logs around.

'Which way – upstream or down?' someone asked.

'Down,' Hrafn replied, nodding towards the right.

'But that will take us back west,' Thure pointed out, still the only one to ever question Hrafn's decisions. 'Isn't that where we've come from?'

'Yes, but it's only for a while. After that it will turn south if this is the right river. Pray to all the gods that it is.' Hrafn touched the Thor's hammer amulet he wore around his neck and muttered something. 'First let's make camp and have a rest and some ale. I think we've earned it. Where are those barrels we bought in Holmgarðr? The others are empty.'

The barrels were found and opened, and a couple of make-shift tents rigged up. The weather had turned rainy, but Linnea noticed that no one's spirits were dampened, especially once the ale began to flow. She still didn't like the stuff and found a stream nearby where she refilled a leather waterskin with fresh liquid. It tasted amazingly good, like the best bottled water from her own time; there was nothing better when you were truly thirsty.

When she returned to the campfire, it was to find Hrafn and Geir head to head and with their arms around each other, grunting and shoving, oblivious to the rain. She glanced at Rurik.

'What on earth are they doing?'

Rurik grinned. 'Wrestling. Our little brother thinks he's big enough to best Hrafn now. I have my doubts, but we'll see.'

'Wrestling?' It didn't look like any wrestling she'd ever seen. 'Er, how do you know who's won?'

'Whoever manages to throw the other to the ground is the winner,' Rurik explained. 'Hrafn is a master at it, but Geir has grown so big now he's not easy to shift.'

The two men grappled for what seemed like ages, pushing each other this way and that, but eventually Hrafn succeeded in unbalancing his brother. Loud applause greeted his victory, but Geir didn't seem to mind.

'I'll get you soon,' he stated confidently.

'He probably will at that,' Rurik whispered to Linnea.

'I heard that.' Hrafn gave Rurik a shove, which only made him chuckle. 'And no, he won't.'

'Honestly, men!' Linnea shook her head, but had to laugh at them anyway.

Thure, who'd been watching with everyone else, came over and clapped Hrafn on the shoulder. 'Good to see you can still keep the youngsters in check. Let's see if I can't beat you in a board game instead. Come.'

That sounded more like a command than an invitation, but Hrafn let it go. 'Very well. Let me just wash first.'

It took two days before the river wound its way in a southerly direction at last. By that time everyone was tired of listening to Thure's complaints and jibes, and Linnea was actually surprised that Hrafn hadn't strangled the man. She was very tempted herself.

That evening, she noticed that Thure wasn't wearing his cloak. The weather was balmy, and growing warmer the further south they travelled. By Linnea's reckoning, at least a month must have passed since they left Sweden, if not more, which meant they were into late June or early July by now. Blankets were only necessary as protection against the ground.

Where had Thure stored his cloak? It had to be in his travelling chest with his other possessions. Linnea knew he had one that was larger than everyone else's – of course – and that it was usually to be found in the stern of his ship these days, as he was doing most of the steering and wanted it nearby. She glanced at the two ships pulled up bow first on the shore. In order to reach Thure's chest, she would have to wade into the water and lean over the side. Perhaps it could be done when everyone else was asleep?

She bedded down as usual, back to back with Hrafn, who had the enviable knack of being able to go to sleep the minute he closed his eyes. There were two guards posted, as always, but they were sitting by the fire, talking in hushed voices. Linnea waited until everyone else was quiet, then slowly got up, pretending to head for the bushes as if she needed to attend to a call of nature. The two guards only threw her a quick look and went back to whispering. Stealthily she made her way to the nearest bush, and from there to the shoreline.

A small crack as she stepped on a twig made her pause, her pulse beating so loudly in her ears she couldn't hear anything else for a moment. She felt slightly sick, but took a deep breath to calm herself and concentrated on listening. A snore, a snuffle, the continued murmuring of the guards, nothing else. *Good!* If she was caught, she'd be branded a thief again, and she couldn't afford for that to happen. She needed to grab that brooch, do what was necessary with it and hope to God it worked.

But what if it didn't?

Don't think like that, she told herself sternly. It had to work. And she had to try. There was no alternative.

In order to make even less noise, she slipped off her shoes and hung them on her belt, using the toggles to secure them. Keeping an eye on the two guards, who had their backs to her, she crept over to the ships and hunkered down next to the hull of the first one, which was Hrafn's. It had been pulled up quite a long way, and she was able to go round the back of it without the water reaching higher than her knees. Checking again to make sure the guards weren't watching, she flitted over to the next ship and paused, peering over the top. Nope, the guards were still busy. It occurred to her that if she could sneak around like this unseen, so could possible attackers, but she'd worry about that later. If there was a later.

Her heart hammering in her chest, she leaned over the side of the ship and fumbled around, trying to locate Thure's chest. There was a little bit of moonlight from time to time, which helped, and there it was. Shaking now, with both nerves and excitement, she lifted the lid – thank God he hadn't thought to lock it – and put her hand inside. She knew his cloak was edged with some sort of fur, squirrel probably, and felt around for its softness. *Ah, there!* She groped the material, pulling it through her fingers until they encountered the round metal shape of the brooch. *Yes!*

'What are you doing?' The deep voice came hissing out of the shadows behind her, and Linnea jumped so violently her chest banged into the ship's hull. She'd withdrawn her hand from Thure's chest instantly, and heard the lid close with a sharp snap.

'Jesus Christ! You . . . you startled me.' She turned slowly to face Hrafn. How the hell had he snuck up on her like that? He must move like a big cat. No one else was stirring.

'I repeat, what are you doing? Are you stealing again?'

'No! I just . . . I needed to borrow something.' It sounded pathetic even to herself, and she knew she'd been caught red-handed. Her heart went into overdrive, and bile rose in her throat as panic threatened to overwhelm her. What did Vikings do to thieves? Did they hang them or . . . or worse? She'd read about people in the Middle Ages cutting the hands off anyone caught stealing. *Dear God, no!* They wouldn't, would they? But she could easily imagine Thure demanding such a punishment and enjoying carrying it out.

Hrafn gripped her upper arm and towed her back towards dry land, throwing an irritated glance at the two startled guards. 'Keep better watch,' he growled at them as he marched past. They had the wits not to say anything; just sat up straighter, scanning the shadows all around them.

He pulled her into the nearby forest out of earshot of the others. 'Do I have to tie you to me at all times?' he snarled, his eyes glittering with fury every time the moon came out from behind a cloud. 'Why were you stealing from my brother?'

'I wasn't . . . I mean . . .'

'What did you take? Show me your pouch.'

'Nothing! I d-didn't take anything.'

He undid her belt with rough movements and checked inside the leather pouch, but she knew he wouldn't find anything other than the amber she'd collected. As if that annoyed him even more, he shoved it back towards her and she caught it to her chest, almost stumbling backwards. 'What were you after, then? Silver?' He was very close, looming over her, and Linnea swallowed hard, trying not to feel intimidated.

How could she explain? There was nothing for it but to tell the truth. 'I want to go back to the future. There is something in Thure's chest that might help me. If it doesn't work, then I'm stuck here, but unless I try, I'll always wonder if . . .' She trailed off. His uncompromising expression showed clearly that he didn't believe a word she was saying.

'It is a great shame that such a lovely exterior hides a devious, unstable mind,' he muttered. 'Rest assured I will be watching your every move from now on. Give me your wrist.'

'What?'

'Hold out your wrist.' He pulled something out of his pocket – a leather thong he used to tie his hair back during the day. Without another word, he proceeded to bind their wrists together with it, then dragged her back to their blankets and lay down. 'Sleep,' he said curtly.

Linnea didn't see that she had any choice. She knew she'd got away lightly. He could have punished her severely, or even given her over to Thure to face his justice – she shivered at that thought – but he hadn't.

Chapter Seventeen

The river, which Hrafn had heard Linnea refer to as the Dniepr, seemed endless. Two weeks passed, if not three – he lost track of time – and he noticed the crew become listless as one day segued into the next. At least they were going downstream now, and although they were still on standby to row whenever necessary, that was mainly in order to stay on course whenever the steering oar wasn't enough to counter any currents.

He allowed them a day's rest at one point and sent half the men into the forest to hunt game. Their diet of fish and barley was becoming monotonous, and he thought perhaps some proper meat would put the spirits back into everyone. Some of the men, Odd and Geir among them, were skilled with a bow and arrow, as well as a spear, and eventually came back with a couple of deer, six hares and a young boar, a veritable feast. Hrafn only hoped the cooking smells wouldn't attract unwelcome attention.

So far they'd not been attacked again, but he kept urging everyone to remain vigilant. He'd had a word with all the men following Linnea's night foray – she should have been caught by those on guard and they knew it – and they all swore to stay alert. It could be that the natives of these parts knew that a ship's crew would become inattentive and bored, and therefore easier prey.

He was determined not to fall into that trap.

'Mmm, I don't think I've ever tasted anything this good.' Linnea sat next to him that evening, licking her fingers after finishing her piece of venison.

Hrafn almost smiled, but he hadn't forgotten her attempt at theft and they'd hardly spoken since. He could tell by her sour looks that she resented being tied to him each night, but what else did she expect? He couldn't understand what she had hoped to achieve. That ridiculous story about needing some item of Thure's in order to return to the future – that was simply a lie. It had to be. Unless his half-brother had some henbane seeds or similar in his chest that Hrafn didn't know about. He'd heard that a *völva* would use such herbs in order to go into a trance and free her soul so that it travelled into the future. Was that what Linnea meant?

But she'd never given any indication of using *trolldomr* or herbal substances. If she was a practitioner of magic, she hid it well. In fact, most days she seemed entirely normal and continued to show signs of great learning. He'd caught her teaching Eija how to read and write runes one day, and later the Roman letters as well.

'Tell me about the future,' he surprised himself by saying. The two of them were sharing a boulder some way away from the others. No one could hear their conversation, and he wanted to keep this strange subject between the two of them.

'What?' Linnea blinked and stared at him.

'Describe the future you have seen. Whether it's in a dream or as part of a ritual, I'd like to know about it.'

'But I thought you didn't believe me.' Her eyebrows came down and Hrafn couldn't help but notice that she was almost as pretty when she was irritated as when she smiled. That was unfortunate. Why couldn't he stop being attracted to her? She was a thief, a liar and quite possibly not sane. And yet he was still irresistibly drawn to her.

'I don't.' He shrugged. 'Well, not the way you mean, but there are those who can see into the future. I think you might be one of them.'

Linnea regarded him for a long moment, as if she was debating with herself. Finally she nodded. 'OK, I'll tell you. I really hope one day I can prove to you that it's the truth.' She took a deep breath and stared into the darkness. 'The world I come from is very different to yours. We see your era as simple, uncomplicated. You live in tune with nature and you work hard for everything, whether you are producing food or everyday items. For us, such things are done by machines.'

'Muh-sheens?' Hrafn repeated the unfamiliar word. 'What are those?'

'It's difficult to explain. They are man-made items that work on their own, using some sort of force that propels them.' Linnea's frown deepened. 'You have seen the power of lightning, haven't you? Well, in the future, man has found a way to harness the forces of lightning and turn them into light, muscle power and many other things.'

Hrafn knew his expression must be sceptical, because she made an impatient gesture.

'Argh! This is so difficult. But . . . imagine you have built a cart and instead of having a horse pulling it, you have a machine inside it that pushes it forward.'

'With lightning?'

'Yes. No. In a way. The point is, we don't need manpower or horsepower because there are better, faster ways of pushing things.'

'I see.' It sounded fantastical to Hrafn, but it wasn't impossible. He learned new things all the time and implements could always be improved upon. He'd heard from his elders that in times gone by, their ships had been smaller and not as fast or as seaworthy. Humans were forever trying to make their objects work in a more efficient manner. 'Is that why you need so much learning? To know how to use such items and how to harness lightning?'

'Yes, in part, although where I come from, people think that having lots of knowledge about as many subjects as possible is a good thing. We are curious, always wanting to learn more. Little children from the age of about five go to special places called schools, where they are taught to write with the Roman letters and count with the numbers from Serkland, and all kinds of other things. What the world looks like, where various countries are situated, their languages, how our ancestors lived, and yes, how to work some of the machines.' Her gaze became distant. 'In a way, I like your way of life better. There are things about my world that are terrible – noise, laziness and foul smoke, and mountains of food that go to waste, while in other countries there are countless poor souls dying of hunger. And there's a lot of arguing about unnecessary things. For instance, there are factions who believe in different gods and they refuse to tolerate each other, saying one set of beliefs is superior to the others. I find that ridiculous.'

Hrafn had to agree. 'There will always be strife between clans and peoples; that is normal. As for beliefs, surely it would be up to the gods to battle it out among themselves?'

A gurgle of laughter escaped her. 'You'd think so, wouldn't you? But since humans never actually see them, how do we know they even exist? There are always those who try to make use of the gods for their own ends. I hate people like that.'

'What have you been taught about the world? You said little children learned things like that.'

'Well, I could draw you a rough map of where we are now, if you like.'

'Do it.' He found a stick on the ground nearby and led her down to the water's edge, where there was a strip of sandy beach. Although she could draw him an image of just about anything, since he would have no idea if it was the truth or not, she did appear to know what she was talking about.

'Right, let's see.' She cleared a large space of sand, smoothing it out with the palm of her hand. 'So this is the country we came from – Svíaríki, or as I call it, Sweden.' She drew an elongated shape and added two smaller shapes on the right-hand side. 'Here's Öland and Gotland, the two islands we passed, and over here is the land of the Balts, Latvia.' A coastline was added, which curved into a large bay, and she pointed to the top. 'Up here is the land of the Finns, but we went this way, along a river to Lake Ladoga.' She drew a huge oblong shape. 'Down the river Volkhov past Aldeigjuborg to Gorodisce, and then there was that other lake, right? Ilmen.'

Hrafn was with her so far. She continued with the river they'd gone down after that, the forested part and now the Dniepr.

'I think the Dniepr is extremely long and we're probably only just at the top of it. Eventually we'll come to Kiev – what you call Koenugarðr, yes? – then continue all the way down to the Black Sea.' Her stick scratched out these details in the sand, although she was running out of space and had to stop and clear a further patch.

'I suppose it could look like that.' Hrafn had no reason to doubt her, as it all accorded with the information he'd been given by other traders.

'It does, I promise. The Dniepr flows into the Black Sea about here.' She pointed. 'And we have to go down to the south-western part of that, where there's an opening into what we call the Mediterranean – the Grikklandshaf, I think I heard you say? The channel – the Bosphorus – is very narrow, and right there at the bottom of it is Miklagarðr.'

Hrafn stroked his beard, which was becoming way too shaggy. He'd have to do something about that when they reached Koenugarðr. 'I don't know if you are telling the truth, but what you have drawn tallies with what others have told me. I'm impressed that you have this knowledge.'

Linnea sighed and threw away the stick. 'But I could have learned it somewhere other than in the future, I know.'

'I didn't say that.'

'But you were thinking it.' She fixed him with her deep blue gaze. 'I'm not stupid and I'm not mad, but I have absolutely no way of proving that to you. I understand how difficult it must be for you to believe me. I wouldn't either if I was you!' She shrugged. 'Maybe it's better if we don't talk about it. Just pretend I'm an ordinary thrall, about to be sold to some disgusting old Serk who's already got twenty other concubines.'

Hrafn's jaw clenched. Was that what would happen to her? Perhaps. She wasn't going to become someone's cherished wife, that was for sure. She'd be used for bed sport. A plaything. He rubbed his eyes and tried to erase the image of someone like Casmir taking her against her will. It made him almost as angry as seeing Thure trying to molest her. *The trolls take it!* She was getting under his skin and he couldn't allow that to happen.

'Time to go to sleep, I think.' He shepherded her back towards the others, ignoring the questioning looks he received from his brothers. It was impossible to explain his conflicted emotions even to himself. No doubt they'd laugh at him and tell him he was going soft. Maybe he was.

But the truth was he was beginning to dread having to sell her.

They reached Koenugarðr after an interminable journey. Linnea would never have guessed a river could be as long as the Dniepr, but then she probably wouldn't have chosen to go down it by boat in her own time either. She could have flown from St Petersburg to Kiev in a matter of hours.

The river widened into a lake before they reached the town, which was on the other side of the open water where it continued southwards. Linnea had read that this was a very important location during Viking times, situated as it was where all travellers – going north or south – had to pass with their goods. She guessed that the inhabitants profited from this by selling food and other provisions that were sorely needed by this point. And no doubt there were those, like Casmir from Gorodisce, who kept an eye out for weak crews and newcomers easy to fleece or rob.

The settlement was on the right-hand bank, which was higher than the other side. Presumably it had been built there for tactical reasons. There were numerous hills, and Linnea spotted some ravines in the distance, but the northern parts of the town were lower, surrounded by forest and areas of bushland. Several islands in the river seemed to be inhabited as well, and there was another largish river that appeared to join up with the Dniepr nearby.

'It's getting very hot, isn't it?' She fanned herself with her hand and wished for a proper fan of some sort. They must be well into July by now, and here in Kiev the air was humid and heavy, while the sun warmed the top of her head unbearably.

Eija nodded, her face shiny with perspiration. 'I have heard that Miklagarðr will be even worse. How will we cope? We're used to the snow and cold of our own lands.' Her expression grew bleak.

'I'm sure we will become accustomed to it.' But Linnea had never been overly fond of warm weather and dreaded Istanbul as much as Eija did. Normally, when going somewhere hot, she'd slather herself in sunscreen to protect her skin, but that wasn't an option now. Perhaps it wouldn't matter, though. Weren't harem ladies kept indoors all the time, locked up? Her stomach plummeted even further at that thought.

'How long are we stopping here for, Hrafn?' Rurik shouted to his brother, asking the question Linnea was sure everyone wanted the answer to. Although it would be nice to have a break from travelling, she didn't feel any safer here than she had in Gorodisce.

'A day or two at most. It depends on how long it takes us to locate provisions.'

Hrafn directed operations as usual, finding them a mooring space at one of the town's wooden quays, then set off with Thure. This time Linnea was glad to see the older man wave away all offers of help from supposedly friendly locals. At least he'd learned that lesson.

'We're to stay here for now,' Rurik told everyone else. 'I'm sorry, but we can't take any chances.'

There was some grumbling among the men, who had apparently been looking forward to finding a willing woman or two. Rurik calmed them by saying they could probably go off later, when Hrafn and Thure came back. This proved to be the case, although they had to take turns so that at least half the men remained with the ships at all times. Surprisingly, Thure took charge this time and sorted out who was to stay and who could go.

Meanwhile, Hrafn went over to where Linnea was sitting. 'Come with me,' he said gruffly

'Where to?' Linnea almost bit her tongue. She really should stop questioning him at every turn – it wasn't her place. But what if he'd decided to get rid of her already? Perhaps he'd found some rich buyer. He still thought her a liar and a thief, and would no doubt be happy to see the back of her. That would scupper her chances of ever returning to her own time, as she'd be far away from Thure and his brooch.

'You'll see.' He stretched out a hand to help her up on to the jetty. To Rurik he added, 'We won't be long, then it'll be your turn to have a look around.'

Rurik just nodded.

They walked in silence at first, with Hrafn slightly in front as if to shield her from the throng of people. After a while, he took her hand. 'Don't want to lose you in the crowd,' he muttered, but he plaited his fingers with hers like a lover, which made Linnea send him a startled glance.

'Are you going to tell me where we're going?' she asked.

'I just thought you might like to have a look at all the stalls. You've been cooped up in the ship for weeks now, and it feels good to stretch your legs.'

'So have all the other women,' she reminded him.

He frowned. 'True. I suppose I'll have to let them go for a walk too.' But he didn't sound very enthusiastic about it. Linnea didn't know whether to be honoured that she was singled out in this way, or annoyed on behalf of the others.

They wandered among the stalls for a while, and she couldn't help but enjoy the sensation of his fingers entwined with hers. His hand was warm, but not too much so, the palms calloused from all the rowing. The slight roughness didn't bother her. It just made them seem stronger, more capable. A shiver went through her as she had a fleeting image of those hands on her body, stroking her soft skin, faintly abrasive in a way that would send tremors right through her . . .

She shook herself mentally. That was crazy, and she ought not to be thinking of him that way.

'Is there anything you need?' Hrafn asked, interrupting her thoughts.

'Um . . . something to protect me from the sun?'

'How about one of those colourful shawls?' He pointed at a

stall that looked like an explosion in a paint factory. Gossamer-thin shawls in all the colours of the rainbow were laid out for maximum effect, and it was a beautiful, if gaudy, sight. 'Would that do?'

'Yes, I suppose. But I have nothing to barter with. I didn't bring the bits of amber.'

'Oh, don't worry about that. It is a gift. Choose one you like.'

A shawl in shades of blue immediately attracted her, and she picked it up. Hrafn nodded. 'Yes, that suits you well. It will match the colour of your eyes, whatever your mood.' He began to haggle with the vendor and eventually parted with a small piece of hacksilver, then took Linnea's hand again and walked off.

'Thank you,' she murmured. It occurred to her that perhaps he wanted something in return. 'I can't buy *you* anything.'

He flashed her a teasing smile, the first she'd seen today, and squeezed her fingers. 'I have everything I need already.'

Linnea felt as though all the air had been knocked out of her lungs for an instant. Did he mean her? But in the next instant, he tugged on her hand and added, 'Come, let us see what else is on offer here.'

They wandered around, looking at the wares on display, but Linnea barely took any of it in. She was too focused on the man beside her, whose fingers stayed deliciously interlaced with hers. It was as if there was electricity between them, tingling sparks shooting up her arm, and she was intensely aware of his gaze on her, rather than on everything around them. The throng of people forced them into close proximity and meant that his arm and shoulder frequently brushed hers, creating even more shivers. And those ice-blue eyes of his seemed to thaw into a deeper indigo whenever he looked at her.

'Are you hungry? There's someone selling apples over there.'

'Oh, yes please.' Linnea hadn't had anything sweet since she'd arrived in Hrafn's time, and the sight of the rosy apples was very tempting.

He bought two, but instead of just giving her one, he took out his eating knife and cut her a slice, which he held out towards her mouth. She opened up instinctively and he popped it inside. As she chewed and swallowed, the freshness of the fruit burst on her tongue; she thought it was one of the most delicious things she'd ever eaten. She must have made some noise of appreciation, because his eyes crinkled in amusement and he chuckled.

'You like it that much?'

'Mmm, it's wonderful.' She was about to wipe a droplet of apple juice from her mouth, but he beat her to it, drawing his finger across her lips while staring at them intently.

Linnea stilled, mesmerised by his gaze. And when he lowered his mouth to hers, replacing his finger with his lips, she didn't move. He ran his tongue along her lower lip, as though savouring the sweetness of both her and the juice, then his arms came around her waist and he pulled her close. She didn't resist. Didn't want to. Her softness fitted the hard planes of his body perfectly, and she only needed to tilt her head upwards a little in order for them to stay connected. At the same time, his mouth began to caress hers, his tongue soon teasingly asking to be admitted. She gave in without hesitation and matched his playful strokes. It made her whole body sing, every nerve end sensitised and wanting more. When he ran his hands up her back, then down her sides again, caressing her softly through the material of her gown, she shivered with delight and pressed herself closer to him.

They were in the middle of a busy market, but Linnea ceased to notice their surroundings. It was as though they were in a bubble, entirely disconnected from the hundreds of people around them. Some bumped into them or brushed against them as they went past, but Hrafn was solid and barely moved. The kissing seemed to go on for ever, but eventually his hands stilled and he pulled his mouth away after one final whisper-soft touch.

He leaned his forehead on hers, his breath as ragged as her own. 'We'd better go back to the ship. I'll arrange for the others to take a walk too. Come.' He stretched out his hand and she took it, walking beside him in stunned silence.

What had just happened? She desperately wanted to ask or at least pull him back for another kiss, but that wasn't an option. Even if he was the best kisser in the world – and she had to admit she'd never met anyone better, although her experience was fairly limited, it had to be said – he was still her owner. Her slave master. She couldn't allow herself to forget that.

When they drew nearer to the quayside, they let go of each other's hand as if by silent agreement.

The fairy-tale interlude was over.

Chapter Eighteen

Hrafn walked back towards the ship in a daze. What in the name of all the gods had he been thinking? He shouldn't have taken Linnea to the market, let alone kissed her in such an abandoned fashion. It was tantamount to playing with fire, and he was definitely the one getting burned. In fact he was burning all over right now, certain parts of his body painfully aware of how much he'd wanted to continue. *Skítr!* She'd surprised him with her willingness, though, and he would swear an oath that that hadn't been her first kiss. No, Linnea knew what she was doing. Was it all a ruse? A spell, even, to entice him into not selling her? It was the sort of tactics a *völva* would use.

If only he knew.

He'd prefer to believe that it wasn't magic, but merely gratitude brought on by the fact that he had been kind to her and bought her a gift. From what he had observed of Linnea so far, she did not appear to be calculating in the least – well, apart from in her quest to steal something from Thure. But did a woman kiss like that out of gratitude? It had felt like something entirely different.

Odin's ravens, but he'd have to ponder this later.

He allowed the most trustworthy of the men to take the other thrall women for walks around the town. It hadn't occurred to him until Linnea reminded him that he was showing favouritism, and he didn't want anyone to accuse him of that, even if it was true. He knew the next part of their journey was fraught with even more danger than before, and he needed everyone to be at their best and in a good mood. Hopefully these jaunts would help.

When they were all back and it was turning dark, the next group of men went off to find a willing woman for the night. 'Aren't you going to take your turn?' Geir slapped him on the back as he prepared to leave the ship.

'Perhaps later.' Hrafn knew he sounded grumpy, but in truth, he wasn't in the mood for bedding anyone, unless it was Linnea. *Aargh!* He was in grave danger of becoming obsessed with the woman. That kiss they'd shared had been spectacular, and he couldn't decide whether it was better to have experienced it or to have remained in ignorance of just how good it felt. The latter would have been wiser, but whenever he was near her, wisdom appeared to escape him completely. Perhaps he ought to sit else-where in the ship so that he didn't have to look at her all day, every day, but it would seem odd if he suddenly changed places now.

Geir's expression showed astonishment and concern all at once, but Hrafn waved him away. 'Go! I'll be along in a while. I don't like this place. It's making me jittery.'

'If you say so.' With one last look through narrowed eyes, Geir left, but Rurik wasn't so easily fobbed off.

'Come along, brother. You look in need of a large draught of ale.' He dragged a reluctant Hrafn to the nearest ale house and sat him down in a dark corner before calling for a serving wench to bring them refreshment. 'What's the matter?' he asked.

'Nothing. I'm fine.'

Rurik smiled and shook his head, undeterred by Hrafn's glower. 'No you're not. I've never known you say no to a bit of entertainment. Is it her?'

'What?' Hrafn turned to look at his brother and swore inwardly. Rurik had always been too clever for his own good. He was also a good listener and extremely observant.

'You spend a lot of time talking to Linnea, and even more of it staring at her.' Rurik's mouth quirked. 'You like her and you're regretting bringing her, aren't you?'

'No. Yes. Well, maybe.' Hrafn dry-washed his face and reminded himself he needed to get rid of his beard. 'I shouldn't talk to her, you're right. She has a way of . . . I don't know, entering my thoughts, twisting them until I feel like I'm the cruellest person in the world for wanting to sell her. But what's so wrong about it? She's a thrall. It's what she's for.'

'Mm-hmm.' Rurik's smile widened. 'Keep talking.'

'Oh, *þegi þú!* I know it's ridiculous, and I *will* sell her. I need that silver or I'll never be rid of Thure.'

'You don't think you'll have enough without that, what with all the amber and other trade goods? Don't forget your share of the profits from Leifr and Olaf's jewellery.'

'Maybe. I don't know.' Hrafn sighed. 'Are you seriously suggesting I should bring her all the way home again? I'll be a laughing stock.'

'Not if she's your mistress. Anyone with eyes in their head would understand.'

Hrafn scowled at his brother. 'You too?'

'No, no.' Rurik held up his hands and laughed, but it sounded forced, and something in Rurik's eyes told Hrafn his brother was under Linnea's spell too. 'She's all yours, but if by any chance you should want to pass her my way . . . well, let's just say I wouldn't refuse. Who would?'

With a final slap on the back and a teasing smile, Rurik jumped to his feet. 'See you later, brother.'

*

It was a relief to set off again along the winding river. They passed lots of islands for a stretch, then went round a big U-bend to the left, followed by a wider part. Linnea still couldn't get her head round how long and wide this river was. One of the longest in the world? She had no idea. There were narrower sections, more lakes, and endless forests.

'I'll be very happy never to see woodland again,' she grumbled to Eija, who agreed.

'Yes, I keep imagining shadows in there, threatening us.' The two women shuddered in unison.

She was also pleased to be away from the market town with all its temptations. She'd seen Hrafn leave with his brother, not half an hour after he'd kissed her. From what the others were saying, she surmised he was heading for a brothel, or whatever these things were called in Viking times, and that stung. How could he kiss her like that one minute, then go and sleep with another woman the next? It felt like a betrayal, and yet she had no right to feel that way. She was nothing to him except trade goods. He hadn't promised her anything.

Best to put the whole interlude out of her mind. It had been nothing but an impulse on Hrafn's part. No point dwelling on it. And yet she did. Endlessly.

About five or six days south of Koenugarðr, the river made a definite turn towards the south. 'This is where it becomes very difficult,' Hrafn told everyone during their evening meal. 'We have now reached the part where there are rapids, and we'll have to carry the ships again. That's not the worst, though – I've been warned there are local warriors lying in wait for travellers along this stretch. They know we'll be struggling with our ships and will perhaps be hoping to surprise us with an ambush. We can't let that happen.' He looked around, fixing them all with his frostiest stare. 'Every single one of you needs to be alert at all times. Whether you are taking your turn at lifting the ship or acting as lookout, you can't afford to waver for an instant. Is that clear?'

There were nods and murmurs of assent.

'I really can't emphasise this enough. We must be prepared for an attack because, make no mistake, it *will* come. It is just a question of when. I suggest we all keep our axes or swords to hand, or hanging inside the ship's sides so that they are easy to reach. Speed might be of the essence and could mean the difference between life and death. If you can, grab your shields if there is an ambush, as they may be crucial.'

Whenever they were on the river, the men's shields hung along the gunwale – the top of the ship's sides – but during portage they had to be put inside so they wouldn't be in the way. Linnea could see that Hrafn had his own sword suspended from a baldric – a sort of leather strap worn diagonally across his chest – and his axe was in a holder hanging off his belt. She shuddered, and as if he'd noticed, Hrafn looked at the women. 'As for you, keep a knife to hand, and if there is an attack, try to stay behind one of us men. We'll do our best to protect you.'

More nods. There were some very sombre faces and Hrafn added, 'Don't look so glum. We are Svíar and we fear nothing! These southern tribesmen will rue the day they decided to trifle with us, right?'

Expressions brightened and a cheer of assent rang out.

'Remember why we're here – the end will justify everything we are going through.'

Maybe for him, but Linnea didn't have that consolation, and neither did any of the other women. They exchanged glances, but stayed silent. What was there to say after all?

'How many of these rapids are there then?' Rurik, as always eager to help his brother, took it upon himself to lighten the mood

213

further by returning to the known facts. 'And didn't you tell me they have names?'

Hrafn chuckled. 'Indeed, other travellers have named them. I believe there are eight or nine larger rapids called things like Sof Eigi – I assume that one never sleeps – Gellandi – perhaps it roars like a dragon – and Hlæjandi, obviously a laughing waterfall. I have been told you can hear some of them at a great distance. We will know when we come closer. Others have more ordinary names, like Holmfors, a waterfall with islands maybe? That sounds strange, but perhaps it is just strewn with treacherous underwater rocks. Oh, and there's the worst of them all: Eyforr, the fourth one along, which is always violent and very dangerous. Also the loudest.'

'It sounds like we have our work cut out for us, but at the same time they'll be a magnificent sight.' Rurik again, clearly trying to put a good spin on things. He winked at Linnea and she couldn't help but smile back, which earned her a scowl from Hrafn. 'What else should we know?'

Hrafn shrugged. 'There are maybe thirty or forty smaller rapids after that, and lots of islands of various sizes to avoid, but I think if we are careful and use the oars to help with the steering, we can stay on the river there. After that, it won't be long till we reach the sea – perhaps a week, no more. There we can hoist the sail and should make good time, following the coastline all the way to Miklagarðr.'

He glanced at Linnea, as if remembering the map she'd drawn for him. She swallowed hard, a feeling of foreboding creeping into her bones. They were nearing the end of the journey, and she still hadn't managed to even come close to stealing that damned brooch. What was she to do? Hrafn watched her like a hawk, and despite the kiss they'd shared, he still tied her wrist to his each night. Her last hope was to simply snatch it off Thure when they reached Istanbul. Knowing him, he'd want to impress the locals, no matter how hot the weather, and he'd wear his cloak and brooch to show off.

Yes, if Linnea could run up to him, pull it off his shoulder – it didn't matter if she ripped the material, after all – and stab herself in the finger while whispering the words inscribed on the silver, everything might be all right. She remembered the inscription clearly, no need to look. It could work.

It *had* to work.

Men grunting and heaving, taking in huge breaths of air. The *thunk* of tree-trunk rollers being thrown on to the ground in front of the ship, the hiss and scraping of its keel along the rollers and then . . . repeat. Four, maybe five feet at a time, in a seemingly endless progress. It was like two giant snails dragging themselves along without hurry. Patches of grass or moss where the ship could slide directly on the ground were extremely welcome, as that sped up the process, but they were few and far between.

The monotony of transporting the ships through the forest, along the edge of the magnificent rapids, was mind-numbing. But Hrafn stayed vigilant, scanning their surroundings incessantly. As he'd said to the others, they couldn't afford even one short moment of inattention or they'd be lost, their endeavours so far for naught.

And then it happened.

He saw a flash of steel through the trees first, a timely warning that might yet save a few lives, and shouted out a warning: 'They're here!'

The men they'd been expecting, possibly Turkic Pechenegs, Khazars or even Bulgars – it mattered not which – came pouring out through the trees and undergrowth, yelling war cries at the top of their voices now they'd been spotted. But Hrafn and his men could be equally as loud, and their own cries mingled with those of the attackers.

Battleaxes and spears were retrieved from the ships or the men's belts, and soon the clang of metal on metal rang out all around. Hrafn had his beloved sword in one hand and a battleaxe in the other, something he'd trained hard to master at home. It gave him the advantage of being able to deflect blows from two directions and inflict more damage, although it meant he couldn't use his shield. But mostly he went on the attack himself, rather than wait for a strike from an opponent, and he made short work of a couple of the fierce-looking men in loose trousers and below-the-knee tunics.

'Watch out, Hrafn!' Linnea's voice alerted him to the fact that someone was coming up behind him, and he whirled around to deal with it. Swinging his sword furiously, he had no time to see how anyone else was faring, but he hoped they were all holding their own. Geir and Rurik stayed close to him, and seemed to be in one piece so far, and Hrafn heard Thure shouting something so he must still be alive. If there was one thing Thure was good at, it was fighting, and he also excelled at self-preservation.

One man went down, struck by a sharp curved sword. Hrafn heard one of the women scream at the sight, although he wasn't sure which one.

'By Thor, how many of them are there?' Rurik yelled angrily. '*Argr!* Take that!'

They were all tiring, Hrafn could tell, and his own muscles were beginning to protest, but it seemed to him that the attackers were being beaten back. He and his brothers moved forward, trying to drive their enemies before them, and shortly afterwards, one of them – presumably the leader – shouted a command and most of them turned and fled back into the forest, leaving their dead behind. Hrafn was just about to breathe a sigh of relief when he heard a shrill cry of distress from Linnea. As he swivelled around, he saw her being manhandled by three of the attackers, who pulled her into the darkness of the trees at breakneck speed.

'Linnea, *nooooo*!' Without thinking, Hrafn set off after them, plunging into the forest.

'Wait!' A noise behind him told him that at least one of his brothers was with him, but he didn't check. He was completely focused on following the men who had hold of Linnea. They weren't going to get her, the cowards. He wouldn't let them take her – the gods only knew what they'd do to her.

His lungs were near to bursting, and he could only imagine what she must feel like, being pulled along forcibly, but he kept calling out to her and she answered from time to time so that he could follow.

'This is madness, Hrafn,' Rurik panted behind him. 'There are only the two of us. What if . . . there's a whole . . . tribe?'

'Don't care.' He bit his teeth together hard and dug even deeper for an extra spurt of energy. And finally he was rewarded.

Linnea must have become so tired she'd collapsed, and Hrafn came upon her and the three attackers in a small clearing. There didn't seem to be anyone else about, so perhaps the others had run in a different direction to their comrades, but even so, it was only a question of time before someone came to their assistance.

'Quickly, Rurik. We need to get back.'

'Don't I know it,' Rurik growled, but he followed Hrafn as he sprinted towards the group.

Linnea was hanging limp in the grip of one of the men, a dead weight, her eyes closed and her chest heaving as though she couldn't get enough air into her lungs. The other two came to stand in front of her.

'Those two first,' Hrafn hissed at his brother.

They were obviously skilled fighters, but Hrafn and Rurik were much bigger and stronger. Launching themselves at one attacker each, Hrafn brought his axe down on his opponent's sword arm, eliciting a high-pitched scream of pain. The man dropped his weapon and Hrafn followed through with a blow to the chin, using his sword hilt for maximum effect. The foreigner dropped to the ground, his eyes rolling up into his head.

Rurik, meanwhile, was still fighting with the second man, dancing out of the way of a lethal curved sword while swinging his axe and waiting for an opportunity to strike. Hrafn trusted his brother to dispatch the man, and turned his back on them. He had a bigger problem. The third man had started shouting in his own language, gesticulating with a vicious-looking knife towards Linnea, who was still being held in a death grip from behind. She opened her eyes and Hrafn saw panic in their depths, but she didn't utter a word.

'*Skítr*, he'll kill her, Hrafn.' Rurik had just dealt a lethal blow to his opponent, and pushed the lifeless body away while staring at Linnea and her captor.

'I know.'

Hrafn was torn. He was so filled with hatred for these cowards who had dared to take Linnea, but through the red mist, reason told him it wouldn't do her any good if he charged at the man who was holding her. Her throat would be slit in the blink of an eye.

More shouting from the third warrior, but as he waved his knife in Hrafn's direction, away from Linnea, she suddenly came to life and headbutted him with the back of her skull, so hard the resulting crunch of bone echoed around the clearing. He staggered and lost his grip on her, and Rurik grabbed her, pulling her out of reach of the knife just as Hrafn ran the man through with his sword. The attacker fell to the ground with a gurgling noise, which Hrafn ignored. Instead he grabbed Linnea's face between his hands, while still holding his sword aloft, and stared at her. 'Are you hurt? Did he cut you? Speak to me, woman!'

He searched her face for signs of damage, but instead almost drowned in her violet-blue eyes, which were luminous and wide with fright. As he forced his gaze lower, he noticed that her mouth was slightly swollen. Had the warriors hit her? *Aumingi!* It was a good thing they were already dead, or else . . . But Linnea was alive and she was his. A sudden urge to kiss her assailed him with such intensity he almost reeled. He wanted to take her in his arms and claim that beautiful mouth, then tell her—

Rurik tugged at his sleeve. 'Hrafn! Let's go. The others could return at any moment.'

'What?' He blinked and came back to reality. 'Yes, of course. Linnea?'

'I . . . I'm fine. I'm not hurt.' She managed a feeble smile and glanced at his sword, which was perilously close to her head. 'But maybe you should lower that before I lose an ear?'

'Yes. Yes, maybe I should.' He let out a shaky laugh, but there was no time for levity. They were still in danger.

As if they'd both had the same thought, he and Rurik grabbed one of Linnea's hands each and started running.

They had to make it back to the others before it was too late.

Chapter Nineteen

Linnea was sure her lungs were on fire and that she'd never breathe again. Several times during that run, she thought Hrafn and Rurik might have been carrying her between them, as she had no recollection of putting her feet on the ground. But somehow her legs moved, and at last they burst through the trees near the river's edge, where the others waited with the ships a bit further upstream.

'Hrafn! Thank the gods. I thought those trolls had taken you all.' Geir hurried towards them with blood streaming from a wound on the left-hand side of his forehead.

'Brother, you're hurt!'

'It's nothing. A mere scratch. I have a hard head, as you know. You've bashed it enough times yourself.' But Geir's face was ashen and Linnea had the impression his words were mostly bravado.

She sank down on to the ground, not caring whether she got dirty or wet. Her legs simply couldn't carry her any longer. They were more like two lumps of jelly. Leaning her head in her hands, she tried to catch her breath, and gradually her lungs began to cooperate, while her heartbeat slowed down. She was safe, for the moment, and she was extremely grateful to Hrafn and Rurik for coming to her rescue. When those tribesmen had dragged her away, she'd thought that either she was about to die or she was in for a life of horrible servitude as a slave to barbarians. With the forest so thick, she'd been sure that no one would ever find her, even if they looked, but she'd heard Hrafn calling out every so often and managed to shout back a few times. Apparently that had been enough for him to follow their trail.

Drawing in a huge breath, she pushed herself to her feet, ignoring her protesting muscles and the urge to cry. This was not the time for wallowing in scary memories – there was work to be done and they needed to get away from this place. There was carnage all around her, and quite a few men sported cuts and bruises. Some of the women too – Ælfgifu was lying on the ground being tended by Mildred. Ada, whom Linnea had seen shielding Gebbe earlier, had a nosebleed as well as sporting a black eye. She was clearly the stronger of the two Frisian girls and fiercely protective of her friend.

'Do you need me to bind any of your wounds?' Linnea went over to them, but Ada shook her head.

'Not yet. There are others we must see to first.'

Two of their men were dead, while Vidar was badly wounded. He had been slashed across one arm and there was a deep gash with blood pouring out of it, which Odd was attempting to staunch by pressing on it with his fingers.

'You need to make something called a tourniquet.' Linnea more or less pushed Odd out of the way, and used her teeth to rip a piece off the bottom of Vidar's shirt. She swiftly wrapped that around his arm above the wound and pulled it tight. The flow of blood slowed considerably.

'We must sew him up quickly.' Eija materialised at Linnea's side holding a cauldron and various other items. 'We'll need a fire to boil the water, as you said last time.'

Linnea nodded and waved Rurik over. 'Can you help us? If we're to save Vidar, we need boiling water, now. And if Thure has any wine left, can I have it, please?'

'He's not much for sharing, but I'll see what I can do.'

While Hrafn directed some of the men in burying their dead and disposing of the bodies of dead attackers, Linnea and the other women tended to Vidar and a few of the others. Vidar wasn't best pleased when she washed his wound with lye soap and then poured wine all over the cut, but he only hissed in a sharp breath and glared at her.

'Was that revenge for Aldeigjuborg?'

Linnea shook her head. 'No. Hopefully it will save your life.'

Wine didn't contain as much alcohol as vodka or stronger spirits, but since she didn't have access to anything like that, it would have to do as an antiseptic. She figured it was better than nothing anyway.

Eija again did the stitching and Vidar remained stoic, not uttering a word. When they were nearly done, he fainted, but Linnea reckoned that was from loss of blood, not because he couldn't take the pain. 'We've got to put him in the ship and keep him warm.' Hrafn had come over to see how they were doing, and she looked up at him. 'Can we borrow some of those furs you've brought? I think he needs to be wrapped up.'

He nodded. 'I'll see to it. Can you take a look at Geir, please? He's a bit too pale for my liking.'

'Yes, I'll just give Vidar some willow infusion first.'

Once the injured man had swallowed some of what he termed 'that vile concoction', Linnea left him in Eija's care and went to have a look at Geir. He was sitting on a boulder with his eyes closed while Ada washed his head wound.

'That looks like it was quite a blow,' Linnea commented. 'Does your head hurt?'

'Yes. It's as though I have ten trolls hammering on rocks inside.' Geir made a face. 'But I've been through worse.'

'Have you been sick?' Linnea hunkered down in front of him while Ada finished winding a strip of linen round his head.

'Yes, a couple of times. It's nothing.' Geir shook his head but winced at the same time.

'No, it's not nothing. I think you have what I would call concussion. No idea how to say that in your language. But you need to lie down flat on your back for at least two days.'

'What?' Geir's eyes flew open. 'I can't! I'm needed to help carry the ship. Especially now that . . .' He didn't finish the sentence but they both knew what he was referring to – they were two men short. 'Thank you,' he added to Ada, who moved off to tend to someone else.

'I'm serious, Geir. If you don't rest your head now, you'll regret it in future. There could be lasting damage. Your brain has been shaken and it needs time to settle down again.'

He snorted, but Hrafn must have come up behind them on silent feet and heard what she'd said. He put a hand on his brother's shoulder. 'I'd do as Linnea says. We can't take the chance of you becoming permanently harmed. The rest of us will carry the ship with you in it. Now go and lie down, please.'

At first Linnea thought Geir was going to protest again, but then the fight went out of him and he just muttered, 'Fine.'

'I'm going to give you some willow bark infusion too, to help with the pain,' Linnea told him. 'I'll bring it to you.'

As soon as Geir and Vidar were settled on the bottom of their respective ships, Hrafn made everyone move. 'Those *níðingar* could come back at any time. The sooner we leave this place, the better.'

Linnea knew that *níðingr* was one of the worst things you could call someone; it literally meant a person who was nothing.

But either way, Hrafn was right, so no one argued, and even the women took turns at helping to move the ships. The fright they'd had gave everyone added strength, and it was a relief when they were able to take to the water once more for a short stretch and then set up camp on an island for the night.

At least they were less likely to be ambushed there.

Thankfully, there were no more attacks, although Hrafn stayed vigilant throughout the rest of their journey down the great river Dniepr. At one point they went past what was left of a ship – nothing more than a pile of planks, some oars and the carved figurehead of a snarling wolf – with bleached human remains lying scattered around it. This served as a stark reminder of the dangers of inattention, although Hrafn was fairly sure none of his crew needed it. They were all alert, and working as silently and efficiently as possible. Even Thure was taking turns at lifting and carrying now – something Hrafn had never thought would happen.

Having to transport the ships on land for long distances slowed them down considerably, and by his reckoning about five or six weeks had passed since they'd left Koenugarðr when they finally reached what appeared to be the mouth of the river. The water widened into a large lake, before narrowing again and finally turning into a delta that flowed into a bay of the Black Sea.

Well, he didn't know if it was actually called the Black Sea, but that was what Linnea had told him and he had no reason to doubt her. It didn't matter either way.

A cheer went up from every man and woman aboard the two ships as the sails were hoisted and they could all relax. Vidar and Geir were both feeling better, although Vidar wasn't able to row yet, so all in all, Hrafn was satisfied. They'd made it this far; now the end of their journey was in sight, even if they still had some way to go.

What appeared to be a large peninsula jutted out into the sea on their left, but once they had passed that, the vast body of water spread out before their eyes. Hrafn had been told that one could sail straight across it in a southerly direction in order to reach Miklagarðr, but he preferred the more cautious option of staying close to the coast on their right. If they followed this they would come upon the great city eventually. It might take a few extra days, but so be it.

'Can we stop along here to buy more provisions?' someone asked.

'I don't see why not. I've not heard that the people hereabouts are hostile.' And Hrafn was conscious of the fact that their food stores were running low.

'At least there should be plenty of fish in this sea,' Geir said. 'Something other than salmon and pike would be nice. Let's buy some fishing nets when next we make landfall.'

Hrafn had to agree. They could no longer hunt, as they had left the forests behind them.

They made good time, with favourable winds, and found the narrow strait that supposedly led to Miklagarðr. What had Linnea called it? The Bosphorus? Something like that. The town was apparently situated at the end of this sea channel where it joined another great sea – the Grikklandshaf – and this proved to be the case. Around midday, about two weeks after leaving the Dniepr, someone called out, 'There it is – supposedly the greatest city on earth!'

It certainly looked vast, but whether it was the greatest remained to be seen.

As he happened to be sitting next to Linnea, manning the steering oar, and was in a decidedly good mood, Hrafn looked at her and smiled. 'Miklagarðr has some of the best markets in the world, and I have heard that a king lives here, more powerful than any other ruler. Is that what you've been told too?'

She nodded. 'It used to be part of the Roman territories – called an empire – so its ruler is not a king, he's an emperor. In your language I believe that's *keisari*, is it not? Or would you call him the Mikla-*konungr*?'

Hrafn laughed. 'No, *keisari* is correct. Not Mikla-anything.'

'Very well.' It was Linnea's turn to laugh, and Hrafn couldn't take his eyes off hers as they sparkled in the sunlight. She had a serene beauty he'd never come across before, and it wasn't just skin deep. He wondered if it was born of a belief in her own abilities, or something else. Of course, he admired her golden hair, glinting now as if there were real threads of gold woven into it, and his body still remembered the feel of her soft figure against him, but that wasn't the only thing that drew him to her. Her keen mind called to him as well, making him want to spend time with her, talking and discussing every subject under the sun, learning from her about all manner of things. And then he'd like to kiss her senseless . . .

But that would be unwise. Very unwise.

Something twisted inside him. Soon he would have to make the decision whether to part with her, but he would try to delay it for as long as possible. They would be here for several weeks; no need to rush things.

'Hundreds of years ago, the Roman kingdom was split into two – a western and an eastern one. I forget why now.' Linnea looked out over the sea and shaded her eyes to better view the approaching city. 'The western one was overrun by Goths, I think, and disappeared, but this one is still strong at the moment. I believe it's called the Byzantine Empire.'

'I'll take your word for it.' Hrafn wondered how much more knowledge was lodged in that brain of hers. She must have spent years listening to her elders in order to absorb it all.

As they sailed closer, he got his first glimpse of enormous city walls built of stone, some very close to the water's edge. If he wasn't mistaken, there were two or three parallel layers to them, with the innermost wall the tallest. These were interspersed with watchtowers soaring into the sky – twenty or thirty that he could see, so perhaps upwards of a hundred if they surrounded the entire area. The walls looked old but impregnable, and beyond lay what appeared to be a shining city with huge stone buildings. When he'd been informed that hundreds of thousands of people lived here, Hrafn had taken it to be a joke or an exaggeration, but now he wasn't so sure. He'd never seen anything on this scale before in his life, and it seemed entirely possible that such a vast number of inhabitants dwelled here.

'Look, there's the Hagia Sophia!' Linnea pointed to a building up on a hill, overlooking the town, with a domed roof of immense proportions. 'It's a place where people worship the Christian god, and it's famous even in my time. It still exists there, although the . . . er, Serks have taken it over.'

'He seems to need a lot of space, the carpenter's god,' Hrafn muttered, which made Linnea smile.

'No, but the people devoted to him like to create beautiful places in which to pray to him and his son.'

The city filled a large peninsula to the south and spread out towards the west as far as the eye could see. The nearer they came, the bigger everything seemed – houses, palaces and buildings of all kinds peeking up over the walls. It was overwhelming in every sense of the word, and Hrafn found himself frowning. How would they fare here? How did you find the right merchants to do business with, especially if you didn't speak the local language?

'You must find an interpreter,' he'd been advised, and someone had given him the name of a trustworthy man, but how on earth was he to locate one man among so many? The people he'd talked to hadn't told him that.

They came to the opening of an estuary of sorts, guarded by watchtowers and walls on either side. Hrafn knew there was a massive iron chain suspended between them that could be raised to stop the town being attacked from the sea. Thankfully it seemed to be lowered today, and they continued towards a harbour on the south side.

'The Golden Horn,' Linnea muttered, not looking as fazed as Hrafn felt by everything around them. She was staring towards a wider stretch of water further in, a basin several hundred feet across.

'What?'

She translated. 'That's the name of this estuary. I'm guessing it's because of its shape if you look at it from above.'

'How are you supposed to see it from above? We're not birds.' Hrafn shook his head – sometimes she said the strangest things.

But his question made her smile again. 'In my time, humans can fly.' At his raised eyebrows, she added, 'Oh, not by themselves, but using . . . um, carriages with wings propelled by—'

'Let me guess – lightning?' he interrupted her. 'Yes, yes . . .' He swallowed a sigh. Her tales were just too unbelievable for words and he didn't want to hear them. 'Well, here's the harbour I was told to aim for.'

The towering walls turned inwards, making the shape of one of those Roman letters meaning five that Linnea had shown him – V. There was a gate into the city on one side, which was apparently the only one they were allowed to use. Through it Hrafn spotted the large storage buildings he'd been told housed enormous amounts of provisions of every kind. And in the distance, he could still glimpse the dome of that Sophia building, or whatever Linnea had called it.

They rowed their ships close to the quayside, which was built of massive blocks of stone, and moored. As soon as they jumped on to dry land, people rushed to greet them, babbling away in a variety of tongues, none of which Hrafn understood until he heard a tiny street urchin shouting, 'I help? I help, master?' in accented Norse.

He waved the boy over. 'You there, come.' He held up his hands and shouted to everyone else, 'Thank you, but we don't need anything right now. Go!' A shooing motion and shake of the head had them backing away, still chattering to each other but with dissatisfied expressions. Hrafn turned to the boy. 'Haluk the interpreter, do you know him? Haluk?' He hoped he was pronouncing the name correctly.

'Haluk? Yes, yes. I find. You wait.' The boy's eyes shone, dark in his sunburned face, and a contrast to his very white teeth. He was wearing a threadbare brown tunic that only reached as far as his little knobbly knees, which were as grubby as the rest of his bare legs and feet. As if confirming how poor he was, he held out his hand. 'You pay?'

Hrafn hid a smile and fished a tiny piece of silver out of his pouch. 'This will be yours if you find me Haluk, but not before, understand?'

The boy nodded but seemed troubled. 'You no ask . . . other?'

'No, I will wait for you, but hurry, please.'

A huge grin showed that the boy was pleased with that answer, and he dashed off with barely a wave.

Thure, who had come up to stand next to Hrafn, muttered, 'Are you sure you can trust such a young one?'

'Who knows? But at least he spoke a little of our language. Let's see if he can help.'

The sun was beating down on them and Hrafn ordered the sails to be rigged as awnings over the middle of the ships. 'We need shelter or we'll all perish from the heat.' Everyone was soon huddled in the shade, shedding their overtunics and trying in vain to waft cooler air inside their shirts.

To Hrafn's surprise, the little boy returned after a fairly short while, followed by a small man in a bright green tunic with a pattern of squares and circles in a contrasting material. Underneath, he had narrow trousers inside black boots that reached to mid calf. His hair was trimmed short and he wore no hat, despite the heat. He made his way along the quayside and bowed. 'I am Haluk. How I can serve?' He waved the little boy away with an imperious gesture, but Hrafn threw the lad a larger piece of silver than the one he'd shown him earlier and called out a thank you. Then he turned to Haluk.

'I was told to find you by a man named Tryggve. He came here some two years past. Do you remember?'

Haluk smiled and then bowed again. 'Tryggve, yes, great man. We did good trade. I help you too, yes?'

'Thank you, yes please.' Hrafn breathed a sigh of relief at having found the man. He'd thought it would be like finding one ant among thousands in a stack, but perhaps interpreters made sure to stay near the harbour. Either that or there weren't many who spoke his language. The gods had certainly been looking out for him today, and he would show his gratitude soon.

'Tell me what you bring,' Haluk urged. 'I find best buyer for goods. I see have pretty womans. Good, good.'

The man was staring straight at Linnea, and Hrafn had to stop himself from snarling that she wasn't for sale. Yet. 'I will, but first I must introduce you to my brother, Thure. He owns the other ship. Ah, here he is.'

Thure seemed uncharacteristically quiet, and Hrafn wondered if he was as overwhelmed as he himself felt. It wouldn't last long, though, and Thure brightened considerably when Haluk, after some haggling, agreed to a favourable rate for his services as interpreter.

'Let us hope we can conclude our business here as speedily as possible,' Thure said, rubbing his hands together in anticipation. 'But first, I would like to sample some of the local food. I can smell it from here!'

The scent of exotic spices hung in the air, and Hrafn's stomach growled in agreement, so Haluk's first task turned out to be easy – to find them a meal.

'Anything except fish,' Hrafn told him with a smile. He'd had enough fish to last him for quite a while.

Linnea had never been keen on spicy food, and would have preferred to cook their usual fare, but it would have seemed rude to refuse, so she ate a little of what she was offered. It was some sort of vegetable stew made with beans or chickpeas, served with coarse bread. That, at least, she enjoyed very much. She didn't think she'd ever gone this long without bread before, and the mere texture of it had her closing her eyes in delight. The scent and taste of olive oil and oregano brought back memories of holidays by the Mediterranean, but she quickly suppressed those. It did no good to dwell on the past – or in her case, the future; she had to focus on the here and now.

'I never thought I'd miss bread as much as I do,' she confided to Eija. 'I used to have it all the time, but we've gone without for months now, haven't we?'

'Yes. I would normally only have some in the autumn, after harvest time. I like this stew, though.' Eija grinned. 'At least it's not made with barley or fish.'

'True.'

They all spent the night on board their ships, which was cramped in the extreme but Hrafn was adamant. 'No point wasting silver on lodgings,' he decreed. 'It will be cooler here by the water, and I'd wager there are fewer bed bugs too.'

'But what about . . . um, there are no bushes or trees here.' Linnea tried to phrase her question as delicately as possible, but heard several guffaws anyway.

'You'll have to use a bucket. We'll rig up some sort of small tent.'

It wasn't ideal, but it was better than nothing.

The following morning, the man Haluk returned. 'We sell fur first,' he told them. 'Before start smell, yes?'

'That sounds like a good idea.' Both Hrafn and Thure agreed. The furs were prepared, the insides dried out, but who knew what the heat and humidity here would do to them?

Linnea watched as the pelts were unloaded on to the quayside, relieved that the man hadn't said that selling the slaves should be the priority.

'Those of you who brought your own furs, come with us. Everyone else stays to guard the rest of our goods, please,' Hrafn ordered.

'What about us women? Can we go for a walk to have a look around?' Linnea dared to ask. Now that she was here, she wanted to experience ninth-century Byzantium in all its exotic glory, and she'd never been to the Hagia Sophia. Besides, there might be an opportunity to snatch Thure's brooch in a throng of people where he'd be hemmed in on all sides. She had to look for a chance, as time was running out.

Haluk, who seemed to have understood her question, scowled at her. 'Womans not walk alone. Not done here. And you thrall, yes? Not sell today.'

Linnea glared back, but it was no use.

'No, stay here, please. I can't guarantee your safety otherwise,' Hrafn added.

She wanted to shout at him. What did it matter? Soon he wouldn't be worrying about her safety in the slightest. It was probably more a question of him not wanting to lose a big fat profit. She sent him a dagger look, but he turned away and there was nothing she could do except stay put.

It was going to be a long, boring and very hot day.

She spotted the little boy who'd helped Hrafn the previous day. He was lurking on the quayside, presumably on the lookout for work of some sort. She beckoned him over. Perhaps he could relieve the tedium by telling them about his city. She'd have to pay him to make it worth his while.

'What's your name?' she asked as he vaulted on board with alacrity.

'Kadir, lady.'

'Well, Kadir, have a seat, please, and tell us more about this place.' Linnea held up a piece of amber. 'I'll give you this if you spend some time with us.'

A huge grin greeted this suggestion. 'Of course, lady. My pleasure.'

Chapter Twenty

Hrafn, Thure and four of their men followed Haluk through the massive gate, weighed down with piles of furs. Dark bear skins at the bottom, followed by tawny wolf pelts, soft mink, marten and fox. The bushy tail and shiny orange-red of a fox's summer coat shimmered in the hot sun, as did the silver grey of their winter ones, the latter mostly caught in the north by Saami. There were beautifully patterned lynx skins as well, bundles of tiny reddish squirrel furs, and larger ones from beaver. Hrafn was certain the merchants here couldn't find a better selection anywhere.

'No weapons. Leave outside,' Haluk told them, although he'd already said that the day before. Apparently a large group of Norsemen had tried to plunder the city some ten years earlier, and the inhabitants had long memories. These days no one was trusted.

Hrafn had hidden a folding knife in his ankle boot, but left his sword and axe on board the ship. Fierce-looking guards by the gate searched them, then waved them through. Either they didn't notice the knife or they didn't consider it a dangerous enough weapon to confiscate. Hrafn was glad – it wasn't much, but it was better than nothing and made him feel marginally safer.

The streets that spread out before them seemed to have been planned in some sort of straight pattern, although there were smaller whimsical alleyways radiating out on each side of the main thoroughfares. As they moved further into the city, some streets had colonnaded walkways with roofs, presumably to protect people from sun or rain, and they were paved with large slabs of whitish stone. It was a far cry from the lanes of Birka or Aldeigjuborg, with their mud and planks, and Hrafn couldn't help but be impressed.

The rows of houses that lined the streets had permanent stalls at the front, selling every item imaginable. Meat, fruit and vegetables vied with spices, perfumes and healing potions, while in other booths shimmering lengths of fabric were spread out. Jewellery, pottery and objects made of glass competed with ivory, silver and bronze. There was so much to look at, it was difficult to know which way to turn first.

'Look at that juggler. He's good, isn't he!' Geir, who had brought almost as many furs as Thure, stared at a street entertainer who was throwing five strangely shaped objects into the air at once, and catching them in turn without ever dropping one on the ground. At the same time, agile acrobats bounced past in their quest to earn a few pieces of silver by showing off their skills, while less fortunate people sat and begged for alms. There were also women with knowing eyes and come-hither smiles sashaying past or standing in doorways, as well as stern men in special robes whom Hrafn took to be servants of the Christian god.

The hustle and bustle was an attack on the senses the like of which he had never experienced before. Added to the sights were the smells of exotic – and sometimes almost suffocating – spices and perfumes, mingling with hot, sweaty humanity and animal excrement. And finally the noise, a more or less deafening cacophony of sounds comprised of sellers crying their wares, people chattering, laughing and arguing, animals braying, and the scuffle of feet and rumble of wheels on paving slabs.

It was too much.

'Over here!' Haluk called, waving them towards a row of stalls that were selling furs of every kind. 'We find good buyer.'

They'd briefly discussed prices the day before, and Haluk informed them that these were decided by state officials and therefore no one could cheat. There were standard weights and measures, and often vendors were checked to make certain they stuck to the rules. Hrafn wasn't sure what he thought about this. On the one hand, it was good that he couldn't be underpaid, but on the other, there was little chance of haggling for a better profit. Still, he hoped to do well enough.

As it turned out, the prices were much higher than he'd expected, and the entire group left the fur merchants' booths very satisfied indeed, their leather pouches clinking with silver.

'Two and a half *dirhams* for just one marten skin! Who'd have thought they would pay that much?' Geir exclaimed happily. 'They're only tiny. And as for the wolf and lynx . . .'

He wasn't the only one who was ecstatic. Thure was in such a good mood, he bought a trinket for Bodil on their way back to the ship, and he kept clapping poor Haluk on the back.

'I told you my furs would do well.' He grinned at Hrafn. 'You should have brought more.'

Hrafn refrained from telling him he was hoping for an even greater profit from all the amber jewellery he had with him. No point spoiling his half-brother's mood.

'Let us buy some food and take it back to the ships,' he suggested instead. There were people selling food and drink everywhere, the only difficulty being what to choose.

'You will like these,' Haluk said, pointing at what looked like little folded pieces of bread. 'Very sweet.'

'Very well, we will try.'

They turned out to be the crumbliest of breads, stuffed full of dried fruits, nuts and honey, and flavoured with something very delicate, which Hrafn immediately loved. Everyone else back at the ships was equally delighted, especially Linnea. Her entire face became suffused with pleasure, almost as if . . . But Hrafn wouldn't allow his thoughts to travel in that direction. He did enjoy the sheer joy in her eyes as she opened them again, having taken her first mouthful.

'Mmm, that was the best thing I've eaten since I arrived in . . . well, at your house.'

'I can see that.' He sent her a teasing glance. 'I never thought a woman could derive so much pleasure from merely eating.'

She smiled back. 'You have no idea. If you ever tasted chocolate, you'd understand.'

'Tchook-lut?'

'No, *chocolate*. It's the best thing in the world.'

'You've clearly never lain with a man.' Hrafn knew he probably shouldn't have said that, but her ecstatic look made him blurt it out. It was exactly how he'd pictured her face after he made exquisite love to her . . . in his dreams. He shook his head at himself. He was in deep trouble, and never had he felt so torn about anything in his life.

Linnea raised her eyebrows. 'And what if I have and I *still* prefer chocolate?'

Hrafn wasn't sure if she was teasing or not, but he had to keep this light or he wouldn't be answerable for the consequences. He raised his eyebrows at her. 'Then you've not slept with the right one.'

To his surprise, she gave him a shove that nearly sent him over the railing and into the harbour. 'You men! Always think you're so good in bed. Well, I don't want to insult your manhood or anything, but I doubt you're that good.'

'Who says I was talking about me?' But as he looked deep into her eyes, they both knew he was. He held her gaze, watching as her cheeks turned pink. He was very tempted to show her then and there what she'd been missing. They were sitting very close together, their arms touching, and judging by the tremor he felt shooting through her, he was convinced she'd enjoy it immensely. As would he. 'Perhaps one day we can put it to the test,' he whispered. The words were out before he'd had time to think them over, and he wanted to punch himself. What a *fífl* he was, to be sure.

Linnea looked as though she wanted to do the same, and the light left her eyes. 'I doubt that too. You'll have to prove it to someone else. I don't think my future owner will want to share me with you.'

With those words she stood up and headed for the makeshift latrine. It was a long time before she came out from behind the hangings.

Linnea was close to tears, but she didn't want to give in to them. She hadn't cried much since just after the accident. The floods she had shed then ought to suffice for a lifetime. But how insensitive could Hrafn be? What was the point of teasing her about his prowess in bed when he must know full well some old Turkish guy was going to get the pleasure of taking her whenever he felt like it?

Stupid bastard!

She wanted to hate him – did hate him right now – but she also knew this was temporary. Every time he came near, she lost all reason and forgot that she was supposed to dislike him intensely. He'd captured her and brought her against her will on this perilous journey where she'd almost been raped and kid-napped and had suffered multiple other hardships. After all that, he was going to sell her to the highest bidder with no thought to her feelings on the subject. And yet . . . if he took her in his arms and kissed her again, the way he had in Koenugarðr, she knew she would melt instantly. There was no way she'd be able to resist him.

She loved him. *Damn him!*

'I don't want to love you,' she muttered, while trying not to breathe in the noxious fumes from the bucket. It was time to get out of here, in every sense of the word, but Linnea was sure that however far she travelled, she'd never be rid of her feelings for Hrafn.

He was a barbarian, a slave trader, a kidnapper and any number of other horrible things, and yet he was also clever, brave, just, strong and focused . . . and unbelievably attractive. Linnea sighed. Was she simply fixated on his handsome exterior? She didn't think so, even though not a day went by without her discovering some new thing about his appearance that she liked. The way his eyes went from ice-lagoon blue to warm Mediterranean indigo when something pleased him. His mouth quirking up on one side when he was secretly amused and didn't want to show it. How his forearm muscles flexed ever so slightly when he had his hand on the tiller and the sun reflected off the golden hairs on his arm. The fact that his eyelashes were almost black even though his hair and beard were different shades of blond . . .

She clenched her fists. 'I don't *want* to notice any of that,' she hissed to herself. Didn't want to remember anything about him when he was gone.

Because soon they would be parted, one way or another, and even if Linnea managed to get back to her own century, Hrafn wouldn't be there. She'd never see him again.

Why did that thought hurt more than contemplating spending the rest of her life in the ninth century?

She must be going insane.

'I obtained a good price for those girls. Turns out you made a great choice for me after all. People here seem to have a liking for Mercians.'

Hrafn stared at Thure. Was he actually pleased with something Hrafn had done for him? *Odin's ravens!* That had to be a first. 'Well, good,' was all he could think of saying.

Haluk had just helped Thure to sell the three thralls who had travelled with him, and Hrafn caught Bodil's look of satisfaction as they departed with their new owners. She clearly thought she was different, but Hrafn knew his half-brother better than that. It was just a matter of time before Bodil met the same fate. The only reason she was still here was because Thure wouldn't want to have to pay for a woman's services during the rest of his stay.

'Your turn, isn't it?'

'What?' Thure's question brought Hrafn's gaze back to him.

'Your thralls. Time to sell them, right? No point paying for food for them any longer. Haluk has plenty of buyers.'

'Oh, that. Yes, but I'm waiting for the best offer,' Hrafn lied. The truth was that having spent months in their company, he had come to like all four women – not just Linnea, even though she was undoubtedly special – and he was finding it harder to part with them than he'd thought. They weren't just thralls, a commodity, but people he'd bonded with. He admired their inner strength and resilience, their quiet dignity and acceptance of their fate. And although he'd not had much to do with the Mercian women during the journey, he had even felt a small dart of regret watching them being led away. What in the name of all the gods was the matter with him? Perhaps he was sickening for something.

'Don't wait too long,' was Thure's parting shot, after which he sent Linnea a long, hard glance. It was fairly obvious that he wanted to see the back of her and was hoping she'd be sold to someone vicious.

That was *not* going to happen if Hrafn had anything to do with it. He'd be choosing her new owner with care.

As if conjured up by Thure's words, Haluk came hurrying along the quayside, accompanied by a young man. In his early twenties, at a guess, the man was a picture of manly perfection – shining blue-black hair cut into a short style, luminous dark eyes, and a chiselled countenance like those of the statues Hrafn had glimpsed inside the city. Slightly tanned skin stretched over a good physique, and as the man came to a halt next to Haluk, his wide smile revealed even, very white teeth. The clothes he wore showed him to be wealthy: his vividly red knee-length tunic was of exquisite silk fabric and covered in woven patterns that included the use of gold thread. He had an ornate belt with a dagger attached, its hilt winking with gemstones, and wore trousers that were tucked into finely decorated leather boots. The best thing about him, however, in Hrafn's opinion at least, was that he did not have the haughty expression he'd seen on some of the others who'd come to the quay to look at Thure's thralls. This man looked happy and carefree, as if he enjoyed life and didn't take his high status too seriously.

Haluk bowed as usual. 'Hrafn, I have here buyer for you's womans. Brother said hurry.'

'Thure said that?' Hrafn could feel his brows coming down in a fearsome scowl. *The black elves take the man!* Why did he always have to meddle? He should stick to his own business.

'Yes, yes, and here perfect buyer. Want two womans. Two!'

Haluk was obviously very excited by this, and held up two fingers for emphasis. 'Them.' He pointed at Linnea and Gebbe, who was undoubtedly the prettier of the two Frisian girls.

'No.' Hrafn surprised himself with the strength of his refusal, then realised he was being stupid and sentimental, something a Norseman should never be. Was he turning soft? He couldn't let that happen or he'd lose all honour. 'At least, not that one,' he amended, pointing at Linnea. 'The other two are sisters. They wish to stay together.'

He had no idea if Ada and Gebbe were related, but he knew they were great friends and they appeared to be glued to each other. Anyone with eyes in their head would have noticed Ada's protective attitude towards Gebbe, and he was loath to part them. Haluk sent him a wide-eyed look, obviously surprised that he would even mention their wishes, let alone take them into account, but Hrafn ignored that. Beckoning the women over, he went to help them up on to the quayside while Haluk translated what he'd said to the prospective buyer.

'You know why I brought you here?' Hrafn said to the two women, speaking in a low voice. He didn't want anyone to overhear them, not even his own men. No, especially not them.

They nodded, looking resigned and sending each other what he could only interpret as a desperate last glance. 'We know,' Ada said. Always the stronger of the two, brave and stoical. 'We are prepared.'

'Would you be content to be bought by the man speaking to Haluk if I make it clear he has to keep you together? He does not look repulsive to me.' Hrafn didn't know why it should matter to him that they approved, but it did. He hoped to Odin no one ever found out that he'd even asked.

They blinked and stared at him with something approaching

hope. 'We'd be living together?' Gebbe had found her voice. 'We won't be separated?'

Hrafn shook his head. 'Not if I make it a condition of the sale.' He shrugged. 'Obviously I can't guarantee that the man is honourable enough to stick to this agreement in future, but it will be up to you to prove that he is better off keeping both of you.'

'We can do that.' Ada was smiling now, and Hrafn saw the buyer's eyes light up when he noticed. She was definitely much prettier when she was happy. Why had he never seen that before?

'Good. Let us talk to him then. Come.'

The buyer seemed much taken with both women's hair, which shone with gold and copper lustre respectively in the midday sunshine. And he exclaimed over their unusual eye colour. 'Blue like sky and grey like storm,' Haluk translated expansively, sensing a good profit here and nodding as if his life depended on it.

'Is he willing to buy both girls and swear an oath to keep them together?' Hrafn asked. 'Else I won't part with them. They go as a pair or not at all.'

Via Haluk, the buyer declared himself perfectly willing and, again according to the translator, swore on his mother's grave. Hrafn thought this a touch too dramatic, and wasn't sure he really could trust him, but he couldn't take the women back home with him, and this seemed a good compromise. Ada and Gebbe were happy – or as happy as anyone could be while still a thrall – and he could let them go with a good conscience.

'What do you say?' he asked them one last time.

'We would rather stay here together than go back to your homeland and perhaps be separated,' Ada declared. 'We will be fine and I have heard thralls can buy their freedom here if they earn enough.'

'Then I hope you do one day. May the gods go with you.'

The transaction completed, the two girls collected their few belongings and said goodbye to Linnea, Eija and the little boy Kadir, who could be found hanging around the ships more often than not. Hrafn watched them go with regret but also relief. He felt that he'd achieved the best possible compromise, and hopefully no one would ever know what it had cost him to part with them. He swore never to trade in thralls again – it simply wasn't for him.

Chapter Twenty-One

Another week went by, and still Hrafn showed no sign of wanting to sell Linnea. She was perplexed, but also frustrated because she wasn't allowed up on to the quay without a guard.

'It is for your own safety,' Hrafn told her when she protested that she'd stay close to the ship.

'But I only want to stretch my legs. Your men can keep an eye on me from where they're sitting.'

'No, I'm not taking any chances.'

If she couldn't walk on her own, there was no opportunity to get near Thure and snatch his brooch. Not that he'd been wearing his cloak much in any case – the weather was far too warm for that. Occasionally, if he was going ashore of an evening, he'd bring it with him, but Linnea could only watch him from afar, always out of reach. And there was no way of sneaking on to his ship to steal the brooch either.

What was she going to do? Time was running out.

She'd contemplated asking Kadir to help her; they were fast friends by now, having spent a lot of time chatting and whiling away the hours by playing board games Rurik taught them. Kadir was quick as a flash, and seemed happy to do almost anything for a small remuneration. But the thought that he might be caught and accused of theft stopped her. Who knew what they did to thieves in this country? Probably something utterly barbaric, and she couldn't risk the little boy having to suffer on her behalf. There had to be another way.

Early one evening, when Hrafn had returned from a particularly good day of trading, Thure came over and climbed on board. He glanced at the bales of silk and bundles of spices being loaded on to the ship and nodded.

'You look pleased, brother, so I thought perhaps some celebration was in order. I brought wine, and an excellent one it is too. Glides very smoothly down the throat.' He slapped Hrafn on the back and sat down next to him without being asked.

'I'm not overly fond of the stuff.' Hrafn shook his head, but Thure was already pouring a measure into a beautiful green glass.

'Just a little in honour of your success. I hear you did well today. And look, Haluk found me these excellent glass cups. Aren't they splendid? I might keep two for myself and sell the others when we get home. *Skál!*' He handed a glass to Hrafn and carefully clinked his own against it. Glass was massively expensive and he appeared to be keeping that in mind.

'Oh, very well, just one. *Skál* yourself.'

Linnea, who was sitting nearby with Eija, quietly contemplating the comings and goings of the harbour, saw Hrafn grimace as he downed his drink. He really didn't seem to like wine, but then it was an acquired taste. She remembered hating it the first time she'd tried it, but later started to enjoy it more.

Thure chattered on about the profit he'd made from some fish teeth he had brought. Linnea knew he meant walrus tusks, which were highly valued here. Hrafn had a few to trade as well, but mostly he seemed to be concentrating on amber and jewellery, plus the furs that had been sold the first day.

'Right, well, I'd best be going. I'm off to find some of that tasty stew Haluk brought us the other day. Better eat our fill of it now, before the monotonous fare of our home journey has to be endured once more.' Apparently full of bonhomie for once, Thure gathered up his amphora and glasses, and climbed on to the quay.

Linnea watched him go, but noticed that he loitered by his own ship for a while, staring over in their direction. What was he up to? She turned to make a comment to Hrafn and saw him slump to one side, falling on to the ship's planks. 'Hrafn? What on earth . . . ? Hey! Someone help me here, please!'

A couple of his men came over, but started laughing when Hrafn emitted a noise like a loud snore. 'Ah, he's just had too much to drink,' one of them said. 'Leave him be. He'll sleep it off.' Joking amongst themselves, and throwing Hrafn amused glances, they went back to the other end of the ship, where they'd been playing a board game and betting on the outcome.

'But . . .' Linnea exchanged a glance with Eija. 'This isn't right,' she whispered. 'You don't get drunk from one glass of wine, and as far as I know, he hadn't had anything else before that.'

'It is very strange, to be sure.' Eija chewed her lip.

'Help me make him comfortable, please.'

Together they laid him out straight, with a tunic for a pillow and his cloak thrown over him.

'Something doesn't feel right about this. Thure is still standing over there, and he drank a lot more than Hrafn.'

'Yes, and he seems in a good mood. I can hear his braying laughter from here,' Eija muttered.

Linnea cast a furtive glance around and saw that the other men were all busy with their game amid much raucous laughter. It was a shame neither of Hrafn's brothers was present – they might have taken this more seriously – but they'd gone off earlier. Since the others were so inattentive, she quickly removed Hrafn's bulging leather pouch and stuffed it into a wooden container half full of dried peas left over from their journey. The pouch was clinking with silver and she buried it deep so that no part of it showed. No point taking any chances; she didn't want Hrafn to be robbed while he slept.

Was that perhaps Thure's intent? Had he given his half-brother some kind of drug so he could take his profits and go home without him? Or surely he hadn't . . . poisoned him? Linnea shivered and reached out to touch Hrafn's neck. No, he still had a steady pulse, thank goodness. She wouldn't put it past Thure to do him harm, but to murder his own brother, that was going too far even for him, wasn't it? Rurik and Geir would never stand for it . . . unless he'd killed them too. Jesus! What was going on here? Her brain started working overtime, coming up with one frightening scenario after another, but reaching no conclusions.

Not long afterwards, however, Thure came sauntering back towards them with a sulky-looking Bodil in tow. He smiled at Linnea and said, 'Come, we are going for a walk.'

She shook her head. 'I don't think so. I'll need to tend to my . . . er, master. You must have given him too much wine. He seems to be unwell.' She glared at him to show that she didn't believe for a second that wine could have such a severe effect, but his smile just widened, growing positively wolfish.

'Oh, he won't be waking up until morning at the earliest, or so the wise woman assured me.'

'Wise woman?' Linnea's insides knotted. So the bastard *had* drugged Hrafn.

'Hálfdan, bring the blonde thrall up to me!' Thure shouted at one of Hrafn's men.

'What?' Hálfdan looked up from the gaming board and blinked.

'You heard me. Be quick about it. My brother has arranged for me to take her to a prospective buyer. Come now, I don't want to be kept waiting all evening.'

'But he never said . . .' Hálfdan looked confused and glanced at the others for help. They all shrugged. As neither of Hrafn's brothers was here, no one dared stand up to Thure, who was technically their master.

'Bring her!' Thure's face took on a look of thunder that had Hálfdan rushing over to Linnea and grabbing her arm.

She tried to resist. 'This isn't right. Hrafn hasn't arranged any such thing. Let me go, you *fifl*!'

But Hálfdan wasn't listening. Linnea guessed that he feared Thure's temper more than anything else, and he wasn't risking his position for the sake of a thrall.

'Eija . . .' Linnea took her friend's hand. 'Tell him as soon as you can,' she hissed.

The Saami girl nodded. 'I will.'

Before she had time to even gather her possessions, Linnea found herself lifted bodily on to the quayside, where another of Thure's men, Dag, took her arm in a firm grip.

'Let's go. Haluk is waiting,' Thure muttered, and set off towards the city gate, tugging Bodil behind him.

'Why do I have to come?' she whined. 'Are you taking me somewhere afterwards?'

But Thure didn't reply.

As they passed through the gate, Linnea noticed Kadir lurking in the shadows but wisely keeping well back. She knew he was very bright and sent him a meaningful look, trying to convey that she was being forcibly abducted. Kadir's brows came down in a scowl, and he nodded at her as if he understood. Obviously there wasn't anything he could do about it, small and insignificant as he was, but the more people who were aware of what had happened, the better. Kadir and Eija could both inform Hrafn, as and when he woke.

Although by then it would probably be too late.

Was she going to be sold? Or . . . killed? No, Thure wouldn't gain anything by that. Perhaps he meant to take his revenge, and finish what he'd started in Aldeigjuborg, and then kill her.

She shuddered. Whatever he had planned, it couldn't be good.

The two women were frogmarched through what seemed like an endless number of streets. At any other time, Linnea would have been fascinated by the buildings and statues and the people milling around, but right now she was dreading their destination too much to care about her surroundings. She vaguely noticed that some streets were for pedestrians only, and blocked at either end by steps that prevented carriages from entering. Others were paved in marble – clearly an upmarket shopping district. Everywhere was surprisingly clean – no emptying of chamber pots into the streets here, the way people in medieval Europe had done – and Linnea guessed that this was due to Roman engineering. They'd been masters at putting in drains and water pipes or channels, making their cities almost as advanced as twenty-first-century ones. The Byzantines had clearly utilised these skills when laying out their streets, and the buildings themselves had a definite Roman look about them.

'Where are we going?' she called out, trying to make herself heard over the din of all the people milling around them, talking Greek and God only knew what other languages. Where was the damned man taking her? He'd said something about Haluk, but normally the interpreter came to them, not the other way round. She tried to hasten her steps so that she'd draw level with Thure. He was wearing his cloak, and if only she could snatch the brooch and run down one of the nearby alleyways, she might have a chance.

'You'll soon find out,' was his infuriating answer.

'I don't think so,' she muttered, and threw herself forward, taking Dag, the man holding her arm, by surprise. She managed to break loose, and lunged for Thure's shoulder. The brooch was big and bulky, and would surely rip the material if she pulled hard enough, but although she got her hands around it, she didn't have time to put all her weight behind the move. Her gaoler was faster than she'd thought and grabbed her from behind, yanking her away.

'*Noooo!*' Linnea's whole being was flooded with despair. She was going to be stuck here in the ninth century for ever, with no way of ever going back to her own time. When Thure left, he'd take her final hope with him.

'What in the name of Odin are you doing, woman?' he snarled. 'Do you think you can steal from me again and get away with it? Hah! Never! Dag, hold on to her tighter and don't you dare let go.' Thure's eyes were spitting fury at her, and he pulled a knife out of his ankle-high boot, brandishing it in front of her face. 'Try that again and I'll cut your throat, profit or no profit. Understand?'

Linnea just sent him a death glare. There was no point replying.

The crowds thinned out as they proceeded further into the city and over to the western side. They passed some fairly seedy-looking tenement buildings, seven or eight storeys high. Linnea knew these were called *insulae* in Latin, although presumably here there was a Greek word for it. Either way, it was where the poorer people lived. Thure kept walking. She guessed no one in this area would be able to afford slaves.

Eventually they reached a prosperous neighbourhood, judging by the size of the houses. These were two-storey buildings with tiled roofs and walls of brick and stone in pleasing patterns. They looked almost like the drawings of Roman villas that Linnea had seen in textbooks. Haluk was waiting outside one of the largest ones, and his face split into a grin as they approached.

'Ah, Thur-eh, you here. Good, good. Lady is waiting.'

'You are sure she wants two thrall women? She won't set them free?'

'No, no, need thralls. She no like husband much. Gived him two sons, enough. Now want peace. Christian woman, no like . . . er, how you say? Concubin?'

'Concubine, yes. If she doesn't like them, why is she buying two?'

'For husband. Keep him away. No touch wife more. Thralls work and if husband look and want, wife no see. What doesn't see . . .' He left the sentence hanging, but his smile said it all.

'Ah, I understand. She's going to turn a blind eye to what the husband gets up to, eh? Clever. Don't see why she couldn't just divorce him, but still . . .'

'Divorce?' Haluk's expression was questioning.

'When you say you no longer want to be married to someone. Divorce and you can marry another person.'

Haluk shook his head. 'No, no, with Christian god, not possible. No divorce. Ever.'

'How strange.' Thure, clearly impatient, changed the subject. 'Well, lead on. Let's proceed with the sale.'

'Follow please.'

As they headed through a central archway and into a large courtyard with a burbling fountain in the middle, Bodil punched Thure on the arm. '*Argr!*' she hissed. 'You said you'd never sell me! *Aumingi!* After everything I have done for you, this is how you repay me? I can't believe—'

Her words were cut off by Thure putting one hand over her mouth and the other round the back of her head, squeezing hard. '*Þegi þú!* You're a thrall, mine to do with as I please, and I've had my fill of you and your whining. Try your wiles on your new master instead. He looks to be rich enough to buy you as many trinkets as you wish. I'm not wasting any more silver on you.' He let go of her with a little shove, which sent her careering into Linnea, and gesticulated around the courtyard. It was undoubtedly opulent, but whether the master of the house would want to spend any of his wealth on two slave women was debatable.

Linnea, who for once felt very sorry for Bodil, steadied the woman and put one hand on her arm. 'Don't bother, Bodil,' she whispered. 'You're well rid of him.' And so was Linnea. At least this time Thure didn't intend to rape her. One consolation in the circumstances.

Bodil looked at her with eyes that were brimming with tears, but then her gaze hardened and she nodded. 'You're right. Thank you. He doesn't deserve me.'

Thure guffawed at this statement, but Linnea gave Bodil's arm a squeeze of solidarity.

She stepped closer to Haluk and hissed, 'Hrafn told you I wasn't for sale unless he said so. He's going to be furious with you, and believe me, you don't want to see him in a bad temper. Hrafn is much more dangerous than his brother – you'll be very sorry you crossed him. Don't do this!'

'Hrafn not master. Thur-eh is,' was Haluk's reply, but there was a flicker of fear in his gaze, and he made sure to scurry away from her and shelter on the other side of Thure.

The utter coward! Linnea was so angry she would have happily punched the man, but with Dag watching her every move, she wouldn't have the opportunity. There was no time to say or do anything else in any case, as the mistress of the house was walking towards them. She was attended by two maids and an older manservant who looked to have some important role in the household, judging by his fine clothes.

The lady herself was dressed in a long, straight tunic of costly material, tightly fitted around the wrists but otherwise fairly loose. The fabric was an intense blue, with geometric designs all over, and it was studded with pearls and jewels that twinkled in the light of nearby torches. It was a very formal outfit, showing the lady's status clearly, and she also wore a jewelled belt, and a large shawl draped over her head and shoulders. A cloud of perfume enveloped her and almost made Linnea cough – it was so long since she'd smelled anything like that, her nose wasn't used to it.

After a short haggling session, a hefty pouch of silver coins was handed over to Thure, and without so much as a backward glance, he and Dag left the way they'd come. Linnea noticed he didn't bother to bow to the lady he'd just done business with. 'Oaf,' she muttered. 'He has no manners, does he?'

'No, never had,' Bodil concurred.

Linnea took a deep breath and turned to Haluk, who looked as though he couldn't wait to escape as well. 'Before you go, please can you translate the lady's instructions for us, as we won't understand a word she says.'

'Just follow other womans. Will show you. Now go.'

He waved them away, indicating that they should follow their new mistress's maids. Since there was nothing else they could do, Linnea took Bodil's hand and nodded. 'Come.'

Chapter Twenty-Two

Hrafn was convinced that the god of thunder himself had taken up residence inside his skull, making an insistent noise that wouldn't give him any peace. It pierced his brain like Thor's bolts of lightning, and he wished he could sink back into oblivion. Eventually he realised that it wasn't a god, but someone shouting his name and shaking his shoulders, while intermittently slapping his cheeks.

'Brother, wake up, in the name of Odin!'

He cracked open one eyelid and squinted against the pearly light of dawn. 'What?' he croaked. His tongue appeared to be glued to the roof of his mouth and there was a foul taste when he tried to swallow. What on earth had he been drinking? Bad ale? Then he remembered Thure's wine and opened the other eye as well, swearing under his breath.

'The trolls take him. Where is he?'

'Where's who?' Rurik came into focus, and behind him, Geir. Both looked extremely concerned, which made Hrafn wake up a little faster.

'Thure,' he muttered. 'Gave me some wine. Going to strangle him when I see him next.'

Rurik shook his head. 'Too late. Someone else got there first.'

'What?' Hrafn sat up too quickly and winced, putting both hands to his aching head. Where in Hel had Thure bought that wine? The after-effects were vile. Quite the worst hangover he'd ever had in his life.

'Thure is dead. Some of his men brought him back just now. Stabbed by someone who knew what they were doing, aiming straight for the heart.'

Blinking, Hrafn regarded his brothers. He wondered if he was still asleep and dreaming, but they looked very real. 'Dead? But why? Thieves?'

'No. Well, perhaps. Dag said they were invited to join a game of dice in a hostelry of some sort. Since Thure had silver to spare after selling Bodil and Linnea, he was in a great mood and decided to join them, and—'

'He did what?' Pounding skull notwithstanding, Hrafn shot to his feet and grabbed the front of Rurik's tunic. '*He sold Linnea?*'

His brother calmly detached Hrafn's hands from his clothing. 'No need to shout. Hálfdan said you'd agreed it and Thure came to fetch her last night. Dag and the others managed to bring back most of the silver, and stopped the cheaters from stealing Thure's big brooch as well, so nothing much was lost.'

'That's not the point! I would *never* have agreed to such a thing,' Hrafn hissed, glaring at his brother even though he was fully aware this wasn't Rurik's fault.

No, it was all his own. He should have been more vigilant. Should have suspected Thure would do something like this. It wasn't as though he hadn't seen the signs, and he knew of his half-brother's malice. Once someone crossed him, they usually lived to rue the day. He'd probably been obsessed with punishing Linnea from the moment she escaped the intended rape. Perhaps even from the moment she'd stolen his brooch and Hrafn had claimed her. '*Argr!*' he shouted. 'We've got to find her. Buy her back. Now, this instant! Let's go.'

'What are you saying? Hálfdan told us she was perfectly willing to go, and you had to sell her at some point. If Thure found a good buyer and we have the silver, then—'

'Loki take the man! I wasn't going to sell her at all. I've changed my mind. Besides, I very much doubt she went willingly.' Hrafn bent to scrabble around on the planks at the bottom of the ship. 'And where is my money pouch? Did the *aumingi* steal that as well?'

'Linnea didn't want to go.' Hrafn had forgotten about the Saami girl, who'd been sitting quietly nearby, but who piped up now. 'Thure took her away by force.'

'Of course he did.'

Rurik and Geir looked at each other. 'But Hálfdan—'

'Fetch him,' Hrafn ordered curtly. 'I'll have the truth out of him.'

'He and the others were playing a board game. I . . . I think they were just used to doing what Thure said,' Eija added.

'Be that as it may, I will hear it from him. Actually, no, wait, I'll go and find him myself. Where is my pouch? Did Thure take that too?' Hrafn stared at Eija.

'No, Linnea hid it so no one would find it. It's in here.' To Hrafn's surprise, the girl rummaged in a container of peas and brought out his fat leather purse.

'Thank you.' He calmed down slightly as something occurred to him and he sank down next to her. 'I mean it, thank you, Eija. You could have taken all this silver and run off, and we would never have known. And yet you chose to stay. Why?'

She looked down and sighed. 'I had to tell you about Linnea. And I didn't want to be alone in this city with all the foreigners. I . . . don't belong here. But if I have to stay, it is better to be someone's thrall, because I wouldn't know how to go on by myself. Not without a husband or family.'

'Is that what you want, Eija? A husband?'

She looked at him as if he was daft. 'Of course, but . . . it's not for me.'

Hrafn put out a hand and squeezed her shoulder. 'Perhaps it is. I'll see what I can do. But first I need to find Linnea. Do you know where Thure was taking her?'

'No, sorry. Just into the city.'

That was no help at all.

After attempting to revive himself with ale – not entirely successfully, since it made him feel rather queasy – Hrafn followed his brothers over to Thure's ship, where the men had laid their leader on the planks near the prow and covered him with his cloak. Some of them stood on the quayside looking uncertain, while a few of the others sat at the opposite end of the ship polishing their weapons in a desultory fashion. In death, Thure seemed peaceful enough; if it hadn't been for the large dark stain that had spread through from his tunic, he could have been asleep.

'What happened exactly?' Hrafn let his gaze roam the assembled company. 'Who was with him?'

'I was,' Dag admitted. 'Thure was in a celebratory mood and wanted some more wine, so we went into a hostelry. There was music and men playing games of dice, and he was invited to join in. He thought it was his lucky night because he won quite a lot to begin with, but then he started losing . . .'

'Yes, and?' Hrafn fixed Dag with an icy glare. Not that the man could have stopped Thure even if he'd wanted to, but to have allowed him to be killed, that was another matter altogether. It was Dag's task to defend his leader at all times, with his own life if necessary.

Dag's cheeks turned a bit ruddy. 'I . . . well, we had all had a fair amount of wine, and it was quite by chance that I saw one of the foreigners cheating. He put his hand over the dice as soon as they'd landed on the table and very quickly flipped one over. I told Thure, who of course became furious and upended the whole table. You know what he was like; his temper flared at the slightest provocation. There was a lot of shouting, but we didn't understand any of it, just that they weren't admitting to having done anything wrong.' Dag shrugged. 'It was a bit difficult to argue against them when we didn't speak their language.'

'Did Thure have a weapon?'

'Of course. He had a knife in his boot and he tried to attack the man who'd been cheating, but one of his friends pulled out an even bigger blade and just stuck it into Thure's heart. I swear, it all happened so quickly, I had no chance of preventing it.'

Dry-washing his face, Hrafn closed his eyes and sighed. He could imagine the scene, and he believed Dag. There would have been nothing he could do. 'So what happened next?'

'I rushed to catch Thure as he fell, and while I was attending to him, the cheater and his friends disappeared. Everyone else pretended nothing had happened and they'd not seen a thing. The owner of the hostelry obviously didn't want any trouble, so he had us evicted as well. It wasn't long before I found myself outside in the street with . . .' Dag nodded at the dead man. 'I carried him back here as quickly as I could.'

No mean feat, as Thure was far from light.

'Very well. What is done is done. We'll have to find somewhere to bury him on the way back. We leave as soon as I've retrieved my thrall woman. Which reminds me . . . Hálfdan, over here, please. I have a bone to pick with you. And Dag, did you see where Thure took Linnea and Bodil?'

'No, it was dark and we walked for quite a while. I doubt I'd

259

be able to find my way back. The interpreter was there, though; he would know.'

'Send someone to find him.'

'Will do. In the meantime, these belong to you.' Dag held out Thure's enormous silver brooch and two pouches of silver and bowed deeply. 'As the next eldest son of Eskil Thuresson, we owe allegiance to you now, Jarl Hrafn. We will swear our oaths to you whenever you're ready.'

'Thank you. I appreciate your loyalty and I will accept your oaths as soon as the pressing matter of my thrall has been re-solved.'

Hrafn hadn't thought that far ahead, but now he realised he had to step into Thure's shoes. Eskilsnes, the settlement at home, was his; as his father's second son, he inherited all Thure's holdings because his half-brother had no children. That was a strange thought, as he'd never expected anything. He'd always been sure Thure would have many sons, which was why he'd been intent on making his own way in the world. Eskilsnes was a wonderful inheritance, but it meant responsibilities he wasn't sure he was prepared for. Still, he'd have to shoulder them. It was his duty.

And at least he could make some positive changes from now on.

Linnea and Bodil followed the servants across the courtyard, which was surrounded by a colonnaded walkway, and headed towards the back of the house. They passed quickly through a magnificent reception room with a marble and mosaic floor, walls painted with beautiful frescoes in fresh colours, and some comfortable-looking couches at one end. She could just imagine the owners reclining on them while having guests for dinner, although perhaps the Byzantines had moved on from that Roman custom and ate sitting up. Who knew?

The back part of the house was less grand, but still impressive, especially when compared with a Viking longhouse. No stamped-earth floor here, no wooden benches with furs to sleep on. Instead everything was of sculpted stone, tiles or stucco, and mostly painted white. Bodil's eyes grew larger with every step they took, and Linnea heard her gasping as they were shown into what looked to be a luxurious bathroom in the Roman style. A sunken bath with steps down into the gently steaming water was positioned in the centre of the room, with stone benches and basins along some of the walls. There were piles of freshly laundered towels on a table, as well as jars of what was presumably soap or bath oil. Two long tunics in the Byzantine style hung on hooks on the wall, and although they were much less ostentatious than that worn by the mistress of the house, the material was good and not in the least threadbare.

'Are those for us, do you think?' Bodil whispered to Linnea. Her voice echoed round the room, making her jump.

'I would guess so.'

The serving women confirmed it with gestures that indicated the two newcomers should take a bath and change into the clean clothing. Linnea didn't know whether to laugh or cry. On the one hand, it would be marvellous to feel truly clean again after so long. Although she and the others had bathed in the rivers, taking turns to keep watch so the men wouldn't see them naked, it wasn't the same as a having a proper bath with heavenly scented soap. And having been sitting in the harbour on board the ship for weeks in the sultry heat, Linnea felt distinctly grubby. She nodded to the women and said, '*Efcharistó.*' She'd been to Greece on holiday once and had learned that one word – thank you; she hoped it was approximately the same in Byzantine times. It seemed so, as she was rewarded with a small smile.

'I'll wash your hair if you wash mine,' she suggested to Bodil.

At least they could enjoy this part of their new captivity, even if what came next was going to be an ordeal to say the least.

She suppressed a shudder. Best not to think about that yet.

'Haluk is nowhere to be found. Everyone just shakes their head when we ask after him, and the other interpreters are pretending they don't know anyone by that name. The *aumingi* must have left the city with the profit he's made from us and Thure. Fenrir and all the *jótuns* take him!'

Rurik threw himself down on the quayside next to Hrafn, who'd been sitting with his legs dangling over the side, staring out across the harbour. The light was fading, the sun sinking into the horizon and creating the most amazing colour display in the sky, but he couldn't have cared less about any of nature's beauty. He only wanted Linnea back. Nearly the whole day had gone by without so much as a single lead as to her whereabouts. How was he going to find her? If no one would help them, it would be like looking for one particular piece of straw in a giant haystack.

He was too restless to be still and jumped to his feet, beginning to pace in front of his brother. 'He must be somewhere. Perhaps we can bribe someone. These people seem to do anything for silver. Wait!' An idea occurred to him and he wondered why he hadn't thought of it before. He stopped and scanned the surrounding area, then beckoned to a couple of street urchins. 'Kadir, is he here? Kadir?'

'*Naí, naí!*' One of the boys nodded and held out his hand.

'For the love of Odin,' Rurik muttered. 'He's telling you no and then expecting a reward? Honestly, these children are all thieves . . . Who brought them up?'

'No, I think that word means "yes", even though it sounds like our "no".'

Rurik made a face. 'Really? They're mad, these Grikkjar.'

Hrafn pulled a silver coin out of his pocket and held it up to the boy. 'Fetch Kadir and it's yours. Go!' He pointed, and the lad nodded again and sprinted off.

A short while later he returned with Kadir in tow. The boy looked wary and reluctant, not at all like his usual ebullient self, and Hrafn saw him glancing around as if expecting to be caught by someone. 'Kadir, what is wrong? Where have you been? I haven't seen you all day.' He threw the promised coin to the other boy while Kadir sidled closer, still visibly on edge.

'You brother here?' he asked, staring at Thure's ship.

'Thure? No, didn't you hear – he is dead. He was killed last night.'

'Dead?' The boy blinked, his brown eyes opening wide, then to Hrafn's astonishment he smiled. 'He dead?'

'Yes, yes, but I don't see why that is cause for celebration. Well, at least not for you,' he amended. For those who had known Thure, he might not seem such a great loss, but Kadir couldn't be aware of that.

'He bad man. He take nice woman.' Kadir pointed at Hrafn's ship and then waved at Eija, who waved back.

Hrafn grabbed the urchin's thin wrist, trying his best not to crush the delicate bones. 'You saw him take Linnea?'

'Yes. Bad man.'

'I know.' Hrafn's patience was wearing extremely thin. 'Did you see where they went? Or do you know where Haluk is? He was going there too, so he would know, but I can't find him.'

'Haluk bad man too.' Kadir's eyebrows came down in a fierce scowl. 'He sell you woman.'

Hrafn took a deep breath to stop himself from shaking the boy. 'Yes. I know. But *where*, Kadir? Where is she?'

'Oh, she at Theodora house.'

'Who is Theodora?' Hrafn wanted to roar in frustration but kept a tight rein on his temper.

'Rich man wife. *Biiiiig* house.' Kadir flailed his arms to show just how enormous. 'I show?'

'Yes! Yes, please. Now! There's not a moment to lose. Rurik, you're in charge here. Make sure everything is ready for departure. We may need to leave in a hurry. Have all the supplies been loaded?'

'I'll find out. Just go, we will be ready.'

Hrafn spun around and took Kadir by the hand. 'How fast can you run? I'll pay you extra if you can keep up with me.'

The little boy grinned and took off so fast, Hrafn was the one nearly left behind.

Chapter Twenty-Three

'I've never worn anything this beautiful. Isn't it pretty? This material is such a deep green colour, and so soft. And look at this belt! All these shiny stones. Oh, I think I'm going to like it here. Thure did me a favour after all. Little did he know!' Bodil's delighted laughter echoed round the small bedroom they'd been allocated up on the second floor of the villa.

Linnea swallowed a sigh. Perhaps Bodil had landed on her feet – the poor woman had been taught by Thure to use her body as a means of advancing in the world, and she was clearly used to it and resigned to this fate by now – but Linnea herself was far from pleased.

It could have been worse and they could be slaving in a hot kitchen at this very moment, being beaten into submission by some evil owner, but somehow even that seemed preferable to what was their likely fate. Linnea didn't want to be anyone's concubine, especially not some middle-aged Byzantine man who would probably sell her as soon as he'd tired of her. And she might still be beaten, because there was no way on earth she'd pretend to be happy about having to sleep with him. She'd fight him all the way.

Just like she'd done with Thure.

The memories from that day hovered at the edge of her mind, but she resolutely pushed them aside. This was different. Her new owner would probably rape her, but not out of malice the way Thure had been hell-bent on doing. He'd be doing it because he felt it was his right. And unfortunately, in the world she was currently inhabiting, it was. A violent shudder shook her body from head to toe, and she bit her teeth together hard to stop them from chattering. The thought of what was to come had her stomach tying itself in knots, and she had to clench her fists as well to keep the panic at bay.

'I think you'll find those stones are bits of glass,' she commented, somewhat acerbically, but Bodil didn't seem to notice. Perhaps to her, anything that glittered was precious. For Viking women, glass beads were a high-status item, so she probably felt richly rewarded already.

Too anxious to sit still, Linnea went to stand by the window, which overlooked the courtyard. There were servants coming and going, silently efficient, and all looking as though they knew their place. She'd be the only one rebelling against her fate, causing a commotion, but she doubted anyone would help her or even feel sorry for her. They'd think she was being unreasonable, needing to be taught a lesson.

Argh! If only she'd managed to snatch that brooch off Thure the night before. She could have been back in her own century and well out of his reach, the bastard. Provided it worked that way, of course, something she'd never know now. But what was the use of what ifs? She was stuck here for ever, unless Eija could persuade Hrafn to do something about it. Why would he, though? He might have been dragging his feet about selling her, but he would have had to do so eventually. That was the whole purpose of bringing her, after all. No point undoing what had already been done. He'd be more likely to demand the silver from Thure and be done with it.

A commotion at the main entrance drew her gaze and she saw a man striding in with a large entourage. This had to be their new master – it couldn't be anyone else. Dressed even more luxuriously than his wife in a baggy knee-length tunic of shimmering yellow with matching trousers tucked into boots, he radiated wealth and power. This was confirmed by the richly decorated belt that encircled his waist, and the jewelled hilt of a dagger hanging from it. His dark hair was cut short and brushed into a neat style, his cheeks swarthy with stubble, as if he'd been travelling all day. He pulled off a cloak and handed it to the nearest servant, walking towards the fountain where his wife waited to greet him with a polite bow. Today the lady had her hair put up in some complicated style and covered by a gossamer-thin veil fastened with glittering pins. From their body language it was clear that Haluk had been telling the truth last night – these two barely tolerated each other.

That was a shame.

'Our master has arrived. Do you want to see?' Linnea gestured towards the window, and Bodil came rushing over.

'Oh! He's very dark-haired, isn't he? Quite a change from Thure.' Bodil leaned forward, then giggled. 'I think he saw me. He was looking this way. Will he like my hair? It's very shiny today now it's been washed. Some of Thure's men were saying the Serks like women with blonde hair because their own women are all dark.'

'I think you'll find he's a Grikkjar, not a Serk,' Linnea muttered, but Bodil waved her comment away.

'What difference does it make? They're all dark-haired.'

Linnea wasn't sure that was the case, but she couldn't be bothered to argue. How soon would they be summoned by their new master? That was the only thing on her mind at the moment, even though she was probably better off not knowing.

*

267

'That's the house he took Linnea to? You are sure?' Hrafn loitered on a street corner with Kadir, and stared towards an enormous building with a reddish roof.

'Yes, yes. Theodora house. I see her.'

'Very well. Thank you for your help. You'd better go home now. I don't want you involved in this any more.'

'In-volved?' Kadir tilted his head.

Hrafn sighed. 'I have to go inside and take Linnea back. If you stay with me, you could be hurt. Or punished.' He mimed a knife cutting the boy's throat. 'Here, I will pay you for your help, then you have to leave. Understand? You can go and help my brother instead.'

He pulled a heavy silver arm ring off his wrist and held it out to the boy. It was much more than the errand had warranted, but he had a feeling he might never see Kadir again, and he wanted the lad to be taken care of. Not to have to scrounge around the harbour looking for the smallest of rewards. He was a bright boy; he deserved better.

'For me?' Kadir's brown eyes rested on Hrafn, serious in the narrow face. 'Too much.'

That made Hrafn smile. Honourable, as well as bright. That was an unusual combination. 'No. It is what you deserve. Thank you for helping me, I am very grateful. I wish you well.'

'I also. Thank you.' In an unexpected gesture, Kadir threw his arms around Hrafn's legs and hugged them tight. Hrafn couldn't resist; he bent to pick the urchin up and hugged him back.

'I will see you again next time I come here,' he murmured. There might not be a next time, but if there was, he would definitely want to meet Kadir again.

'Yes, yes, next time. I be here.' The boy's eyes shone and he waved happily as he set off back towards the harbour.

Hrafn's smile dimmed. It was time for serious business. He'd briefly contemplated asking to buy Linnea back, but he knew Thure well enough to be sure he would have sold her to someone unreasonable. And if he knocked on the door asking for her, but was then refused, they would know who had taken her if he managed to steal her away later. Also, they'd be much more on their guard. But how was he going to enter that house and snatch her back? Because he wasn't leaving this place without her.

He'd rather die.

A serving woman had brought them an evening meal, but Linnea wasn't hungry and only nibbled on a piece of bread. It was made with olive oil and rosemary, lovely and fresh, but to her it tasted like sawdust and she had trouble swallowing it.

'Isn't this stew wonderful? So rich, and the smell is just . . . *mmm*. And this cheese – I've never tasted anything like it!' Bodil was still enthusing about everything and it was trying Linnea's patience, her already jangling nerves stretching to breaking point.

'I wouldn't know. You can have mine too, if you want.'

'Really? Oh, thank you!' Bodil was either supremely thick or completely self-centred, as she didn't seem to notice Linnea's dark mood at all. Possibly both. It seemed that nothing could take away her euphoria at having landed in such an opulent environment. Linnea felt mean for even wanting to try to dampen her spirits. Why not let her enjoy it?

The sounds coming from downstairs indicated that some sort of dinner party was going on; there was much chatter and laughter, as well as music floating out into the courtyard. How long would that go on for? And would the master want entertainment later? Linnea hoped he'd send just for Bodil, as he had only seen her so far. Perhaps he'd be satisfied with one blonde at a time?

Probably not.

Sitting by the window, leaning her chin in one hand, she stared desultorily into the darkness until something made her straighten up. There was a small noise from the entrance passage, where it seemed a servant was posted as a guard at all times. The man had been walking back and forth, but he disappeared from view suddenly, and although Linnea waited, she didn't see him again. Instead, a dark shadow flitted into the courtyard and along the colonnaded walkway, blending in with the darkness against the wall. There were torches in sconces at intervals, but the shadowy figure managed to keep away from those for the most part.

What was going on?

At one point there were two torches close together – more difficult to avoid – and Linnea gasped as they shone briefly on a dark-blond head. Hrafn? It couldn't be. Her heart did a somersault, hope and joy suddenly flooding her whole being. He hadn't abandoned her after all. Peering into the gloom, she tried to make out his shape, but he had disappeared. Soon afterwards, however, she heard footsteps along the balcony walkway outside their room. She knew their door was locked, but she ran over to it, and as the footsteps passed by, she called out softly, 'Hrafn! In here!'

There was a brief silence, then she heard a whispered 'Linnea?'

'Yes, yes, I'm here.' She scratched on the door with her nails, not daring to make more noise than that.

'What are you doing? Who are you talking to?' Bodil looked up from the last morsels of her meal, licking her fingers. 'Oh!' Her eyes opened wide as the key turned in the lock and the door opened, admitting Hrafn, who closed it behind him as stealthily as he could.

'Thure hasn't changed his mind, has he? No! He can't make me go back.' Bodil's mouth set in a mulish line.

'Shh.' Hrafn looked them up and down. 'Are you well?' he whispered. 'Have they hurt you?'

'Don't be stupid. Look, we are treated like queens!' Bodil stood up and did a twirl, showing off her tunic and belt. 'And you should see their bath house and the room downstairs. It's like a palace!'

'Shh!' Both Hrafn and Linnea shushed her now and she flashed them an angry glare.

'Well, I'm not leaving. Tell that oaf he can find himself another woman. I want no more to do with him.'

'Thure is dead,' Hrafn hissed. 'He was killed last night in a brawl. So you can safely come back with us. Quickly! We must leave now, before it's too late.'

Bodil crossed her arms over her chest. 'I told you – I'm staying right here! You go if you want to, but you can't make me come with you.'

'Are you absolutely sure?' Linnea put a hand on Bodil's arm. 'You don't know that man downstairs yet. What if he's worse than Thure and . . . hurts you?'

'He won't, I'll see to that. If I please him, why would he?' Bodil grinned. 'And I know how to please a man, trust me.'

'Leave her, Linnea. There's no time for this.' Hrafn had opened the door a crack and was peering out. 'I think I hear footsteps. We have to go now.'

'Bodil?'

But the woman made a shooing motion. 'Go, I tell you. I want to stay, honestly. Enjoy your life, as I'll enjoy mine.'

Hrafn grabbed Linnea's hand and pulled her towards the door. 'Come!'

Together they tiptoed out and ran on silent feet along the balcony towards a staircase. Hrafn's hand felt big and safe around Linnea's, and she revelled in the sensation. *He came for me!* She had hoped he would, but had not dared to believe it. But they weren't safe yet. She was another man's property. She doubted her new master would part with her even if he got his coins back. And Hrafn didn't seem like he was in a bartering mood anyway.

Just as they reached the bottom of the stairs, a cry was heard from the entrance.

'*Skítr!* They've found the guard. I had to knock him senseless.' Hrafn glanced around and ducked into a doorway. 'Is there another way out of here?'

'I don't know. We've spent all day in our room, and yesterday we only walked through the main area and the bath house.'

'Which way is that?'

'Over there.' Linnea pointed and Hrafn set off in that direction.

They made it to the bath house, but there were shouts behind them now and the sound of running footsteps upstairs. Linnea's escape must have been noticed. A cold dread settled in her stomach and she had a hard time breathing, even though they weren't running very fast.

'There has to be another door,' Hrafn muttered as they came to a halt near the sunken bath. Torches lit this room and those nearby, as though they had been made ready for use later on. The illumination helped them to evaluate their options. 'In there maybe?' He pointed to a doorway, but when they looked, it only led to a small changing room.

They dashed across to the other side of the bath and through another door. Hrafn slammed it shut behind them, and as it had some type of miniature bar as a locking mechanism, he pushed that in place to seal them in.

But it was a dead end.

Linnea stared at him. 'What are we going to do? They will kill us both for this.' She had sudden visions of beheadings or other gruesome types of execution and wanted to be sick.

'They'll have to get past me first.' His mouth tightened with determination and he pulled a knife out of his ankle boot.

'You can't beat a whole group of people with just a knife.' Linnea knew he could hold his own in most fights, but the odds against him were astronomical. The servants here were bound to be well armed, at least compared to Hrafn's single small blade, and he was but one man.

'I can try.' He laid the knife down on a bench for a moment and came towards her, putting his arms around her and pulling her close. 'No one is taking you away from me, Linnea. It will have to be over my dead body, and I assure you I will wound a good few of them first. Perhaps that will give you a chance to escape. Run down to the harbour if you can. Rurik and the others are waiting, ready to leave.'

Linnea wound her arms around his neck and shook her head at him. 'You're mad, do you know that? But thank you, I appreciate what you are trying to do.'

He nodded. 'I may never have another chance to do this, so . . .' He looked deep into her eyes, then bent to give her a soft kiss.

Perhaps he had meant that to be it, but Linnea had other ideas. She pulled him closer and kissed him back, putting her heart and soul into it. He didn't seem to mind in the slightest, and reciprocated, caressing her mouth with his, using the tip of his tongue to tease a response from her that had her toes curling in their worn Viking shoes. It felt as though the kiss went on for ages, but at the same time it was only moments before there was banging on the door and angry voices shouting what were presumably Greek swear words and commands.

They pulled apart slightly, while still holding on to each other, and Hrafn put his chin on the top of her head. Linnea in turn leaned against his shoulder, but there was something hard and cold in the way. At first she just moved her cheek, annoyed at the obstruction, but then the implications of what was right in front of her eyes sank in.

'Hrafn! You have Thure's brooch!'

He regarded her with raised eyebrows. 'Yes, and . . . ?'

'It could be our way out of here. If it works, that is. Let's try. What have we got to lose?'

'What are you talking about? What has the brooch got to do with our current plight?' He scowled at her as if annoyed that she wasn't taking their situation seriously.

'Don't you remember what I told you? This was what I meant, the thing I was looking for in Thure's chest, that made me travel through time. Maybe it can do the same for both of us now.' Linnea reached up and started to unfasten the big silver circle from his cloak, but he put his hands around her wrists.

'Linnea, I thought you had stopped with that ridiculous tale. Honestly, I don't care about your background; you don't need to make up stories to account for your knowledge and—'

'Shush!' She put her fingers over his mouth. 'Hrafn Eskilsson, you listen to me and listen carefully. I. Am. From. The future. That is a fact. Now, if you let me hold that brooch for an instant and do as I say, I will prove it to you, I promise.' She pinned him with a stern gaze. 'Are you not even a tiny bit curious? What if it turns out I'm telling the truth?' He was vacillating, she could tell from his narrowed gaze. 'After that kiss, can you not trust me just a little?'

He drew in a deep breath and pushed his hair away from his face with one hand. 'Very well, we have nothing to lose. They'll be through that door any moment now.' It was true. Linnea could hear the sound of wood splintering. Someone must have fetched an axe. 'Here.' He swiftly unpinned the brooch and held it out to her. 'What do you want me to do?' He picked up his knife and held it in one hand while she grabbed his other one.

'I'm going to prick our fingers with this sharp pin, and at the same time you must say the words "*Með blóð skaltu ferðast*" out loud.'

'*Með blóð skaltu ferðast?*' He looked doubtful, but she gripped his hand tightly and positioned one of her fingers close to his.

'Yes. Are you ready? We have to do it at the same time or it might only work on one of us. In fact, I don't even know if it will transport more than one person, but . . . Never mind. Hold on to me, and for the love of Freya, don't let go. On the count of three. *Ein, tveir, þrír . . . Með blóð skaltu ferðast!*'

As they said the words, she stabbed at their fingertips with the pin and saw blood welling up on both of them. She held tight to the silver brooch, and to Hrafn's arm with her other hand, as her head started spinning and the world tilted on its axis. Vaguely she heard him exclaim something, but she didn't register his words. She was too busy trying not to be sick as the spinning intensified and that weird noise, as though a thousand voices were shouting and whispering at the same time around her, started up inside her head.

Just as she was sure she couldn't stand another second of it, everything went black.

Chapter Twenty-Four

Hrafn registered unfamiliar noises at first, and then the fact that his head had finally stopped whirling. He'd never felt so nauseous in his life as when Linnea had stabbed his finger with Thure's brooch – no, his brooch now – and he couldn't account for it. The sight of blood had never bothered him in the slightest. So what had happened?

He opened his eyes and saw a multitude of colours, as if he was lying inside the rainbow. Had someone killed him and dumped him on the Bifröst bridge? But he didn't remember dying, and surely he would have felt something?

'Hrafn? Hrafn! We did it!' Linnea's face appeared above him, as if she'd sat up abruptly, and she was grinning down at him. 'It worked! It really worked – I don't believe it.'

Slowly, in case the nausea was about to return, he raised himself on his elbows and looked around properly. He wasn't on the Bifröst bridge, but in a small room filled with shawls of every possible colour. Hundreds of them, neatly stacked on shelves, hanging off pegs, draping over each other. Some encased in what looked like clear glass, others not. And a couple tied on to hideous sculptured heads without faces. He chuckled. 'So much for dying,' he muttered.

'Dying? What do you mean? We're safe. No one can kill us now.' Linnea looked around. 'Although we probably shouldn't stay here or they'll think we're thieves. Can you stand up?'

'Of course I can.' Hrafn shook his head, which seemed fine now, and got to his feet. 'Is this a merchant's booth? I've never seen one like this before.'

'I suppose so. But if I'm right, we're in Istanbul now, not Miklagarðr, and it should be the year 2017. We need to leave. No one has noticed us yet, so let's just walk out of here calmly and keep walking if anyone calls out to us. Pretend you don't hear them.'

She took his hand and Hrafn let her lead him towards a doorway that was also draped with shawls. Pulling these to one side, she stepped through and he followed, walking into a booth with more shawls – honestly, how many could one man sell? – and out through a door that opened on to a busy street. The merchant did shout something, but Linnea just held up their joined hands to show they hadn't touched anything, and apparently that was enough to convince the man they weren't thieves.

'Come. We need to find our way down to the harbour.'

Hrafn sent her an amused glance. 'You sound like you are in charge. What happened to my meek thrall?'

She snorted. 'I was never that! And here, there are no thralls, so we are equals. Keep that in mind, will you? And try to remember what I told you about women in my era.'

Hrafn was about to reply, but just then he was forcibly made aware of his surroundings as something honked like a goose behind him, only twenty times louder. 'Odin's ravens! What is that?' He stared in disbelief at the wagons driving past him at speeds he had never even dreamed about. And not just wagons, but strange contraptions with only two wheels that somehow stayed upright even with a person sitting astride them, as though

277

riding a horse. The wagons were mostly covered and . . . was that glass underneath the roofs? It couldn't be. He'd never seen glass like that, only drinking vessels and beads.

'Those are cars and motorcycles. Oh, and bicycles and buses.' Linnea pointed up into the sky as the foreign words came pouring out of her. She seemed excited and happy, whereas Hrafn felt mostly confused. 'And up there are the aeroplanes I told you about, remember? The wagons that fly people across the sky. They are real, see?'

Staring up into the clouds, Hrafn saw a metal tube with wings and round glass panels that did indeed appear to be flying. 'Are you telling me there are people inside that?'

'Of course. It looks small because it's so far up, but each one of those can carry more than a hundred people,' Linnea assured him.

Humans flying? The year 2017? This had to be a dream. He looked around him again. Nothing was familiar. Everyone in this street was wearing strange clothing and clutching unfamiliar things that they poked at with their fingers or held up to their ears. The wagons, whose names he had already forgotten, made a terrible noise and emitted foul-smelling clouds of smoke, and the buildings . . . they were like nothing he'd ever seen before. Huge windows made of what also seemed to be clear glass. Many, many storeys, one on top of the other, soaring into the sky as far as the eye could see, formed of materials the likes of which he couldn't identify.

And the sheer number of people was overwhelming too. If he'd thought Miklagarðr was busy, this was hundreds of times worse.

'This is unbelievable. By Thor's hammer, I must be dreaming!'

Linnea stopped and smiled at him. 'Do you really think your mind could make all this up? I've never told you exactly what my era was like, so you wouldn't have any way of knowing what to imagine.' She gave his hand a squeeze. 'I'm sorry, but you actually have to believe me now. I did travel through time and ended up with you, and now you've done the same, only you're here with me instead.'

He tried to take it in, but it was too much. Gazing around him at all the amazing and occasionally downright strange things that Linnea's era consisted of, he could feel his brain being overloaded with impressions, sights and sounds. It would take him years to process all this. Years to become used to it, if he ever did. What if he didn't want to? But did he have a choice?

What if he was stuck here for the rest of his life?

'Linnea?' He pulled her to a halt. 'What am I going to do here? Do you have traders in your era? Will anyone want to buy amber?' Not that he'd brought any, but he could probably travel back to the land of the Balts and search for more.

And would she stay with him to guide him through it all, or would she take revenge on him by leaving him to fend for himself? He suddenly realised that he didn't understand a single word anyone was saying as they walked past, whereas presumably Linnea did. Was this how she had felt when he found her? By all the gods, no wonder she'd been confused and angry.

To his surprise, she started laughing, and he scowled at her. 'What is so amusing?'

'I'm sorry, it's just the idea of you living here. I don't think it will work.'

'Why not? What else do you expect me to do? I can learn. I'm not stupid and I am not afraid of anything.' Not even those noisy wagons that thundered past at deadly speeds. 'Although I suppose I will need new clothing.' He was starting to notice the strange looks they were receiving.

Linnea reached up and kissed his cheek in an oddly tender gesture. 'I know you're not stupid, and yes, you probably could learn to live here, but you'd be like a fish out of water. You don't belong here.'

'So what do you suggest?' He was still glaring, but really, what did she expect?

'We're going back to your time. I just have to find someone who can tell me how to get down to the harbour.'

'What?' He tugged on her hand. '*We* are going back to my time? You mean you would be willing to go back and be my thrall again?' He waved one hand around to encompass their surroundings. 'And leave all this?'

She hesitated, then stared at the ground. 'Well, no. I want to be a free woman, obviously, but . . . I do want to stay with you. If that's what you would like too. Although if you'd prefer to go back on your own, then . . . that can be done.'

He regarded her for a while longer, uncomfortably aware of the magnitude of what she was saying. What she was willing to sacrifice for him. This was her time. She had been telling the truth all along, and the gods had somehow sent her to his era, but now she had the chance to resume her former life. Presumably she had family somewhere, loved ones. And yet she wanted to go with him. It was more than he deserved.

He lifted her chin with his fingers, willing her to look him in the eyes. When she did, he saw doubt mingling with something else. Love? Desire? He wasn't sure, but he knew one thing – he couldn't bear to leave her if there was the slightest chance he didn't have to. 'I do wish you to come back with me, stay with me. From this moment on, you are free.' Although in truth, he didn't think he had ever really owned her. She had always been a free spirit, a law unto herself. He just wanted her to belong to him in some way, but realised now it had to be on her terms. Of her own free will. 'But are you sure? What about your family? You will be leaving them behind again.'

Her expression clouded over. 'I know. I . . . need to think about this some more while we walk. I have to let them know I'm safe, of course, but I have no idea how to tell them everything that has happened. Or that I might not be coming back . . .' Her voice broke. 'Oh why does everything have to be so difficult?'

He pulled her close, just holding her for a moment. It seemed an impossible choice, but only she could make it. Eventually, she let go of him and held out her hand. 'Come, I will find someone who can give me directions. I think better when I'm moving.'

They walked for what seemed like ages, but Hrafn was so busy trying to absorb all the impressions that he hardly noticed where she was taking him. Eventually she spotted a small hut and told him it said 'Tourist Information', or some such thing.

'They'll have a map, for sure. Um . . . a piece of vellum that tells us where to go.'

She turned out to be right, and was given a bit of calfskin so thin Hrafn thought it would break at any moment. On it was a drawing of a city, seen from above, and she pointed to a spot marked with red. 'This is where we are, apparently. We need to go to where the Prosphorion Harbour used to be – I think that's where your ship is. Well, was. The lady kindly googled it for me. As far as I can see, there's a railway station there now, the Sirkeci station. We'll have to go in there and hope we are in the right place.'

'A what? Googled?' She was using even more of her strange language, but he didn't really want to know. In this alien world, he'd just have to take her word for it.

Linnea was trying very hard to make sense of her emotions, and to come to some sort of decision about the future. She was aware that time was of the essence – Hrafn had to go back to his own era quickly. There were people waiting for him, depending on him.

His brothers wouldn't leave without him, but at the same time they might be at risk if her new owner came looking for her. Hrafn had stolen her away unlawfully; it was possible Rurik and the others could be punished for this when the two of them weren't to be found. She had to make up her mind fast, but how did you decide about something so momentous on the spur of the moment? And yet in her heart she already knew what she wanted.

She'd been on such a high when she realised the time-travel brooch had worked in the other direction, which meant that it wasn't a once-in-a-lifetime device. It could, presumably, be used any number of times, and that was extremely comforting to know. She ought in theory to be able to go back and forth whenever she wanted, so that even if she stayed in Hrafn's time, she could visit her family.

Her first thought on waking here had been to contact her parents – perhaps she could ask to borrow someone's mobile to send them a text message – but when she considered the implications, she realised it would be extremely difficult to explain everything by text. They might not even believe her, and would think she'd gone insane. Or that someone was playing a cruel prank on them, pretending to be their daughter.

No, she'd have to speak to them in person, but then they would definitely try to dissuade her from going back to the ninth century.

Would it be better to let them know she was safe and well when she was back in Sweden? Perhaps. At the moment, she desperately wanted to stay with Hrafn and travel home with him. The kiss they'd shared just before arriving back in Istanbul had shown her that there were deep feelings between them. He'd seemed to want her as intensely as she craved him. They belonged together. She'd felt their emotional connection time and time again, although she had tried to ignore it. Now that she was a free woman, their relationship could develop in a more normal direction. She wasn't his slave any longer, but his equal.

She sighed, her thoughts returning to her parents. Contacting them to tell them she was fine was the obvious thing to do, but what if she then went back with Hrafn and died on the way to Sweden? It was a perilous journey after all, one she was only willing to undertake because she loved him. She'd been gone so long now, her parents probably thought her dead already and had done their grieving. Wouldn't it be cruel to give them a crumb of hope only to disappear a second time? Yes, best to leave it be for now, but oh, how she longed to hear their voices, just for a short while.

'I'm not going to tell anyone I'm here,' she declared, startling Hrafn, who appeared to be walking around in a daze. And no wonder – there was a lot for him to take in.

'You're not?'

'No. If I'm going back with you, there is no point. They would only try to dissuade me, and if I refuse to listen to them, they'll be upset. I've been gone for months, disappearing without a trace, and they must have been through so much already. It would be cruel.'

Yet again, he pulled her close, and the feel of his arms around her reinforced her decision. This felt right. She belonged with Hrafn, no matter how much she loved her family.

'It has to be your choice,' he murmured. 'But I can't fault your reasoning.' He held on to her for a while longer. 'What about your friend? The one who almost died with you.' He nodded towards the traffic whizzing past them. 'I can see now why people are easily killed if they are travelling at such speeds. You were indeed very lucky.'

'Sara? Yes, I wish I could let her know I'm OK, but the same applies to her. And you're right about the cars – they do go so much faster than any wagon in your era; it's a wonder more people aren't killed every year.' She shuddered, blocking the inevitable thoughts of the accident.

He hugged her tight. 'It must have been truly terrifying. I understand your nightmares even better now.' Pulling away slightly, he gazed at her. 'Perhaps when we are back at Eskilsnes, you could use the brooch to visit everyone? Do you think that would work?'

'Yes, that's what I was thinking. If it takes us back to your time again today, then it should be possible.' She attempted a smile, although it was a wobbly effort as she was close to tears, feeling torn and emotional. 'I will definitely try.'

'Good. I will gift you this brooch as soon as we are back at my ship. It's too heavy for your clothing, I think, so I will keep it for now.'

She considered it. 'Yes, it's a real lump of a thing, isn't it? But beautiful.'

'It used to be my father's. I never thought I would inherit it. Nor Eskilsnes, and yet now it's all mine. Strange.'

'Well, that supposes that we can return to your time and make our way back to Svíaríki.'

'Hmm, yes.' Hrafn sighed and scanned their surroundings. 'Do we have far to go?'

'No, but before we continue, I'd kill for something to drink.' It was late summer and extremely hot and humid in Istanbul, not to mention dusty. The traffic fumes were making her cough, and she realised she wasn't used to the polluted air. It really was foul.

Hrafn blinked at her. 'You want me to kill someone so you can have some ale?'

Laughter gurgled out of her before she had time to stop it. 'No, no, don't be so caveman. I didn't mean it that way.'

'Cayve man?'

'Never mind. I just meant that we don't have any coins that are acceptable here so we can't buy anything to drink.'

'Why, don't they like silver in your era?'

'Oh yes, but you don't use it to purchase anything with. Not in little pieces anyway.'

He shook his head as if it was all too much for him to take in. It probably was. After all, it had taken Linnea weeks to truly believe that she was in the ninth century. She couldn't expect him to accept the opposite in just a matter of hours.

'You know, it might work, though. Give me some of your coins and I'll try.' She held out a hand and he took some silver dirhams from his belt pouch.

There was a street vendor selling chilled bottles of still water and bars of Swiss milk chocolate. After a major charm offensive, Linnea managed to make him part with two of each in exchange for what she told him were antique coins. 'Honestly, take them to any dealer and I swear you'll get loads of money for them. Please? Someone stole my wallet and this is all we have left.'

The guy, who was young and handsome, and obviously fancied himself as a bit of a ladies' man, gave in. 'OK, but if you lie, I'll come find you,' he threatened good-naturedly.

'I'm not, I swear! Thank you so much.' Linnea grabbed the water and chocolate, and told Hrafn to follow her into the shade of a building. There was a low wall and she sank down on it while he seated himself next to her.

'He seemed very taken with you. What did you promise him?' He had that caveman look again, which made Linnea want to laugh, but this time she suppressed her giggles.

'Nothing, except that your coins were worth trading with. Here, drink this and try a bite of chocolate.'

'Oh, is that the food you were talking about once?' He accepted the bottle and drank half the contents in one go. 'Ah, that is good.'

He squeezed the container gently and frowned when it made a crackling sound, the plastic caving inwards from the pressure of his fingers. 'This is a strange material. Like glass, but soft.'

'It's called plastic and it's very useful, but terrible for nature.'

'How so?' He was still examining it, turning the bottle this way and that.

'It's a long story. I'll explain it some other time. Now try the chocolate and you'll see what I meant about that. It is the food of gods.'

'Huh.' He took a bite and Linnea watched as the taste hit him with full force. 'Oh! Oh, *skítr*!' His eyes grew round and he chewed and swallowed, staring at the small bar in his hand. 'I do believe you were right about this too!'

This time Linnea couldn't hold in her laughter, nor the 'I told you so' that followed.

He grinned back, giving her a teasing look. 'But I still don't think it beats a night with me.'

Something inside her stomach flipped and she sent him a flirtatious glance. 'Oh really?'

'Yes, really.' He took another bite and his eyes twinkled, sending her an unmistakable signal. 'But I'll admit it probably comes close. You'll have to judge for yourself. If you want to, that is.'

Stupidly, she felt herself blush, and turned away murmuring, 'Hmm, we'll see.' But there was no doubt about it. She did want to find out if his lovemaking skills were as good as he boasted. In fact, she wanted him right now, and just knowing that he desired her too was making her even hotter than she'd been before. But this was not the time. The priority was to get back to his ship.

She finished her water and stood up. 'Are you ready? We have some time-travelling to do.'

Chapter Twenty-Five

'This doesn't look like a harbour to me.' Hrafn stared at the long, low brick building with a larger section in the middle. It had some sort of domed roof and a small tower either side. There were glass windows everywhere of all shapes and sizes, and although he was becoming used to them now, it was still awe-inspiring to think that glass could be used in this way and in such vast quantity. 'Where's the water?' he grumbled.

'It's gone. In my time they have filled some of the harbour in and built this, I think. We need to get as close to the water as we can, though. This way.'

Linnea led the way into the most enormous hall Hrafn had ever seen. The roof soared far above them, painted in cream and pink colours, while below were windows and doors picked out in brown. The flooring appeared to be polished stone and the whole room gave an impression of airy opulence.

'I want floor like this at Eskilsnes,' he murmured, wondering what everyone would say about that. Not that he'd know how to obtain it, but still . . .

Linnea hardly spared it a glance, though, and continued to the other side and through a door. This took them on to some sort of colonnaded walkway with a gap dug in between it and a similar structure on the other side. At the bottom of the gap were long metal structures, evenly spaced and lying parallel to each other.

'What is this?' Hrafn gazed around him just as a giant wagon came gliding along the metal bars, pulling other wagons behind it.

'A railway station. That is a train. It can transport many more people at a time than the, er, wagons you saw outside in the street,' Linnea explained. 'Actually, we can't really do this in public. Let's go into the toilet.'

'The what?'

'The privy.'

Hrafn spluttered with laughter. 'Right, but . . . Oh, very well. That might be a good idea anyway.'

She sent him a stern glance, but acknowledged that using the conveniences before travelling through time again was practical. 'You go into that one first, it's for men only, and do what you have to do, while I go in here. Then we're going into the disabled one together.'

'Whatever you say.'

He was becoming used to her ordering him around now, but once they were back in his time – if they managed to get there – that had to change. No matter how much of a free woman she was, he was the leader of their trading expedition and she would have to accept that.

Once he had used the strange metallic basins the way he saw other men doing, Linnea pulled him into another such room but with only one basin in it surrounded by a lot of metal poles. 'I won't explain about this as it will take too long and we need to hurry. If someone saw us go in here together, they'll alert the authorities. They'll probably think we're . . .' She turned an interesting shade of pink that Hrafn would have liked to discuss, but he knew this was not the time.

As if confirming her words, someone hammered on the door, shouting angrily. Hrafn ignored it. 'Very well. Here's the brooch. I'll prick our fingers this time. Give me your hand.' She held it out. It felt small and fragile in his, but he knew she was a strong, capable woman. Hadn't she proved it by not grumbling all through their long journey down the rivers of Garðaríki? Or at least she hadn't complained much in comparison to what she could have done, given what he now knew to be the truth about her background. 'On the count of three again?'

She nodded, and after he'd counted them down, he swiftly pricked their fingers.

'*Með blóð skaltu ferðast . . .*'

It was dark when Linnea opened her eyes. At first she wondered if the time-travelling had failed this time. Or what if they'd ended up in a completely different era? Jesus! She hadn't even considered that. But at least they were on dry land – she'd been worried they might end up in the water of the harbour if she miscalculated their position.

'Linnea, are you awake?' Hrafn's voice rasped out of the darkness next to her and she felt him searching for her hand. She gripped his fingers and was flooded with relief when he entwined them with hers. At least she wasn't alone.

'Yes, I'm here. Why . . . why is it so dark?' They'd left Istanbul in bright sunshine, but now she could barely see a thing, although her eyes were slowly adjusting and she was beginning to realise there was faint moonlight.

'Well, it was night-time when we left Miklagarðr, and if this has worked, we should be back there the same night. I think we're just outside the harbour gate. Look, can you see the outline of ships over there?'

Peering into the shadows, Linnea made out the shapes of masts and furled sails, bobbing gently up and down. 'Yes! Is that your ship, do you think? Oh, what if we're in the wrong place?' Or time . . .

'Only one way to find out. Come.' He stood up and pulled her to her feet, tugging gently on her hand as he strode off in the direction of the ships.

As they neared the water, Linnea's eyes adjusted even more, and she started to make out the shapes of several ships, as well as the edge of the quayside.

'Who goes there?' A gruff voice halted them in their tracks.

'Rurik?'

'Hrafn! By all the gods, you're back!'

Linnea put a hand to her heart to stop the sudden fluttering caused by that harsh question, and also the sheer relief that they hadn't ended up in the Stone Age. The brothers hugged briefly, and held a whispered conversation bringing each other up to speed with what had happened, although Linnea noticed that Hrafn left out the part about travelling to the future. No point going into that now – if at all.

'Dawn isn't far off,' Rurik said. 'And everything is ready.'

'Then we must wake the others and be sure to leave as soon as we can see where we're going. I hope that chain is lowered early enough so that we can get through. The sooner we are away from here, the better.'

'There have already been men here searching for you. Hopefully they won't return too soon.' Rurik sounded serious. 'They said you'd committed a crime, but we allowed them to search the boats and they were satisfied that you must be hiding elsewhere.'

'Good, but we can't take any chances. Wake everyone on Thure's ship – you're in command of that from now on – and I'll take care of this one. Linnea,' Hrafn turned to her, 'can you make sure Eija knows what is happening and keeps quiet, please?'

'Yes, of course.' Happy that the Saami girl would be travelling back with them, she followed him over to his ship and he helped her to climb down. While he made his way along the bottom, whispering with his men, she went over to Eija and shook her awake. In just a few words, she explained the situation.

'I'll be quiet,' Eija assured her. 'And so will he, right, little one?'

'What?' Linnea blinked and made out a small head that had popped up next to Eija. 'Kadir! What are you—'

'Shh. Don't tell the master, please,' Eija begged. 'He's coming with us. Said the men were after him too for helping Hrafn. We can't leave him.'

'Oh, right. Very well. Let's just sit and wait quietly then.'

As she settled down next to Eija and the boy, Linnea prayed to every god she could think of. Surely she hadn't come all this way only to be imprisoned by Byzantines?

In the end, they were able to escape without any problems. They slipped out of the harbour at first light, rowing as carefully as possible so as not to make any noise. The men were all experienced rowers and worked together as one. The two ships skimmed the surface, and as there was hardly any breeze yet, their keels glided smoothly and silently through the water. No alarm was raised, no one came after them, and there wasn't any shouting on the quayside.

Hrafn breathed a sigh of relief as they steered north towards the Black Sea. He watched the sun rise in all its glory to their right, turning the sky from pale gold to burnt umber, ochre, deep orange and then yellow, before blue took over. Thank the gods he was back in his own time and not stuck in Linnea's chaotic and noisy era. That had been nigh on unbearable. The peace out here on the sea enveloped him and settled like a cloak around his shoulders. Although he was rowing as if his life depended on it, wanting to put Miklagarðr as far behind him as possible, his actions were steady and calm, and he had the sense that all was right with the world.

Linnea was right – this was where he belonged.

They rowed for several hours and didn't make landfall at all. Instead, Rurik pulled his ship up alongside Hrafn's as soon as they were clear of the narrow channel and out on the wide sea, and they all shared a quick meal while resting for a while. Hrafn, who had been sitting near the prow for once, lost in his own thoughts, was surprised to hear a small voice asking if he wanted more ale. He looked up to find Kadir standing next to him.

'Kadir? What do you here? How—'

'I coming with.' The urchin looked both fearful and determined, lifting his chin and staring at Hrafn as if defying him to throw him overboard. 'Eija said. Bad mans take me if stay. No have mother, father. I come, yes?'

Hrafn took a steadying breath and nodded. 'Did someone see you helping me, is that it?'

'Yes. Ask questions. Hurt my arm. I run.' Kadir pointed to a large bruise on his skinny upper arm where someone had clearly grabbed him too hard. Hrafn swore inwardly. He should have been more careful and made sure no one knew of the boy's involvement with his rescue of Linnea.

'Very well. From now on, you are my foster-son, understand? Like a son, but not born of my wife.'

Kadir's face split into a huge grin and his eyes sparkled. 'Yes, yes! I son of Hrafn.'

'*Foster*-son, but almost the same. Did everyone hear that?' Hrafn raised his voice. 'Kadir is as a son to me and you will all treat him accordingly. Come here, you *fifl*.' He pulled the boy in for a fierce hug and felt joy flowing through him as he ruffled the urchin's hair. Not only was he going home with Linnea, but he hadn't had to leave Kadir behind either. Perhaps he should have thought of taking him with him before, but he'd always imagined the boy had parents somewhere in the city who would miss him.

Remembering his promise to Linnea, he added loudly, 'And one more thing – Linnea and Eija are both free women now, not thralls. They belong to no one unless they themselves choose to.' He glanced at Linnea and saw her blush as his meaning sank in. Hopefully she would want to belong to him, but he couldn't force her. She had to decide that for herself. That was not to say he wouldn't do his utmost to persuade her, but still . . .

'Right, we'd best continue. I've decided to sail straight across, rather than close to the shoreline. It seems wise in the circumstances. Let's hoist the sails, I feel the wind coming up!'

It wasn't ideal, especially for Rurik's crew, who had to put up with having the dead Thure on board, but no one voiced any complaints. They made good time throughout the day, and although Hrafn had seldom had to steer at night, he found it easy here. The sky was very clear and all the stars visible. There was no problem locating the ones he needed in order to keep the ship going in a northerly direction. He remembered the map Linnea had drawn for him, and only hoped she had been right and this would take them exactly where they wanted to go.

Linnea felt contentment flowing through her, and for most of the day she simply enjoyed the sensation of the wind and the sun on her face, the salty spray from the sea settling on her skin, and the quiet companionship of Eija and the others. With a jolt, she realised she was experiencing a profound sense of belonging. She was one of them.

A Norsewoman. Who would have thought it?

The panic that had been ever-present in the beginning was gone. Although she missed her parents and siblings, as well as

Sara, she had hope of seeing them again one day, and for now, that was enough. She glanced in Hrafn's direction. He had moved to take charge of the steering oar and shouted out instructions about the sail from time to time, but whatever he was doing, she was supremely aware of him.

As if he'd sensed her gaze on him, he turned his face to look at her. She could tell that he was tired, as there were dark shadows under his eyes, but when he smiled at her, he was still the handsomest man she'd ever come across. The only one she wanted.

He took her hand with his free one and gave it a squeeze. 'You are looking beautiful this morning, *unnasta*. I could wish that there were fewer people surrounding us,' he whispered.

She leaned into his shoulder and closed her fingers around his. 'Me too, but I like sitting here with you all the same.'

His smile widened, and those amazing eyes turned a melting indigo. 'Then, knowing that you feel the same, I am content to be patient.'

Linnea wanted to tell him that she was actually bubbling with *im*patience, but they had the rest of their lives to explore whatever this was that was developing between them. For that, she wanted privacy. How long would it be before they reached the Dniepr delta? And would they be able to sneak off into the forest alone, or was it too dangerous?

She swallowed a sigh at the thought that they might not be entirely alone until they reached Aldeigjuborg. If they even survived the journey, which, she suddenly realised, was a big if. And it was one hell of a long way.

'Why don't you tell me a bit more about your world, the future?' Hrafn suggested. 'It will help pass the time, and with this strong breeze, no one can hear us.'

'What do you want to know?'

'Everything! But you can start by telling me about the strange material that held my water . . .'

They encountered some heavy seas at one point, and Hrafn saw the fear in Linnea, Eija and Kadir's eyes, although they all pretended not to be affected. He himself had sailed through worse and just kept the steering oar steady, shouting to Rurik not to lose sight of him. His brother nodded and managed to keep the second ship close until the weather calmed down again and they could sail side by side. Although the men hadn't been afraid, they all still drew a collective sigh of relief when seagulls began to swarm above them and they saw the coast appear on the horizon.

Hrafn was still going by the map Linnea had drawn, and which he'd memorised, and before they reached the coast, he turned towards the east. This proved to be the right thing to do, for soon afterwards, the large spit of land signalling the entrance to the Dniepr hove into view.

'Yes! This is it, is it not?' Geir shouted. 'I remember this part because we were so relieved to see it last time as well.'

'Indeed. We should be entering the river soon. From now on it will be hard work, though, as we'll be rowing against the flow.'

'When is it not?' someone piped up. It was Dag, from the other ship, daring to be cheeky. Hrafn grinned at him to show there were no hard feelings. The man had acted on the orders of his leader, Thure, as was his duty, and he couldn't fault him for that.

They made a brief stop to bury Thure at the top of a small hill. Everyone worked together to fashion a grave worthy of a jarl, and Hrafn had no hesitation in burying his half-brother with all his belongings. He wanted none of them for himself, apart from the brooch, which he kept for Linnea as promised. The ornate sword and dagger were placed beside Thure's body, as well as his battleaxe and various provisions for his journey to the afterlife. Smiling slightly at the irony, Hrafn added two of the glass cups that had so nearly ruined his own life, but which he knew Thure had valued. Once everything was arranged to his satisfaction, they covered the body with earth, then searched for stones from the surrounding landscape, which they heaped on top to form a cairn in the shape of a ship. It was the best they could do and it would have to be enough.

Linnea and Eija stood with Kadir behind the others. Even though she didn't mourn Thure, she felt the solemnity of the occasion, and admired Hrafn for the dignified way he was burying a half-brother he'd had no liking for. He could have exacted vengeance posthumously by throwing the body into the sea. Instead, he was making sure Thure was sent off to the next world with everything he could possibly need. It showed what a truly honourable man he was and made her love him even more.

To her surprise, things became even more serious when they were done. Hrafn turned to head for the boats, but stopped when he saw that no one else was moving. The men were standing in a semicircle, and all bowed to him as one.

'We wish to swear our oaths of allegiance.' Dag stepped forward. As Thure's right-hand man, he seemed to have taken charge of the proceedings. 'Will you hear us, jarl?'

'I will.' Hrafn went over to sit down on a nearby boulder and pulled out his sword, which he placed across his knees, holding it so that the hilt stuck out on one side.

Dag dropped to one knee in front of him and gripped the hilt. 'I, Dag, son of Thorkil, make this oath and swear by this sword, and by my own weapons, to fight for you and yours, Hrafn Eskilsson, to always be by your side in battle, to protect you, and to avenge your death should you be unlawfully slain. I further swear to offer you my counsel and advice, always with your best interests at heart. May the mighty Odin smite me and this sword pierce me, should I fail in any of my duties towards you. And may Tyr, the god who allowed Fenrir the monstrous wolf to bite off his hand so that the creature could be eternally fettered for the good of everyone, bear witness that my oath is binding henceforth and for ever more until the end of time.'

Linnea knew that the god Tyr was considered the guardian of oaths, and therefore such a pledge was serious indeed.

'Thank you, Dag,' Hrafn replied. 'Hereby I declare that I accept your oath. In turn, I, Hrafn, son of Eskil, swear upon this sword to lead you in battle, to be a just and generous jarl, a protector and provider to you and yours, for as long as I shall live. May the same gods bear witness to this my oath, and please accept this gift as a symbol of the pact between us.' He pulled a silver armband off his wrist and held it out.

'Thank you, my jarl.' Dag accepted the arm ring, bowed again, then stepped back to allow the next man forward.

Linnea had noticed that Hrafn had been wearing an awful lot of silver armbands during the last few days and guessed that he must have anticipated this ceremony. He gave one to each man as seemed to be the custom. She watched as they all swore fealty to him in turn. It was very moving and brought a lump to her throat.

She could see in the men's expressions that they did not hesitate for a moment to make these oaths. It was clear that they were doing so because they genuinely respected Hrafn, and not because they had to, as must have been the case with Thure. It made her see him in a new light, and she also realised the heavy burden he'd taken on. As jarl, he was expected to look after their welfare and make sure they and their families were provided for.

But just like these men, she had complete faith in him.

Chapter Twenty-Six

Probably the toughest weeks of their lives began – rowing all day, guard duty at night, as well as hunting and fishing to keep their strength up with nourishing food. Linnea and Eija insisted on taking their turn rowing, and Hrafn let them, even though he knew they would tire faster than the men.

'It is good that you build your strength up,' he told them. 'You'll be better able to help us move the boats across land when that time comes.'

They bought food supplies wherever they could, stopping at small settlements along the river, and he also bought some sheepskins. Autumn was upon them, and even when they all slept huddled together in the ships, it was much colder. Having a sheepskin covering as a base helped no end. He also encouraged Geir and the other hunters to go after animals with luxurious pelts whenever they came across them. There was no time to prepare the skins as normal, but even in their raw state they gave welcome warmth, despite the slight stench.

With the cold also came illness, unfortunately.

'My throat is . . . um, full with sharp knives,' Kadir complained one morning, 'and head hurts.' He wasn't the only one. Soon there were bleary eyes, red noses and hacking coughs coming from every direction.

Hrafn had suffered through colds many times and knew of no cure. 'You'll soon feel better,' he told the youngster. The boy had to learn to be a man, but Linnea had a soft spot for him.

'Hrafn, did you not buy honey when we stopped at that farmstead the other day?'

'Yes, but . . .' He'd been saving it to sell, as he knew he'd get a good price for it in the larger settlements.

'Good. Then I'll make everyone a soothing drink.' She boiled water and added honey to half of it, distributing the mixture to everyone afflicted with a sore throat. The other half she used to steep willow bark and made them swallow this concoction every so often.

'She's a godsend,' Rurik croaked, following her with his gaze. 'That willow bark has helped my head no end, and the honey water is wonderful.'

'The sickness would have passed anyway,' Hrafn muttered, not wanting his men to go soft or Rurik to gaze at her in that adoring fashion, but he was grateful to her, and doubly so when his own throat turned raw.

They came to the dangerous rapids. Here, they were always on high alert, and Hrafn was pleased they'd managed to replace the two men they had lost last time they passed this place. Two Svíar who had been serving in the Byzantine emperor's army had tired of this and wanted to go home. It had seemed ideal for them to join Hrafn's crews, and he was pleased to see they took their guard duties as seriously as everyone else. But either the marauders recognised them and remembered their previous defeat, or they weren't bothering travellers at this particular time of year, because no attack came.

As they passed Koenugarðr and continued up through the

forests, then along the small river to Lake Ilmen, they were left alone. By the time they finally rowed past Holmgarðr, and floated down the Volkhov river towards Aldeigjuborg, winter was coming ever closer and everyone cheered at the sight of the jetties.

'At last we'll be able to sleep in a warm house! Thank the gods!' Vidar expressed what everyone else was thinking after they had woken to frosty mornings the last week.

'Yes, I'm hoping Olaf can find room for us all somewhere.' Hrafn knew his friend would happily try to squeeze them all in, but he didn't want to inconvenience Mila to that extent, especially since she must now be hugely pregnant. Thankfully, Thure's acquaintance agreed to take Rurik and his crew, while Hrafn and the rest stayed with Olaf as before.

'It's good to see you, my friend!' Olaf greeted them with much back-slapping and a knowing look in Hrafn's direction when he caught sight of Linnea. 'So you couldn't let her go, eh? I thought that would happen. Should have left her here with us rather than dragging her all that way, poor woman.'

'It was good for her and she never once complained,' Hrafn replied, although that probably wasn't quite true. She had been stoical, however, especially on the journey back, putting up with the cold nights without a word of protest. 'I do wish, though . . . but never mind.' Although he'd sneaked a kiss or two whenever possible, and they'd slept next to each other every night, they hadn't managed any time alone during the journey. Hrafn knew it was too risky to stray from the others, especially after dark, and it wasn't worth losing your life for the sake of making love, even assuming she would agree to it. But now . . .

Olaf chuckled. 'Aha, I think I see your dilemma. Would you perhaps care to borrow our box bed tonight?'

'Oh, no, I couldn't ask that of you, and Mila would have my head, no doubt.'

'Never! She's a keen matchmaker, is my wife. You wait and see. I'll have a word with her. For now, come and sit by the fire. You look half frozen to death!'

'Wait, what are you doing?' Linnea tugged on Hrafn's hand as he attempted to pull her in the direction of what looked like a cupboard with a mattress inside it. 'We can't go in there! That is Olaf and Mila's.'

'It is, but they're lending it to me. To us. He's extremely pleased with the profits I brought him, and he owes me as it's more than he imagined.' Hrafn put his head to one side, his expression suddenly serious. 'That is, if you want? I mean . . . I would be honoured if you would consent to spend the night with me. To sleep with me. I thought . . . Oh, the trolls take it! I'm making a hash of this.' He lowered his voice and whispered, 'Linnea, I want you so badly, I'm going out of my mind. Please say you feel the same. Or am I making assumptions?' He brought her hand to his mouth, kissing each knuckle in turn while still gazing at her intently.

Linnea's heart pounded and her legs turned to jelly just looking at him. There was no doubt in her mind whatsoever. This was the reason she had gone back to his time. 'Yes,' she murmured. 'I . . . I'd like that. But . . .' She was painfully aware that several people were sending them covert glances.

Hrafn put his hand in the small of her back. 'Let us shut the world out at least. I want to hold you without everyone else looking on.'

Linnea found herself hustled inside before she could say anything else, and the cupboard doors closed behind them. There was a small oil lamp standing on a shelf above their heads, which threw a soft light over the clean bedding. Hrafn knelt before her and put his arms loosely around her waist.

'I have waited such a long time for this, *unnasta*, but if you are not ready, just tell me and I won't do more than kiss you, I swear.' His voice was husky and the words sent a thrill right down to her toes.

This was it. They were finally alone, and Hrafn wanted to make love to her. She could see the desire in his eyes, feel the proof of it brushing her stomach through her tunic. They *had* waited a long time and she'd never been more sure of anything in her life. She wanted him.

'I'm ready,' she whispered, and tugged at the hem of her woollen tunic.

'Here, let me help you and you can help me.' He pulled the tunic over her head, then bent to shower soft kisses along her cheek, jawline and throat. 'Undo my belt, please.'

She wrestled with the belt buckle, trying to concentrate on that while being distracted by his kisses. As soon as the belt was off, he flung the tunic over his head and pulled her closer, kissing her mouth. Softly at first, then more fiercely, showing her exactly how much he wanted her. The constant nearness throughout their travels combined with the frustration of seeing but not being able to touch had been driving Linnea mad. The occasional brushing of hands and stolen kisses had stoked the fire in their blood, and now it was ready to boil over. They were both on their knees, facing each other, and Hrafn put his hands on her behind, rubbing softly and pushing her body harder against his.

'Linnea,' he breathed. 'Are you sure this is what you want?'

'Oh, yes, definitely.' She trembled as he deepened the kiss while allowing his hands to roam up along her waist and to the underside of her breasts. 'Yes please!'

'We're wearing too many clothes. Let me rid you of this.' He pulled her linen undergown off in one go and drew in a sharp breath. 'Odin's ravens, but you are perfection!' For a moment he just stared at her, and although Linnea knew she ought to have felt embarrassed, she didn't. With him looking at her like that, she did feel perfect. She revelled in the heat in his eyes as he devoured her with his gaze, before he leaned forward to take first one, then the other nipple into his mouth to suck gently.

'Take your own clothes off, for the love of Freya,' she told him sternly as a delicious shiver snaked down her spine. She might not be embarrassed, but she didn't want to be at a disadvantage either.

'I like it when you order me around.' He grinned and gave her nipple a lick before starting to undo his trousers. 'Within reason, of course.'

'Hah! Don't start telling me you want to be my master or something equally caveman,' she muttered, helping him off with his shirt and then becoming distracted by a very nicely sculpted male chest covered with a smattering of dark-golden hairs. She ran her palms and fingers over his taut skin and stored the feel of it in her memory.

'Hmm, you're going to have to explain that to me sometime, but not just now . . .' Hrafn had obviously had enough of talking, and playfully wrestled her down on to the mattress, leaning over her while being careful not to crush her. He started raining kisses all over her body, beginning with her mouth and moving down her throat, chest, breasts and stomach, until he reached the parts of her that were already burning for him.

'Hrafn . . .'

'I know, *unnasta*, be patient. I promised this would be better than chuk-lut, didn't I?'

As his tongue and fingers began to work their magic on her, Linnea was forced to reconsider her words. He was turning her entire body into a quivering mass of nerve endings, all clamouring for just one thing – him. 'Hrafn, now, *please*!' she begged. She'd never done this before but she was absolutely sure that if he didn't take her soon, she'd die.

He obliged, plunging into her quickly and then stopping, allowing her to adjust to the sensation of having him inside her. 'Did I hurt you?' he whispered.

'No, no, just . . .'

She didn't have to say anything more. He started to move, and she was so ready for him, it was only moments before her entire being exploded. She cried out, but he covered her mouth with his and continued to move. More waves of pleasure built up and crashed through her, making her moan and move frantically to increase the friction between them. He moved with her and didn't let up until she felt him shiver and, with a groan, find his own release just as her senses erupted once more. She closed her eyes and allowed the feelings to engulf her.

Breathing heavily, he stayed inside her but pulled her close. 'Tell me if I'm crushing you.'

'No, it feels . . . good.' Linnea smiled into the semi-darkness. That was an understatement. It was better than good. It was the most amazing thing that had ever happened to her in her life.

He raised himself on his elbows and kissed her. 'And?'

'What? Oh.' She grinned. 'Very well, I'll admit you were right. This is better than chocolate.'

His smile was smug, but she allowed him that. 'Can we do it again?' she asked, startling him into laughter.

'Um, yes, if you'll give me a moment.'

She wriggled underneath him. 'Take your time.'

He laughed again. 'Well, if you continue doing that, it might not be so long, my golden treasure . . .'

They stayed at Aldeigjuborg for a week, recovering from their long journey and building up their strength with wholesome food. Mila told them they'd just had the big autumn slaughter and there was plenty of meat of every kind. Hrafn loved this time of year, when you could sink your teeth into a satisfyingly large chunk of meat, rather than having to survive on stews and vegetables with tiny amounts of smoked meat or fish. Autumn was always a time of plenty, and one had to make the most of it.

His appetite for Linnea was just as voracious. Olaf and Mila graciously allowed them to continue to borrow their box bed, and Hrafn spent his nights teaching Linnea all the delights of love-making. He was astonished that she'd actually been untouched, as he'd had a suspicion she might not be. The thought that he had the privilege of being her first and only lover was a heady one.

'Are you going to marry her?' Olaf sent him a keen glance as they walked through the town towards the ships. Hrafn was due to take his turn on guard duty and Olaf had said he'd like some fresh air.

'Marry her? I don't know.' In truth, Hrafn hadn't thought much beyond the present haze of lovemaking and sleeping. Somehow he'd imagined that he and Linnea could simply continue their relationship when they were home at Eskilsnes, but of course that would make her his official concubine rather than his wife.

'You seem made for each other. What's to stop you?' Olaf looked baffled.

'Well, I've inherited my father's holdings now and they are quite considerable. I am probably expected to marry a rich neighbour's daughter to increase my lands.'

'Pfft.' Olaf made a face. 'You've never cared about lands and suchlike before. And judging by what you've told me, your father owned plenty, so why would you need more? No, my friend, do not let this woman slip through your hands. I'm telling you – she may be happy to bed you now, but she'll expect more than just being your mistress. Can you see her, in a few years' time, in the role of that unfortunate woman your half-brother was dragging around with him?' He snorted. 'I can't. Your Linnea is different.'

His Linnea. Hrafn swallowed hard. Of course Olaf was right. He couldn't do that to her, and what did it matter if she came with no dowry or status? He cared nothing for such things, never had. And he didn't want any other woman, only her. 'Yes, you're right,' he conceded. 'I'll have to speak to her when we get back. There may be more time for private talk then.'

Olaf slapped him on the back. 'You do that, but don't wait too long or someone else with eyes in their head will snap her up.'

Hrafn unconsciously curled his hands into fists. That was not going to happen. 'That reminds me – have you any marriage plans for your apprentice?'

'What, Einarr? No, why?'

Hrafn smiled. 'A little bird told me a secret, so I have a proposal for you . . .'

'Is always s-so c-c-cold in Hrafn land?'

Kadir was sitting next to Linnea, huddling so close she wondered if he was trying to climb inside her cloak. Olaf had offered to let them stay for the winter, as the first snows had arrived, but Hrafn and the others were hell-bent on reaching home before the rivers and lakes froze. She'd knitted Kadir two sweaters and Eija had made him a hat, socks and mittens. He was also swathed in a wolf pelt Hrafn had bought for him, but still he shivered.

She couldn't really blame him. A journey across the Baltic Sea in what was nothing more than a glorified rowing boat really wasn't pleasant at this time of year. In fact, it was downright miserable. Linnea didn't think she'd ever been this wet or cold, and she wasn't sure her extremities would be able to recover from the ordeal. What if she got frostbite and her fingers fell off? She shivered even more at that thought and dug them into her armpits to prevent it. But for Kadir's sake, she had to try and stay positive.

'No, it's warm in summer,' she soothed. 'And you'll get used to this, I promise. Let's ask if we can do some rowing – that will make us feel warmer. We could perhaps share an oar, you and I?'

They'd left an ecstatic and blushing Eija behind with her intended. Einarr hadn't hesitated for a moment in accepting Olaf and Hrafn's plans for him, saying he'd been on the verge of asking to come with Hrafn to his homeland just to be near Eija. As it was, they were both content to stay with Olaf, where Einarr could continue to learn his trade and Eija would be with Mila. The latter was a little put out at first, since she liked to be the one match-making, but when appealed to for help in teaching Eija how to be a good wife, she completely forgot her sulks and became happy and animated. Linnea was thrilled that everything had turned out so well.

They sailed straight for home; Hrafn decided to bypass Birka for now and see his merchant friend there some other time.

'As long as he gets his profit eventually, it won't matter if he has to wait a while.'

It was therefore an enormous relief when they finally sighted Eskilsnes and everyone could be hustled into the welcome warmth of the longhouse. Estrid was there to greet them. She'd been in charge of the household while they had been gone, and an uncle on Thure's mother's side, Knut, had looked after the farmland as there were no other relatives from the male line who could do it.

'Well, I had quite given up hope of seeing you this side of winter,' Estrid said, frowning in Linnea's direction. Hrafn was holding her hand and she hadn't thought anything of it until now. Discreetly she let go of his fingers, and as he was busy talking, he didn't seem to notice.

Linnea hustled Kadir over to the hearth and rubbed his little hands, even though hers were just as frozen. 'It's going to feel like someone is sticking needles into you for a bit, but don't worry, that's normal and it will pass,' she told him in a whisper.

'Where is Thure then?' she heard the older woman demanding.

Hrafn and the others told of Thure's misfortune, although they glossed over the fact that he'd been killed because of his temper and his own idiocy in playing dice with people he didn't know. There was also the bad news to deliver to the families of the two men who had died during the ambush on the way to Miklagarðr, which put a dampener on everyone's mood. Eventually, however, Estrid rustled up a celebratory meal, not too difficult at this time of year with all the surplus meat and produce from the harvest, and the atmosphere became more jovial.

Hrafn took the seat that had been Thure's before and waved Linnea over to sit beside him. She felt Estrid's disapproving glance, but as he was the head of the household now, she figured no one could argue with him. During the cold voyage across the Baltic, she'd started to think about what would happen once they arrived here, and she'd realised that Hrafn hadn't once mentioned marriage. Not that she was old-fashioned enough to demand that a man should marry her just because she'd slept with him – she'd been very willing after all – but she was acutely aware that here in the ninth century, things were different. Still, it had only been a few weeks and their relationship was very new.

Estrid sat down next to Knut, and Hrafn threw them a surprised glance. 'What's this? Am I missing something?'

His aunt looked coy and gave a small smile. 'Oh, Knut and I decided to marry. It seemed . . . expedient. You know, having to run this place together, it made sense.'

I bet! Linnea wondered if Hrafn realised that his aunt must have thought he wasn't coming back. That none of them would be coming back. If that was so, Knut would have inherited everything as the closest relative, and Estrid would have been the mistress of Eskilsnes. Linnea regarded the older woman over the rim of her ale mug. Was Estrid even pleased to have her nephews back?

'Well, congratulations!' Hrafn seemed oblivious as he toasted the couple, but Linnea knew he was far from stupid. He'd have worked it out.

'I don't think your aunt likes me much,' she commented as Hrafn pulled her into the bedroom that had been Thure's. It was small, but there was a proper bed with what looked like a feather mattress and clean covers. Utter bliss! And best of all, there was a door they could close and bar, and Linnea wouldn't need to worry about anyone hearing what they were up to. It had made her blush just thinking about what others might have thought, listening to them night after night in the tiny cupboard at Olaf's house.

'Estrid? Oh, that's just her way. She's always looked strict and forbidding, but underneath she is a good woman.'

'Are you sure? She looks at me like I'm dirt. And her and Knut . . .' Linnea let the sentence hang.

Hrafn made a face. 'Yes, I can see that she was planning for her future, but can you blame her? If we hadn't returned, her status would have been lost to whoever Knut appointed or married. I know he's old, but old men who suddenly inherit large holdings can expect to marry very quickly. I'd say she was clever to trap him while she could, but then he's never been very bright, poor man. Kind and fairly competent at running a farm, but not clever in any other way, so he won't have given any thought to what would happen. Estrid is more than a match for him.'

'Well, I hope you're right.' Linnea hesitated. 'What happens when you marry? Would she be content to hand over the reins to your wife?'

'She wouldn't have a choice, but knowing her, she'll be hoping

I marry someone young and inexperienced so she can guide her.'
Hrafn chuckled. 'I'd make sure that didn't happen.'

She waited for him to say something about her own status here
– she'd given him the perfect opening after all – but he was more
interested in removing all her clothes. As always, once he'd ignited
her desire, she forgot everything else. There was always tomorrow.

Chapter Twenty-Seven

Hrafn was kept very busy for the next few days catching up on everything that had been happening at Eskilsnes. Knut had done a good job of running the farm, but his long-winded explanations of why he'd slaughtered this particular animal or mated others nearly drove Hrafn to distraction. He just wanted to take up the reins himself and get on with it.

'Thank you, Knut, I appreciate all your hard work. It must seem sad that you did all this for your nephew when he's now dead and I've inherited instead. I assure you, I never had any expectations in this direction.'

Knut clapped him on the back. 'I know. I've known you since you were a boy, and although I could see that you and Thure didn't get on, never once did you try to usurp his place. I wish you nothing but well. As soon as you take a wife, I'll remove Estrid from here. We can live on my small farm, as I've always done.'

'There's no rush. You are always welcome here, Knut.' And Hrafn meant it. He liked the old man, although he could see that taking Estrid away would probably be a good thing. He knew her well enough to realise she'd not be content to have to defer to his wife, especially not if that was Linnea. She'd already hinted that he ought to make a match with their neighbour's daughter,

Christina Courtenay

Gudrun, who apparently came with a large dowry. He'd brushed her off, but it was worrying that Estrid still seemed to view Linnea as a thrall, even though he'd explained to everyone that she was a free woman now. Perhaps he should have waited to bed her, but since they were both eager, where was the harm? He'd marry her soon, but best to let Estrid and everyone else get used to her presence and new status first.

One thing at a time, and he had a surprise to plan.

The first opportunity he had, he visited Rurik, who seemed to have taken up permanent residence in the Eskilsnes smithy.

'You're making yourself at home, I see,' he commented, noticing that his brother had appropriated a corner of the workshop and made it his own. Bodolf, the smith who made all the tools and other necessary items for the farm, didn't appear to mind, and the two men were working happily side by side. Rurik took up little space in any case, as silversmithing was not as bulky as fashioning things out of iron.

'For the time being. I'll need to set up a business elsewhere, but it can wait for a while.'

'Good. I was hoping you'd stay.' Hrafn smiled. He'd prefer to have both his brothers around all the time, but knew they would want to make their own way in life. 'That wasn't what I came to discuss, though. I was wondering if you could possibly make a special item for me. It would need to be your very best work.'

'Of course.' Rurik almost looked offended. 'As if I'd do anything else.'

'I know, sorry. What I meant was, it has to be perfect.' He bent to whisper, even though Bodolf was banging away at a piece of iron and probably couldn't hear a thing. 'I need a ring for Linnea and I want it to be truly stunning.'

'For Linnea? So you . . . ?'

Hrafn nodded. 'As soon as you're done, yes. I love her. There will never be anyone else for me.'

He thought he caught a fleeting expression of regret on Rurik's face, which surprised him, as he hadn't thought his brother would mind him marrying a former thrall, but then Rurik smiled and clapped him on the shoulder. 'I wish you all the happiness in the world. Now tell me what you had in mind . . .'

'Please may I have some yarn? I need to make Kadir some more socks.'

Linnea had ventured over to the corner of the longhouse where Estrid and some of the other women sat and spun, carded or worked on weaving cloth. During the cold winter months, it would seem these activities had been moved in here as presumably the little hut outside wasn't heated or was maybe too dark. They all looked up, but no one said anything except Estrid.

'Spin some yourself. Or make him do it – I've no idea why Hrafn saw fit to bring back a grubby little Grikkjr to live among us. He needs to learn his place, that of a thrall.'

Linnea counted to ten before saying in an even voice, 'Kadir is Hrafn's foster-son, not a thrall, and I think he's being taught sword-fighting and the like, not spinning. As for me, I'm sure you remember that I don't know how to spin. Perhaps someone could be kind enough to teach me if there's no yarn available.'

She could see that there was, though. A whole basketful, in fact, sitting by one of the women's feet. But if she had to do things the hard way, she was prepared to learn.

'I'm afraid we don't have the time. We are very busy here, as I'm sure you can see.' Estrid looked her up and down as though she was a particularly nasty bug. Linnea stared back, sending the old lady a death glare.

'Very well, I'll have to find someone else to teach me then. I'm sure Hrafn can point me in the right direction. I apologise for intruding.'

She heard Estrid snort as she walked away, and there were titters of laughter from some of the other women. It made her fume, but there was nothing she could do about it right now. If Hrafn ever did marry her, she'd make them pay. Contrary to what she'd said, though, she wasn't going to run to him telling tales. She'd sort it out in her own way. The socks would have to wait; instead she asked him if he had any old clothes she could adapt for Kadir.

'He's growing all the time, now that he's being given proper food every day, and he still feels the cold, poor boy.'

'Of course. Have a look in my chest, I'm sure you'll find some old things that can be altered for him.' Hrafn gave her a quick kiss. 'Take whatever you need. Or ask Geir – he grew something fierce the year before we left for Miklagarðr. He's bound to have garments that are too small for him.'

'Thank you.'

He seemed to be in a hurry and there was always someone waiting to speak to him. She supposed that being the head of the household carried many duties as well as privileges. Duties that she was sure Thure had neglected for years. Hrafn was different and he'd want to do things right. But it meant Linnea was left on her own a lot of the time. Very much alone.

With a sigh, she found some of his old clothes and started to cut them down to Kadir's size. At least she had some needles and thread. If she'd asked Estrid, the woman would probably have told her there were none to spare.

Two weeks went by. Hrafn was settling into life back at Eskilsnes and the place felt vastly different now that he was in charge. It wasn't so much that it had been run-down before – Estrid had always made sure the house and outbuildings were kept scrupu-lously clean and in good repair, even if Thure took no interest in such matters; it was more that the atmosphere seemed lighter. Not that he wanted to boast or expected any thanks for it, but people didn't have to tiptoe around any longer, wondering when their master's temper was going to erupt next. And Thure's glow-ering presence in the chair at the end of the room didn't hang over them. Hrafn liked to think that he was keeping everyone in good cheer.

The only fly in the ointment was Estrid, who still hadn't taken to Linnea. He watched with a frown as the older woman blanked his lover, acting as if she wasn't there most of the time. The few occasions when she had to address Linnea directly, there was a distinctly frosty tone to her voice. He couldn't understand it. Linnea seemed to be doing her utmost not to antagonise anyone.

He'd have to ask Rurik to hurry up with that ring – the situation was becoming urgent.

He cornered Estrid one morning when she was on her way to the smokehouse.

'Good morning, aunt. May I have a word?'

'Certainly, but if it's about your thrall concubine, I don't want to hear it.'

'Estrid! I—'

She cut him off. 'You're not thinking with your head, nephew, only other parts of your body. You need to consider your future and the good of all the people living here. For their sake, as well as your own, you should make an advantageous marriage, not throw everything away for a pretty face. I'll grant you she's lovely, and she's clearly happy to let you have your fill of her, but what happens when you tire of her? You'll have a wife who brought you nothing, and you don't even know where she came from so you won't be able to send her back to her kin. That's even supposing you can persuade her to divorce you. Look what happened to your friend Haukr. He was trapped with a wife he hated for years.'

Hrafn drew in a long breath and tried to stay calm. He did know where Linnea hailed from, but of course he couldn't tell Estrid that. He also knew he'd never tire of her. She was the first and only woman he'd ever wanted to spend more than one night with. The only one he could see as the mother of his children, and as a travelling companion when he went on his trade journeys. Each day he discovered more things about her that he liked. Of course he wasn't stupid – he understood that marriage wasn't just based on lust, and desire would fade with time, but Linnea was different. She had a keen mind, and after their shared experiences, he didn't think they'd ever run out of things to talk about. He simply enjoyed being with her.

'That was different. I don't want anyone else,' he told Estrid firmly. 'And if you can't live with that, then you will have to make your home elsewhere.'

Her face turned pale, then her eyes flashed dangerously. 'You are being hasty. At least give it some more thought. I'm convinced you're making a mistake.' Her voice rose. 'Gudrun is the woman for you. I had Knut ask her father whether he'd be agreeable to a match, and he is. Please, I beg you to consider the good of everyone here at Eskilsnes.'

Hrafn bit his teeth together hard to prevent himself from saying something he'd regret. 'Very well, I will think about it.' But not for long. Then he'd reject the idea, but he wasn't going to tell her that yet.

To his astonishment, she threw her arms round his neck and clung to him, hugging him tight. 'Thank you, dear nephew, you make an old woman very happy.'

Speechless, he disentangled himself as soon as he could and walked off.

*

Linnea ducked back behind the smokehouse. She'd just been to the privy and had caught the tail end of Hrafn's conversation with his aunt. It made her insides turn as icy as the weather. A fierce shiver shook her from top to toe.

So he was considering marrying his neighbour's daughter after all, was he? And what of her? Did he think he could keep her as his concubine? Or was he going to discard her before the wedding, passing her on to someone else? No way.

She marched towards the house, intent on telling him exactly what she thought of this idea, but Estrid was suddenly blocking her path. The woman held up a hand. 'One moment, please.'

'What? I don't want to speak to you,' Linnea snarled. This was all Estrid's fault. The old biddy had had it in for her right from the start, and if she hadn't been sowing seeds in Hrafn's mind, perhaps he would have proposed by now.

'Wait! I'm sorry you had to hear that. I understand that you are not best pleased, but did you really think a man like Hrafn would marry a woman who's been a thrall? He owes it to his position here, to everyone who depends upon him, to make the best possible match and enrich his holdings. You can bring him nothing but yourself.' Estrid grabbed Linnea's hand. 'He might think that is enough right now, but do you honestly believe he'll still be of the same mind in five years' time? When you've borne him several children and he's tired of bedding you? Trust me, I know what men are like. The word that describes all of them is fickle.'

Linnea swallowed hard. Estrid was a horrible woman and she didn't want to listen to her. The old crone was clearly thinking mostly about herself. Her position here would be diminished if Hrafn married Linnea, but perhaps there was also some stigma attached to such a match that would tarnish the family's status and reputation, something Estrid obviously valued highly. Did Linnea really want to be responsible for that? For ruining the family's standing in the community? And what if Estrid was right about the other things? Hrafn was certainly enjoying making love to Linnea right now, but they had no birth control, and if she stayed with him, she'd be bearing a lot of children. With each one, her body would become less enticing and more matronly. Who could blame him, then, if he tired of sleeping with her?

'I can't stay here and be his concubine,' she said between gritted teeth. That would be unbearable, even if this Gudrun would put up with it, which she doubted.

'No, I can see that would be distasteful.' Estrid shook her head and pretended a compassion Linnea was sure she didn't feel at all. 'If I were you, I'd leave. Take some of his silver – I'm sure he wouldn't mind, and I'd be willing to persuade him he owed you that much – and make a life for yourself elsewhere.'

'I don't want his silver.' Linnea drew herself up to her full height, which was quite a few inches more than Estrid's, and glared at her. 'I'm not a thief, never was.'

'No, no, but I'm only thinking of your welfare. You need some way of existing until you can begin to earn a living.'

Something in Estrid's eyes told Linnea the old woman probably thought selling her body was the only thing she was fit for, and taking some of Hrafn's silver would help set her up somewhere to ply this trade. *The complete and utter bitch!* Although to be fair, in this century perhaps she was right.

She hesitated. Should she discuss it with Hrafn? Find out what his plans were for her future? But did she really want to know? It would spoil all the wonderful memories she now had of their time together. And she couldn't possibly make love to him again tonight, knowing he wasn't really serious about their relationship, that she was just a pleasant interlude before his real duties beckoned.

No, she couldn't stay here. She needed to go back to her own time. Now. There was just one problem. It was winter, and even if she'd been able to make her way back to the spot where Hrafn had found her, she was sure Lars and his archaeologists would be long gone. She'd end up somewhere out in the countryside with no means of contacting her family. Eskilsnes could be a complete wilderness in her own century. Linnea didn't want to be lost in the middle of a vast forest with no idea of how to get out of it. Another plan was needed, and something occurred to her.

'Could you arrange for me to be taken to Haukr's settlement?' She remembered going past it on their way to Birka, and she knew now why his name had seemed so familiar to her.

Estrid frowned. 'He is married,' she said, inadvertently confirming that she'd been thinking exactly what Linnea had suspected.

'Yes, yes, I know, but I am . . . er, slightly acquainted with his wife, Ceri, and I think she might help me.'

'You never said.' Estrid peered at her suspiciously. 'Were you thralls together somewhere? Although it was my understanding that Haukr brought her straight here from Bretland.'

Had Ceri been a thrall? Linnea wasn't sure she'd been aware of that, but it didn't matter now. 'No. I met her elsewhere. Look, I was a bit confused when I arrived here that first time and didn't realise they lived so close.' Linnea almost laughed out loud. She'd also had no idea she was in the ninth century and able to talk to people she'd only ever read about on a rune stone. The settlement where Haukr and Ceri lived had, in time, become her parents' summer cottage. As a six year old, Linnea had been present when they dug up a rune stone that mentioned their names. She was convinced it had to be the same place, and if so, there was a telephone and she knew where the key to the door was always hidden. Where better to try and time-travel to?

'Very well. I'll see that you are taken there whenever you are ready.'

'I want to go now. Just give me a moment to gather a few things.'

She only prayed that Hrafn wasn't wearing Thure's brooch today. That was the only piece of silver she intended to take with her.

Chapter Twenty-Eight

'Where is Linnea?' Hrafn ruffled Kadir's hair affectionately. The boy was sitting on a bench, staring at the floor and kicking his heels against the wooden panel.

'Gone to visit friend. Said I had to stay with you.'

Hrafn lifted the lad's chin and frowned at the sulky expression. 'What do you mean? She doesn't have any friends around here.'

She didn't even seem to have any at Eskilsnes, come to think of it. He hadn't once seen her sitting with the other ladies, laughing and gossiping the way they normally did. Most days he'd found her in their bedroom, which inevitably led to his being distracted from noticing anything other than her proximity to their bed. Perhaps he ought to have paid more attention to what she did the rest of the time.

'Ask old woman. Said man row Linnea to friend.'

A worm of unease wriggled inside Hrafn and made him scan the room for his aunt. He found her where she always was, near the loom and other female implements. Leaving Kadir to his sulk, he strode over to her. 'Aunt? What's this I hear about Linnea?'

'Hmm?' Estrid turned limpid eyes his way. 'Oh, er, she said to tell you she's gone to visit some friends. She hoped you wouldn't mind her borrowing Vidar and one of the rowing boats, but I said I was sure that was fine.'

'What friends would those be?' Hrafn was aware that his voice sounded harsh, but Estrid appeared unconcerned.

'I believe she mentioned someone called Ceri. A former thrall, like herself.'

Clenching his fists so as not to throttle his aunt, Hrafn narrowed his eyes at her. 'Haukr's wife? Linnea doesn't know her.'

'Oh, but she assured me that she does.' Estrid shrugged. 'You'll have to ask Vidar when he returns. I told him to come straight back, in case the water starts to freeze. We've not had any ice yet, but it can't be long now.'

Hrafn didn't stay to hear any more. He *knew* Linnea had no friends in his time, so if she was heading for Haukr and Ceri's settlement, there had to be another reason. Stomping into their bedroom, he began to look through their things. He'd had a chest made for Linnea to store her clothes in, and most of her spare garments were still there. Her thick cloak was gone, as were her hat and mittens, but nothing else. Looking through her meagre pile, he suddenly felt ashamed that he hadn't thought to give her something more fitting to her new status. She'd not complained about wearing the same old tunics as before, but it was no wonder really that his aunt and the others had still viewed her as a thrall. She'd been dressed like one.

'*Skítr!*'

He slammed down the lid of her kist and opened that of his own. At the bottom was a smaller chest containing his wealth. It was locked, with the only key hanging off his belt, but he knew she wouldn't have taken his silver in any case. She only had to ask and he'd give her whatever she needed. His clothes were all there, obviously – she'd have no need for those – and nothing else was missing, not even his spare belt. Although . . . wait a moment.

Where was Thure's brooch? He'd left it behind because the weight of it was annoying when he was trying to work, and instead he was wearing his old one, which was lighter and simpler in design. He quickly riffled through the chest once more.

'*Noooo!*' He banged his fist on the nearest wall. The brooch was gone. Of course it was, and he knew why. Linnea was going to go back to her own time.

When he looked over towards the bed, he saw a large piece of birch bark with slightly curled edges. He picked it up. On it were scratched a whole lot of runes. He started to read with hands that shook.

> Hrafn – thank you for our time together. I will never forget you, but I do not belong here. Be happy and live your life to the full as I intend to do mine.
> Your *unnasta*, Linnea

With a vile oath, he threw the piece of bark across the room, although being so lightweight it didn't go very far, which unaccountably annoyed him even more.

Standing stock still, he considered his options, but there was really only one. He had to go after her and hope that she hadn't already left by the time he reached Haukr's settlement.

'Thank you, Vidar, I'll be fine now. You can go straight back, like Estrid told you.'

'Are you sure? Should I not go with you up to the hall? What if they are away and—'

'No, no. Look, you can see that someone is at home. There is smoke coming out of the gables.' Linnea pointed up at Haukr's longhouse. She had no intention of going there, but Vidar couldn't be allowed to find out. 'Please, I don't want you to get into trouble.

323

I can manage by myself, I promise.' For good measure, she added, 'I'll see you soon. Estrid will let you know when to fetch me back.'

He vacillated, but eventually gave in and started rowing back the way they'd come. Perhaps he'd hoped for a warm drink or some stew before another long, cold journey, but Linnea couldn't let him stay. He might think she was still punishing him for the role he'd played in Thure's attempted rape of her, although she'd long since forgiven him. Be that as it may, she didn't want anyone to see what she was about to do next.

She waited until he was out of sight, then glanced around, making sure there was no one else about. Since it was a dark and dreary day, with needle-sharp sleet that was coming down almost sideways due to a strong wind, everyone seemed to have had the sense to stay indoors. They wouldn't venture out unless they had to visit the privy or tend to animals in the byre. Now was a good time for her to disappear.

She huddled by the shore in the lea of a large boulder near the jetty and pulled open the leather pouch hanging off her belt. Hrafn had given it to her and she would treasure it always, but right now the clasp was proving difficult because her fingers were stiff with cold. Her plait, thickly coated with snowflakes, which made it heavier than usual, fell forward, hampering her further, but at last she managed to bring out the clumsy brooch. Its long pin was stuck in the leather and she had to wriggle it to release it. 'Bloody thing,' she muttered. 'You'd better work your magic one last time, because I just can't stay here. Do you hear me?'

She almost laughed. Here she was talking to an inanimate object now. Was she going insane? No, but she would if she didn't get out of here soon.

'Right.' She held the brooch up and read the runic inscription one last time. It was definitely the last time, because she didn't intend to take it with her. Before, when she'd time-travelled, she'd held on to the brooch, but she'd decided to let go of it now. It wasn't hers to keep; it was Hrafn's, even if he thought it as ugly and cumbersome as she did. His inheritance from Thure, along with everything else that was slowly but surely pulling him away from her and towards his duty as the heir.

Blinking back sudden tears, she swore under her breath. 'I will not think about that now. Come on, Linnea, focus.'

Gripping the brooch firmly with one hand, she steeled herself – deliberately pricking your skin with something sharp went against every instinct and wasn't easy. She inhaled deeply and stabbed at a finger on the other hand while repeating the inscription – *Með blóð skaltu ferðast* – out loud. As soon as she'd done it, she threw the brooch away from her. She vaguely saw it land near the path that led to the house from the jetty. After that, everything became a blur and the nausea assailed her with a vengeance. She knew what to expect, but it was horrible each time it happened even so, and she gritted her teeth in order to endure it.

It had to be this way, and soon she'd be home . . .

'Hrafn, this is a surprise! What are you doing out in this foul weather?'

Haukr greeted him with a smile, but there was a crease between his brows that spoke of concern. No one in their right mind travelled at this time of year unless they had to.

'I'm looking for Linnea, my intended. Did she come here? She told my aunt she was coming to visit you, and my man Vidar says he left her on your jetty earlier today.'

He'd met Vidar on his way here, but they'd only spoken briefly, as Hrafn was in a hurry to carry on with his journey. At least he knew he was heading to the right place.

'No. As far as I know we've not had any visitors today. Ceri!'

He shouted for his petite wife, a woman Hrafn liked very much. She was as tiny as Haukr was large, but somehow they were perfect together and anyone could see they were very much in love. In a moment of blinding clarity, Hrafn realised he wanted exactly the same kind of close and warm relationship. He'd had it with Linnea, only now it might be too late for him to tell her that.

Skitr!

Ceri confirmed that no one had arrived that afternoon and Hrafn headed back towards the door. If she wasn't in here, she had to be outside. As it was starting to snow properly now, perhaps there would be footsteps to follow if she'd gone on somewhere. He had to look.

'Wait, I'll come with you!' Haukr grabbed a cloak, hat and some mittens and hurried after him. On the way down towards the jetty, Hrafn decided to tell his friend the truth. He'd trust Haukr with his life, and this was one secret he couldn't keep to himself right now. In as few words as possible, he tried to explain what he feared could happen. Or had already happened. Haukr stared at him, blinking away the snowflakes that were settling on his eyelashes. 'The future? Are you sure?'

Hrafn stopped at the end of the jetty and turned to look at his friend. 'I know, it sounds completely insane, does it not? But I swear to you, on all the gods, that it is the honest truth. I give you my word of honour, my oath, whatever you want. We know there are things in this world we don't understand, and the gods have mysterious powers. Well, this is clearly one of them, and they chose to show Linnea – and me – what they could do. I have myself travelled to the future, although briefly, and I am entirely sane. I could describe things to you the like of which you would scarcely believe. But right now, I have to find Linnea. If I don't, my life is over. It's as simple as that.'

Haukr put his hand on Hrafn's arm. 'I understand, and I

believe you. I know exactly how you are feeling and I will help you as best I can. We start here?'

'Yes, it makes sense. This was the last place she was seen.'

They followed the jetty back to the shore, scanning the planks for evidence of her presence, but the snow was settling on it now and showed no anomalies. As they set foot back on land, however, Hrafn saw something glinting more brightly than the snow itself. With an exclamation, he bent down and grabbed it. 'Thure's . . . I mean, my brooch! She *has* been here.'

But the emphasis was on the past tense. Linnea had been there but she wasn't any longer. She'd done what she said she would and travelled back to her own time.

'D-Dad? It's m-me, Linnea.'

Her teeth were chattering so much she was finding it difficult to speak, but she'd wanted to hear her father's familiar voice as soon as she'd entered the cottage. Time enough to get the wood-burner going later.

Amazingly, the cottage was here, exactly where she'd thought it would be. And the key, as usual, was hidden under a flowerpot. Her stepmother always said that if someone wanted to break in, they would, key or no key, and there would be less damage if they just unlocked the door. A sentiment Linnea was very grateful for right now.

'Linnea? *Linnea!* How is this possible? Where are you? Are you OK? Have you been kidnapped? Held prisoner? What the—'

'Dad. *Dad!* C-calm down. I'll explain everything, but I'm f-fine. Just very c-cold. I'm at the cottage. Can you come?'

'I'll be there in ten minutes. Don't go anywhere, you hear me?'

'I won't.'

He hung up, and Linnea sank to the floor. Her legs just wouldn't hold her upright any longer, and there were tears pouring down her cheeks. She wasn't sure if they were tears of relief at being back here, sheer emotion at hearing her dad's voice, or unbearable sadness at knowing she'd never see Hrafn again. Probably a combination of all three.

After a while, she managed to stand up and get a fire going in the woodburner. She was huddled in front of it with a blanket round her shoulders when her dad, Haakon, came barging through the front door and rushed over to pull her into his arms. 'Linnea! Sweetheart . . .'

She could feel his tears running into her hair, but she knew those were definitely tears of joy. 'Oh, Dad!' She buried her face in his shoulder and inhaled the familiar scent of him.

Since she was a little girl, he'd always been there for her, making sure she was OK. Her mother, Sofia, his ex-wife, was a flaky socialite who never stayed in one place for long and was always moving on to the next exciting thing, while Haakon and his second wife, Mia, were the rocks in Linnea's life. With them she'd had a safe haven, calm and orderly, and they'd given her siblings as well as a home environment she could thrive in. They made sure she spent time with her mother too, but it was always a relief to be back with them. Secure. Comfortable. Home. That was how it felt now, and Linnea almost sagged with relief.

For a while they just stood there clinging to each other, but eventually Haakon pulled back and scanned her face. 'Are you really all right? No one has hurt you? Where the hell have you been? We thought you were . . .' His voice broke.

Dead. They'd thought her abducted and murdered probably, as she'd suspected, but he couldn't say it out loud.

'No, no one hurt me. I've had to work hard – just look at these muscles – but I don't think that's damaged me in any way.' She jokingly flexed her biceps and thought about the incredible slog of transporting Hrafn's ship along rivers and through forests, and all the other physical labour she'd done. It had toughened her up but it hadn't harmed her. The only thing that hurt was not being loved by him. But she'd get over that.

Probably.

'Come, let's sit down. You have to tell me everything, but only if you feel strong enough. Do you want anything? A drink? Some food? There might be a tin of soup or two here.' He was going into parent mode, but she held up a hand to stop him.

'Not now, Dad. I'm not hungry. Yes, let's sit on the sofa and I'll tell you where I've been. But you've got to promise not to send me straight to a mental institution. I swear to God I'm not crazy. Do you believe me?'

He frowned. 'Of course. Why would I think that? Have you been brainwashed or something? You've not been . . . radicalised, have you?' He suddenly seemed to notice her clothing. 'I mean, is that a . . . a kaftan? You're not wearing a headdress.'

Hysterical laughter bubbled out of Linnea, and she tried to stop it. 'No, no, I haven't been radicalised.' More laughter. 'At least not unless being indoctrinated with Norse beliefs counts. Surely you of all people should recognise this type of clothing.' He was, after all, an expert on Viking archaeology. She took a deep breath and tried to get a grip.

'What? Norse, but—'

'Listen, Dad, and I'll tell you my story. Just let me finish before you comment, OK?'

'All right.'

She began with the metal detector and carried on telling him everything that had happened to her since the early summer, only leaving out the last part about sleeping with Hrafn. Her dad didn't need to know that and it would probably only complicate matters. Fathers could be very possessive about their daughters, and although she was twenty-two – no, wait, she'd

329

turned twenty-three while she'd been gone – he still saw her as his little girl. When she was done talking, Haakon stared at her for several long moments, the silence in the cottage only broken by the occasional hiss and crackle from the fire.

'Ninth century?' he said finally, blinking. 'Seriously?'

'Yep.'

'And you met Haukr and Ceri? Who lived here?'

'Not met, exactly, but I was told their settlement was here, and when I asked to go to their place, this was where I was taken. Hrafn's people clearly knew Haukr well.'

'Bloody hell . . .' Haakon looked shell-shocked, and she couldn't blame him. She'd had six or seven months to get used to the idea, while he'd had mere minutes.

She leaned over to hug him. 'I know it sounds completely insane, but I can tell you details about Viking life you'd probably never know otherwise. And I'm completely fluent in Old Norse now, including all the swear words, which I'd bet Daniel would give his right arm to hear.'

The thought of Daniel made her frown. She realised she didn't miss him one little bit; she hadn't even remembered his existence until this very moment. The thought that she'd once had a crush on him seemed ludicrous now. He was so not what she wanted in a man. Nothing like . . . She cleared her throat. She refused to think about Hrafn now. That could be done later, in private.

'But what made you decide to come back? And why didn't you try it earlier, once you knew you could?' Haakon was peering at her, his eyes searching hers. 'We were going out of our minds!'

Damn. Fathers weren't just possessive; they also knew their children better than you thought.

'Well, that's another long story . . . Um, can we do that one later, please? I'm a bit tired now, Daddy.'

She tried for her best cajoling voice, the one that had always worked on him before, and he fell for it. 'Of course, sweetheart. I'm sorry, you must be exhausted. Why don't you go and have a long, hot bath – the water should be nicely heated now – and I'll call Mia. She's probably going spare, wondering why I haven't rung.'

'Sure, good idea. Give her my love.'

Mia was a great stepmum and they'd always got on well. Linnea loved her and the half-siblings she and Haakon had produced – a brother and a little sister – as well as her foster-brother Ivar. Mia and Haakon had taken him in when he became an orphan and he'd been part of their family ever since. As she made her way up to the bathroom, she smiled at the thought that she would see them all soon.

Although when she found them waiting for her downstairs half an hour later – every last one of them, plus Sara and Uncle Lars – she was more than a little surprised. She hadn't thought they'd arrive quite so soon, and en masse.

Chapter Twenty-Nine

Hrafn knew what he had to do, and he told Haukr his plan. 'There's no time to go back and inform Rurik, but he and Geir will understand as I've told them about Linnea being from the future. Will you swear to me you'll let them know if I don't come back? Rurik is next in line to inherit Eskilsnes, and he'll make a good leader.'

'Yes, of course I'll speak to them,' Haukr assured him, 'but hopefully it won't be necessary.'

'No, maybe not. We'll see. Give me a week before you do anything, as I don't know how long it'll take. Now, please, stay and watch, because if nothing else, this will convince you I'm telling the truth.'

Haukr smiled. 'I can't wait, my friend.'

If he was being ironic, Hrafn knew he'd have to eat his words. As long as the brooch worked, that was. He wasn't quite sure why it was still here, since last time it had been used for time-travelling they'd taken it with them, but the churning sensation in his stomach told him it might be Linnea's way of letting him know she didn't want to come back. By leaving the brooch here, she wouldn't even have the option.

Well, he'd just have to persuade her.

He'd had a quick word with his aunt just before he went after Linnea, and it had made him realise why Linnea had left, and without discussing it with him first.

'Yes, I did speak to her earlier, just to help her to comprehend why it's necessary for you to make a more advantageous marriage,' Estrid admitted. 'She'd overheard us, you see, and was upset, poor girl. Entirely understandable. I'm sure she thought you'd carry on the liaison for much longer and—'

'Aunt Estrid, *þegi þú*! I've heard quite enough. I am aware that I owe you a lot, but this is one matter I cannot allow you to have a say in. What Linnea and I have is not a mere liaison.'

'But Hrafn, if you married Gudrun, you'd soon have other children, and—'

'Other children? What do you mean? Kadir is only my foster-son and . . . No! Linnea is with child? She didn't say.'

'Well, I don't know for certain, but someone said they'd seen her being sick behind the privy. Honestly, you've saved yourself the trouble of having to put a child out in the forest. Always so difficult and distressing for the mother.'

But Hrafn hadn't stayed to hear any more. *The trolls take Estrid!*

'Right, I hope to see you again soon, Haukr. Farewell for now.'

Hrafn focused on the brooch, read the words to make sure he remembered them correctly, and pricked his finger with the pin. As blood rushed to the surface, he recited the words out loud and waited, gripping the heavy silver item hard. It wasn't long before the familiar nausea and all the other strange sensations came, pulling him into a dark vortex as before. He didn't fight it, just endured.

The last thing he heard before the void claimed him was Haukr's exclamation of surprise.

333

When he opened his eyes, he became aware that something was hurting his hand. He looked down and saw that he'd been clutching the brooch so hard it had made an impression on his palm. He loosened his grip and sat up, brushing off the snow that was now clinging to him everywhere. It was cold, but he barely noticed. Instead, he let his eyes roam the immediate area. The jetty was still here, but it looked a lot smaller than the one he'd just left, and peering up the hill, Haukr's longhouse was gone. All his buildings, in fact, had disappeared. In their place was a small white and yellow house with lots of glass panels, and smoke coming out of a tall part sticking out of the roof.

He'd come to the future, but was he in the right place? And if not, how would he find Linnea? Because it suddenly hit him that he wouldn't be able to communicate with anyone here without her.

'Madison! Ivar! And Storm!' Linnea embraced her little sister, foster-brother and brother before turning to give Mia a hug, followed by a squealing session with Sara while Lars waited his turn. 'Wow, this is quite the family reunion.' She beamed at them all and blinked away the tears that threatened to fall.

'We can't believe you're alive and well.' Lars looked like he was choking back tears too. 'You have no idea how many times I've blamed myself for letting you go off on your own like that. I should have made sure someone accompanied you.'

Linnea gave him an extra hug. 'No, please, don't blame yourself for anything. I've had . . . an adventure, and if it wasn't for you, none of it would have happened. It didn't quite turn out the way I wanted it to, but hey, not everything does. And I've learned so much.' She suddenly remembered Karin and her runic prophecies. 'Those runes were definitely right about transformation and awakening,' she mused, 'not to mention the rest . . .'

'What runes?' Lars frowned in confusion.

Linnea patted his arm. 'Never mind, that's another story.'

'But where did you go?'

'Yes, come on, spill! We want to know *everything*!' Sara, who seemed to be completely recovered from the accident now, was almost bouncing up and down. It was wonderful to see her so animated and happy, despite everything she had been through. Linnea realised her feelings of survivor's guilt were considerably lessened by the knowledge that Sara was truly all right, in every sense of the word. They both were, and it was time to concentrate on living their lives rather than looking back.

'OK.' Linnea glanced at Mia. 'I think we're going to need tea, and lots of it. Or maybe hot chocolate if you can stretch to that.'

'Absolutely.' Mia smiled. 'We stopped on the way here and stocked up on a few things.'

When they were all sitting around the table with their preferred hot beverage, making the little cottage seem extremely cramped, Linnea told her story again. When she'd finished, you could have heard an ant walking across the floor; the silence was absolute. Then Storm exploded.

'No *way*! That's fucking *awesome*! You rock, sis!'

'Storm!' Mia frowned at her son, but he just grinned, so she turned back to Linnea instead. 'You are being absolutely serious? This isn't some elaborate ruse to protect your kidnappers? Because if you're that worried about them, we can all swear not to report them to the police, if that's what you want.'

Linnea shook her head. 'No, I swear on my honour, this is the whole truth and nothing but the truth. I actually travelled through time. You have my oath on it, as Hrafn would say.'

'Um, this Hrafn, he wouldn't happen to be quite hot, would he?' Madison teased. At fifteen, she was just discovering boys in a big way, and Linnea saw Haakon roll his eyes.

'As a matter of fact, yes, I suppose you could say that,' she admitted. What was the point of lying? He was, and always would be, the hottest man on the planet as far as she was concerned. Even if he'd been dead for over a thousand years.

'Uh-huh, thought so.' Madison high-fived Storm and the two of them grinned at each other.

'But that's not the point. The point is he's a Viking – well, *was* a Viking – and I met him. In the ninth century. For real.' Linnea sighed. 'Look, I know you probably don't believe me, and I wouldn't believe it either if one of you told me a story like that, but it really did happen. Now can you all please swear to keep it to yourselves and then we can put it behind us. I'm here, I'm fine, and I'm ready to embrace twenty-first-century life again. Starting with chocolate. Who's hogging the Kit Kats?'

Ivar handed her one with twinkling eyes. He was the only one who hadn't commented, and Linnea raised her eyebrows at him. 'You OK?'

He nodded. 'Just digesting what you said. It's a shame you didn't go into the house to visit Haukr and his wife. You might have met my ancestor, Thorald.'

'Sorry, I didn't think about that. I was kind of in a hurry to get out of there, and I didn't want to be seen. I mean, they'd have probably freaked out big-time if I disappeared right in front of their eyes.'

Ivar laughed. 'Good point. Shame you left the brooch behind, but anyway . . .'

Haakon and Lars took turns asking her questions about Viking life for a while, until Mia finally told them to desist. 'Let the poor girl be. She must be exhausted and should be tucked up in bed. Haakon, will you stay here tonight? Then you can bring Linnea home tomorrow, after she's rested. We can't all fit here, so the rest of us had better drive back now.'

'Yes, of course. We can—'

A banging on the door interrupted him and everyone stared at it. 'What the hell?' Storm muttered, checking his watch. 'It's a bit late for visitors, isn't it? Or did you tell anyone else about Linnea?'

'No one. Go on, open it!' Mia shooed him away, as he was sitting closest to the front of the house.

Storm opened the door a crack, but a gust of wind blew it into his shoulder. 'Ouch! What the . . . ? Who the hell are you? It's not Halloween, is it?'

But the person outside didn't reply. Instead he strode into the room and regarded them all in turn, as if he was looking for someone.

Linnea felt the world tilting on its axis, and black spots danced in front of her eyes. 'Hrafn?' she whispered. But it was all too much, and her mind took a dive into oblivion.

'Odin's ravens! I didn't mean to make her faint. Let me go, *fifl*!'

A man and a young boy were attempting to push Hrafn up against a wall, and he let them, because he understood it was out of concern for Linnea.

'You are Hrafn?' The man, who looked to be about Hrafn's own age, seemed to speak passable, if halting, Norse, and Hrafn breathed a sigh of relief. So Linnea wasn't the only one in the family with language skills – excellent.

'Yes,' he said. 'And I am not here to hurt her, upon my honour.'

The man turned to translate for the others, and a tall blond man, who was possibly Linnea's father, judging by the similarity in looks, waved at the pair to let Hrafn go. They did, but kept a wary eye on him, as if they suspected he was going to jump on her and kill her. If only they knew how far off the mark they were . . .

337

He wanted to rush over and take her in his arms, but when she stirred and opened her eyes again, her gaze was far from friendly.

'What are you doing here?' she hissed. 'You weren't supposed to come after me.'

'Oh yes? That must be why you left me the brooch then,' he countered.

'No! I didn't ... I mean, it's your brooch. I didn't want to be blamed for stealing it again.'

'That would be difficult if it was in your era and not mine,' Hrafn pointed out.

'Well, I ... *Aargh!* Why are you here?' Linnea stood up and waved away all her fussing relatives, muttering something to the nearest one. Then she walked over to stand in front of Hrafn and stared up into his eyes.

'I came to fetch you,' he said. It was the truth, although perhaps that wasn't quite the right way of putting it, judging by the way her eyes glittered dangerously.

She poked him in the chest. 'And what if I don't want to go back with you? I'm no one's concubine, do you understand? I'm not willing to be your plaything until you tire of me and go and marry that Gudrun, or whoever. Did you really think I'd accept that? And what of her? How awful to marry someone only to find there's another woman in their bed already!'

'Linnea—' He strove for a calm tone, but she interrupted him, smacking him on the arm this time.

'No! You've had your chance and you didn't take it, so now I'm staying here. You can just go back and do your duty, the way your evil aunt wants. I don't care.' But there were tears hovering on her lashes that told him she was lying.

She did care. And that made what he had to say so much easier.

'*Ást mín.*' She was his love, there was no doubt about it. '*Ek ann þér.* I love only you, and if I can't marry you, I will never marry at all. In fact, if you don't want to come with me to Eskilsnes, I'd be happy to stay here. As long as I can be with you, I don't care what I have to do, how menial the work. I want to spend the rest of my life with you. You are everything I want and the trolls can take both Estrid and Gudrun, whoever she is – no, I've never met her, and I don't want to either – and anyone else who tries to stand in my way. Please tell me you feel the same. Linnea?'

She'd gone pale again, and he put his arms around her to support her in case she fell. There was a collective gasp from everyone else in the room, but both Linnea's father and the man with the language skills held up a hand to stop them rushing to her aid. Hrafn gathered they had understood at least some of what he'd been telling Linnea and were waiting to hear her reply. As was he.

She took a deep breath and regained some colour in her cheeks. 'You . . . you want to marry me? Even though I have no dowry and no connections?'

'Yes. Such things do not matter to me; I already have more than enough. You are the only important thing in my life. I never thought to inherit Eskilsnes, and to be honest, I'm not even sure I wanted it. But the thought that I would sacrifice my happiness just to increase my holdings is ludicrous. If I can't share it with you, it is not a home. It's worthless to me. Please, will you marry me?'

He put his hand in his pouch and brought out the ring Rurik had finally completed. Hrafn had no idea why it had taken so long, but the wait was worth it. His brother had surpassed himself and created a unique piece of jewellery, a ring of gold made up of a raven ensnared in tiny flowers. Linnea flowers, set with pale pink stones to show their colour. 'I was only waiting to ask you until Rurik could finish this for me. I wanted something special, something just for you.'

'Oh!' She took the ring and studied it, her cheeks turning pink. He hoped it was pleasure staining them now and not anger.

He glanced at the faces surrounding them and sighed. 'I do realise what you'll be giving up and I would understand if you can't bear to live in my time, but . . . we can always visit. Unless you'd prefer me to stay here?'

She blinked, and a fat tear rolled down one cheek, but she swiped it away as a slow smile spread across her beautiful mouth. 'No, I wouldn't ask that of you. You're a true Norseman and you'd never be happy here.'

'Then . . . ?' He tugged her a little closer and felt his own mouth quirking into a smile when she didn't resist. The usual pull of attraction between them had him squirming with impatience. He wanted her, the way he always did, with a fierceness that took him by surprise every time. But her family were present and this was not the moment to persuade her like that.

Her smile became radiant. 'Yes! Yes, I'll come with you. Yes, I'll marry you. But if you ever – *ever* – so much as look at that Gudrun, I'll kill you, understand? Even when I'm ugly after bearing too many children.'

'What are you talking about? You'll never be ugly to me, and I want lots of children.' Hrafn decided they could argue about that later and instead pulled her in for a kiss. A kiss that went on for so long the younger boy started whistling, joined by his sister. When Hrafn looked up again, everyone in the room was staring at him and Linnea, but they were grinning now and her father shook his head.

'I see I lose her again,' he said in halting Norse, and pointed at Hrafn. 'You look after. Well!'

Hrafn nodded and let go of Linnea long enough to bow to his future father-in-law. 'You have my oath.'

After that, there was a lot of talking, laughing and hugging, and Hrafn just watched with a smile as Linnea tried to make herself heard among her relatives. It would seem he was marrying into a noisy clan, but that was fine by him. For Linnea, he'd marry into any family in any realm, even Loki's.

Chapter Thirty

'Are you sure you're going to be OK, sweetie? You've got all the medicines and, um, contraceptives and stuff, and if you or your children ever get ill, you promise you'll come back?'

'Mia! I'll be fine. Women did survive in Viking times, you know, even without all our knowledge.' Linnea's cheeks were hot with embarrassment. She so didn't want to discuss birth control with her stepmother, or anyone else for that matter. But it made sense to bring something with her, unless she wanted her body to be worn out with childbirth within a few years. Much better to space the pregnancies out a bit to give her a chance to recover from each one. Because she knew there would be quite a few even so. And she couldn't wait.

'We're going to miss you terribly, but it's wonderful to know that you are alive and happy at least. A huge improvement on imagining you murdered and hastily buried somewhere.' Her dad was trying to keep it together, she could tell, and would probably manage it until she'd gone. Then Mia would have to console him. And she would, Linnea was counting on it.

'We'll visit, I promise. Hrafn says we'll bring our firstborn to see you as soon as it's safe for the baby to travel through time.' Linnea giggled. 'Doesn't that sound crazy? I honestly still wake up sometimes wondering if I'm dreaming.'

'Yes, completely insane.' Haakon sighed. 'But it seems to be real, so just take care of yourself, OK?'

'Will do. If I survived a journey to Byzantium, I'm sure I'll be fine at Eskilsnes. Oh, and you should definitely do a dig there, Dad. I bet you'll find all sorts of great stuff. I'll make sure to hide a few goodies for you.'

'Thanks. Good idea.'

The time had come for her and Hrafn to leave, and after the last goodbyes, they made their way down to the jetty.

'Are you ready?' Hrafn took her hand. 'I'm not asking too much of you, am I? I want you to be happy, and this must be so difficult.'

Linnea stood on tiptoes to give him a hard kiss. 'I want to be with you and this is the best way. No regrets. Let's go, quickly, before I freeze to death. We don't want to kill our first child by frostbite.'

'Our first . . . You mean Estrid wasn't lying?'

'Estrid? What does she know about it? I never told a soul.' In fact Linnea hadn't been sure herself until she'd done a test from the pharmacy the previous day.

'She said you'd been seen being sick behind the privy and that it was a sign.' Hrafn looked stunned, but his eyes shone bluer than usual in the sun reflected off the snow.

'I think that was just something I ate, because I haven't been sick at all, but yes, I had it confirmed yesterday. You'll be a father in about six months' time.'

He gave her a kiss that more than matched the one she'd given him. 'Then we had better hurry. I want to share the good news with everyone. Hold out your hand.'

Their journey – if you could call it that – back to the ninth century went as well as could be expected, although Linnea was sure she felt even queasier than the previous times. 'Urgh, I don't think I'll ever get used to that,' she muttered, getting up on to her knees in the snow.

'No, it's vile, but the end justifies the means, right? Come, let us go up to Haukr's hall. They'll have to put us up overnight. I'm not travelling in the dark in this weather.'

Linnea had been told that Haukr knew their secret, but the big man didn't let on that there was anything unusual about their visit. He and his wife made them very welcome, and after a convivial evening and a good night's sleep, she and Hrafn rowed back to Eskilsnes. They thanked the gods that the water still hadn't frozen. Linnea definitely didn't fancy walking all the way.

'Here we are.' Hrafn pulled the boat up on to dry land, as it would be broken if it was still in the water when the ice came. 'Estrid had better lay on the best feast of her life, or she's not welcome to stay here any longer. In fact, I'll let you decide her fate – you deserve to.'

He took Linnea's hand as they walked up from the lake towards the longhouse. As they entered, a cheer went up, instigated by Rurik and Geir, who came rushing over to greet them.

'Brother! You're back! And with your . . . er, Linnea in tow. Excellent!'

'Not "er, Linnea", but Linnea my wife-to-be. Prepare yourselves for feasting, everyone; we will marry tomorrow!' Hrafn let his gaze roam the room and Linnea saw him sending hard looks at several people, especially the women, some of whom blushed scarlet. The harshest glare he reserved for Estrid, though, and the old woman's mouth pursed even as her face turned pale. 'Aunt, will you welcome my bride into the family?'

Estrid stood up slowly and walked forward, fiddling with something hanging off her brooch. As she reached them, Linnea realised it was the set of keys that showed her status as the most important woman at Eskilsnes.

'Welcome. I wish you a long and happy life together. I believe these are now yours.' Estrid held out the keys and Linnea glanced at Hrafn, who nodded imperceptibly.

'Thank you, I'll take great care of them.' Linnea took the keys and tucked them into her pouch. For Hrafn's sake, she wanted peace here, so she added, 'Since I don't have your vast experience of running a household, I would very much appreciate your guidance, Estrid.'

A hush fell on the assembled company as everyone waited to hear the woman's reply. After a slight hesitation, Estrid nodded. 'It will be my pleasure to teach you, niece.'

At that point, Rurik and Geir erupted into whoops again, which set everyone else off. Hrafn bent to hug his aunt and added a quiet 'thank you', while the rest of the people of Eskilsnes seemed intent on starting the celebrations immediately. Linnea smiled – there was nothing as rowdy as a bunch of Vikings in feasting mode, as she'd already learned, but she was looking forward to this one since it was in her honour.

Hrafn took her hand and brought her over to his big chair, where he sat down and pulled her on to his lap. 'Thank you for being gracious to my aunt. It was more than she deserved and she knows it,' he whispered.

'You're welcome. I hope we can keep the peace now.'

'I'm sure you will.' He nuzzled her ear. 'Not regretting this?'

She put her arms round his neck and leaned her forehead against his. 'No, never. I love you, Hrafn, and I always will. Are you sure you don't regret not selling me when you had the chance?'

'Absolutely not! I wouldn't sell you for all the gold and silver in the world. You are my very own golden treasure and I'm not letting you go, ever!'

Christina Courtenay

The kiss he gave her had everyone hollering their approval, and Linnea smiled against his mouth before breaking off the kiss to shout at Rurik.

'*Þegi þú*, brother! You'll be next to fall in love.'

She was going to enjoy living here, and she wanted everyone to be as happy as she was.

346

Acknowledgments

I have dedicated this novel to the Romantic Novelists' Association, which is celebrating its 60th anniversary this year. It was a lucky day for me when I discovered this amazing organisation – I would never have persevered with my writing without them. The friends I have made in the RNA, the events and workshops I attended, and the incredibly supportive mentors I met along the way, made a huge difference to me. I thank them all from the bottom of my heart!

As this is a sequel, the same people who helped with book one were instrumental in assisting with this one – thank you all. And as usual, special thanks are due to my lovely author friends Gill Stewart, Henriette Gyland, Myra Kersner and Sue Moorcroft; you are my rocks when the writing gets tough.

There were a few additions: Dr Joanne Shortt Butler, who has taken over answering all my questions about Old Norse and Viking customs – thank you, Jo, you've been amazing! (As before, any grammar/vocabulary mistakes are entirely my own). Vasiliki Scurfield – *efcharistó* for help with the Greek for 'thank you'! And Nicola Cornick, Anna Belfrage and Alison Morton – it's a huge pleasure working with you to promote the time slip, time travel and alternative history sub-genres we all love!

Christina Courtenay

I would also like to thank the world's best neighbour, Åsa Johnsson Humphries, for always being around for *fika* and chat – living in our little village wouldn't be half as much fun without you!

A special thank you to my wonderful editor Kate Byrne and her team at Headline, as well as Lina Langlee, agent extraordinaire, for all your support and encouragement – I'm so happy to be on this journey with you all!

To Richard, Josceline and Jessamy – thank you and I love you more than I can say!

The Runes *of* Destiny

Bonus Material

Christina Courtenay
Reveals . . .

If I had to go back in time and choose another career . . .
Archaeologist! As a teenager I was lazy and wasn't sure I could handle all the studying involved, but it would have been so worth it. You should always go after your dreams, I know that now!

My dream holiday destination . . .
Always Japan – despite having lived there for three years I can never get enough of visiting that amazing country. The food, the sights, the people, the shopping . . . there is an endless amount of things to do and I will keep going back for as long as I am able to.

The first album I ever bought . . .
When I was little my dad used to travel a lot with his job and every time he went to the UK he brought me back a gift. He bought me my first album – The Beatles' *Sgt. Pepper's Lonely Hearts Club Band*. I loved it and almost wore it out I played it so many times!

The book I've read the most times . . .
Cotillion by Georgette Heyer – even though I know it so well, it never fails to make me laugh!

The item I have more of than anything else . . .
Um, that's a tough one as I'm a collector (no, not hoarder, I can
still move round my house!) – Foo dogs (aka Staffordshire mantle
spaniels)? Blue and white porcelain items? Boots? No, actually –
books!

The thing I could never give up . . .
Chocolate! I have tried and did go several years without at one
point in my life, but it is always calling to me so I couldn't quite
let it go.

My choice of superpower . . .
I'd like to be like the *Star Wars* jedi who can 'suggest' thoughts to
other people to make them do what they want – how useful is
that!

If I could pick any actor/actress to play my latest lead character . . .
Chris Hemsworth (in his *Thor* guise) would be perfect for any/all
of my Viking heroes ☺

The best play I've seen . . .
I don't actually go to the theatre very often and prefer really old-
fashioned plays like *The Mousetrap* or *The Importance of Being
Earnest*. There's something about the 'olde-worlde' feel to them
that just suits a theatre stage so well.

The one piece of advice I would give my teenage self . . .
Stop caring so much about what other people think! And be
braver.

The comedian who makes me laugh the most . . .
Sadly they're no longer with us, but I loved all the films with Marty Feldman and Gene Wilder. Together they were comedic genius!

My favourite city in the world . . .
Could I have two, please? London because I love the architecture, the history, the museums and sights. Wherever you go, you can get a glimpse into the London of the past and there are lots of intriguing places to explore. And Venice – I've only been there once but it was an incredible place – the faded grandeur, the slowly sinking buildings, the architecture and the vibrant atmosphere, it was all fascinating!

If I had to eat the same meal for dinner every day for the rest of my life . . .
Probably sushi or alternatively tomato and mozzarella with vinaigrette (love that stuff!).

If I want to relax . . .
I read a book I know I'm going to enjoy or I go to the cinema to see a feel-good film, armed with a huge bucket of salted popcorn (movies are never as enjoyable without popcorn).

If I could go back to any time in history . . .
Either the Viking period (of course!) or the Regency, but it would have to be as someone of wealth and standing because otherwise either era would probably be miserable!

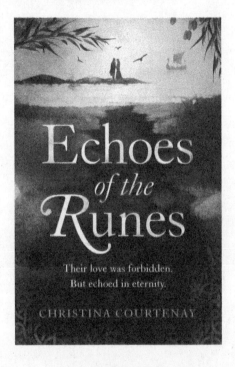

Read on for an early preview of Christina Courtenay's
next enthralling love story

Whispers
of the
Runes

Coming soon from

REVIEW

Prologue

Stockholm, Sweden, August 2019

'Oh, come on, don't be a chicken! It's not like anyone believes in fortune-telling anyway. It's just a bit of fun, right?'

Sara Mattsson sighed and sat down next to her best friend's little sister, Maddie, who was shaking a small leather pouch full of stones. The teenager had learned to read the runes as a way of passing the time when her parents took her to Viking re-enactment weekends, and jokingly claimed to be psychic now. She often pounced on anyone who came to the family's home for dinner, offering her services as seeress.

'And anyway, I need the practice to keep my skills up, you know. Please?' Maddie wheedled.

'Fine, but I don't want to hear anything about tall, dark strangers, OK?' That would just remind her of her ex.

Maddie grinned, but then grew serious as she went through the ritual of closing her eyes, selecting three stones from the pouch, and dropping them on to a tablecloth with three circles drawn on to it. Each stone had a different rune painted on its surface and the girl leaned forward to study them. 'Look, they've all ended up in the circle for your future. Excellent!' She picked one up. 'This is Raidho. Means you're going to travel.'

'Well, yes, I know. I'm going back to the UK tomorrow.' Sara had been visiting family and friends in Sweden, but it was time to go back to her fledgling business in England.

'Hmm, it should be more exciting than that, but whatever. This next one is Berkana, the rune of birth and growth. It promises new beginnings and, um, possibly desire and love?'

Sara snorted. 'Not very likely. I told you, none of that rubbish, please.'

Maddie sent her a stern look. 'I'm not making this up, I'm just interpreting your runes.' She pointed at the final stone. 'So that one basically says you've got to be strong. There's going to be some delays or restrictions, and you have to rely on your inner strength.'

'What? My plane will be late?'

Maddie leaned forward and gave her a playful shove. 'No! It can mean that you have to face your fears, endure, survive. Be determined and patient. Stuff like that.'

Sara shook her head. Wasn't that what she'd been doing already, this past year or more? And it wasn't getting her anywhere. 'Well, thanks for the reading. Can't say I believe a word of it, but I wish you luck as a fortune-teller.'

'Hey! The runes never lie.' Maddie pretended to look offended, but her sparkling eyes gave her away.

'Hm, well, hopefully your next customer will be less sceptical.'

For herself, she'd just carry on working hard until the painful memories faded.

Chapter One

North Sea, Haustmánaður/September 873 AD

'Are you sure we shouldn't go back? That old fisherman said there's a storm brewing.'

'Don't be ridiculous! Anyone can see the weather is perfect for a sea crossing. Besides, that was two days ago – it's a bit late to turn around now.'

Rurik Eskilsson listened as the two men at the stern of the ship bickered. One was its owner, Sigvardr, the other a passenger just like himself, although much older than Rurik's twenty-two winters. Well past his prime, in fact, the worry-guts was clearly not comfortable with being on board, and had been violently sick for most of the journey so far. His face held a grey tinge and if he'd had anything left inside him, he'd probably still have been hanging over the gunwale.

A quick glance at the sky showed only an expanse of blue, but towards the horizon clouds were undoubtedly gathering. Sigvardr was right though – there was no point in turning around as they were already more than halfway across the North Sea, having left Ribe in the land of the Danes the day before yesterday. Rurik touched the large Thor's hammer amulet hanging around his

neck and hoped the gods would keep them safe. His future plans did not include drowning in the salty depths of the ocean. Rather, he was on his way to a new life, an adventure, far from his family and friends, and he didn't want anything to stand in his way.

He'd had to get away from *her* before he went insane, her golden loveliness as far out of his reach as it could possibly be . . . but he refused to think about that now.

'Tie the sail tighter! Not like that, you *fífl*, properly!' Sigvardr shouted out his orders, and Rurik hoped the man knew what he was doing and it wasn't all bravado. He'd been in charge of a ship himself a few times, and as far as he could tell, Sigvardr was an experienced sailor. For a brief moment though, he wished he was travelling with his older brother Hrafn instead. He had his own ship and had offered to take Rurik to his destination, but it was past time to cut the ties between them and strike out alone.

The swell of the waves increased, their tops foaming like horses that had been worked too hard. At first, the large ship cut through them smoothly without any problems, but when the wind picked up, the clinker-built vessel began to buck and creak as it rode the hills and troughs of water. It was superbly constructed and Rurik didn't doubt it could withstand much worse treatment, however. Norse vessels were made to be flexible, yet strong, and it would take a lot to break it.

'We should be sighting land towards dusk,' Sigvardr commented. His voice was loud and carried across the wind so that everyone heard him, but the only one who replied was the worry-guts.

'If we make it that far . . .' was his ominous muttering. Rurik sent him a death glare, hoping to shut him up. No one wanted to listen to his fears, and he was the only one there who was scared. If they were meant to die this day, they would. You couldn't change your fate – the Norns, ancient goddesses of destiny, had decided that ages ago – so what was the point of fretting?